INTRIGUE

Seek thrills. Solve crimes. Justice served.

The Sheriff's Baby

Delores Fossen

Under Lock And Key

K.D. Richards

MILLS & BOON

THE SHERIFF'S BABY
© 2024 by Delores Fossen
Philippine Copyright 2024
Australian Copyright 2024
New Zealand Copyright 2024

First Published 2024
First Australian Paperback Edition 2024
ISBN 978 1 038 93522 9

UNDER LOCK AND KEY
© 2024 by Kia Dennis
Philippine Copyright 2024
Australian Copyright 2024
New Zealand Copyright 2024

First Published 2024
First Australian Paperback Edition 2024
ISBN 978 1 038 93522 9

MIX
Paper | Supporting responsible forestry
FSC® C001695

Published by
Harlequin Mills & Boon
An imprint of Harlequin Enterprises (Australia) Pty Limited (ABN 47 001 180 918), a subsidiary of HarperCollins Publishers Australia Pty Limited
(ABN 36 009 913 517)
Level 19, 201 Elizabeth Street
SYDNEY NSW 2000 AUSTRALIA

Printed and bound in Australia by McPherson's Printing Group

The Sheriff's Baby

Delores Fossen

MILLS & BOON

Delores Fossen, a *USA TODAY* bestselling author, has written over 150 novels, with millions of copies of her books in print worldwide. She's received a Booksellers' Best Award and an RT Reviewers' Choice Best Book Award. She was also a finalist for a prestigious RITA® Award. You can contact the author through her website at deloresfossen.com.

Books by Delores Fossen

Harlequin Intrigue

Saddle Ridge Justice

The Sheriff's Baby

Silver Creek Lawman: Second Generation

Targeted in Silver Creek
Maverick Detective Dad
Last Seen in Silver Creek
Marked for Revenge

The Law in Lubbock County

Sheriff in the Saddle
Maverick Justice
Lawman to the Core
Spurred to Justice

Mercy Ridge Lawmen

Her Child to Protect
Safeguarding the Surrogate
Targeting the Deputy
Pursued by the Sheriff

Visit the Author Profile page at millsandboon.com.au.

CAST OF CHARACTERS

Sheriff Duncan Holder—Sheriff of Saddle Ridge, Texas. He'll do whatever it takes to protect his ex, Deputy Joelle McCullough, and their unborn child.

Deputy Joelle McCullough—She's five months pregnant, and even though things are strained between Duncan and her, she'll work with him to stop the threat to their baby.

Molly Radel—A dispatcher who's kidnapped the same night someone attempts to abduct Joelle. It's possible these attacks are linked to the murder of Joelle's father, which happened five years ago.

Al Hamlin—A PI who claims he's looking for his missing pregnant sister, but it's possible he's the one behind the attacks.

Brad Moreland—He has an axe to grind with everyone in Saddle Ridge for what he feels is a wrongful arrest of his now ex-wife.

Shanda Cantrell—Brad's ex-wife. She miscarried after being arrested by Joelle's father, who was then sheriff. She insists she's gotten over the past but could be planning revenge.

Kate Moreland—Brad's mother. She's been linked to the illegal sale of babies, so she might have her own agenda for wanting to kidnap Joelle.

Chapter One

The sound instantly woke Deputy Joelle McCullough, but it took her a moment to realize it hadn't been part of the dream.

The nightmare.

There were no blasts of gunshots that had killed her father. No, this had been a clicking sound like that of someone shutting a vehicle door.

Rubbing her eyes to help her focus, Joelle checked her phone for the time. Just past 2:00 a.m., which meant it wasn't anywhere near a normal visiting hour. Added to that, she wasn't exactly on the beaten path since her house was a good mile outside of her hometown of Saddle Ridge with no other houses within sight of hers.

There were no texts from her three siblings or any of her friends. None either from anyone at the Saddle Ridge Sheriff's Office where she'd been a deputy for seven years now. So, no alerts from anyone she knew well enough to contact her before just showing up at her place, but it could be a neighbor coming to her for help.

Everyone in Saddle Ridge knew where she lived, knew that she was a cop. That meant this could be some kind of emergency that had warranted a face-to-face rather than a call or text.

She threw back the covers, immediately reaching for her

Glock 22 that she kept on the nightstand. Grabbing her firearm when off duty hadn't always been her automatic response. Not until five months ago when her father had been gunned down at his home. Since then, things had changed.

Everything had changed.

And Joelle no longer trusted that a neighbor's emergency—or whatever this was—wouldn't end in gunfire. Her father hadn't been armed when he'd answered his door that night. He obviously hadn't been alarmed that whoever had come calling was there to kill him.

She couldn't make the same mistake.

It was the reason she'd had a top-notch security system installed, and it was turned on and armed. If anyone attempted to get in through a door or window, the alarms would start blaring, and the security company and the sheriff's office would be alerted. Most importantly, *she* would be alerted, and she could use her cop's training to put a stop to a threat.

Despite the urgency and worry building inside her, Joelle took her time getting out of bed. She'd learned the hard way that standing too quickly would make her lightheaded.

One of the side effects of being five months pregnant.

She ran her hand over her stomach, trying to soothe the baby's sudden fluttering. Not hard kicks. Not yet, anyway. Just soft stirrings that reminded her of the precious cargo she was carrying. Reminding her again of why she couldn't risk what'd happened to her father.

Once her heartbeat had steadied enough so that it was no longer thrumming in her ears, Joelle listened for any other sounds. Nothing except for the hum of the air conditioner and the spring breeze rattling through some of the tree branches outside her house.

She went to the front window and peered out, but it

took her a moment to spot the vehicle. A black car that she didn't recognize. It was parked not in her driveway but off to the side beneath a pair of towering oaks. The headlights weren't on, and the door was indeed shut.

There was no sign of the driver.

Because of the angle of the parked car, Joelle couldn't see the license plates, and she didn't waste time figuring out what was going on. Not with every one of her cop's instincts now telling her that something was wrong. She stepped to the side of the window so that she wouldn't be seen or in the line of fire, and made a call to the Saddle Ridge dispatcher.

"This is Deputy Joelle McCullough," she said, keeping her voice at a whisper just in case the driver of that vehicle was close enough to hear her. "I need backup at my house."

She wasn't sure who was on night duty at the sheriff's office, but it wouldn't be her brother Slater. He was staying the night in San Antonio, a thirty-minute drive away, since he was on the schedule to testify at a trial. If Slater had been in town, she would have called him directly since he lived just up the road from her.

After she'd done a thorough visual sweep of the front exterior of her house, Joelle went to her kitchen window to check the backyard. Thankfully, there was a full moon to give her some visibility, but there were also plenty of trees and shrubs dotting the five acres she owned. Lots of places for someone to hide if that's what a person wanted to do to try to get back at a cop.

She wasn't aware of anyone specifically who wanted to end her life or get revenge on her, but her father's killer was still unknown and at large. Since no one was certain of the reason her dad had been gunned down, she might be on the killer's hit list, too.

With her phone in her left hand and the Glock still gripped in her right, Joelle stayed positioned to the side of the kitchen window while she continued to watch and listen. Nothing.

And that in itself was troubling.

If this was someone she knew, they would have already come to the door or made themselves known. Added to that, the person would have parked in front of her house and not off to the side like that.

The minutes crawled by until Joelle saw the slash of headlights as they turned into her driveway. Backup, no doubt. She didn't breathe easier, though, because she needed to let the responding deputy know there was someone out there, maybe someone waiting to fire shots.

She hurried back to the front and silently cursed when she glanced out the front window and recognized the dark blue truck. Not a deputy but rather Sheriff Duncan Holder. Once, he'd been a fellow deputy but had been elected sheriff after her father's death.

Duncan was also the father of her unborn child.

As always, she got a serious jolt of conflicted feelings whenever she laid eyes on Duncan. Memories. Heat. Guilt. Grief. A bundle of raw nerves mixed with the old attraction that Joelle wished wasn't there.

Because she didn't want Duncan or anyone else to be gunned down tonight, Joelle fired off a quick text to let him know about the unfamiliar black car and the out-of-sight driver. Duncan responded just seconds later with a thumbs-up emoji, and he pulled his truck into her yard and closer to her porch. He sat there for a few moments, still on his phone, and Joelle figured he was probably running the license plate on the visitor's vehicle since he'd likely have a good view of the one on the rear of the car.

Duncan finally put his phone away and stepped from his truck, keeping cover behind the door while he fired glances around the yard. He, too, had his Glock drawn and ready.

Her heart did that stupid little flutter it always did whenever she was around him, and for the umpteenth time, Joelle wished she could make herself immune to him. Hard to do, though, with those unforgettable, heart-fluttering looks. The dark brown hair, blue eyes and a face that had no doubt gotten him plenty of lustful looks.

More seconds passed. Her heart raced. Adrenaline pumped through her. Her stomach tightened.

The gusts of wind sure didn't help, either, with her raw, edgy nerves. Those gusts kicked up, stirring seemingly everything at once, including an owl that sounded agitated by the noise. It was bad timing since the owl's hoots and squawks could conceal any sounds her visitor might make.

Duncan finally moved away from his truck, coming up the porch steps, and that was her cue to use her phone app to disarm the security system and unlock the door. He stepped in and brought the scent of the fresh night air with him. His own scent, too, one she wished wasn't so familiar to her.

"You're not on shift," she muttered, well aware that her tone wasn't exactly friendly.

"No. I couldn't sleep so I went into the office to do some paperwork. I was there when you called. Have you seen anyone around that car or the house?" he tacked onto that.

He met her gaze for just a fraction. She was betting that he was also trying to make himself immune to her.

Joelle shook her head, locked the door and reset the security system. "I heard the car door shut about fifteen minutes ago. It woke me, and when I got up and didn't see anyone, I called dispatch." She'd tried to make her voice steady, as if giving a report to her boss. Which she was. But it was hard to keep the emotion out of it.

Duncan glanced at her pale yellow gown that in no way concealed, well, anything. It was thin and snug enough to show the outline of her breasts and baby bump.

Yes, definitely hard to keep the emotion out of this.

"I ran the plates," he told her. "The vehicle belongs to Alton Martinez in San Antonio."

She repeated the name to see if it rang any bells. It didn't. "Does he have a record?"

"I'll know in the next couple of minutes." Duncan stepped around her and went to the kitchen window to look out as she'd done.

He'd been in her house before but not in a while. Not since that night her father had died. In fact, Duncan had been here in her bed while her dad was being gunned down. Joelle knew she stood no chance of forgiving herself for that.

For years, Duncan and she had resisted the scalding attraction that'd been between them. They'd believed resisting was a necessity since they were fellow deputies, working side by side in sometimes dangerous situations. They hadn't wanted to risk a failed relationship that could have interfered with them doing their jobs. They'd resisted time after time, year after year. Until that night of her father's murder.

And it'd had disastrous consequences.

One good one, though, too.

Joelle hated she hadn't been with her father to try to stop his death, but she loved the baby she was carrying, and the pregnancy was the main reason she was managing to hold her life together. Duncan had helped some with the managing, too, by making sure they were on different shifts so she wouldn't have to see him that often. That's why it'd been such a jolt to have him respond to her call for help.

"Have you gotten any recent threats that I don't know about?" Duncan asked, the question yanking her out of her thoughts and forcing her to focus on the here and now.

"No. And I haven't made any recent arrests, either," she added, even though as sheriff, he would have already known that.

Of course, it wouldn't have to be anything recent to continue to be a threat. Sometimes, when criminals got out of jail, they went looking for anyone who'd had a part in their incarceration. No one immediately came to mind, though.

Duncan's phone dinged, and he tore his attention from the window to read the text he'd just gotten. "Martinez doesn't have a record, but about four hours ago, he reported his car stolen."

Joelle's chest clenched, and another wave of adrenaline washed through her. She had steeled herself up for the worst, but she'd hoped this would turn out to be nothing. The fact it was a stolen vehicle meant it was almost certainly something bad.

Staying on the other side of the window, she peered out, searching again for whatever sort of threat this might be. Her mind was having no trouble coming up with some awful scenarios. Especially one.

"Before I went to bed, I accessed some internet newspaper articles on my father's murder and my mother's disappearance," she told him.

No need for her to explain either of those incidents. Her father had been murdered, and on the same day, her mother, Sandra, had simply vanished. Both incidents had gutted her. Both had left her in desperate need of answers.

"I read any and every article connected to my parents," Joelle added to let Duncan know that wasn't anything out of the norm. "In one of them, a journalist mentioned that she was continuing to look into the murder and would post updates. I knew it was a long shot, that she probably didn't know anything we didn't, but in the comments, I asked if she'd found anything."

Duncan looked at her, their gazes connecting, and even in the dim light, she could see the sympathy in his eyes. Could practically hear the sigh that Joelle was certain he wanted to make.

"And you think…what…that your father's killer saw the comment and believed that maybe he or she wanted to stop you from digging?" he asked. He still didn't sigh. Nor did he dismiss it. "I saw the article. Saw the comment you posted."

Joelle figured she shouldn't have been surprised. Duncan felt guilty about her father's murder, too, and he was a cop just as she was. This was a crime they both wanted solved, and that meant digging through any and all possible leads.

"It's been five months," Duncan went on a moment later. "If the killer had planned on coming after one of us, you'd think that would have happened before now." He paused. "But the car was stolen, and the driver is nowhere in sight. So, I'm not writing anything off right now."

Good. Joelle had wanted him to take this seriously because she certainly was.

"We can work this a couple of ways," Duncan explained a moment later. "We can wait for the driver to show himself, or I can go ahead and call in every available deputy. We can flood the grounds with headlights and maybe spook the person enough for him or her to come out."

Joelle knew that no one in law enforcement wanted to be woken up at this hour, but her fellow cops, including the reserve deputies, would gladly come if they thought it meant catching her father's killer. Every member of the Saddle Ridge Sheriff's Office wanted justice for their former boss.

"Bring in the deputies," she advised. She glanced down at her gown again. "I'll hurry and change and then will keep watch at the front of the house."

Duncan made a sound of agreement, and while she hurried to her bedroom, she heard him call dispatch who in turn would contact the deputies. Since a few of them lived only a mile or so away, it shouldn't take long for them to start arriving.

Joelle wanted to believe that the extra help would mean a killer could be captured tonight. A capture that'd take place when she had plenty of backup so as to lessen the risk to her unborn child. But she had to stay grounded since this might not even be related to her father's death or her mother's disappearance.

Moving as fast as she could, Joelle pulled on a pair of maternity jeans, a loose top and her boots, and she hurried back into the living room. However, she came to a quick stop when she caught a whiff of something.

"Smoke," she heard Duncan say from the kitchen.

This time, the adrenaline came as a hard slam. Because Duncan was right. There was the faint scent of smoke in the air.

Duncan came barreling out of the kitchen and toward the front. "I don't see any signs of a fire in the back," he relayed to her as they both hurried to the living room window.

Joelle's heart was thudding now, and the fear came. A fire could be a ploy to get them out of the house. Or rather to get *her* out of the house. So she could be gunned down. But she didn't see flames anywhere.

"The scent's coming from here," Duncan muttered, glancing at the east wall of the living room.

The only windows on that particular side of the house were what was called clerestory, which meant they were above eye level and had been designed to let in natural light. That didn't stop Duncan. He dragged over a chair, anchoring it against the wall and hefted himself up to look out.

He cursed.

"There's a fire right next to your house," he told her, causing her heart to race even more. "It's already at least four feet high."

The exterior was wood, and while Joelle hoped it wouldn't easily ignite, her visitor must have believed that would be the result. Either that, or he or she had wanted Duncan and her just to go running out.

Duncan made another call to dispatch, this time to alert the fire department. Something the person outside must have figured they would do. And that meant the seconds were ticking down. If Duncan and she waited until the firefighters arrived, the house could be engulfed in flames, putting them and the baby at risk. But the risk could be there if they ran, too.

"My car's in the garage," she let him know.

The vehicle wasn't bullet resistant but then neither was Duncan's truck, which was parked by her porch. Still, if they were in her car, at least they could try to drive out of there if the fire overtook the house.

Duncan made another of those sounds of agreement, and he took her keys from her when she scooped them up from the foyer table. That meant he was no doubt planning on being behind the wheel and that he would insist she get down. The cop part of her hated she had to make such concessions. However, the baby changed her priorities, and Joelle knew that both Duncan and she would do anything and everything possible to keep their child safe.

"I have to disarm the security system until we're through the garage door," she relayed to him, using her phone to do that. The moment they were inside her car, though, she reset the alarm.

In the distance, Joelle heard the welcome sound of a cruiser's siren, but her relief over the backup was short-lived.

Because the next sound she heard was a blast.

Some kind of explosion roared through the house and garage, shaking the very foundation. Paint cans and gardening tools fell from the shelves and hooks, smashing onto the concrete floor. Each crash only escalated the urgency and fear.

So did the smoke.

The scent of it got much stronger, and Joelle could see whiffs of the smoke seeking beneath the mudroom door and into the garage. Thankfully, there was no smoke around the garage door itself, and that was likely the reason Duncan started the car and hit the remote on her visor to open the door.

"Stay down," he ordered her.

Joelle did. She strapped on her seat belt and sank down as low as she could. She also kept her gun ready in case she had to return fire.

Duncan threw the car into reverse and hit the accelerator, bolting out of the garage. Because of the way she was positioned, Joelle couldn't see the person responsible for the fire, but she had no doubts that Duncan was keeping watch.

The sirens got louder, and she saw the whirl of the blue lights slashing through the darkness. That would almost certainly get their attacker running. Or so she thought.

But she was wrong.

The bullet slammed into her windshield, crashing through the safety glass on the driver's side. For a heart-stopping second, she thought that Duncan had been hit, but he pressed even harder on the accelerator and got the car out of her driveway and onto the country road that fronted her house. He stopped just as the cruiser pulled in next to them.

"It's Luca," Duncan told her, referring to Deputy Luca Vanetti. "Text him and tell him to stay put until the others arrive. We have an active shooter. Tell him to let the other deputies know."

Joelle fired off a quick text, then braced herself for another shot. Or an explosion. Her house was burning, she was sure of that, but she couldn't deal with the sickening dread of losing her home and everything she owned. For now, she just had to focus on staying alive, and then she could figure out who was doing this.

And why.

She especially wanted to know the why in case that led her to her father's killer.

There was the sound of another siren. More whirling lights. Two more vehicles arriving on scene. What didn't happen was another round of gunfire, which meant the shooter was likely already on the run. Joelle prayed, though, that someone would spot the person.

Because she was so focused on listening for their attacker, Joelle gasped when the sound shot through the car. But it wasn't a bullet. It was her phone, and Joelle saw a familiar name on the screen. Molly Radel, a former deputy who'd transferred to working as a dispatcher after she got pregnant. Even though Molly was on leave, awaiting the birth of her baby, it was possible she'd been called in to assist in some way.

"Molly," Joelle answered, and she was about to give the woman a quick explanation as to what was going on, but Molly spoke before Joelle could do that.

"You have to help me," Molly said, her voice trembling and frantic. "Someone's breaking into my house."

The words had no sooner left Molly's mouth when Joelle heard the woman scream.

Chapter Two

Even though Joelle hadn't put the call on speaker, Duncan heard the woman's scream loud and clear. Since Joelle had greeted Molly by name, he also had no trouble figuring out that something was seriously wrong.

"Put the phone on speaker," Duncan told Joelle, and the moment she'd done that, he tried to figure out what the heck was going on. "Molly?" he asked.

He could hear what he thought were the sounds of a struggle, but the dispatcher didn't answer. And that caused Duncan to curse. He had every available lawman responding to the situation here at Joelle's. A situation that might escalate even more if the attacker continued to shoot at them. But Duncan knew he had to go to Molly, and he had to do that now.

"Use my phone to let the deputies know that I'm heading to Molly's place," Duncan relayed to Joelle. "I want Luca to follow us as backup."

Of course, that meant he'd be taking Joelle with him since there wasn't time for him to get her safely into a cruiser. He got confirmation of that when he heard Molly scream again. The woman was obviously fighting for her life, and there wasn't a second to lose.

Duncan gunned the engine to get them out of there,

and he kept watch around them as he headed for the road. Thankfully, no shots came their way. That was the good news. The bad news was that could mean the shooter had stopped firing so he could go in pursuit of them.

Joelle finished a quick call to Luca to request backup and then went back to her own phone. "Molly?" she tried again.

The sounds of the struggle had stopped. No more screams. Nothing. And that tightened every muscle in Duncan's body. Hell. The sounds of her screams had been terrifying, but the silence was even worse. Because the screams meant she'd at least been alive.

He thought back to the petite, young brunette who'd been a dispatcher for about six months now. She was pregnant, and she wasn't married but had instead opted for artificial insemination to have a child. Molly's parents were dead, and since she had no siblings, she would almost certainly be alone. It was info that everyone in town knew, and it was possible that someone had used that particular info to go after her.

But why?

"This can't be a coincidence," Joelle muttered, taking the words right out of Duncan's mouth.

Yeah, Duncan was leaning that direction as well. Two pregnant women attacked on the same night in the same small town. That would, indeed, be one hell of a coincidence if the incidents weren't related. Still, it was possible that there were two forces at work here. Duncan just didn't know exactly what those two forces were right now, but he'd need to find out and fast.

When there was an attack or kidnapping involving a pregnant woman, it was usually connected to some kind of domestic dispute. In fact, the number one threat to a pregnant woman was being murdered or seriously injured by the woman's partner. But there were also those crimes that involved kidnapping or killing a pregnant woman so the baby could be taken. With Molly so close to giving birth, that was definitely a motive at the top of Duncan's list.

But that didn't explain the attack on Joelle.

She was in her fifth month of pregnancy. Still a long way from delivering their child. A kidnapper would have to hold her for months. Not exactly a comforting thought, but then none of this was anywhere near comfortable.

Duncan cranked up the speed when he reached the road and headed toward town. Since he'd known Molly his whole life, he knew where she lived and didn't have to look up her address. He just drove and tried to figure out how to make this trip as safe as possible for Joelle.

A safety she likely wouldn't want if she was thinking like a cop.

But if necessary, he'd need to remind her that she was on desk duty until the baby arrived. That wasn't a personal preference on his part simply because she was carrying his child. It was standard practice in the sheriff's office, and it was something her father would have insisted on had he still been alive.

Beside him, Joelle continued to try to get some kind of response from Molly by calling out the woman's name into her phone. Molly didn't answer. But there was a response in the form of a dead line. When she tried to call again and got the same thing, Duncan knew that someone had switched off the phone.

"I'll call dispatch to have Molly's phone tracked," Joelle told him.

He could hear the fear and nerves in every word she'd spoken. Fear that was there for a reason because they both knew that whoever was attacking Molly could have also disabled the phone, making it untraceable. Duncan hoped like the devil that hadn't happened, though, because if Molly wasn't home, the phone would be their best bet in tracking her.

Thankfully, there was no other traffic on the rural road at this hour so Duncan continued to press on the accelerator, eating up the distance between Joelle's and Molly's. Luca stayed right behind him in the cruiser.

Duncan's phone rang, and when he saw Deputy Ronnie Bishop's name on the screen, he took the call on speaker. "Is everyone all right?" Duncan immediately asked since he knew Ronnie was at Joelle's.

"So far," Ronnie quickly assured him. "No signs of the shooter, though, and there's been no gunfire since Joelle and you left. No one's attempted to get to the stolen black car, either."

If the gunman had, indeed, been coming after Joelle and him, that would mean he or she had a second vehicle. And likely a partner. Either that or the gunman had positioned a second vehicle earlier and then driven the stolen one to Joelle's. Duncan couldn't think of a good motive for a would-be killer to do that, but the reason could be a clue to who had attacked them and why.

"How many deputies are there?" Duncan asked Ronnie.

"Six, including me. The fire department is here, too, but they're holding off until they get the word from you that it's safe to try to put out the fire."

It wasn't safe. Not with a gunman, maybe two, in the area. Hell, there could be even more than that if this was some kind of coordinated attack. No way could Duncan risk the lives of his deputies and the firemen when Joelle wasn't even there. Yes, she might lose her house to the fire, but the goal was to get everyone out of this alive and then catch the SOB responsible.

"Everyone stays in their vehicles for now," Duncan instructed, "but have two of the deputies go to the end of Joelle's road and keep watch for anyone trying to sneak away from there. Two more should stay put in case the shooter isn't done. Send the other two to Molly's."

If Molly had been kidnapped, or worse, then Duncan figured he was going to need as much help as possible.

Ronnie gave a fast assurance that he'd do as Duncan asked, and they ended the call just as Duncan finally made it to the turn to Molly's. It wasn't a typical subdivision or neighborhood like in a city but rather a spattering of homes that had been built on multi-acre lots. With all the trees and natural landscape, it was more like living in the country, which made for a peaceful lifestyle.

It also meant Molly's neighbors might not have been able to see or hear what was going on.

Added to that, Duncan was well aware that her nearest neighbors were all senior citizens. That was the reason he hadn't called any of them to go check on Molly and try to stop whatever was happening. Duncan hadn't wanted to risk any of them being hurt or killed. This was definitely a situation for law enforcement.

"I want you to stay down," Duncan told Joelle, and he made sure it sounded like the order it was.

She didn't protest. Not with words, anyway. But he knew this was eating away at her. Especially since someone was threatening and maybe had already harmed someone she knew well.

Duncan sped into Molly's driveway, his gaze immediately firing all around. There were no vehicles in front of the house. Nor was there anyone in sight. Just the darkness and the milky yellow illumination coming from the porch light.

"The front door's open," Joelle murmured.

It was. Duncan had noticed that right away, but he aimed a quick scowl at Joelle to let her know if she had seen that, then it meant she wasn't staying down. Joelle muttered some profanity and slipped lower into the seat.

With Luca's cruiser squealing to a stop behind him, Duncan hurried out of the car, and while keeping watch, he ran toward the porch. He couldn't risk sitting around, waiting to see if he could figure out what was going on because at this exact moment, Molly could be inside fighting for her life.

Duncan barreled up the porch steps, taking them two at a time, and pinned his focus to the open door. If Molly's attacker was still in there, he had to be prepared in case the guy shot at him. That's why Duncan tried to listen for any sounds of a struggle or movement.

He heard nothing.

And knew that wasn't a good sign. Ditto for what he spotted on the porch just to the right side of the welcome mat.

Drops of blood.

Duncan was sure that's what it was, and cursing, he stepped around the drops and went inside. Of course, just his mere presence could contaminate the scene, but again, Molly was the priority here. He had to hold out hope that the blood belonged to her attacker, that Molly had somehow managed to fight him off and sent the SOB running.

"Molly?" he called out.

No need for him to stay quiet since there was no element of surprise here. If the attacker was still inside the house, he would have heard the car that Duncan had been driving and the cruiser. Molly would have, too, and that meant if she'd been capable of calling out for help, she likely would have already done it.

Trying to steel himself for the worst but praying for the best, Duncan went into the house, staying low and leading with his gun. His attention whipped to the right, then the left. He took in the toppled lamp on the floor, but it seemed to be the only sign of a struggle.

Room by room, he made his way through the place, recalling the time or two he'd been here with his folks when they'd visited Molly's parents. Years ago, even before Molly had been born. Duncan was thirty-seven and Molly just twenty-four so he'd been plenty old enough to recall coming here for her folks to show off their baby girl. Maybe that was one of the reasons Molly had wanted to raise her child here. Her home. A place where she'd no doubt felt safe.

That last thought twisted his gut into knots so Duncan kept moving, kept searching, all the while listening for, well, anything. In addition to being able to hear anything in the house, he also needed to make sure nothing was going on outside with Joelle and Luca. So far, he wasn't hearing or seeing anything. Nothing out of place except for that lamp.

Until he made it to one of the bedrooms.

Molly's no doubt, and there were plenty of signs of a struggle here. The bed was empty, but the covers had been dragged off, and the clock and lamp that'd almost certainly been on the nightstand were now on the floor.

"Molly?" he called out again and still got no response.

The overhead light was off, but there was a nightlight plugged in the outlet near the door to the adjoining bath. It was enough for him to see more of those blood drops.

Hell.

Duncan moved faster now, checking out the bathroom for any signs of Molly. Nothing. So he kept moving, hurrying to the other rooms. They were all empty, but he got another jolt when he saw the nursery all decked out in shades of pink. Since Joelle's and his baby was also a girl, it made the gut punch even harder.

Pushing that aside, he made his way back through the house and was careful not to touch anything. Whoever had taken Molly might have left prints or some kind of trace evidence in the struggle, and Duncan didn't want to compromise that any more than he already had.

He went back to the porch and saw that Luca was out of the cruiser and near Joelle's vehicle. The deputy immediately looked up at him, but Duncan had to shake his head.

"Molly's not here," Duncan relayed to them. "And there's blood on the porch and in the master bedroom. I want a BOLO for Molly and a CSI team in here right away."

That got Joelle coming out of the car. "There's a garden shed in the back," she said, already moving as if to head in that direction. "Molly could be in there."

Duncan cursed and went after her. "I know about the shed and was about to check it out." He was about to order her back to the car, but she spoke before he could manage to say it.

"I have to help," she insisted.

Joelle wasn't crying. She was too much of a cop for that. But her voice was shaky, and he figured that applied to the rest of her as well. Along with the mother lode of adrenaline, she was also battling the overwhelming fear that a woman they both knew had been kidnapped or killed and that the same thing had nearly happened to her.

"Stay close to me," Duncan finally agreed.

He'd make this search quick so he could get Joelle into at least some minimal cover. Then, he could take her to the sheriff's office while they regrouped and figured out their next move.

As he'd remembered, the shed was in the backyard, not far from the porch that wrapped around the entire house. Duncan made a cursory look of the area, then a quick glance into the shed just to see if by some miracle Molly was hiding there. She wasn't.

"Molly?" he called out one last time.

When he got no response, he hurried back to the car with Joelle and got her inside. "Start calling her neighbors," Duncan instructed. "I want to know if anyone saw or heard anything."

He doubted that'd been the case, though. If so, those neighbors would have already headed over. Still, it was possible that someone had heard something that would give them clues as to who had taken Molly.

There was the howl of sirens in the distance, and Duncan knew it wouldn't be long before more deputies arrived. Good. He'd have them check around the place while he got on the phone with the Texas Rangers and Highway Patrol. Both agencies would get word of the BOLO, but Duncan wanted to emphasize that Molly was pregnant and she worked for law enforcement. Molly was one of them, and that would hopefully get her the highest priority.

Duncan took out his phone, ready to get started on those calls, but he stopped when he caught some movement from the corner of his eye. He pivoted in that direction, in the same motion taking aim with his Glock. Then, he stopped when he spotted something.

The woman walking toward them.

Correction: staggering toward them.

It wasn't Molly. No, this woman was older and had graying black hair that was tangled around her face. She was barefoot and wearing a ripped shirt over stained gray yoga pants.

Duncan's first thought was this was Sandra McCullough, Joelle's mother who'd deserted her family the day her husband had been murdered. No one had seen or heard from her since. But it wasn't Sandra, and Duncan had no idea who she was.

Joelle got out of the car, taking aim as well. So did Luca, but Duncan could see both of the woman's hands, and she wasn't armed. Still, this could be some kind of ploy so he approached her with caution.

"Who are you?" Duncan demanded. "Are you hurt?" He didn't see any signs of injury, but it was possible some of the stains on her clothes were dried blood.

"I'm sorry," the woman said as she came even closer.

That put some ice in his veins. "Sorry for what?" And because it had to be asked, he added. "Are you the one who took Molly?"

She didn't answer but rather just kept walking, her feet dragging through the yard. Her eyes looked vacant. Robotic, even. As if someone had forgotten to turn on a switch. Duncan was betting she'd either been drugged or was in shock.

"This is all my fault," the woman muttered. Her voice was flat and barely a whisper. "Everything that's happening is my fault." She dropped to her knees, her gaze shifting to Joelle. "I'm so sorry, but he wants you dead."

A hoarse sob tore from her throat, and the woman collapsed into a heap on the ground.

Chapter Three

While Joelle sat in the waiting room of the emergency room of Saddle Ridge Hospital, she tried to keep her breathing level and tamp down the worry that was threatening to cloud her mind. Worry wouldn't help—not her baby, not Molly and not her. What she needed right now was for Molly to be found alive and well and for her to find answers as to what the heck was going on.

Duncan was clearly after those answers, too, and he had been on the phone nonstop since they'd arrived at the hospital with the mystery woman. The woman who'd delivered that sickening message.

I'm so sorry, but he wants you dead.

That was definitely something Joelle hadn't wanted to hear, and it'd left her with even more questions. Who was the woman and who was the *he* she'd proclaimed wanted to kill her? Was he the person who'd driven that stolen car to her house and set the fire? It was hard for her to believe that it wasn't connected, but until the woman regained consciousness, all Joelle could do was speculate and deal with her own phone calls. So far, none of those calls had given her any good news.

Plenty of bad, though.

Her house was basically in ashes now because the fire

department hadn't been able to move in to try to save it since there'd been the threat of an active shooter. There were no signs of the shooter now, though. No sign of Molly, either. And the now-unconscious mystery woman had had no ID on her so they didn't even know who she was.

However, Joelle had gotten some good news, not from a call but rather the checkup she'd had shortly after Duncan and she had arrived at the hospital. Despite the traumatic situation she'd experienced, the baby was fine. The monitors had shown a strong, steady heartbeat and lots of movement—signs that had fulfilled a lot of Joelle's prayers. Her baby was okay.

Now, Joelle had to make sure she stayed that way.

The only instructions the doctor had given her was to get some rest, and Duncan had been there to hear that part. Which meant he'd soon be trying to get her off her feet. She was exhausted, no doubt about that, and exhaustion wasn't good for the baby, but neither was having shots fired at them. To make sure an attack like that didn't happen again, they needed answers fast.

Since Duncan was still on the phone, Joelle went after some of those answers by making a call to dispatch to check if there'd been any missing persons' reports in the area of someone matching their mystery woman's description. There hadn't been, but Joelle had known that was a long shot, that the woman could have come from anywhere and maybe wasn't missing at all. She could have arrived shortly before she'd staggered toward Joelle's house.

Emphasis on *staggered.*

She hadn't been steady on her feet at all and seemed dazed, perhaps even drugged. But it was also possible she had been experiencing some kind of medical emergency that had created those symptoms. If so, the woman might not have even been aware of what she was saying.

I'm so sorry, but he wants you dead.

Though she certainly hadn't seemed so dazed or drugged when she'd spoken those words. She'd seemed adamant about delivering a warning with a potential deadly outcome.

Joelle was about to text one of the deputies to see if there'd been any signs of a vehicle that the woman could have used to get to or near her place, but before she could press the number, she got an incoming call from one of her brothers, Ruston McCullough, a homicide detective with San Antonio PD.

It wasn't Ruston's first call of the morning. That initial one had come while Duncan and she were en route to the hospital. She had assured Ruston and her other brother, Slater, and their kid sister, Bree, that she hadn't been harmed, but Joelle knew they were worried about her. Knew, too, that the calls to check on her would continue until they could see her face-to-face and make sure the baby and she were, indeed, okay.

"Anything?" Ruston immediately asked. His tone was brusque as it usually was, but Joelle was aware that the question covered a lot of bases, including her own state of mind.

"No. We're still in limbo when it comes to any info that'll help." She paused, had to because of the sudden lump in her throat. "Still nothing on Molly. Someone took her, and she has to be terrified."

Joelle refused to believe it could be worse than that. She wouldn't accept that Molly could be hurt or dead. She had to cling to the hope they would somehow find her and bring her safely home.

"Any ransom demand?" Ruston questioned.

Joelle had to repeat her "no." But in a way, a ransom demand would be a positive sign. It meant she'd been taken for money and would presumably be released unharmed if the money was paid.

Ruston sighed and paused a long time. "I'm sorry about your house. You've got the keys and security code to stay at my place, but I don't want you there alone. Just hang with Duncan until I can get there. I want to keep coordinating with the Rangers to try to locate Molly."

"Keep on that," she insisted. She would have also told him she would come up with a safe place to stay, however, when Duncan ended his latest call and started her way, she put the rest of this conversation on hold. "I have to go," she told Ruston. "I'll let you know if I get any updates."

She ended the call and stood to face Duncan. He definitely didn't look to be the bearer of good news, and that caused her heart to sink again. She prayed he wasn't about to tell her Molly was dead.

"We haven't found Molly yet," Duncan immediately said, probably picking up the worst-case-scenario vibe from her expression. "Some of the reserve deputies are canvassing the area around her house to find out if anyone saw anything."

The late hour wouldn't help with that, but maybe Molly had managed to scream or something. If so, that would have already been reported, but Joelle had to hang on to the hope that they'd get a viable lead.

"The CSIs are going through Molly's house and the stolen car left at your place," Duncan continued. "They're still looking for her vehicle, too." Even though it wasn't necessary for him to identify what *her* he was referring to, he tipped his head to the exam room where the medical staff had taken the mystery woman. "She didn't have any ID on her."

"And there's no missing person's report matching her description," Joelle provided.

Duncan nodded. "Apparently, she drifted in and out of consciousness when she was in the ambulance so when we're able to speak to her, she might be able to tell us who she is. And why she issued that warning," he tacked onto that.

Yes, that was vital for the safety of their baby, and Joelle reminded herself that there were a lot of people working to get answers and make sure that *safety* happened.

"Do you think this woman and the warning are directly connected to Molly?" Joelle came out and asked.

Duncan's gaze locked with hers. Something they usually avoided because of the heat that was always there between them. Heat that came despite any and everything going on. There'd always be an intimate connection, especially now that she was carrying his child, but because she was so worried about Molly, it was easier for Joelle to shove that heat aside.

"Yes," he admitted. The sigh he added was long, heavy and weary. "That's why I made a call to the FBI. I wanted to see if they were aware of any black market baby rings or perpetrators in the area who could be targeting pregnant women. Nothing like that is on their radar, but they're checking to see if this is someone from out of state."

Joelle had tried to maintain a stoic expression, her cop face. She tried not to let the possibility of something like that give her this jolt of fear. But it did. Mercy, it did.

Duncan muttered some profanity and took hold of her arm. Probably because she looked ready to collapse. Joelle was almost certain that wouldn't happen, almost, but she allowed him to help her back into one of the chairs, and he sank down on the one beside her.

"Deep breaths," he advised her. "Count to ten. Tell me the latest names you're considering for the baby."

Part of her resented Duncan for seeing the weakness in her and knowing she needed help. Part of her also resented that such measures might be necessary to keep herself from spiraling. But the resentment was really for herself, for feeling this clawing terror all the way to the bone. Those sort of emotions didn't help. In fact, they could hurt, and she didn't want anything else that could hinder them in this investigation.

"I'll be all right," she muttered, hoping it was true.

The sound Duncan made let her know that he wasn't so sure of that at all, and she might have launched into more attempts at convincing him if her phone hadn't rang. "It's my sister again," she muttered, and even though Joelle wasn't in the mood to talk to her, she had to answer it or it would cause Bree to worry even more than she was already was.

"Bree," Joelle greeted. "I'm all right."

"So you say." Her sister's sigh was plenty loud enough for Joelle to hear. "I'll believe it when I see it. I'm coming home, but I can't get there for at least a couple of days."

Joelle groaned. Bree was a lawyer working on a special task force in Dallas, six hours away, and she knew Bree had used all her vacation time and then some when she'd come home after their father's murder and disappearance. Since Joelle figured she stood no chance whatsoever of convincing Bree she was fine and didn't need her sister to be there, she went with a different tactic.

"Everyone in the sheriff's office is tied up with the investigation," Joelle spelled out. "And right now Saddle Ridge isn't the safest place to be."

"I'm coming home," Bree insisted, and then she paused. Sighed again. "I need to see you. There are things I want to talk to you about."

Joelle didn't like the sound of that, especially since she and her sister communicated at least weekly either by phone call or text. "Is something wrong?" Joelle came out and asked.

It was a valid question. Like her, Bree had been devastated with what had happened to their parents. Added to that, Bree had broken up with her longtime boyfriend, Luca. Then again, Luca and Bree had had an on-again, off-again thing going on since high school. Since Bree was often involved in high-profile legal cases for the state and was gone a lot, both Luca and she had had other relationships. But something had happened between Luca and Bree to make her sister pull the plug and now things were permanently off.

Or so Bree had said.

Luca wasn't offering up anything so Joelle wasn't sure what had happened. Maybe it was something similar to what had gone on between Duncan and her. Too much pain and grief. Too much guilt. Too much, period.

"I should be home by early next week," Bree added a moment later. "In the meantime, you stay safe. I love you, Joelle."

"I'll certainly try," Joelle assured her. "And I love you, too," she said, ending the call just as the door to the exam room finally opened.

It wasn't the mystery woman who came out, of course, but it was a familiar face. Dr. Chase Benton, one of the doctors who worked at Saddle Ridge General Hospital.

Dr. Benton spotted them and walked their way as Duncan and she headed to him. "Is she awake?" Duncan immediately asked.

"She is, for the moment anyway," the doctor said, but there was caution in his voice. He stepped in front of Duncan when he started toward the exam room. "I'm well aware that you need to see her," he quickly added. "I've heard what's going on, and I understand you have to question her, but you should know that she's still unable to stay awake for more than a couple of seconds. Unable to tell me her name as well. I suspect she's been drugged, and that the drugs combined with a head injury are the reasons she's lapsing in and out of consciousness."

That wasn't a surprise to either Duncan or her, and that led them to more questions. Who'd drugged her and why? Hopefully, they'd know the answers to that soon.

"Her blood pressure is high as well," the doctor continued. "And that means when you question her, you can't push too hard. I can't give her anything right now for the blood pressure until I find out what other drugs are in her system."

Duncan groaned. "I have to push," he insisted. "Molly Radel and her baby's life could depend on it."

Dr. Benton's eyes widened. "You believe the patient had something to do with that?"

"I think the likelihood is high that there's a connection. It's possible the woman can tell us who took Molly."

Despite Duncan's use of *likelihood* and *possible*, the doctor nodded and stepped to the side. "All right, you can question her, but I have to be there. And trust me, I will pull the plug on the interview if I feel she can't handle it."

Duncan nodded, too, while he was already on the move. With Dr. Benton and Joelle right behind him, Duncan stepped into the ER room where the woman was lying on the bed. She was hooked up to a monitor and had an IV in the back of her hand. Joelle also spotted some injuries.

There was a gash on the side of her head, some bruising as well and her feet were covered with cuts and scrapes.

"She obviously walked barefoot through some rough terrain," the doctor pointed out. "There was also powder on her clothes. The kind of powder you'd get from a deployed airbag."

So maybe she'd been involved in a car accident. However, that didn't explain what had happened to her shoes or why she'd ended up walking to Molly's. Or the ominous message she'd delivered.

The woman's eyes were open, and when she lifted her head, her attention went straight to them. Joelle didn't see any recognition in her expression, only wariness and confusion. Added to that, her gaze still had that dazed look she'd had when she arrived at Molly's.

"I'm Sheriff Duncan Holder," he said, stepping closer to her. He tipped his head to Joelle. "And this is Deputy Joelle McCullough. Could you tell us your name?"

The woman looked at the doctor and then shifted her attention to Joelle. "I came to see you," she muttered, her voice a ragged whisper.

That gave Joelle some hope. If the woman remembered that, then she might recall other things, too.

"You did," Joelle verified. She started to remind her of what she'd said before she collapsed but decided to press for an ID instead. "Who are you?"

She shook her head as if trying to figure that out, and then murmured. "Kate Moreland."

Duncan got out his phone as she spoke the last syllable, and he fired off a quick text, no doubt to get someone at the sheriff's office to run a background check on her.

"Kate Moreland," Joelle repeated, mentally testing out the name, but it didn't ring any bells. "You know me?"

Kate shook her head. "I know of you." Her voice broke into a hoarse groan. She eased back onto the bed and closed her eyes. "I had to warn you."

Another positive sign that she'd remembered that. Of course, the warning she'd delivered hadn't been positive at all.

"You said someone wanted me dead," Joelle reminded her. "Who?"

She didn't open her eyes, and it was at least fifteen seconds before she answered. "My son," she finally said, and she broke down into a heaving sob. A reaction that caused the numbers on the monitor to spike.

"You need to leave," Dr. Benton insisted. "Her blood pressure's too high. Step out while I try to get her stabilized." It wasn't a request, and the doctor practically muscled them out of the room.

Duncan cursed and took out his phone. "Slater's running the background check on her. I'll see if he's got anything yet." However, Duncan's phone rang before he could call her brother.

"It's Ronnie," he relayed to her, and he put the deputy's call on speaker.

"We found a car, a dark blue Audi," Ronnie said right off. "It looks as if the driver hit the east side of the bridge and lost control. It was off the road and all the way down on the banks of the creek."

The creek was only about a half mile from Molly's, and if it did, indeed, belong to Kate, then the woman had likely been traveling from the interstate. If she'd been coming from town, then the collision would have probably happened on the west side of the bridge. Also, if she'd been coming from town, Duncan or one of the responding deputies would have spotted her on the road before she'd made it to Molly's.

"I'm running the plates now," Ronnie continued. "But there was a purse and a phone in the vehicle. According to the driver's license, the purse's owner is Kate Moreland. She has a San Antonio address."

San Antonio was a half hour away, which meant Ruston could no doubt help with getting them any info they needed on her. And her son. Joelle wanted to know his name and why Kate had believed he might want to kill her.

"When you do a thorough search of the car," Duncan said, "check her GPS to confirm if she was heading to Molly's or Joelle's. And let me know if you find anything we can use."

Ronnie assured him that he would, and Duncan ended the call to make one to Slater. Her brother answered on the first ring.

"Kate Moreland," Slater immediately said, and he rattled off an address in San Antonio. "Age fifty-three. Divorced. No criminal record. She's a very wealthy businesswoman who owns a half dozen martial arts and workout gyms."

"You have the name of her son?" Duncan pressed.

"Yeah. Brad. Age twenty-eight, and I'm just scratching the surface on him. Why? Is he part of this?"

"Kate seems to think so," Duncan quickly verified. "She believes her son might be out to kill Joelle."

Slater cursed. "He's got a record for assault during a bar fight, but I don't see any connection to Joelle or Saddle Ridge..." His words trailed off, and he cursed again. "But his ex-wife, Shanda Cantrell, does. My dad and you arrested her nearly two years ago for reckless driving and resisting arrest. Either of you remember that?"

"I do," Duncan said.

"So do I," Joelle murmured, trying to zoom in on any info that was lingering around in her memory. The info had plenty of gaps in it so she took out her phone and started searching while she continued. "I recall Dad and Duncan bringing in a woman for those charges. They had me search her for weapons, and because she was being so combative, Dad put her in a holding cell."

"A definite yes to her being combative," Duncan agreed. "She tried to take a punch at me. And she cursed and spat at Joelle. Cursed the sheriff, too."

Slater must have pulled up the file right before she did because he was the one to add more. "She ended up pleading guilty, paid a fine and did some community service. Dad worked it out so she could do that service in San Antonio so she wouldn't miss any work at her job as a florist." Slater paused a moment. "Had she been drinking?" he asked. "Was that the reason for the reckless driving?"

"No alcohol," Joelle was able to provide. "She admitted to having been in a heated argument with someone on her phone. She was also speeding when she rammed into a mailbox, swerved and nearly hit another car." Then, she paused. Had to. Because she spotted something in the file notes. "Shanda was three months pregnant."

Both Duncan and Slater went silent, but she could hear Slater clicking away on a keyboard. "She has no children listed. Neither does Brad."

So either Shanda had miscarried or the baby had died. Either way, that might play into motive. If there was motive for Shanda, that is. Kate hadn't said a word about her ex-daughter-in-law, only her son. Maybe then, losing a child had something to do with why Kate had come here to issue that warning about Brad.

"I'll obviously want a conversation with both Shanda and Brad," Duncan insisted.

"I can arrange that," Slater volunteered. "When I call him, how much do you want him to know about his mother?"

Duncan's forehead bunched up while he gave that some thought. Joelle definitely wanted to hear how he was going to handle this, but her phone rang, and her chest tightened when she saw *Unknown Caller* on the screen.

"This could be the ransom demand," Joelle muttered, answering the call on speaker and hitting the record function on her phone.

She steeled herself up to hear a snarled threat and demand from the kidnapper. But it wasn't.

"Help me," the woman said.

It was Molly.

Chapter Four

"I'll have to call you back," Duncan told Slater the moment he heard Molly's voice.

He didn't wait for Slater to respond. Duncan ended the call and went closer to Joelle.

"Where are you?" Joelle asked Molly. "Are you all right?"

Molly didn't answer, but Duncan could hear some kind of shuffling around, and several moments later, someone spoke. But this time, it wasn't Molly.

"Don't ask any questions," a man said. His voice was muffled and practically a growl. No doubt because he was trying to disguise it. Did that mean Duncan knew this person? "I made a mistake, and I'm trying to fix it."

Despite the man demanding no questions, Duncan had so many of them. Joelle no doubt did, too. But at the top of their list had to be if Molly had been harmed.

"We're listening," Duncan prompted so the man would continue.

"A big mistake," he muttered, adding some profanity. "I'll leave the woman somewhere you can find her."

Duncan jumped right on that. It wasn't the ransom demand—or any other kind of demand—he'd been expecting. "Where?"

"I'll call you once I've dropped her off, tell you where

she is, and you can come and get her," the man was quick to say.

Of course, that meant the guy would probably be long gone by the time they arrived to get Molly. But this could also be a trap to draw Joelle and him out.

"Is Molly all right?" Duncan asked, hoping that Molly would be able to answer that for herself.

"She's shaken up but fine. Like I said, taking her was a mistake."

Duncan wanted to press for more. He wanted to know why kidnapping Molly had been a mistake. Had this been a case of the wrong person being taken? Had Joelle been the target? He needed answers to all of that, but he especially wanted to know whose blood was in the house and on Molly's porch. If it was Molly's, then she was more than just shaken up.

"Leave Molly somewhere now," Duncan bargained. "She and her baby need to be checked by a doctor."

Silence. For a long time. And Duncan hoped like the devil that the guy was considering that. The sooner they got Molly, the better.

"I'll call you when I call you," the man finally snarled, and he ended the conversation before Duncan could say anything else.

Duncan immediately cursed and tried to call the kidnapper back. It wasn't a surprise, though, when the guy didn't answer. Still, Duncan reminded himself that the call was a positive sign. Molly was alive, and the man who'd taken her wanted to return her.

Supposedly.

He cursed again and looked at Joelle. "He could be using Molly and her baby as bait," she muttered.

"Yeah." But Duncan didn't need to spell out the rest.

He'd have to go to Molly even if a trap was a high probability. Which it was. He'd have to go even if there was only a slim chance they'd get Molly back.

"You'll take backup," Joelle said, proving that they were thinking the same thing. "And you'll be careful."

Duncan shouldn't have felt good about her adding that last part. But he did. There'd been so many weeks of tension between Joelle and him. So much guilt. Now, though, they were on the same side again, and he realized just how much he'd missed this. He'd had a thing for her for years, that wasn't going away, but he missed working with her almost as much as he missed being with her.

Almost.

He glanced up the hall when he saw someone approaching, and his body braced. But it wasn't a threat. It was Luca who'd gone back to Joelle's after he'd escorted Duncan and her to the hospital.

"No sign of the gunman yet," Luca reported. "No other shots fired after you left the scene. How are you two? Were either of you hurt?"

"We're fine," Joelle assured him. "We just got a call from the kidnapper." She handed him her phone. "The recording of the conversation is on there, but the kidnapper claims he intends to return Molly."

That put some hope in Luca's intense brown eyes. Hope that disappeared as fast as it'd come. "You believe him?"

"Too soon to tell," Duncan muttered.

Luca's phone rang. "It's the fire department," he explained. "I'd better take this." He stepped away to do that, and Duncan turned back to Joelle.

"When the kidnapper does call back, you won't be going with me to pick up Molly," he told her.

Her mouth tightened, but she didn't argue. She had to

know if this was a trap, then she was likely the intended target.

Well, maybe she was.

"You don't resemble Molly," he said, thinking out loud. "You live miles from each other. Yes, you're both pregnant, and she's a former cop, but that's about it."

Joelle nodded. "Maybe it wasn't about mistaking Molly for me but he could possibly see the kidnapping as a mistake. It's possible he didn't know she was pregnant." She paused. "Or he could have just changed his mind."

That was true, but it still didn't explain the attack on Joelle. Or maybe it did. "If someone wanted to kidnap pregnant women, there could have been two teams operating. The one that hit your place and the one that went after Molly."

Joelle made a sound of agreement but wasn't able to add anything else because the door to Kate Moreland's room opened, and Dr. Benton came out.

Benton was quick to shake his head. "You won't be able to speak to Ms. Moreland for at least a couple of hours. Maybe longer. Her blood pressure isn't stable, and she's at risk for a hypertension crisis, which could lead to a stroke or heart attack. I'll give you a call when it's safe for her to have visitors."

Duncan couldn't press to continue the interview, not when it could put the woman's life in danger. But there were also more pressing dangers than Ms. Moreland's health.

"Ms. Moreland was worried about her son, Brad," Duncan told the doctor. "She thought he might want to harm Joelle in some way. That's why she was heading to Joelle's place, but she was near Molly's when she was involved in a car crash."

A crash that might or might not have been an accident.

That was yet something else Duncan would need to find out about.

"If she's right about her son, he could be dangerous," Duncan went on. "I'll keep Deputy Vanetti standing guard outside her room now," he added, motioning to Luca who was only a few feet away and still on the phone. "And I'll get a reserve deputy in to replace him." That's because Duncan needed all his best trained deputies on the investigation.

The doctor nodded and gave an uneasy glance around. "I'll alert security, too, that there could be a potential problem."

Security was basically one guard who monitored the cameras positioned in and around the hospital. Duncan didn't know who was on duty tonight, but a deputy would be the best bet to keep Kate safe.

"I'll contact a reserve deputy," Luca volunteered after the doctor had walked away, already on his phone. No doubt to call security. "And I'll get the hospital guard a photo of Brad Moreland so he can keep an eye out for him."

"Good idea," Duncan told him and added a thanks before he got Joelle moving.

"You want me to walk with you to the exit?" Luca asked.

It was tempting, but he had to shake his head. "Best to stay on Kate's door. But I will use your cruiser."

It was bullet-resistant and parked right outside the ER. A safer way to get Joelle to the sheriff's office than using her car.

Luca immediately handed over the keys, and while Joelle and Duncan started down the hall, she typed out a text. "To Slater," she explained. "I want to fill him in about what's going on."

Good idea because Slater and all the other deputies needed to know about Kate and her son. About Shanda as well. Even though they didn't have any direct proof, the attacks on Joelle and Molly might, indeed, be related to Shanda's arrest two years ago. That was a long time to wait to act out on a grudge, and that's why they had to learn everything they could about the woman.

Duncan stopped at the ER doors and peered out into the parking lot. He didn't see any immediate threat. In fact, because of the early hour, there wasn't anyone around.

No one visible, anyway.

Of course, there was always the threat that a gunman had positioned himself to wait for them to come out. And that's why Duncan had to test the waters. Something Joelle wasn't going to like. The cruiser was close, but he wanted it as close to the ER doors as possible. That would minimize Joelle's time for being out in the open where she'd be an easy target.

"Wait here," he instructed.

Nope, she didn't like it, but she didn't voice her objection. However, she did take out her gun and started glancing around to make sure he wasn't about to be ambushed.

Duncan also took out his weapon and hurried to the cruiser. He kept an eye on Joelle as well because if she was a target, then an attacker could use this opportunity to go after her. But he held out hope that Molly's kidnapper believed her abduction to be a mistake. If so, then maybe going after Joelle had been, too, and it could mean she was no longer in danger. Duncan had to hope for the best and prepare for the worst, though, and that meant making this trip to the sheriff's office as safe as possible for her and their baby.

Thankfully, no one fired at him when he raced outside and to the cruiser, and he moved fast to bring the vehicle closer to Joelle. Duncan lifted his hand in a wait gesture, though, and didn't give her the go-ahead to move until he'd gotten back out of the cruiser first to open the passenger's side door for her and also so he could shield her as best he could.

All of these security measures had to be both a blessing and a curse for her. After all, Joelle was a good cop, as good as they came, and she was normally in the role of the protector. Added to that, it was probably especially uncomfortable for her since he was the one doing the protecting. But like him, she needed to take all available precautions for their child.

The moment Joelle was inside the cruiser, Duncan hurried back to the driver's seat, and he got them out of there fast. Again, though, he had to keep watch since it was possible for a sniper to be perched on top of one of the buildings that lined Main Street. Thankfully, they made it the six blocks without anyone trying for round two of an attack.

Duncan parked right out front, and they both hurried into the building. Which was practically empty. No surprise there since he had the deputies working the crime scenes at Molly's and Joelle's and others out looking for the gunman. The sole occupant was Carmen Gonzales, a reserve deputy who'd retired several years earlier but still made herself available for emergencies. This was definitely an emergency.

"Any word about Molly?" Carmen immediately asked.

"Nothing confirmed, but her kidnapper called and claims he'll release her," Duncan explained, and he tacked on a question of his own to that. "Are there any reports from the deputies in the field?"

Carmen shook her head. "Nothing that I didn't forward to Luca and you." She glanced down at the laptop she'd been using when Joelle and he had come in. "I'm doing the background checks on Kate Moreland, her son and his ex-wife, Shanda."

"Good. Keep on that," Duncan instructed, though he wanted to do some digging in those areas as well. "Do you have the son's contact info?"

Carmen checked the computer screen again and nodded. "I'll forward it to you. The phone number for his ex as well."

Duncan muttered a thanks and put his hand on the small of Joelle's back to get her moving first toward her desk in the bullpen where he grabbed her laptop. Then, he picked up his from his office before heading to the break room at the back of the building.

"The doctor said you should rest," he reminded her.

"I can rest and work at the same time," she was quick to respond.

Duncan had expected that and already come up with a compromise. He took her to the break room with him where there was a fairly comfortable sofa, had her sit and then handed over the laptop.

"I want you to contact the techs at the crime lab and see if they can get anything from the number Molly's kidnapper used to call us," Duncan instructed. "That's priority."

Even though both of them knew that was a long shot. The kidnapper had probably used a burner that couldn't be traced. Still, they might get lucky.

"After that, if you're not ready to get some actual sleep, I need any and all preliminary reports from the CSIs and fire department," he continued.

"I won't be ready to sleep," she assured him. "Not with the adrenaline still burning through me."

Yeah, he knew all about adrenaline overload. Hard to come down from that, and when you did, it was a crash.

Joelle would no doubt soon be exhausted. Maybe enough that she'd actually grab a nap.

He went to the small fridge in the corner and took out two bottles of water and one of Joelle's yogurt cups she kept stocked. He set one of the waters, the yogurt and a spoon on the end table next to her.

"Also, if you still have any bandwidth left after dealing with the techs and getting the reports, go through the file of Shanda's arrest. See if there are any red flags that could have predicted something like this."

It wasn't busy work, and Joelle knew that because she got started on it right away. All were necessary steps in the investigation. So was what Duncan had to do next. Despite the fact it was barely five in the morning, he used the contact info Carmen had just emailed him and called Brad Moreland. There was no answer for four rings, and just as Duncan thought the call might go to voice mail, someone finally answered.

"What?" a man snarled, and judging from the grogginess in his voice, Duncan had woken him up.

"I'm Sheriff Duncan Holder from Saddle Ridge. FYI, this call is on speaker, and I have a deputy listening. Are you Brad Moreland?"

The man cursed. "Saddle Ridge," he spat out like venom. "Yeah, this is Brad Moreland, and anything you want to say to me should go through my lawyer. We're going through with the lawsuit for what you did to my wife."

"Your ex-wife," Duncan corrected. "And what lawsuit?" He figured he'd get that out of the way before bringing up the reason for this call.

"My wife," Brad snapped. "Shanda and I are reconciling. And as for the lawsuit, you'll soon know all about that because we're filing a civil suit for my wife's unlawful arrest and detainment. An arrest and detainment that was so traumatic she ended up miscarrying."

Bingo. There it was. The motive all spelled out. Though it did seem odd that they'd file a civil suit, which would draw attention to themselves. That could mean they weren't behind the attack and Molly's kidnapping. Or else they wanted to use the civil suit as a sort of reverse psychology. Why go after them physically when they were already going the legal route?

"We're going to sue you and your department into the ground," Brad threatened. "And then we'll go after your personal assets. You and your deputies aren't above the law, Sheriff." Again, he used that venomous tone for the last word.

Since Shanda's arrest had been justified, Duncan seriously doubted there'd be a payout of any kind, but a civil suit was an annoyance since he would still have to defend the actions the former sheriff had taken. That would in turn stir up bad memories for Joelle.

One look at her face confirmed it was already doing that.

"You and the deputies are going to pay for—"

"I'm calling about your mother, Kate Moreland," Duncan interrupted.

Brad clearly hadn't expected him to say that because it stopped his tirade, and after a few seconds of silence, the man muttered, "What about her?" There was concern, but then the anger returned. "Did you come up with some reason to arrest her?"

"No." Duncan took a moment to consider what he intended, and didn't intend, to say. "She was involved in a car accident and was taken to the hospital."

Brad cursed. "Is she alive?"

"She is." And he waited to see how Brad would react to

that. If Brad did, indeed, have criminal intentions as his mother claimed, then the man might have wanted the news that the car crash had been fatal.

"I need to see her," Brad insisted. "Where is she?"

"She's in the hospital and in protective custody."

There was some more cursing. "*Your* protective custody. This from the sheriff's office that killed my child and wrecked my life—"

"It's odd that you'd mention someone being killed because that's what your mother claimed you wanted to do."

That brought on the silence. "You're lying."

"I have witnesses," Duncan pointed out.

Brad huffed. "Witnesses who you coached no doubt because you want to get ahead of the lawsuit and try to defame me."

"I didn't know about the lawsuit before I called you. Now, explain why your mother would accuse you of plotting to kill a cop." Duncan made sure that wasn't a suggestion but rather an order from a sheriff.

"I have no idea." Now there was plenty of defensiveness in Brad's voice. "You said she was in a car accident so maybe she got a head injury and was confused."

Duncan hadn't missed the fact that Brad hadn't asked about his mother's injuries right from the start. Most people did once they understood their loved one was alive. Brad had demanded to see her, but he hadn't pressed about her condition.

"Is my mother in the hospital there in Saddle Ridge?" Brad finally said after a long silence. "If so, I can be there in under an hour."

"She can't have visitors. Doctor's orders. But even if she could, I won't let you in to see her unless I'm convinced your mother was wrong about you wanting to kill one of my deputies."

"Deputy Joelle McCullough." Brad said her name like profanity. "She was one of the cops who arrested my wife. Oh, her dad was the head honcho in that, but he's dead so the lawsuit will be aimed mainly at his daughter and the other cops involved. Molly Radel and Ronnie Bishop."

Everything inside Duncan went on alert, and he mouthed for Joelle to send Ronnie a heads-up about being a possible target.

"It's interesting that out of the three people you just named," Duncan continued with Brad, "one was kidnapped and the other attacked. According to your mom, she specifically came to Saddle Ridge to warn Deputy McCullough."

Brad's next round of profanity was quick and raw. "Like I said, my mother was mistaken. Sure, I've talked about Deputy McCullough and Deputy Radel but I'll go after them in the courts for what they did. I'm not on some vendetta."

"So, you have an alibi for the past five hours?" Duncan fired back.

"I was in bed at my house. Alone," Brad tacked onto that in a mutter. "That doesn't mean I did those things."

Maybe. But it didn't look good, not with his mother accusing him and with no alibi. "I want you here at the Saddle Ridge Sheriff's Office in three hours. That'll give you time to arrange for your lawyer to come with you."

"You better believe I'll have a lawyer. And I'll expect to see my mother when I'm there."

"You can expect it, but you might not get it," Duncan snarled right back. "Be here in three hours," he repeated, and he ended the call.

Duncan immediately fixed his gaze on Joelle, prompting her to give her take on the phone call.

"Brad's angry enough to come after Molly and me. And he has plenty of money to hire someone to orchestrate the attacks," she amended and then paused. "But if he hired that gunman and the kidnapper, then why didn't he establish an alibi for himself?"

Yeah, that was the thing that stood out for Duncan, too. "Maybe Brad didn't know his mom was going to rat him out. He also might not have thought we'd connect the kidnapping and attack to what happened to his ex-wife nearly two years ago."

Still, a guilty person should have thought of those angles and covered his butt. Brad hadn't. Was that cockiness, sloppy work or was he actually innocent?

Joelle's phone dinged with a text, and she sighed when she read it. "While you were talking to Brad, I texted the tech guys with the kidnapper's phone number. They obviously took me at my word when I said it was high priority because they checked it right away. It's a burner, and it's no longer in service."

Duncan went with a sigh of his own, even though it was expected news.

"Of course, the tech guys will keep searching to see if they can link it back to anyone," she added.

That was standard operating procedure, but it was a rarity when they found those links. Still, it was all they had at the moment.

"I'm hoping the kidnapper will arrange for us to pick up Molly before Brad comes in for his interview," Duncan said, and he checked the time. "Why don't you try to get some rest—" He stopped when his phone rang. Unknown caller. And his heart raced at the possibility of this being the kidnapper who was using a different phone.

"Sheriff Holder," Duncan answered. He hit record and put the call on speaker. But it wasn't a man's voice who greeted him.

"Sheriff," a woman said. It definitely wasn't Molly, either. "I'm Shanda Cantrell. I just got off the phone with Brad, and he was very upset."

Duncan would have preferred for this call to be about Molly and her release, but he'd intended to call Shanda so this saved him the step of having to get her number.

"A lot of people are upset right now," Duncan verified. "And by the way, I have you on speaker, and one of my deputies is listening. I'm also recording this conversation."

That brought on a couple of moments of silence. "All right," Shanda finally said. "I'm calling because Brad told me his mother was delusional and talking out of her head," Shanda went on. "Kate accused Brad of intending to commit a crime."

"Did he?" Duncan asked, figuring that was the fastest way to cut to the heart of this conversation.

Shanda didn't gasp or make a sharp sound of surprise. Instead, she sighed. "No. Not that I know of," she tacked onto that.

Interesting. Those weren't the words of a woman jumping to defend her ex-husband. "But it's possible he committed a crime," Duncan pressed.

"Not that I know of," she repeated, and this time there was an admonishment to her tone. "I can tell you that the relationship between Kate and Brad is strained right now, so if Kate sustained a head injury or something, that might have caused her to say what she did."

Duncan disregarded the last part of that and went for the meat of the remark. "Strained how? Why?"

Shanda sighed again. "It's because of me. Brad wants to get back together and Kate loathes me."

When Shanda didn't add more, Duncan went with a prompt. "Brad wants to get back together. How about you? How do you feel about that?"

"It's complicated." Shanda groaned. "I know that's a cliché, but in our case, it's true. Brad and I share a very painful past."

Duncan could relate, what with Joelle and him blaming themselves for not stopping her father's murder. So the cliché of complicated fit them, too.

"I'm not sure if Brad and I will be getting back together or not," Shanda finally admitted. "It won't happen unless he's willing to get the counseling he needs. So far, Brad hasn't shown up at any of the appointments I've scheduled for him."

Maybe because the man didn't want to forget the past but rather get revenge for it.

"Counseling has really helped me," Shanda went on. "I had a difficult childhood, and according to my therapist, that created some anger issues. Issues, too, with using people. And, yes, I used Brad. Or rather I used his money. Don't get me wrong. I loved him, and that's why I married him, but I wasn't careful with his money."

Shanda sounded a lot different than she had from the night she'd been arrested. Maybe the counseling had worked. Or maybe this was all an act.

"Why does Kate loathe you?" Duncan asked, circling back to what Shanda had said earlier.

"This is all very personal," Shanda muttered.

"You bet it is," Duncan snarled. "Someone tried to kill

one of my deputies and kidnapped a former deputy who's now a dispatcher. For me, that's as personal as it gets, and if you have any information that can help me find the person responsible, then spill it."

"Yes," the woman said, her voice heavy with emotion now. "Brad told me about that, and he thinks because of what Kate said, he's now a suspect in those crimes."

"He is a suspect," Duncan verified. "And you're a person of interest. In fact, I'll need you to come into the Saddle Ridge Sheriff's Office for an official interview. When we're done talking, go ahead and arrange for that. Bring your lawyer if you want, but I expect you in this morning. The earlier, the better."

"I see," Shanda said in a whisper. "You believe the attack and the kidnapping are connected to what happened to me nearly two years ago."

"Are they?" Duncan was quick to ask.

"No, I don't think so." She paused. "Look, I understand you have a job to do, but that incident was very painful for me. I had a miscarriage, and since I couldn't deal with the grief of losing my child, I fell apart. It ruined my marriage."

Duncan listened for any signs of bitterness and rage, but he didn't pick up on anything. What was there was the pain and grief of trauma. Then again, maybe that's what Shanda wanted him to hear.

"As I said, I've gone through counseling," Shanda went on. "Lots and lots of it. It's helped, but Brad seems stalled in that deep rut of loss over our baby. You see, I'd had a hard time getting pregnant and gone through many fertility treatments. The pregnancy was a miracle, and it was snatched away."

Now there was some bitterness, but Duncan figured it was a drop in the bucket to what Brad had revealed.

"I understand Brad has filed a civil lawsuit over what happened," Shanda went on. "I'm trying to talk him out of that because I don't think that will help with his healing. He needs to heal," she emphasized.

Duncan had to wonder just how "broken" Brad was. Maybe Kate was dead-on when she'd accused her son of going after Joelle.

"Any idea why Brad would wait two years to file the lawsuit?" he pressed.

Shanda sighed. "He's talked about it for a while, months. And I know he interviewed several lawyers before he finally found one who actually encouraged him to go through with it."

So, Brad had shopped around to find someone who had told him what he wanted to hear. And once Brad had that approval, maybe he did more than just start a legal battle. Maybe he decided to get full on revenge.

"Could Brad have been responsible for the attack and kidnapping?" Duncan came out and asked.

"I don't want to believe he is," Shanda admitted. Then, she stopped and muttered something Duncan didn't catch. "I'll contact my lawyer and see if he can meet me right away so we can go to the sheriff's office together. As soon as I have a time for our arrival, I'll let you know."

"I want you in before ten o'clock," Duncan insisted.

"I'll let you know," Shanda repeated, and then she ended the call.

Duncan put his phone away and began to process everything he'd just heard. Judging from the way Joelle's forehead had bunched up, she was doing the same.

"Shanda believes Brad could be guilty," Joelle concluded. "Along with Kate's statement, maybe that's enough for us to get access to Brad's financial records to see if he hired the gunman and the kidnapper?"

"Maybe," Duncan muttered, but he could already hear Brad's lawyer putting up an argument about that. An argument he might win since Kate's own mental state couldn't be verified right now. Still, it was worth a try.

Duncan texted the assistant district attorney to put in the request. He'd have to follow that up with some paperwork, but he might be able to get enough out of Kate and Shanda to justify the warrant.

"You want to try to get some rest now?" Duncan asked her after he'd finished his text.

Joelle opened her mouth, no doubt to argue, but was cut off by the sound of footsteps. Moments later, Carmen appeared in the doorway.

"There's a PI here to see you," Carmen said. "Al Hamlin."

Duncan repeated the name, but it didn't ring any bells. Joelle shook her head to indicate she didn't recognize it, either.

"Did he say what he wants?" Duncan asked.

Carmen nodded. "He claims he knows who kidnapped Molly and tried to kill Joelle. And he says he has proof."

Chapter Five

Joelle slowly got to her feet, her attention fixed on Carmen. She immediately had a bad thought, that this was one of the gunmen using this visit as a ploy to come after Duncan and her again. The concern must have shown on her face, too, because Carmen spoke right up.

"Hamlin didn't set off the metal detector," Carmen pointed out, "but Luca's back, and he frisked him. He was armed with a Glock that he's licensed to carry, but Luca is holding onto that and keeping an eye on him." She shifted her gaze to Duncan. "Do you want to see him, or should Luca interview him?"

"Oh, I want to see him," Duncan assured her. "Take him to interview room one. Joelle and I will be in there in a minute or two."

Carmen nodded, stepped away and then backtracked. "While Luca was frisking him, I ran a quick background on Hamlin. He is a PI from San Antonio but currently living in Austin, and he's twenty-three. That's all I have on him right now, and I'll dig for more, and if anything comes up while you're talking to him, I'll let you know."

"Thanks," Duncan said. "Dig, but finding Molly is the top priority, and I want you to sit on the lab to get the results on the blood that we found at Molly's place. So, don't spend much energy on Hamlin because this visit might turn out to be nothing," he added in a mutter.

Joelle knew Duncan was right about both things. Molly being the priority and this turning out to be nothing. Crackpots surfaced all the time during investigations, and even though there hadn't been that much time between this PI showing up and the attack and Molly's kidnapping, word of it would have already gotten out. Still, Joelle felt herself clinging to the hope that this Allen Hamlin could give Duncan and her some much-needed answers.

"I won't insult you by asking if you're up for doing this interview," Duncan told her once Carmen had left. "But if you want to keep on the searches you're doing, I can handle Hamlin solo."

"I want to hear what he has to say," Joelle was quick to let him know. Oh, yes. That hope was burning bright and hot in her.

Duncan studied her a couple of seconds, not with the heat that was sometimes in his eyes when he looked at her. All right, there was some heat. Always was, but Joelle was certain he was trying to make sure she was holding up okay. She was barely holding on and now battling the dreaded adrenaline crash, but there was no way she would sit this one out.

He finally nodded and tipped his head toward the interview room just down the hall. Judging from the sounds of footsteps and voices, Carmen was already escorting the PI there.

Because Joelle was behind Duncan, she didn't get her first glimpse of Hamlin until they were in the room with him. He looked even younger than twenty-three and was wearing khakis and a white button-down shirt. His short cropped hair was a pale blond. Actually, pale described the rest of him, too, what with his light skin tone and gray eyes. He had a thick envelope tucked under his arm.

"Let me know if you need anything," Carmen muttered to Duncan before she left them.

"Sheriff Holder," the man immediately said, and he extended his hand for Duncan to shake. Duncan did, but before Hamlin had released his grip, he looked at Joelle. "Deputy McCullough. I'm Al Hamlin."

Joelle was a little uneasy that Hamlin could identify them when she was reasonably sure she'd never seen him before. "Have we met?" Joelle came out and asked.

Hamlin shook his head. "I followed news of your father's murder so that's how I knew who you were. Both of you and the other deputies were mentioned in the press a lot."

Father's murder. No way for her not to react to that, but Joelle tried to mask the quick punch of grief. But Hamlin was right about the press. No one in her family or the sheriff's office had escaped the publicity.

"Thanks for seeing me so early," Hamlin said, glancing at both Duncan and Joelle. "You're going to want to hear what I have to say."

Duncan motioned for Hamlin to take a seat, and when he did, Duncan and she sat across from him. "You told my deputy that you had information about two crimes that were committed a few hours ago."

"I do." Hamlin handed Duncan the envelope. "There's a lot of information in there so I'll try to summarize and hit the high points. Five months ago when Sheriff McCullough was murdered, he was investigating a missing pregnant teenager."

"Mandy Vernon," Duncan automatically supplied while he opened the envelope. He took out what appeared to be police reports.

"Yes," Hamlin agreed. "Some thought Mandy had just run away because she wasn't getting along with her folks or her boyfriend, but Sheriff McCullough thought she might have been kidnapped or lured into the hands of someone who wanted her for the baby she was carrying."

Joelle knew that was also true. Her father had been insistent that something bad had happened to Mandy.

"I believe Sheriff McCullough was right," Hamlin went on, and then he stopped and took a long breath as if steeling himself up. "A month ago, my own sister, Isla, went missing. She's seventeen and was seven months pregnant at the time she disappeared. I swear on my life that Isla wouldn't have just left. Like Mandy, I believe someone took her for the baby."

Joelle glanced at the reports again. "Do you have proof?"

"Circumstantial but yes, there's proof," Hamlin insisted. "Over the past year, eight pregnant teenage girls have gone missing in the state, and none has been seen or heard from since." He leaned in, putting his arms on the table, and he looked straight at Joelle. "I believe there's a black market baby ring operating, and that your father found something that could have gotten him killed."

This wasn't a total news flash. Joelle, Duncan and everyone in law enforcement in Saddle Ridge had looked at that connection since it was a case that had occupied a lot of her father's time. But if her dad had actually found anything big related to the investigation, he hadn't put it in his reports. Nor had he mentioned it to anyone. Since three of his kids were cops, Joelle thought he would have told them.

If he'd gotten the chance, that is.

It was possible he'd been murdered before he could reveal something he'd learned.

"Bottom-line this," Duncan said, holding up the one-inch

thick stack of papers he'd taken from the envelope. "Is there proof of any kind for who killed Sheriff McCullough? And for the attack on Deputy McCullough and the kidnapping of the dispatcher?"

Joelle expected the PI to hedge and repeat his *circumstantial*. But he didn't.

"Yes," Hamlin stated, and he gathered his breath again. "Since Isla went missing, I've been digging, and talking to every informant I could. One name kept popping up when people would whisper about a black market baby ring." He paused a heartbeat. "Kate Moreland."

Of all the names Joelle had thought he might say, that wasn't one of them. "Kate?" she questioned.

Hamlin gave a firm nod. "Don't ask me how I got access to her financial records, but something doesn't add up. The woman's bringing in a lot more money than her businesses."

Joelle scowled, and she was certain Duncan was doing the same. "I will ask how you got her financials," Duncan stated, "because if you obtained them illegally, then you don't have proof."

The PI muttered some profanity and shook his head. "The proof is there for someone who can get it through legal channels. I took some shortcuts because I wanted to see if there were any red flags, if this woman could possibly be the person responsible for the disappearance of my sister and other teenage girls. I believe she is," he added with what sounded to be absolute certainty.

"Spell it out for me," Duncan ordered.

Joelle figured Duncan wasn't forgetting about those short cuts that Hamlin had admitted to taking. He'd no doubt get back to those, but if Kate did have some part in Molly's kidnapping, then that was the priority here.

"I have a statement from two women who say that Kate Moreland brokered the sale of their babies," Hamlin went on.

"Their names and details are in here?" Duncan asked, motioning toward the papers again.

"They are." Now Hamlin paused, and some of his enthusiasm waned. "But those incidents happened over ten years ago. There are some more recent," he was quick to add. "However, those women wouldn't go on record."

Playing devil's advocate, Joelle tried to see how this all might have played out. "Isn't it possible that Kate didn't broker the sale of the babies but rather just put the teenagers in contact with prospective adoptive parents?"

Though, so far, Joelle hadn't come across any reference to Kate having done that sort of thing. Still, info like that didn't usually turn up in background checks unless there had been something illegal about it.

"Kate might try to say that," Hamlin answered, "but she'd be lying. The girls said Kate paid them five thousand for the babies."

"Is there any kind of concrete proof of that?" Duncan asked.

"The statements from the girls." Hamlin's voice turned hard, and he huffed. "I figure Kate's been doing this for years, and that she then sells the babies for a whole lot more than five grand." He paused, looked Joelle straight in the eyes. "I also believe when she couldn't find a readily available teenager to give up their kid, then Kate had pregnant adults kidnapped. And I think that's what your father uncovered."

Part of Joelle wanted to latch on to this since it would be a lead not only in Molly's kidnapping but also her father's murder. But as working theories went, it wasn't nearly as strong as Brad's and maybe Shanda's motive. Or what had happened to her father. Because maybe Brad or Shanda had had her dad killed because of the arrest and miscarriage.

Maybe Kate had the same motive as her son.

But then why would the woman have shown up proclaiming Brad was behind the attacks? That didn't make sense, unless…

Joelle's mind followed that through. If Kate was, indeed, guilty of everything that Hamlin was saying, she might want to set up her son to take the blame. But certainly, there'd be someone else, someone not in the woman's gene pool, to try to frame.

"Read the files," Hamlin said after another huff. "You'll see the connections, and you'll see that Kate is guilty."

Duncan made a sound that could have meant anything. He certainly didn't jump on the "Kate did this" bandwagon.

"I'll definitely read through all of this," Duncan assured him, "and I'll want to talk to the two women who gave you their statements about selling their babies to Kate."

Duncan stood, signaling an end to the meeting, and Hamlin clearly didn't approve of what he obviously thought was a brush-off.

"Kate did this," Hamlin snarled. His gaze fired to Joelle. "Arrest her if you want your father's killer behind bars."

"If Kate did it, trust me, she'll be arrested," Joelle confirmed.

That brought on another huff from Hamlin, and he stood and stormed out. They followed him to make sure he did leave the building. After all, everything Hamlin had just told them could have been done to get closer to them, to get them to let down their guard.

Because Hamlin could be one of the gunmen who'd attacked her earlier.

They went into the bullpen, and Hamlin didn't linger. He went straight past Carmen and Luca and out the door.

"Did he actually have proof of anything?" Luca immediately wanted to know.

Duncan lifted the papers. "To be determined. Until we know for sure, though, call the deputy who's guarding Kate Moreland and tell him or her to keep a very close eye on the woman. I doubt Kate's in any shape to leave, but I want to make sure she stays put." His gaze slid to Hamlin who was now on the sidewalk. "And tell the deputy to make sure that guy doesn't get into her room."

Luca glanced at Hamlin, too, and took out his phone to make the call.

Duncan shifted his attention to Carmen. "Get me anything you can find on Hamlin and Kate Moreland. Use the techs to help with that, but I need thorough background checks on both of them."

Carmen nodded and hurried back to her desk.

Joelle looked at the papers. "I can start going through those."

Duncan hesitated, and she knew why. There was probably a lot in there about her father's murder. A lot that would take jabs at some still raw, painful memories.

"It needs to be done," was all Joelle said, and Duncan handed over half the papers to her. He'd almost certainly be poring through the other half.

They went back to the break room but had barely made it inside when Joelle's phone rang. Her heart jolted when she saw *Unknown Caller* on the screen, and she nearly dropped the papers when she fumbled to answer it.

"Joelle," a woman said.

Molly.

Joelle fumbled the papers again to put the call on speaker. "Molly."

Since her voice had way too much breath and hardly any sound, Joelle repeated the woman's name. Duncan sprang into action, taking out his phone and contacting tech so they could try and trace the call.

"Are you okay?" Joelle asked Molly. "Where are you?"

Molly didn't answer right away, but Joelle could hear someone muttering in the background. Even though she couldn't make out the words, she guessed it was the kidnapper giving Molly instructions about what not to say.

"I'm not hurt," Molly finally answered. "And the baby's moving and kicking so I think she's fine, too."

Joelle had so many things she wanted to ask, but she blurted out the first thing that popped into her head. "There was blood at your house."

"It's not mine," Molly said, but then stopped when there was more muttering in the background.

Duncan's gaze flashed to Joelle, and then he fired off a text. And she knew why. If the blood wasn't Molly's, then it likely belonged to the kidnapper, and they could use it to identify him.

"I'm to tell you that he's releasing me in a couple of hours," Molly went on several moments later. "But you're to send him ten thousand dollars to this account." She read off a series of numbers, and Duncan typed them into the notes on his phone. "You can get the money from my savings. I have an inheritance from my grandmother, and once the money's in the account, he'll call you with the location where he's dropping me off."

Ten thousand. That wasn't a huge ransom so maybe the kidnapper just wanted some cash to get away. Joelle was betting that the account would be offshore and not traceable. But they still had the blood.

"He also said I was to tell you not to look for him," Molly added. "Please don't look for him," she said, her voice breaking into a sob. "I just need this to be over, and it won't be if he gets spooked. I need to come home."

"We'll get you home," Duncan promised, but he was talking to the air because the call had already ended.

Duncan took her phone and immediately tried to call Molly back. There was no answer, and Joelle suspected in a minute or two the burner phone would be disabled.

A flood of emotions slammed through Joelle. The relief, the fear, all mixed together with the adrenaline crash. It was a bad combination because she started to shake. She headed toward the sofa so she could drop down onto it, but Duncan pulled her into his arms.

"We will get her home," he repeated, and he eased her even closer to him. Until they were right against each other.

Joelle knew she should move away. But she couldn't. She needed this. Needed Duncan. Even though there'd be a high price to pay for it. This kind of closeness could lead to dangerous feelings. Ones that would drown her in guilt because Duncan was the ultimate reminder that she hadn't saved her father. That she might have been able to stop him from dying or her mother from vanishing if she hadn't been with Duncan.

"I'm okay," she managed to say.

It wasn't anywhere close to the truth, but when the heat came, swirling in with the other emotions, Joelle forced herself to move. Not far. Just one step back, and she made the mistake of looking up and into Duncan's eyes.

Yes, the heat was there. But there was so much more. He was worried about her. Heck, she was worried about herself, about what the stress of this was doing to their baby. The best way to minimize that worry, though, was to try and forget the heat and focus on getting Molly safely home.

"I can transfer the money into that account," she said. Her voice was still shaky. So was the rest of her, but Duncan must have realized, too, that the work was what they both needed now. "I can get it from my savings so we don't have to go through the bank to get it from Molly's."

"Use the sheriff's office funds and instruct the bank to delay releasing the money," Duncan told her. "The kidnapper will see the funds deposited and maybe go ahead and release Molly. Once we have her, we can try to trace the kidnapper's location when he or she attempts to withdraw or transfer the money."

Like her, he didn't seem hopeful of that happening, but they had to check and double check. Even if Molly was safely returned, a serious crime had been committed. The kidnapper, and anyone who hired him, should pay and pay hard.

Since Joelle had never done a transfer like this, it took her several minutes to work through the process of it. While she did that, Duncan called the tech who'd been trying to trace the call. They were both still busy with their tasks when Carmen appeared in the door. She had her laptop balanced in the crook of her arm and continued to read whatever was on the screen until Joelle and Duncan finished.

"The kidnapper was using another burner," Duncan said. "Couldn't be traced, and like the other, it's already been disconnected." He glanced at Joelle. "Did the transfer go through?"

Joelle nodded, and she looked at Carmen. "The kidnapper called again and had Molly tell us that he wanted ten grand."

"Is Molly okay?" Carmen immediately asked.

"She said she was," Joelle relayed. "I hope that's true."

"So do I," the other deputy muttered, and she turned her attention back to her laptop.

"Please tell me you have something on the blood that was found at Molly's," Duncan said to Carmen.

"No. Luca's calling about that now. But I got a preliminary report on Hamlin. Since his sister went missing, he's focused only on that. No other clients."

Duncan huffed and put his hands on his hips. "It's hard to earn an income when you don't have clients."

"He inherited life insurance money from his parents who died in a car accident three years ago. It was about half a million, so I'm guessing he lives off that and apparently devotes all his time to finding his sister. There's no sign of her, by the way," Carmen added. "But Austin PD believes she ran away with her then boyfriend since he went missing, too."

"Is there anything in that prelim report to indicate that Hamlin could have been behind the kidnapping and attack on Joelle?" Duncan asked.

"No criminal record or anything like that, but I'll keep digging. I should be able to get access to the background that would have been done on him to get his PI license. That would give us a bigger picture of him."

"Do that," Duncan said just as his phone rang.

Joelle immediately got to her feet, and everything inside her went tight again until she remembered the kidnapper would likely be calling her number, not Duncan's.

"It's Dr. Benton," Duncan relayed, answering the call. "I'm putting you on speaker so my deputies can hear. I hope you're about to tell me we have the green light to question Kate."

"Not yet. She's sedated, and I want her to stay that way for at least another hour or two," the doctor explained. "I'm calling because I got back her tox results, and I thought you'd want to know."

"I do," Duncan verified. "She was drugged?"

"There were traces of a prescription sleep aid in her system. Doxepin. Traces," the doctor emphasized. "There certainly wasn't enough of it to cause unconsciousness."

Joelle frowned, and she waited for Duncan to ask the question she knew had to be on his mind. "Do you think she faked her symptoms?"

"Hard to say, but it's possible she had some kind of allergic reaction. I'll be checking for that. When I checked her online medical records, there weren't any allergies listed. Not only that, she's been prescribed this particular sleep aid for years. Still, it's possible the drug in combination with something else caused the disorientation and the unconsciousness. As I mentioned earlier, that *something else* could have caused the car accident."

Yes, that could explain it. Joelle recalled seeing the cut on the woman's head.

"How serious is that injury to the head?" Duncan wanted to know.

"We ran a CT scan, and there was no obvious signs of brain damage or even a concussion," Dr. Benton was quick to say. "Once the patient is out of sedation for her blood pressure, I'll do some neuropsychological evals since a CT scan doesn't always confirm a concussion. It's possible, too, that the trauma of the car accident is playing into her reactions."

Duncan's expression let Joelle know he was skeptical about that. But why would Kate have pretended to be drugged? The woman had literally staggered onto Molly's property and then collapsed. Why do that?

Unfortunately, Joelle immediately came up with an answer. A bad one. If Hamlin was right about Kate being a criminal, then maybe her behavior was meant to make her look innocent while also pointing the blame at Brad. But Kate could have also done this to get closer to them. So she could try to do to Joelle what was done to Molly. Still, that seemed an extreme ploy especially since the woman hadn't been on their radar before she'd shown up at Joelle's.

"I still want to talk to Kate once she's awake," Duncan stressed. "I'll also want the results of those tests you mentioned."

"Is she a suspect in the attacks?" the doctor asked.

"A person of interest, but some information has come to light that I need to question her about. It could be related to the murder of Sheriff McCullough."

"I see," the doctor muttered after a long pause. "I'll let you know the moment you can talk to her," he assured Duncan.

When the call ended, Duncan stared at his phone for a moment before his gaze shifted to Joelle. "We really need to dig into Kate's background."

She couldn't agree more. "I'll do that and check for any updates from the CSIs, techs and lab." They had a lot of cogs going in this particular investigative wheel, and any one of them could provide them with answers.

Maybe, *finally*, answers about her father.

Joelle couldn't fully process that. Couldn't deal with the emotions that would bring. She had to rely on the work not only bringing a closure to the case but to help her find the mental healing that had so far eluded her.

Of course, the healing would only be partial. She would still need to know what had happened to her mother.

"I'll get that PI background report on Hamlin," Carmen said, and she headed back toward the bullpen.

Joelle forced her hands to steady on the laptop keyboard while she checked for those updates. There was one which had come a little too late to say that the blood at Molly's hadn't been hers. That comparison had been fairly simple because her DNA was on file. Now that Molly had been ruled out, the sample would have to make its way through the database to see if there was a match.

Since Duncan was already at work on his laptop. Joelle didn't relay the blood news. She just moved on to the next task—finding out if Kate Moreland had something to hide. The basics about the woman meshed with what they had already learned. She owned a lot of businesses she had inherited from her father who'd died a decade earlier.

Joelle continued looking into the woman's personal life. Divorced, ex-husband deceased and only one child. Brad. There were plenty of social media posts about Kate's fundraisers, parties and such, but there were no recent mentions about Brad. Joelle had to go back five months to find them, and she immediately saw a pattern. Before five months ago, Kate had posted many photos of her and her son together. Then, nothing.

Joelle had to wonder about the timing since her father had been murdered five months ago.

From across the room, Duncan's phone rang, immediately getting her attention since it could be news about Molly. "It's Ruston," he said.

She automatically sighed. Her brother was no doubt checking on her again and probably thought she'd try to gloss over how she was doing. Which she would have done. No way did she want her brothers worrying about her any more than they already were.

"Ruston," Duncan greeted, and unlike the other calls he'd been getting, he didn't put this one on speaker.

Joelle couldn't hear what her brother said, but whatever it was had Duncan slowly getting to his feet. "Hell," he spat out.

That caused Joelle to stand as well, and she went to Duncan. "What's wrong? What happened?" And too many worst-case scenarios started flying through her head.

Duncan lifted his finger in a "wait a second" gesture. "You're sure it's her?" Duncan asked Ruston.

The answer he got caused Duncan to curse again, and then he added, "Yeah, call me the moment you know anything." He pressed end call, and he looked at her.

"Is it Molly?" she managed to ask, even though Joelle's throat had seemingly clamped shut.

Duncan shook his head. "It's Shanda Cantrell. She's been murdered."

Chapter Six

Duncan drank more coffee and paced with his phone anchored between his shoulder and ear while he waited for Joelle's brother, Detective Ruston McCullough, to take him off hold and give him the update on Shanda's murder.

It'd been over an hour since Ruston's initial call to deliver the shocking news that Shanda had been found dead just outside her house in San Antonio, and Ruston had only been able to provide the basics. Apparently, Shanda's lawyer had found her dead when he'd gone to her place. Cause of death had likely been a gunshot wound to the chest.

"Sorry about the wait," Ruston said when he came back on the line. "I just got another call from the CSIs out at Shanda's house, and I wanted to hear what they had to say so I could pass it along to you. And Joelle. She's there, right?"

"I am," Joelle verified. She looked too exhausted to pace, the way Duncan was in an effort to burn up some of this adrenaline and nerves. She was on the sofa, watching and waiting.

"How are you holding up?" Ruston asked, and Duncan knew that question was for Joelle.

"We need answers," she replied, clearly dodging her brother's question.

Ruston sighed because that dodge had given him the

answer. His sister was exhausted and worried about everything that had gone on not just since the attack but the events of the last five months. All of this could be linked, and that was a connection that wasn't going to allow Joelle, or the rest of them, to get much rest anytime soon.

"All right," Ruston continued, "here's what I have. At approximately 6:45 this morning, Shanda's lawyer, Frank Salvetti, arrived at her residence in San Antonio. She had called him about a half hour before that and instructed him that she needed him to accompany her to Saddle Ridge right away."

Hell. A lot had gone on in these hours following Joelle's attack. It was barely six in the morning, but it felt as if they'd been at this for days.

"That's a fast, and very early, response for a lawyer," Duncan pointed out.

"Yeah," Ruston agreed. "I'm guessing it's because Shanda either pays him well or else they have a personal relationship that made him react so fast. Not lovers. I've found no proof of that but maybe just friends. Anyway, he found her lying partway inside her door and on her porch, and he called 911. The ME just confirmed that cause of death was the gunshot wound to the chest. No surprise there. I was one of the first on scene, and it was obvious that she'd been shot and bled out."

"Any witnesses?" Joelle asked.

"None, and there were no security cameras. But it's definitely not suicide. No other weapons around, and even though I don't have the report back on it yet, it'll turn out that she was shot at point-blank range. What it looked like to me was that she opened her door to someone, maybe thinking it was her lawyer or possibly because she knew the person, and then she was shot."

Duncan groaned. Ruston was a good cop so his account

was almost certainly what had happened. But with no witnesses and Shanda dead, they didn't have an ID on the shooter.

"Shanda called me about an hour before she was killed," Duncan explained. "I was going to question her about the attack on Joelle and Molly's kidnapping."

Ruston made a sound of acknowledgment. "Joelle had messaged me about that." He paused. "Shanda's arrest could be linked to Dad's murder. Who else knew that?"

"My three suspects," Duncan was quick to say. Technically, he should be using the "persons of interest" label, but in his mind, they were solid suspects. "Shanda's former mother-in-law, Kate Moreland, who's still hospitalized. Shanda's ex-husband, Brad. A hothead who blames your dad, Joelle and a few others for Shanda's miscarriage following her arrest. The third suspect is Al Hamlin, a PI who showed up out of the blue to point the finger at Kate."

Duncan paused to give Ruston some time to consider all of that.

"Who's your top suspect?" Ruston asked several moments later.

"Well, it would have been Shanda before she was murdered," Duncan admitted. "After all, she's the one who lost the baby, and she's got the funds to hire a gunman and a kidnapper." He stopped again, cursed. "And she could have done just that. Hell, maybe one of her hired thugs wasn't pleased with her and killed her. Molly's kidnapper said what he'd done was a mistake so maybe this is the way he dealt with it."

"You have a name for the kidnapper?" Ruston wanted to know.

"Working on it. We collected some of his blood from Molly's house, and it's being processed now."

If the kidnapper had a record, then they might get a quick match. Rarely did he hope someone was a criminal, but in this case, it would make getting the ID much easier.

"Kate Moreland is in the hospital with a deputy guard on her door," Duncan added to Ruston. "I've been trying to call Brad, but he's not answering."

"He's not answering my calls, either," Ruston supplied. "I've sent two uniforms out to his place to check on him. Brad didn't answer the door and didn't appear to be home. Of course, he could be on his way to see his mother before he's due to come in for his interview."

True, and he might not answer his phone if he was on the road. But it occurred to Duncan that Brad could be dead as well, and if so, he wasn't sure how that would have played out. Maybe Kate had gotten fed up with both Shanda and Brad and hired someone to kill them? Or maybe Brad was very much alive and just dodging cops. If so, that moved him to the top spot of suspects.

Duncan heard the sound of approaching footsteps, and he expected to see either Luca or Carmen step into the doorway. But it was Joelle's other brother, Slater, who was the senior deputy in the sheriff's office. He was definitely a welcome sight since there was plenty to do.

Like Ruston, Slater was the spitting image of a younger version of their late father. Tall and lanky with black hair and green eyes. Joelle had gotten the black hair, but she had her mother's misty gray eyes.

"Let me know if you get any updates," Duncan said to Ruston. "I'll do the same for you."

He ended the call and watched as Slater gave both Duncan and his sister long examining looks. Slater sighed because he could no doubt see the exhaustion on Joelle's face.

"I just did a report with the case updates," Joelle said,

maybe to cut off her brother's insistence that she get some rest. "I'll fill in what Ruston just told us and forward copies to you and the other deputies."

Slater didn't address that. He went to Joelle, eased her off the sofa and into his arms. He brushed a kiss on the top of her head and touched his hand to her baby bump. "How's my niece?"

The argument that had been in Joelle's eyes instantly faded, and she returned her brother's hug. "I think she's swimming around in there."

"Good." Slater leaned down and put his mouth to Joelle's stomach. "Hang in there, kid. I just ordered your mom a huge breakfast to be delivered from the diner. Get ready for all kinds of goodies."

"Thank you," Joelle muttered.

Duncan sent him a look of thanks, too, and wished he'd thought of it. Of course, Joelle might not eat. She hadn't touched the yogurt he'd given her earlier, but maybe Slater could give her a brotherly reminder that eating would be good for the baby.

"I managed to postpone my testimony in the trial," Slater explained, going toward Duncan now. "I figured you could use me back here."

"I can," Duncan verified. "We're hoping the kidnapper will be contacting us soon about releasing Molly, and we need a lot of research done on our suspects."

"Brad Moreland, his mother, Al Hamlin," Slater named off. "I saw the report Joelle did about Shanda's murder so she's off the list. As soon as I had Hamlin's name, I contacted a PI friend who lives in San Antonio, and I asked her about him. This particular PI is a *Girl with the Dragon Tattoo* sort of computer whiz, and she's created all these programs to mine data from old internet articles and social media posts." He paused. "And yeah, she sometimes hacks to find what she wants."

Duncan didn't approve of doing something illegal since they wouldn't be able to use the info in court. But at the moment he was for any and everything that helped them solve this so they could get Molly back.

"Did this PI find something?" Duncan prompted.

Slater nodded. "On the drive back here, she called me with what she'd dug up. Six years ago when Hamlin was seventeen, he and his then pregnant girlfriend were accused of trying to extort money from a couple who wanted to adopt the baby. They were convicted as juveniles so that's why the record didn't pop in a normal background check."

Joelle went closer to them. "Of course, Hamlin didn't mention that to us. What happened to the baby?"

"Unknown. The baby's mother, Erica Corley, was only in juvie lockup for two months, and she was released when she was eight months pregnant. She disappeared shortly thereafter, but my PI friend is trying to track her down."

"Good," Duncan muttered. "Because it'd be interesting to find out if Hamlin and she did sell the baby. It also makes me wonder if Hamlin's missing sister left because he was pressuring her to sell the child."

"Since I was wondering the same thing, the PI will be looking into that as well," Slater said. "People put all sorts of stuff on social media so she might be able to find something that'll clue us in to Isla Hamlin's disappearance."

Duncan made a quick sound of agreement just as he heard a shout coming from the bullpen. And the shout came from a voice he instantly recognized from the phone conversation he'd had with him.

"Sheriff Holder?" Brad called out.

So Brad had surfaced after all, and Duncan was a little

surprised that he'd actually come in as scheduled without being further prodded. Surprised and very much interested in what the man had to say. With Slater and Joelle following him, Duncan went into the bullpen to find the sandy-haired man struggling to get past Luca who was trying to frisk him. Carmen had stepped in to help, but Slater moved toward the trio, too.

"Settle down," Slater snapped to Brad. "You don't get past this point until we're sure you're not armed."

"I'm not armed," Brad snarled, and he aimed a venomous glare at Duncan. "Shanda's dead. Dead," he repeated, his voice breaking on the word. "You should have stopped that from happening. You shouldn't have allowed her to die."

Brad's voice didn't just break that time. He began to sob, tears spilling down his face. He also stopped struggling with the search.

"He's not armed," Luca told Duncan. "What do you want me to do with him?"

"Interview room one," Duncan said. Because one way or another, he intended to get answers from Brad.

Since Brad wasn't steady on his feet, Slater took one side of him and Luca took the other. They maneuvered him to the interview room, sat him in the chair, and Joelle got a box of tissues and a bottle of water. What none of them did was give Brad any sympathetic looks because they all knew this could be an act.

That they could be looking at a killer.

"Let me know if you need me," Luca muttered, heading back toward the bullpen.

"Same here," Slater said. "I'll do some more of that digging we were talking about."

That no doubt meant Slater was going to try to find Hamlin's old girlfriend, Erica. Duncan hoped he could manage it since Erica, who'd now be in her mid-twenties might be able to provide them with some insight into Hamlin.

Duncan and Joelle sat across from Brad and didn't say anything for several minutes. They just waited for Brad to cry it out. When he finally reached for a tissue to dry his eyes, that was Duncan's cue to get started. However, Brad beat him to it.

"Who killed Shanda?" Brad asked. The anger was back in his voice now. "Was it my mother?"

Duncan didn't respond to that. Well, not a direct answer, anyway. Instead, he read Brad his rights, and he didn't think it was his imagination that Brad became more incensed with each line of the Miranda warning.

"Do you understand your rights?" Duncan asked when he'd finished.

"Of course, I do," Brad snapped. "You're covering your butt, but there's no need. I didn't kill my wife."

"Do you understand the part about your right to have your lawyer present?"

"I do, and he'll be coming in soon, but I don't want to wait for him to get answers. I need to know now. Did my mother do this?"

"Your mother is under guard at the hospital," Duncan reminded him. Of course, that didn't mean Kate hadn't hired someone to do it. He leaned in and stared at Brad. "Did you kill Shanda?"

Outrage bloomed across his face, and his mouth dropped open. "No, I did not." Brad snapped out each word. "I loved her, and we were getting back together."

"Maybe," Duncan concluded. "I talked to Shanda right before she was killed, and she didn't confirm a reconciliation. Just the opposite."

No trace of Brad's tears remained, and his eyes narrowed. "I don't believe you. You're lying to provoke me."

"I'm repeating to you what she told me."

Duncan withheld anything else about that conversation he'd had with Shanda, and he let the silence roll through the room. In his experience, most people being interrogated or interviewed were uncomfortable enough with the silence that they started talking.

It worked.

"Shanda wanted me to see a shrink," Brad finally admitted. "She wanted me to rehash the past."

"Isn't that what you're doing with the civil suit?" Joelle asked.

Now Brad turned those narrowed eyes on her. "No. That's retribution. That's payment for a wrong that you and your father did." He stopped and visibly reined in some of the anger. "I thought the best way for Shanda and me to move on was to get back together and start that family she's always wanted."

Interesting. Not the family *we'd* always wanted. "You wanted to have a child with Shanda?" Duncan came out and asked.

"Of course." Brad had gone back to snapping. "And now that won't happen because she's dead."

Brad made the sound of a sob, but Duncan saw no fresh tears in his eyes. Being the cynic that he was, Duncan wondered if the man had tapped his supply of fake drama.

"I understand you called Shanda after you and I had our phone conversation," Duncan said, shifting the conversation a little.

Brad nodded, attempted another sob, and he must have given up on that because he pressed a tissue to his eyes. "I told her what was going on, and I said I wanted to see her. She said we could meet for lunch after I was done with my interview." He stopped again. "If I'd gone over to her place then and there, she might not be dead. I could have stopped her from being killed."

Maybe that was true. But not the truth if Brad had been the one who'd pulled the trigger.

"Where were you from the time you got off the phone with me and Shanda's murder?" Duncan pressed.

"Home," Brad was quick to say.

Duncan was just as quick with a response. "Can anyone verify that?"

"I was alone," the man snapped. "But I tried to make some calls to my mother so it's possible those can be pinpointed to my house."

Yeah, it was possible. But it wasn't proof. Someone could have used Brad's phone to make it look as if he were home. And even if Brad had personally made the calls, it didn't mean his hired gun hadn't been doing his bidding. Still…

"I want permission to get access to your phone records," Duncan insisted. "If you don't agree, I'll assume you have something to hide, and I'll get a search warrant."

Brad didn't seem especially bothered by that. "I'll give you permission," he said, making Duncan silently groan. It meant any communication Brad might have had with hired guns had likely been done through a burner. Maybe one like the ones Molly's kidnapper had been using.

Next, Duncan went with an outright lie, something he was allowed during questioning. "We have footage from security cameras up the street from Shanda's. It's being analyzed as we speak, but I already know there was a vehicle in the area. A vehicle matching the description of one registered to you."

Brad sprang to his feet. "It wasn't mine. I wasn't anywhere near Shanda's this morning."

That might be true. Might be. But Brad could have hired someone to kill her. And that led Duncan to motive.

"Here's my theory," Duncan started. "You arranged to have Deputy McCullough killed or kidnapped. Ditto for the dispatcher who was also a deputy during Shanda's arrest two years ago. Shanda either found out what you'd done or you told her, and when she said she was going to the cops, you made sure she wouldn't be talking to anyone."

If looks could have killed, Brad would have finished off Duncan and Joelle on the spot. He sank back down into his chair. "This interview is over," he insisted, taking out his phone. "I'm not saying another word until I have my lawyer here."

Duncan didn't press, and he figured he could use the time before the lawyer arrived to assemble as much of a case as he could against Brad. What he needed was some physical evidence, something that would get him an arrest warrant so he could take Brad off the streets. Of course, if Brad was the killer, it was possible he'd already set hired guns in motion for another attack.

Joelle and Duncan stepped outside the interview room, closing the door behind them, and they looked at each other. "You believe him?" Joelle whispered, taking the question right out of Duncan's mouth.

Duncan had to shrug. Then, he groaned and scrubbed his hand over his face in frustration. "I want to believe he's the killer, but I'm not sure."

Since he didn't want Brad to overhear any part of this conversation, he motioned for Joelle to follow him back to the break room.

"Everything we have on Brad is circumstantial." He took out his phone. "I'll have Carmen get Brad to sign the agreement to get his phone records. If he's still willing to do it, that is. And there might be something in his call history that could help us get a warrant for his financials."

Duncan fired off a quick text to Carmen, but before he got a reply, his phone rang with an incoming call from Dr. Benton. Duncan couldn't answer it fast enough.

"Kate is awake, and she's insisting on seeing Joelle and you," the doctor said without a greeting. "Obviously, I'd like for her to hold off on that for another hour or two, but she got agitated when I suggested it. Can the two of you come to the hospital now?"

"Absolutely," Duncan readily agreed. "We'll be there in about ten minutes."

Joelle and he hurried back to the bullpen, and Duncan saw the instant alarm on the three deputies' faces. "Brad decided to wait for his lawyer," Duncan explained because the deputies had obviously thought Brad had done something to provoke them. "Joelle and I need to get to the hospital to question Kate Moreland."

"I can go with you for backup," Slater immediately volunteered.

Duncan nodded and got them moving toward the door. After he'd checked to make sure there were no threats lurking around, they got into the cruiser with Joelle in the back seat, Duncan in shotgun and Slater behind the wheel.

As expected, it was not a peaceful, relaxing ride. They were all very aware that the hired guns could be nearby, ready and waiting to strike. It was the reason Duncan had considered asking Joelle to stay behind. But not only wouldn't she have agreed to that, Kate had asked specifically to see her. It was possible the woman would say something to Joelle that she wouldn't to Duncan.

When they reach the hospital, Slater parked by the ER doors so that Joelle and he could hurry inside. Slater got out as well, and Duncan knew he would stand guard, watching for any kind of danger. Simply put, if any hired guns came into the hospital after Joelle and him, Slater would be the first line of defense against that.

Also as expected, there was a reserve deputy outside Kate's room. Anita Denny. Since she obviously recognized Duncan and Joelle, she opened the door and motioned them inside.

"She's waiting for you," Anita, the reserve deputy, informed them.

They stepped into the room and saw that Anita was right. Kate was, indeed, sitting up and clearly expecting them. She didn't look drowsy but rather alert and very worried.

"A friend of mine called the hospital and left a message to tell me that Shanda had been murdered," Kate immediately said. "Is it true?"

Later, Duncan would want to know the name of that friend. For now, though, he basically did a death notification.

"I regret to inform you that Shanda was murdered earlier this morning," he told her while he carefully watched her reaction.

A reaction that included widened eyes and a shudder of her breath. Kate touched her fingers to her mouth that trembled. "I'd hoped it wasn't true. I didn't want it to be true," she amended.

Duncan didn't have time to treat this like a normal death notification. He needed to jump right into questions that had to be asked. And he had to start with the basics.

"I'm going to Mirandize you," Duncan stated. "It's to cover the legal bases and make sure you're aware of what your rights are."

Kate didn't ask why he was doing this. She merely sat

and listened while he finished, and then she nodded when he asked if she understood everything he'd just spelled out.

Since Kate didn't voice any kind of objections, Duncan continued, "From what I've heard, Shanda and you didn't have a good relationship. You were at odds. In fact, when I spoke to Shanda before she died, she claimed that you loathed her."

Kate didn't show any flares of temper as Brad had done. The woman sighed and shook her head. "I did loathe her," she admitted. "I thought she didn't handle her miscarriage and divorce nearly as well as she could have, and I believe she never actually loved Brad."

Duncan lifted an eyebrow. "I didn't pick up on that last part from either Brad or Shanda."

"You wouldn't have." Kate glanced away, groaned softly. "Brad was blindly in love with her, and he couldn't see Shanda for what she was. A gold digger. That big house she lives in? That was part of her divorce settlement. She took half of Brad's money when she divorced him."

Now there was some anger, but she kept her gaze pinned downward while she picked at the sheets covering her. Duncan had to wonder if she was looking down so he wouldn't be able to see some truth that she couldn't conceal in her eyes.

Truth that she was glad Shanda was dead. And that she was the one who'd made that happen.

"I should tell you something in case it comes up later," Kate said. "I don't want you to think I'm withholding anything."

"I'm listening," Duncan assured her.

"On the night Shanda was arrested, she and I were arguing on the phone. A very heated argument," Kate emphasized. "I'd called her about some charges I saw on Brad's credit card. Shanda had gone to a high-end boutique and treated herself to the best the place had to offer. I'm talking nearly ten grand. Shanda said that Brad had given her the shopping trip as a surprise gift, and I told her that Brad wasn't paying the bills, that I was." She stopped. "Anyway, Shanda was yelling at me and that's probably why she was driving erratically."

Duncan had known about this. It'd been in the statement Shanda had given. Well, she'd given a thumbnail of it, anyway. She'd told Sheriff McCullough that she'd been having a dispute with her mother-in-law.

"You must have been very upset when you found out that Brad and Shanda were getting back together," Joelle threw out there. All sympathy. Fake, of course. But Duncan knew she was going for the "good cop" angle here. That gave Duncan the leeway to go badass.

"I was," Kate muttered. "I thought it would only lead to Brad being crushed all over again." Now she finally looked up, her attention going to Joelle. "Crushed," she emphasized. "Brad was never the same after the miscarriage and his marriage breaking up."

That was Duncan's cue to jump in. "Is that why you went to Molly's to accuse Brad of trying to kill Joelle?"

On a heavy sigh, Kate closed her eyes. But she nodded. She took in a few shallow breaths, opened her eyes and looked at Joelle again. "I'm sorry, but Brad blamed you and your father for what happened to Shanda. He should have blamed Shanda herself. She's the one who got herself arrested. Instead, Brad decided she wasn't at fault and that the cops involved needed to pay."

"Pay by killing me and kidnapping a former deputy?" Joelle supplied.

Kate nodded again and repeated her apology. "I think

my son has had some kind of mental breakdown. I blame Shanda for that. She led him on, making him believe she'd get back together with him, but there were always new conditions for a reconciliation. One day, she'd say he had to go to counseling. The next, she'd tell him he had to cut me out of his life." She paused. "And he did."

Neither Brad nor Shanda had mentioned that so Duncan had no idea if it was true. However, it was something he would definitely ask Brad about.

"It must have hurt when Brad did that," Joelle murmured.

"It did." There was another flash of anger in her eyes, but Kate seemed to quickly shut that down. "It cut me to the core."

"And that cut made it easier for you to go to Joelle and tell her that Brad wanted her dead," Duncan pointed out.

Kate's mouth tightened for a couple of seconds. "Yes, it did make it easier," she confessed. "If my son hadn't basically disowned me, I might not have been willing to believe the worst about him. But I do believe it. I think Shanda convinced him to go after the people who arrested her. I think this was all her doing."

That was possible, but there was a big question mark in that theory. "Then, why is Shanda dead?"

"Maybe she hired the wrong people to do her bidding, and it backfired." Kate offered that up so quickly that it was obvious she'd given it some thought. "If you play with fire, sometimes you get burned."

"So, you don't think Brad would have killed her?" Joelle asked.

Kate stayed quiet a while. "I don't want to believe he would, but it's possible. Shanda broke him, so anything is possible."

Duncan wasn't sure about the broken part, but it was obvious that Brad had some serious issues. Obvious, too, that he could have certainly murdered his ex-wife.

"I saw your tox results," Duncan said, and he noted the flash of surprise in Kate's eyes. She hadn't been prepared for a quick shift in topics. "There didn't seem to be enough of the sleeping aid in your system for you to behave the way you did when you arrived at Molly's."

Kate stared at him and touched her fingers to the bruise on her forehead. "This must have caused the wooziness," she said. "That and maybe my blood pressure." She paused again. "But I don't recall taking any of my sleeping pills that night. In fact, I'm sure I wouldn't have since I'd planned on driving to Saddle Ridge to see Joelle."

Duncan and Joelle exchanged a glance, and it was Joelle who voiced what they were thinking. "You believe someone might have drugged you with them?"

"Yes," Kate muttered. She squeezed her eyes shut for a moment. "Brad came to see me as I was getting ready to leave. He was furious because I'd shut off his accounts and canceled his credit cards. I was paying him a hefty salary to manage some of my businesses," she added. "I figured since he'd disowned me, then he shouldn't have access to that money." Her mouth tightened again. "He'd planned on buying Shanda another big engagement ring and was enraged when his credit card was declined."

"You two argued?" Duncan prompted when Kate went quiet.

"Yes. A loud ugly argument. I poured myself a shot of scotch, and it's possible Brad could have put one of my sleeping pills in it."

Now Duncan was the one to shake his head. "Why would he have done that?"

"I don't know. To get back at me," Kate suggested. "Maybe

because he realized I was going to see Joelle. I didn't tell him that, but it's possible he guessed since just the day before he'd been ranting about how much Joelle needed to pay for what'd happened to his precious Shanda."

Duncan still wasn't convinced. "If Brad wanted to drug you so you couldn't drive to Saddle Ridge, why not put more than one pill in the drink?"

"Because he might not have wanted to risk me tasting it," Kate answered without hesitation. "And I probably would have. I did notice a funny taste after I drank the scotch in a big gulp, but I didn't think anything about it. Not until later, when I was here at the hospital."

Everything the woman was saying could be true. Or it could all be lies. Duncan knew he was going to have to compare Kate's and Brad's responses side by side and try to figure how this had actually all played out.

Joelle's phone rang, the sound shooting through the silence that had fallen over the room, and he saw *Unknown Caller* when Joelle showed him the screen.

"We have to take this," Joelle said, and Duncan and she went out into the hall. They moved away from Kate's door before Joelle accepted the call.

"Thanks for wiring me the money," the man said. "I'm taking Molly to the drop off now."

It was the kidnapper, the same one who'd called earlier.

"Where?" Joelle asked.

"You'll know soon enough," the man said. "Keep your phone ready because in exactly twenty minutes, I'll be calling you back to come and get Molly."

Chapter Seven

Even though Joelle knew that Duncan still had plenty more questions for Kate, that would have to wait. Twenty minutes wasn't a lot of time to get ready for the kidnapper to drop off Molly.

Or for the kidnapper to put the finishing touches on a ploy to draw Duncan and her out.

Joelle was well aware that might be the case. So was Duncan, and he would almost certainly insist that she stay at the sheriff's office. That wasn't what Joelle wanted to do, but she figured she would end up going along with it. There was no need to put the baby at even greater risk.

"I'll have to come back to finish this interview," Duncan told Kate, and he didn't wait for the woman to respond. He motioned for Joelle to follow him, and they headed out the door.

"Keep a close watch on Kate," Duncan muttered to Anita. "And if she makes any calls, I want to know about it."

Yes, because Kate could be behind whatever was about to happen, and she might want to make a call to someone she'd hired to do her bidding.

They hurried back toward the ER doors where Slater was waiting for them. The moment they were back in the cruiser, Duncan took out his phone. "I need to assemble some backup," he muttered.

Yes, that was a must, and Joelle could see how this could play out. She'd man the sheriff's office, probably along with Luca and Carmen, and then every other available deputy would go with Duncan. Joelle prayed that would be enough protection if something went wrong.

Before Duncan could even make a call, her phone rang, and Joelle frowned when she saw the *Unknown Caller* on the screen. She showed it to Duncan, and the sudden alarm on his face no doubt mirrored hers. Joelle answered, put it on speaker, and the kidnapper's voice poured through the cruiser.

"Molly's at the former sheriff's house," the man snarled.

Oh, mercy. *There*. It would be there. The house where Joelle had been raised. But where her father had also been murdered. She hadn't been able to step inside the place since the initial investigation.

In the background, Joelle heard Molly call out, "Joelle." That was all Molly managed to say before the kidnapper issued an order for her to shut up.

"If you're not here in ten minutes, the deal is off," the man warned them.

"But you said twenty minutes," Duncan snarled right back.

"Ten," the kidnapper repeated.

Slater and Duncan both cursed. "I want proof of life," Duncan demanded.

The kidnapper cursed, too. "You already got it. You heard her yell Joelle's name."

"That could have been a recording," Duncan pointed out.

Joelle hadn't considered that, but it was possible. Likely, even, if the kidnapper had already dropped off Molly somewhere else and was putting some distance between him and her. Added to that, Duncan didn't really have any bargaining power since the money had already been transferred. They'd had no choice about that, though, since it had been the kidnapper's only demand for Molly's release. Now these new demands with the quick time restraints spelled trouble.

More cursing from the kidnapper. "Tell him you're alive," the man growled.

Seconds ticked off, and Joelle had to breathe because her lungs were starting to ache. "I'm alive," Molly finally said.

"Where are you?" Duncan asked her.

"I'm not sure. I'm blindfolded, but it's possible I'm at the McCullough ranch like he said."

Possible. But maybe the kidnapper had her elsewhere. Still, Molly was alive, and Joelle was going to latch on to that.

"Don't be late," the kidnapper added. "You wasted one of your minutes with all this yakking. Be here in nine minutes, Sheriff." He ended the call.

"This is a trap," Slater spat out, and his gaze met Joelle's in the rearview mirror.

She couldn't disagree. It had all the markings of a trap, but there was another factor here.

"He has Molly, and we have to get her back," Joelle stated. "The cruiser is bullet-resistant, and I'll stay inside. Yes, this might be a ruse so he can come after me, but he could do that at the sheriff's office, too. In fact, that might be what he has in mind. Get all of you hurrying there to the ranch while he's already right here in town."

Both Slater and Duncan knew that was true, and this was definitely a "damned if you did, dammed if you didn't" situation. Duncan seemed to be having a very short mental debate about that.

"Go to your dad's house fast," Duncan instructed, and like Slater had done to her earlier, he looked at her, the worry in his eyes. "I'm sorry," he muttered.

"Don't be. Let's go get Molly," she said. "Who should I call for backup?"

A muscle flickered in Duncan's jaw when it tightened. "Have dispatch send all available deputies to the location."

Joelle made the call, already calculating how long it would take them to arrive. Too long probably, and the kidnapper would likely know that. Would likely know, too, the emotional punch that her father's house would have for her. She hated these sick mind games. Hated the person who'd set all of it into motion.

She checked the time. They'd already burned one of those nine minutes, and she didn't know the exact time it would take them to get to the ranch. At the speed Slater was going, though, they should make it with maybe a minute or two to spare. A minute or two they wouldn't have had if Duncan had insisted on taking her back to the sheriff's office.

The question was what would they face once they were there at the ranch?

"You want me to call my ranch hands and have them meet us there?" Slater asked Duncan.

"Do that. Have them stay back, though, until they get the word we need them."

He was thinking this could turn into a gunfight. And it possibly could. Joelle tried not to think of the risk this would be to her baby. Especially since Molly and her child were in even greater danger.

While Slater threaded the cruiser around the curvy country roads, Joelle fixed the image of her family's ranch in her head. Of course, she knew every inch of the house and grounds. Knew, too, that there were plenty of places for someone to lie in wait for them. It didn't help, either, that there was no one working full-time at the ranch. Slater often sent over his own hands just to check on the place, but there likely wouldn't have been anyone around when the kidnapper had set all this up. Which could have been hours ago. Heck, he could have been holding Molly here all along, though that would have been risky since eventually, when Duncan had had the manpower, he would have sent someone out to check the place.

"The second floor of the house will be a good place for a sniper," Joelle said. "Not the roof, though, because of the steep pitch."

"There are four front-facing windows on that second floor," Slater added.

Duncan had been to the ranch many times so he no doubt knew all of this, but Joelle thought it wouldn't hurt to spell out the potential points for an attack.

"From the barn loft," she went on, "there's a direct view of the road so anyone there would be able to see the moment we arrive."

Duncan muttered a sound of agreement and took out his gun. "Try to call the kidnapper again and see if he'll give us Molly's exact location. Yeah, it's a long shot," he grumbled.

It was, but Joelle tried anyway. As expected, he didn't answer. It rang out, and she figured he was already in the process of disabling it. Not that they would have the time to trace it. No. This was coming to some kind of showdown fast.

The minutes ticked away but so did the miles as Slater drove toward the ranch. He took the curves at a higher speed than he probably should have, the tires squealing in protest, but her brother kept control of the cruiser and ate up the miles.

Joelle had to force herself to breathe again when the ranch's pastures came into view. She hadn't needed proof that things weren't the same as they had been five months ago, but she got that proof, anyway. There was no livestock in the pastures. None of the beautiful palomino horses her father had loved. Those had already been moved to Slater's ranch.

The sun was fully up now, but the morning mist was still hovering over the pasture grass, giving the place an eerie, otherworldly feel. The mist hung around the house, too, and while it wasn't dense enough to conceal a shooter, she couldn't help but think of the smoke. And the fire that had destroyed her house. It was possible the kidnapper would do that here, too.

Slater cursed again, and Joelle soon saw why. There was a man at the end of the long driveway that led to the house. He was standing next to a black truck.

Hamlin.

"What the hell is he doing here?" Duncan grumbled, taking the question right out of her mouth.

"He's armed," Slater was quick to point out.

Joelle had noticed that as well. Hamlin had a gun in his right hand, and he jerked as if about to aim it at them. He didn't, though. Nor did he relax the grip he had on the weapon.

Her first thought was he was the kidnapper, and this was that showdown they'd expected. But she was betting none of them had expected the man to be out in the open like this.

Slater pulled the cruiser to a jarring stop just a few feet away from Hamlin. "Do you see anyone else?" he asked, his gaze already combing the house and grounds.

Joelle and Duncan were doing the same thing. Looking for hired guns that Hamlin might have brought with him, but there was no one visible in any of the second-floor windows or the barn.

Duncan lowered his window a fraction. "Stay put, Hamlin," he called out when the PI began to walk toward the cruiser. "And drop your weapon."

Hamlin glanced at his gun and scowled. Then, he huffed. "What the hell is this? Did you set me up or something?"

"Drop your weapon," Duncan repeated. His voice had a bite to it, but he added even more with the repeat.

On another huff, Hamlin tossed the gun on the ground and lifted his hands in the air. "I haven't done anything wrong," the PI protested.

"Then, why are you here?" Duncan demanded.

"Because you texted me and asked me to come." Hamlin's response was quick. Maybe rehearsed.

"I didn't text you," Duncan informed him, and Joelle noticed that Duncan was continuing to look for anyone else.

Hamlin shook his head. "But you did. My phone's in my pocket. I can show you."

Duncan didn't take him up on that offer, probably because he knew the text had been sent by someone else to set this all up. But what was *this*? "We're here looking for a kidnapped woman, and the kidnapper gave us this location."

That put some alarm in Hamlin's eyes, but since Joelle was plenty skeptical when it came to the PI, she figured that, too, could have been rehearsed. "I don't know anything about that, and I haven't seen anyone else since I got here."

"He could be telling the truth," Slater whispered. "Brad, Kate or the kidnapper could have arranged for Hamlin to come here to muddy the waters. Of course, if it's Brad or Kate, then it means they know all about Hamlin."

Yes, which would mean they'd know he was investigating the sale of babies. And that he believed Kate was behind that. However, Brad could have arranged this, too, if he wanted the cops looking at someone else other than him for Shanda's murder, the kidnapping and the earlier attack.

"There's only a minute left on the kidnapper's deadline," Joelle reminded them. Though she wasn't sure if that deadline applied any longer since they were, indeed, at the ranch.

Where there was seemingly no sign of Molly.

"Yeah," Duncan muttered, and he seemed to take a breath of relief when there was the sound of sirens in the distance. Backup would be there soon. "Hamlin, get face down on the ground, and don't block the road."

Joelle looked at Duncan, but she already knew what he had in mind. He'd leave backup to deal with Hamlin, and the PI would no doubt be handcuffed so he wouldn't be a threat. Good, because Joelle had the sickening feeling they already had enough threats to deal with.

And priority was finding Molly.

"Find out who's in that cruiser and let them know what's going on," Duncan told her just as his phone dinged with a text. "Never mind. It's Woodrow Leonard and Ronnie Bishop. They were on their way back from your place."

That explained how they'd gotten there so fast. It would have put them miles closer since her house was only an eight-minute or so drive from here. And that was a reminder they were already out of time for finding Molly. Of course, the deadline might not mean anything since it could have simply been part of the ruse to get them here, but Duncan apparently wasn't going to take the risk that those ten minutes had been part of the ploy.

"Joelle, text Woodrow or Ronnie and tell them to cuff Hamlin and take his gun," Duncan instructed. "Tell them to be careful and watch for gunmen. Slater, drive closer to the house."

She typed out the text, but Joelle also continued to glance around at their surroundings. Specifically, looking for any signs they were about to be shot at. But no bullets came.

Not yet, anyway.

Slater went slow, no doubt doing his own checking, and he finally came to a stop in the circular drive in front of the house. He positioned the cruiser close to the porch steps but still had a good view of the barn. Of course, that meant any gunman would have a view of them, too.

"Woodrow and Ronnie will deal with Hamlin," Joelle relayed after she got a response from Ronnie. "They'll cuff Hamlin, put him in the back of the cruiser and drive closer to assist."

"Good," Duncan muttered, and he turned to her. "You're staying put. I'm going inside the house to look around."

Oh, that gave her a nasty jolt of fear. "You're not going in there alone."

Duncan's mouth tightened, and she saw the debate in his eyes. "I want Slater to stay here with you in case you're attacked again."

She shook her head. "You're just as likely to be attacked in the house. Slater can go with you, and I can crawl over the seat and get behind the wheel." Her baby bump wasn't so big, not yet anyway, to prevent her from doing that. "Then, I can move the cruiser if necessary."

Joelle didn't want to think of what might make that necessary, but it would almost certainly mean some kind of attack. Maybe a firebomb to the house. But if that happened, she wouldn't be driving away unless Duncan and Slater were out of harm's way and with her.

The debate in Duncan's eyes continued a moment longer, and when he cursed, she knew he'd made his decision. So did Slater. They both reached for their doors.

"Don't get out of the cruiser," Duncan warned her one last time. He looked as if he wanted to add more, so much more, but thankfully he didn't. Now wasn't the time to bring up anything about "if the worst happens."

"Find Molly," Joelle said as they exited the cruiser.

The moment the doors were shut, she climbed over the seat and got behind the wheel while she continued to keep watch. Behind her, she saw Woodrow and Ronnie's cruiser pull to a stop, and in the distance, she heard yet more sirens. More vehicles, too, and Joelle spotted Slater's ranch hands as they arrived. Good. The more, the better.

But "more" didn't help Slater and Duncan right now.

Joelle quickly lost sight of them after Slater unlocked the front door and they hurried into the house. She could imagine, though, that they would immediately start the room-to-room search. It was a big house, and that meant there were plenty of places to check.

Plenty of places for a killer to hide, too.

Added to that, the house didn't have an open floor plan so Duncan and Slater wouldn't be able to do a quick visual sweep to determine if anyone was there. It'd be a slow process, searching through all eight rooms on the bottom floor before going to the second floor and then likely the attic if there was no sign of Molly before then.

She purposely didn't watch the time because she didn't want to mark off the seconds and minutes of the search for Molly. That wouldn't help her stay focused. Just the opposite. She didn't want to think of the extreme danger Duncan and her brother were in. Molly, too.

The baby stirred, a reminder of why she had to stay safe. It was also a reminder of Duncan. For the past five months, she'd worked so hard to keep her distance from him. Worked hard not to feel anything. Because those kinds of feelings also deepened the guilt and grief. But it was impossible to keep him out of her thoughts when they were thrown together like this. The closeness and the danger were breaking down barriers she'd fought to keep in place.

She forced all of that aside for now and tried to get a glimpse of the upstairs windows, to see if Duncan and Slater had made it to the second floor. It was impossible, though, with the way Slater had parked. The eaves of the porch blocked her view.

Another cruiser pulled in behind the others, and her phone dinged with a text. From Luca. We're coming closer, he messaged.

Hamlin is cuffed in the cruiser. Woodrow, Ronnie and I are going to check the barns and the other outbuildings. David will be here any minute now to help.

Deputy David Morales who normally worked the swing shift. Obviously, he'd been called in, and he would probably have his usual partner with him, Deputy Sonya Grover. Since Sonya and Molly were also friends, the woman would have insisted on coming to help.

All possible help would be needed since in addition to the big barn adjacent to the house, there were two smaller barns farther away and four other smaller outbuildings scattered around the grounds. There was even a fishing cabin on the banks of the creek that snaked through the ranch.

Joelle responded to let Luca know that she understood the plan, and she watched as they sprang into action. Not just the two cruisers but the three ranch hands from Slater's ranch. They didn't park near her, though, but rather between the house and the barn, and soon the deputies and hands began to pour from their vehicles. That didn't make her breathe easier, though.

It just meant a gunman would have more targets.

Her phone dinged again, and the relief washed over her when she saw it was from Duncan.

First and second floors cleared. Molly's not there. Heading into the attic now.

That rid her of any relief she'd just gotten. Yes, Duncan and her brother were still safe, there was no gunfire, but Molly wasn't there. It sickened Joelle to think of where the woman could be. And if she'd been hurt or worse. Now Duncan and Slater would have to basically climb a ladder to get into the attic, and there could be a gunman waiting for them.

She caught some movement from the corner of her eye and turned to the side of the house that was on the opposite side of the barn. Joelle immediately saw the white rectangular spots on the ground. Not the lingering morning mist. These appeared to be sheets of paper.

Joelle didn't want to move too far from the front door in case Slater and Duncan had to come running out, but she backed up the cruiser, keeping close to the porch so she could have a better look. Definitely paper and not some kind of explosives. She inched the cruiser back even farther, and she looked down.

Photos.

Four of them.

And her heart skipped a beat. Because they were pictures of her father. Not crime scene photos, either. These had been taken just as the blood had started to seep out from beneath his fallen lifeless body.

Oh, mercy.

The killer had taken these. And had left them for her to see.

Joelle's gaze immediately fired around. Just as there was a blur of motion. A man came charging at the window of the cruiser. Since he was wearing jeans and a gray work shirt, at first she thought it was one of the ranch hands or a deputy.

It wasn't.

She had a split second to realize this wasn't someone she knew, and she drew her gun. Too late, though. The man had a gun rigged with a silencer, and he immediately jammed it against the window.

And he fired.

The point-blank shot blasted through the cruiser, deafening Joelle and creating a half dollar-sized hole in the bullet resistant glass. The pain shot through her head and quadrupled when he fired another shot. Then, another.

For a horrifying moment, she thought she'd been hit. But no. He wasn't aiming at her. He was tearing the glass apart so he could get to her.

He managed it, too.

She turned her gun toward him, ready to fire, but his fist came through the hole, and he knocked her gun away. In the same motion, he unlocked her door from the inside and opened it, dragging her out of the cruiser.

The pain was still ramming into her head and ears, but Joelle didn't allow that to make her forget her training. She had to protect herself. She had to protect her daughter so she tried to ram the heel of her hand into his throat.

He dodged the blow, and before she could try to deliver another one, he grabbed her hair, dragging her in front of him.

"Stay back or I'll kill her," the man snarled.

That's when she realized Luca, Woodrow and two of the ranch hands had their weapons trained on her attacker. There was no sign of Duncan or Slater, but she figured they were racing out of the attic to the sound of that gunfire. Yes, the gunman had used a silencer, but the shots had still made some sounds that cops would have recognized. Added to that, there'd been the breaking glass. That would have alerted them, too.

"Let her go," Luca demanded.

"Not a chance," her attacker growled, and he began to walk backward with her.

He was pulling her hair hard, causing more pain to shoot through her, but Joelle was gearing up to start fighting him. He stopped her with a single sentence.

"Don't do anything stupid to get your kid hurt," he whispered right against her ear.

She didn't pivot and try to throw the punch she'd been planning. Nor did she attempt a kick. Joelle froze for a moment. Her baby. He was threatening to hurt her baby. And he could do it. That's why he'd said it, and he likely thought it was cause her to give up.

It wouldn't.

No way was she going to let her baby be at the mercy of this SOB. If he managed to get her away from the ranch, then heaven knew where he'd take her. And what he'd do to her and her precious child.

Joelle braced herself and got ready to do what she had to do.

Fight.

Chapter Eight

Everything inside Duncan went cold when he heard the shots. Three of them, one right behind the other.

He forced himself not to think, especially about Joelle and their baby. Duncan just scrambled down the attic ladder and started running. Fast. As if Joelle and the baby's lives depended on it.

Because he had the sickening feeling that it did.

Duncan took the stairs two and three at a time to reach the first floor, and he was about to barrel out the front door when something from the living room window caught his eye.

Joelle.

Hell. She wasn't in the cruiser but on the side of the house, and there was a hulking thug with one hand twisted in her hair and the other holding a gun that was pointed at her head. He was dragging her toward the back of the house. Maybe toward a vehicle he had stashed somewhere on the ranch.

Duncan turned around and headed for the back door, and he cursed when he had to waste precious seconds fumbling to get a deadbolt open. He finally managed it. Finally, got onto the back porch. But he didn't run. In fact, he tried to stay as quiet as possible when he made his way to the side and peered around it.

Duncan silently cursed. Then, he prayed.

The thug had his back to Duncan and was manhandling Joelle. The grip he had on her hair had to be excruciating, but she was alive, and Duncan couldn't see any blood. However, he could see Joelle trying to shift her feet as the would-be kidnapper maneuvered her over some kind of photos on the ground. Later, he'd see what those photos were all about, but for now he had to figure that Joelle was attempting to get into a position so she could fight back.

Duncan had to admire her grit, but this was a situation that could get her killed. Even if that wasn't the thug's intention. The fact he was dragging her somewhere meant he wanted her alive, but he might accidently shoot her if this turned into an outright scuffle.

Still, something had to be done. And it wouldn't be a shot since Duncan didn't have a clean one. The guy was big, at least a head taller than Joelle, but he was well aware of that and was hunkering down enough so that someone wouldn't put a bullet in his brain. Even Duncan couldn't risk shooting him from behind because the shot could go through him and into Joelle.

Duncan glanced over his shoulder when he sensed the movement. Not another thug but rather Slater who was quietly making his way to the end of the porch next to Duncan. Slater didn't curse when he saw what was playing out in the side yard, but Duncan suspected there was plenty of silent profanity going on. Plenty of questions, too. Well, specifically one question.

How the hell had this snake gotten Joelle out of the cruiser?

He suspected that a trio of gunshots in the same exact spot and a hefty sized gun had something to do with that. The cruiser was bullet-resistant, but shots could still get through. Or maybe something had happened to force Joelle out of the cruiser. Later, he'd want the answers to that, but for now he focused on keeping Joelle alive.

Duncan kept his gun aimed and ready, and he watched as the thug continued to drag Joelle. Duncan had to duck back out of sight, though, when he saw the guy turn to look over his shoulder. Thankfully, Slater did the same.

Since Duncan didn't want to risk the thug seeing him, he just stood there and waited. It felt like a couple of lifetimes. Bad ones. Long grueling moments with the stakes as high as they could get.

When the thug finally came into view, Duncan could see that Joelle was still squirming, still trying to fight this snake with her bare hands. The guy turned to take another glance behind him.

And that's when Duncan knew he had to make his move.

It was a risk. Anything he did at this point would be. But he tossed his own gun aside and launched himself off the porch, right onto the guy's back.

Duncan didn't do anything to break his fall. Or the thug's. Duncan didn't care if he broke the SOB's neck. Instead, he focused on knocking away the gun that was pointed at Joelle. That was the danger now. That had to be his priority. That and making sure Joelle didn't get hurt in what was about to happen next.

The thug grunted in pain when Duncan slammed into him and then yelled when Duncan's tackle rammed him onto the ground. Duncan didn't try to break his own fall but rather Joelle's. He hooked his right arm around her, cushioning her as best he could. He wasn't sure if it worked, but she didn't cry out in pain.

He hoped that wasn't because he'd knocked her unconscious.

But he soon felt her move, scrambling away from them. Good. Though Duncan knew Joelle wouldn't be running. She would no doubt be looking for a way to help him win this fight. He didn't especially want her to do that, but this was Joelle, and there'd be no stopping her.

Cursing, the thug used his elbow and jammed it right into Duncan's jaw. He could have sworn he saw stars, but he didn't let the pain faze him. Couldn't. Duncan grabbed the guy by the throat and punched him right in the face. There was a satisfying popping sound, followed by a spray of blood that let Duncan know he'd broken the man's nose.

Duncan didn't stop there. He rammed his fist into his throat, a maneuver he knew would disable him. And it did. Sputtering out a hoarse sound that was akin to a death rattle the SOB dropped back on the ground, clutching his throat and gasping for air.

Slater was suddenly right there, with his gun aimed at the man. Joelle was, too, and Duncan guessed that she'd grabbed the thug's weapon and was now ready to use it on him. Duncan was hoping that wouldn't be necessary.

"It's best if he's alive so we can question him," Duncan managed to say.

It was a reminder that he thought Joelle needed because she had her steely gaze pinned to her attacker, and the look in her eyes told Duncan she was ready to put a bullet in the guy if he tried to attack them again. The man wouldn't be able to do that, though, because he'd need breath to manage it, and it'd be a while before he got that back. Added to that, it'd be suicide for him to try to move with two cops—no, make that five—holding him at gunpoint.

Duncan got to his feet as fast as he could. "Where's Molly?" he demanded. "Point if you can't speak."

The guy kept groaning, kept gasping, but he still somehow managed a defiant look. Added to that, he tried to mutter something, and Duncan thought it was "go to hell, Sheriff."

So, he wasn't going to bend. Not at the moment, anyway.

"Cuff him and get him to jail," Duncan told Woodrow and Ronnie. "Charge him with attempted kidnapping and murder of a police officer. No bail for that." He turned to Luca and the others. "Keep searching for Molly. She might be in the vehicle this SOB used to get here."

With those steps set in motion, Duncan took hold of Joelle's arm. She was trembling, but she wasn't in shock, and other than a few red marks on her temple and neck, she didn't appear to be injured. He sent up a whole load of thanks for that.

"It's not safe for you to be outside," Duncan reminded her. "This guy might not be alone."

She looked at him, their gazes connecting, and it seemed as if she was using him as some kind of anchor. A way to stop herself from falling apart. It was one thing for a cop to be involved in an altercation, but it was much worse when the cop was the target. And there were no doubts about that. Joelle had been the target.

Again.

Joelle managed a nod, and she lowered the thug's gun to the side of her leg. Duncan eased it from her hand and passed it to Luca.

"Bag that," Duncan told him, and he got Joelle moving. First, up onto the porch and then into the house since it had already been searched.

The moment they were inside, he pulled Joelle into his arms. Yeah, it was unprofessional, but he'd been scared out of his mind about her getting hurt, and he needed this. Mercy, he needed it.

She dropped her weight against him, melting into his arms, and she made a hoarse sound. Not a sob. He figured she'd fight tooth and nail to stop any tears. But she couldn't totally stave off the effects of an adrenaline slam like this.

"Are you okay?" he asked. "All right, dumb question. Of course, you're not okay, but were you hurt?"

Joelle dragged in a few quick breaths. "I wasn't hurt. And the baby's fine because she's moving around."

That gave him a punch of relief that was even more powerful than the elbow slam the thug had managed into Duncan's jaw. He'd still need Joelle examined, which would mean checking the baby's heartbeat and such, but they'd come out of this a whole hell of a lot better than he'd imagined when he'd first seen the thug dragging Joelle through the yard.

"He shot out the window of the cruiser at point-blank range," Joelle said, her voice a shaky tangle of breath and nerves. "But he could have shot me. He didn't. He was going to kidnap me."

Yeah. Duncan had already gone there, and the "there" would give him some hellish memories for the rest of his life.

"With him being alive, we might be able to find out if he's a hired gun," Duncan said. "Or learn if he's actually the one who orchestrated these attacks." If so, the man wasn't on their radar. "Did you recognize him?"

Joelle shook her head, the movement causing his mouth to brush across her forehead. And that caused her to look up at him. Their gazes connected again and held firm.

She had to be experiencing a whirl of emotions right now. He certainly was. And Duncan figured those emotions played into him lowering his head and touching his mouth to hers. Just a touch, but it packed another punch.

Man, did it.

The heat would have rolled right through him, and he wanted to take her mouth as he'd done the night they'd landed in bed. And they would both pay dearly for that lapse, too. Joelle and he already had enough regrets, and Duncan didn't want this to be one of them. He figured Joelle felt the same.

But he was wrong.

Joelle came up on her toes and kissed him. Not a touch this time. It was a whole lot more. It was hard, hungry and filled with so many of those emotions. So much heat. She seemed to be using it as an anchor, too. Or maybe something that would help her remember she was alive.

"Thank you," she said when she finally pulled back. "You saved my life. You saved the baby."

In the moment, it felt as if they'd crossed some kind of threshold, that some of the old guilt might be lessening. But Duncan figured this was literally just that—*in the moment*—and that once Joelle leveled out from this attack, then she wouldn't want to be kissing him. Well, she might still want the kiss. Might want *him*. But after a little while, that guilt would hold her back just as it had for the past five months.

Duncan didn't have time to dwell on that. Or on the heat the kiss had notched up. He heard Slater call out his name, and Duncan knew he had to make sure nothing else had gone wrong.

"Wait just inside the door," Duncan told Joelle, and he reached down into his boot and came up with his backup weapon.

Since her gun was still somewhere out in the yard, he wanted her to have a way to protect herself. Of course, he was hoping with all the hopes in the universe that she didn't have to do that. Joelle had already been through way too much.

Duncan opened the back door and stepped onto the porch. He had his own gun ready as well, but he didn't see any immediate signs of danger. However, Slater, Woodrow and Ronnie were hurrying toward an outbuilding that Duncan knew Joelle's father had used to store ATVs and other equipment. At least Duncan thought that's where they were going, but they stopped about six feet in front of the shed.

"Ronnie spotted this," Slater added, reaching down and picking up a piece of green fabric that was almost the same color as the grass.

While Joelle did as he'd asked and remained in the doorway, Duncan went down the steps to have a closer look. He couldn't be sure, but it looked like the torn sleeve of a pajama top. Since Molly had been kidnapped when she likely still would have been in bed, the fabric could belong to her.

Slater went to his knees and began pulling at something. Some kind of flat circular metal cover the size of a tire. It was obviously heavy because Slater was struggling with it, and Ronnie dropped down to help him.

Behind him, Joelle gasped, and Duncan whirled around to make sure no one had come up behind her. She was alone, but she had gone pale, and she pressed her fingers to her trembling mouth.

"It's an old well," she said. "It terrified me when I was a kid, and Dad had that cover put on it to make sure no one fell in. It weighs too much for kids to move it. But..." She stopped, groaned. "But a kidnapper could have done it. Molly could be in there."

Hell. That got Duncan hurrying out into the yard to help them.

"The cover's been moved recently," Slater said, still focusing on the task. "You can tell from the grass around it. But whoever moved it put it back in place."

Duncan growled out another "hell," aloud this time. And he hoped if Molly was in there, she was still alive. By the time Duncan reached them, Slater and Ronnie had already dragged the cover to the side.

"Molly?" Slater called out, looking down into the gaping hole in the ground.

The opening was definitely wide enough that a person could be shoved in there, but if Joelle's dad had had it capped up like this, it had to be deep. Probably deep enough to kill a person if they fell or were pushed in.

"Molly?" Slater shouted again.

No response. Not from the well, anyway. But Duncan heard something coming from the outbuilding. Not a voice but a barely audible thump. It was enough to get the three of them running toward it.

"Woodrow and Sonya, keep an eye on Joelle," Duncan told the deputies who had just come out of the barn. They'd obviously been searching it for more gunmen and Molly.

Slater reached the outbuilding first, and Ronnie and Duncan both readied their weapons while Slater threw open the door and then immediately darted to the side in case someone was about to fire at him.

But no shots came.

A sound did, though. Another of those thumps, and when Duncan looked inside, he saw Molly on the floor.

Alive.

Duncan couldn't add the "and well" part to that, though. Her eyes were wide. Her forehead, smeared with dirt and maybe even some blood. Her hair was a tangled halo around her face. But she was very much alive.

He quickly saw that Molly was gagged and tied up, and

she was bumping the side of her leg against the tire of an ATV, the only movement she could have managed, considering the way she was positioned in the shed. That bumping had likely caused the sounds they'd heard. They would have no doubt found her in the search, but that had allowed them to get to her even sooner.

Slater hurried to her, easing down her gag while Ronnie got to work on the ropes around her feet. Duncan called 911 for an ambulance. The moment the gag was off her mouth, Molly cried out in pain.

"Hospital," she managed to say. "I'm in labor."

Chapter Nine

The images came at Joelle hard and fast. The blood. So much blood. And it was on those photos she had seen in the yard at the ranch. The ones she'd been forced to walk through when the kidnapper had her.

Joelle groaned and tried to yank herself away from those images. She had to climb her way out of this nightmare because she couldn't be here. She couldn't—

"Joelle," someone said.

Duncan.

And she thought that was his hands on her arms. It was enough to yank her back, and her eyes flew open. Yes, Duncan. He was right there, hovering and looking very concerned.

"I'm okay," she managed to say. "It was just a nightmare."

A nightmare she'd lived when the kidnapper had her. Oh, this was going to stay with her for a while, and she didn't need any new horrific memories to blend with the others she already had.

"No, you're not okay," Duncan said, sitting beside her. "But you soon will be. Just level your breathing. In and out," he instructed.

She tried to do that. Tried, too, to push away the lingering bits of the dream. Then, she remembered the rest of what happened. Remembered where she was as well. She was in a hospital bed. Not because she'd been injured. No, both the baby and she were fine. The doctor had told her that during the exam he'd given her after they'd arrived at the hospital.

With Molly.

Molly wasn't okay. Joelle had seen the cuts and bruises on her face, and she remembered Molly had been in labor.

"Did Molly have the baby?" she asked. "Are they all right?"

"She's okay. She's still in labor so the baby hasn't come yet." He dragged in a weary breath, and there was plenty of worry on his face. Some of that worry was no doubt for her and their own child. "The doctors have assured me that six hours isn't that long when it comes to labor."

Six hours. That's how long it'd been, and Joelle realized she'd slept nearly a full hour of that. Well, slept and dreamed anyway.

"The last update I got was that Molly was about seven centimeters dilated," Duncan explained. "So, maybe it won't be long now." He paused a moment and eased a strand of hair off Joelle's cheek. "Molly's injuries aren't serious, thank God. And the baby seems to be perfectly fine."

Joelle felt the relief shove aside some of those remnants of the nightmare. "Good." And she repeated it several times.

"Obviously, we haven't been able to ask Molly about the kidnapping," Duncan went on. "There'll be time for that later after the baby's born."

She figured he was wishing he could question Molly since the woman might be able to tell them more than they already knew. And it occurred to her that Duncan might know a whole lot more than he had when she'd fallen asleep.

"Sonya is with Molly in labor and delivery," Duncan went on before she could ask him for an update on the investigation. "Sonya went to childbirth classes with her and is Molly's coach. It's possible Sonya and Molly have been talking in between contractions." He eased off the bed and lifted a white bag. "The hospital food didn't look that good so I had this delivered from the diner. A grilled chicken sandwich, a fruit cup and milk. You should eat."

Joelle's stomach growled at the mention of food, and she realized that despite everything that'd gone on, she was in fact hungry. Duncan took out the items he'd mentioned, laying them out on the rolling table that he pulled over.

Apparently, she wasn't the only one hungry because he took out another sandwich, a bag of chips and a bottle of water for himself. He hadn't gotten his usual can of Pepsi, though, and she suspected that was because he knew it was her favorite as well but that she'd given up soda for the duration of the pregnancy.

"You've been here the whole time I've been sleeping," she commented, already knowing the answer. Duncan wouldn't risk leaving her, not when there were those two gunmen still at large. "Did you get any rest?"

He tipped his head to the chair in the corner. "Some."

Which meant maybe a catnap at most. Since there was also a laptop on the chair, it likely meant he'd spent the bulk of those six hours working. Joelle felt a little guilty about that, but then she reminded herself that her resting had been necessary. Doctor's orders. Yes, she and the baby were all right, but the doctor had said some sleep would remedy the effects of stress caused by the attack.

They ate in silence for a few moments, but she didn't miss the glances he kept giving her. Often, she could pinpoint what was on Duncan's mind just by looking at him, but there had to be plenty on his mind right now. Joelle plucked out one of the possibilities.

"Have you managed to ID the man who tried to kill me?" she asked.

"Not yet."

She hadn't thought it possible, but just admitting that tightened his jaw even more. Of course, everything about this bothered him because the attacks were aimed at her which meant they were also aimed at the baby.

"And we had to let Hamlin go," Duncan added a moment later. "I can't prove he didn't send that fake text to himself. Hell, I can't prove anything that'll land him in jail."

Yes, definitely plenty of frustration mixed with the worry and exhaustion. Not a good mix.

"Did you see the photos of my father in the yard?" she added.

Of course, she knew that he had. He wouldn't have missed something that big at a crime scene, and even though he'd left with her to follow Molly in the ambulance, Duncan had likely gotten a glimpse of them. He'd probably had more than a glimpse by now since one of the other deputies would have bagged them for processing and sent him pictures of them.

He nodded and continued to study her. "The man we have in custody won't talk about them, but I'm guessing he's the one who put them there. Is that what caused you to drive the cruiser to that part of the yard?"

It was Joelle's turn to nod. And to wince and shake her head. "It was a trap, and I fell for it. He was right there, hiding, waiting for me."

"If you hadn't driven over to them, he likely would have just come after you where you were parked," Duncan was quick to point out. "It was a risky plan, what with cops and ranch hands all over the place."

Yes, it had been risky. And it'd nearly worked.

"The man was wearing Kevlar beneath his shirt," Duncan went on, "but he could have been shot elsewhere if someone had spotted him charging at you."

That was also true. "Does that make him an idiot, cocky or desperate?" she wanted to know.

"Maybe all three." He took a bite of his sandwich, motioned for her to do the same, and she did. "His name is Willie Jay Prescott," he added after he'd washed the bite down with some of his water. "At least we think that's his name. The lab got a match on the blood found at Molly's, and it belongs to this Willie Jay. Since the guy who tried to take you had a cut on his arm, we're guessing Molly wounded him and he left some blood behind."

That made sense. Well, maybe it did. "There were at least three gunmen involved in the combined attack on me and in Molly's kidnapping," Joelle reminded him.

He made a quick sound of agreement. "When I'm able to talk to Molly, I'll show her Willie Jay's picture and ask if he was the one with her the whole time. It's possible he wore a mask around her, but she might be able to ID him."

Since Molly was a former cop, Joelle was betting the woman would be able to do it, too. Even though Molly would have been terrified during her captivity, she would have no doubt paid attention to the man holding her.

"My father's killer or his accomplice is probably the one who took those photos," she said. Again, this wouldn't be a surprise to Duncan. "That means Willie Jay could have been the one who murdered him?"

"Possibly." Duncan added a heavy sigh to that response. "But it could have been someone else. I'll try to come up with a way to get Willie Jay to open up about that. Hell, to open up about anything because right now, he's refusing to say a word."

"Has he lawyered up?" she asked.

"Not so far, but he also won't confirm he even understands his rights. That means a psych eval. I've already scheduled one to give the official determination that he's competent enough to be charged with kidnapping, forced imprisonment, attempted kidnapping of another police officer and any other charge I can tack onto that."

The attempted kidnapping charges would definitely stick since there were plenty of witnesses. A crime like that would send him to jail for a long time. But it'd be a heck of a lot longer if they could prove he'd been the one to take and hold Molly.

And if he'd killed her father.

She doubted Willie Jay was just going to confess to that.

"We could maybe build a circumstantial case for murder if we can connect Willie Jay to those photos," she said, thinking out loud. "Because only the killer or someone who had knowledge of the killer would have those."

Even if Willie Jay was only an accomplice in that particular crime, it would carry the same penalty as the murder itself. Which would put Willie Jay on death row. Joelle wanted that. She wanted her father's killer to pay.

But she also wanted answers.

Why had her father been gunned down? And had Willie Jay orchestrated that, or was he merely a hired gun? Added to that, why had he wanted her? As she'd told Duncan earlier, he could have killed her, and he hadn't. He had intended to kidnap her. It was possible that was so he could get the baby, but there had to be an easier way to get his hands on a pregnant woman.

And that circled her back to the pictures.

Then, back to their suspects.

"If Brad, Kate or Hamlin are connected to Willie Jay," Joelle said, hoping this idea made sense when she spelled it out, "then, maybe you can use that as a trigger to get Willie Jay to talk. Maybe let Willie Jay believe you'll let one of them get access to him. *Bad access*," she emphasized. "As in the kind of access to have him murdered because he can link one of them to the attacks, Molly's kidnapping and my father's murder."

Of course, there was no way Duncan would actually allow a prisoner to be hurt or killed like that, but it might work if Willie Jay thought Duncan would do something that drastic. Judging from the sound Duncan made, he agreed.

"Willie Jay might tell us something that'll pinpoint who's responsible for what happened. Including your father's murder," he added. "Because I think it's highly likely that someone hired Willie Jay. There's nothing in his background to lead me to believe he's capable of putting together something like this. I could be wrong, but I don't think so."

Since Joelle hadn't had a chance to pour through what they'd learned about Willie Jay, Duncan's assessment was enough for her to believe the man was a lackey. It was his boss they wanted.

"What about Brad?" she asked as they continued to eat. "Is he still at the sheriff's office?"

Duncan shook his head. "His lawyer showed up and insisted Brad had to leave to make funeral arrangements for Shanda. Brad apparently broke down, and Carmen thought he might need to be sedated."

Joelle raised an eyebrow, and Duncan must have picked up on the question she was about to ask.

"I have no idea if Brad's grief is real," he said, "or if he's the one who killed Shanda, but since we had so much going on, I had Carmen reschedule the rest of the interview for tomorrow. Ruston arranged for some SAPD cops to tail Brad to make sure he doesn't try to flee. By the way, Ruston's on his way here to check on you."

She didn't groan, though Joelle hated that her brother was taking the time to do that. Especially since there were so many other things that needed to be done. But she also knew that talking Ruston out of a visit would be impossible. He was her big brother, and he no doubt felt an obligation to make sure she was all right.

"Kate is clamoring to get out of the hospital and go home," Duncan said a moment later, continuing the update of all three of their suspects. "She claims she's in danger." He lifted his shoulder. "She might be if Brad or Hamlin want her dead, and that's one of the reasons I'm keeping a deputy on her door."

Yes, and the other reason was to make sure Kate didn't leave before they had a chance to find out if she was the mastermind behind what was going on.

The silence came again. So did some memories. Recent ones. Or rather a recent *one*. And Joelle knew they needed to talk about it.

"I should apologize for kissing you," she said.

Duncan laughed. "Joelle, you never need to apologize for that. But I know where this is leading," he was quick to add. "Kissing me brings back a lot of bad stuff for you."

It did. But it brought back good stuff, too. Specifically, the heat. "It's a distraction neither of us need right now," she pointed out.

No way could Duncan disagree with that, but he certainly didn't jump to say she was right. "There are a lot of different distractions," he said, his gaze sliding to her stomach. "The baby's the top priority."

Joelle was thankful he'd spelled that out. Despite the bitter feelings between Duncan and her over her father's murder, she knew he was committed to this baby. That he loved her. And right now, Joelle very much needed that.

"I always figured when I had a baby, that my parents would be around to share the experience," she said. Of course, that brought on a wave of bitter memories. "They very much wanted to be grandparents."

"They did," Duncan muttered.

She heard something in his voice, some of his own bitter memories, and she thought this went beyond what'd happened in the past five months. Duncan hadn't had the loving childhood she had. Just the opposite. From the bits and pieces he'd told her, his bio-dad had never been in the picture, and when he'd been six, his junkie mother's boyfriend had killed her in a domestic dispute. Duncan ended up in foster care and bounced around from place to place until he landed with an elderly aunt who lived in Saddle Ridge. The aunt had died when Duncan was a senior in high school so he had no family to speak of.

Well, no family except this baby she was carrying.

"You'll be a good dad," she muttered.

It was the truth, but part of her wished she hadn't spelled it out like that. It broke down yet even more of the barriers between them. So did the look he gave her.

A long lingering look that started at her eyes and landed on her mouth.

Thankfully, they didn't have time to make the mistake of another kiss because there was a tap on the door, and Duncan practically came to attention. He moved away from the food, positioning himself between her and whoever opened the door a moment later. Duncan slid his hand over his gun. But it wasn't a threat.

Ruston stuck his head inside.

"Good," her brother said. "You're awake." Ruston glanced

at Duncan's stance and nodded his approval. "Glad you're here and taking precautions."

They had a suspect just up the hall and a possible missing gunman. Joelle figured there'd be a lot of precautions until they made some arrests.

Ruston went to her, helped himself to one of the grapes from her fruit cup, and then leaned down to kiss her cheek. He took hold of her chin, turning her face while he examined her. He frowned when his attention landed on the bruises on her neck and temple. The ones on the neck had happened when Willie Jay had put her in a choke hold. The other was from the barrel of his gun.

"The SOB will pay for that," Ruston snarled.

Joelle didn't huff or remind her brother that she was a cop and such things happened to those in law enforcement. Yes, she was a cop all right, but she would always be his little sister. So would Bree, even though there wasn't a wide age gap between any of them. Each of the McCullough offspring had been born two years apart with Ruston the oldest at thirty-seven. Slater, thirty-five. She was thirty-three, and Bree, the baby of the family, was thirty-one.

"I can give you something that I think will help you make the SOB pay," Ruston added to Duncan, and he took out his phone. "On the drive over here, one of the techs called me. Shanda didn't have security cameras, but there was one on the street."

Ruston pulled up something on his phone and held it out for them to see. It was the grainy image of a nondescript dark-colored car, but the graininess didn't extend to the part of the photo of the driver.

"Willie Jay," Duncan and she said in unison.

"Yep," Ruston verified. "This was taken just up the block from Shanda's house, and if you look at the time stamp, it means he was there right around the time Shanda was being murdered."

Joelle felt a welcome wave of relief. Willie Jay would end up in jail for a long time, maybe even on death row. But that wouldn't convict him of her father's murder. Not unless they found a connection.

"We have Willie Jay's gun," Duncan explained. "The lab can see if it's a match to the one used to kill Shanda."

"Good," Ruston muttered. "Since Shanda was murdered in San Antonio, SAPD will be charging Willie Jay with that, but I don't want him to go unpunished for what he did to Molly and Joelle. I'd like to see him convicted on all charges with the sentences running consecutively. That way, even if he doesn't get the death penalty, there'd be no chance that he'll ever see the outside of a jail cell."

Joelle got another wave of relief, but there was still that nagging thought running through her head. "I want to find a connection between Willie Jay and Dad's murder. He might have been the one to pull the trigger."

Since there was absolutely no surprise on Ruston's face, Joelle knew that had already occurred to him. Of course, it had. Ruston had probably read every report connected to what had happened.

"I'm working on it," Ruston assured her just as there was another knock at the door.

Like earlier, Duncan braced. So did Ruston. But it was Sonya who peered in, and the deputy was smiling.

"Molly had the baby," Sonya announced. "A perfectly healthy girl. Seven pounds, three ounces, and I can attest to the quality of her lungs because she yelled plenty when she finally came out."

Tears watered Joelle's eyes, but these were definitely of the happy variety. "How's Molly?"

"She's great." Sonya didn't seem to be lying about that, either. "She's totally in love already with her baby girl." Now she paused. "I think that'll help her get over the trauma of what happened."

"Did Molly talk about the kidnapping?" Duncan was quick to ask, but the question had also been on the tip of Joelle's tongue.

"Not much. And I didn't press her on it," Sonya admitted. "Molly mainly just wanted assurance that her kidnapper was behind bars. He still is, right?"

"He is," Duncan verified.

"Good. Because I'm sure Molly will ask when she sees you. You can see her now," Sonya added. "A really short visit, though, after the pediatrician is finished examining Annika. That's what Molly's naming her."

Joelle got up out of the bed, intending to head to see Molly right away, but Duncan's phone rang.

"It's Luca," Duncan relayed. "You're on speaker," he added to Luca when he answered. "Give me some good news."

"I might be able to do just that," Luca replied. "I've been digging into Willie Jay's background, and I found out something very interesting. Willie Jay used to work for one of our suspects."

Chapter Ten

Hamlin.

Duncan wouldn't have been surprised no matter which of their suspects Luca had named. Kate, Brad or Hamlin. At this point, Duncan considered the three to all be sharing that top spot for their number one suspect.

Too bad he couldn't eliminate two of them, and then he'd know which one of them was responsible. Well, maybe. The gut-twisting possibility was that the culprit hadn't even surfaced, that Willie Jay's boss was someone other than Hamlin.

Still, Willie Jay had worked for Hamlin so that was a start.

"Arrange to have Hamlin brought in right away," Duncan told Luca, and Luca assured him he'd do just that.

Duncan ended the call and slipped his phone back in his pocket. "Sonya, I figure you didn't get much rest, what with being called in early and Molly's birth coach, but do you have the bandwidth to stay here with the baby and her until I can get someone else to guard them?"

"I can stay as long as needed," Sonya quickly assured him. "In fact, I'd like to stay the night. Molly and I are friends, and I think she'd be more comfortable with me than with someone else."

"I agree," Duncan told her, "but if you feel yourself start to fade, then let me know."

Duncan checked the time. The hours were just racing by, and they had so much to do. But it was a priority now to see Molly. Not just because she might be able to give them answers but also because she was part of their Saddle Ridge Sheriff's Office family, and she'd been through a hellish ordeal. Then, Joelle and he could go back to the sheriff's office and wait for Hamlin. Duncan had no doubts that Luca would be able to locate the PI and get him in there fast.

"I take it you're up to this visit with Molly and the baby?" Duncan asked Joelle.

"Absolutely." Her answer was quick and resolute.

Ruston checked his watch as well, and he leaned over and brushed another kiss on Joelle's cheek. "I'll head back to San Antonio and work the arrest warrant there. I just wanted to see for myself that you were all right. Are you going to Slater's tonight or will you stay with Duncan?"

Obviously, the question threw her because she gave him a blank stare for a couple of seconds. "To be determined," she said at the same moment Duncan said, "I'll take her to my place."

"Good," Ruston concluded, but he didn't spell out why he felt that way.

"Good," Joelle murmured, not sounding nearly as pleased about staying with him as Ruston had been.

They went into the hall with Ruston heading for the exit, and Sonya, Duncan and her going in the direction of labor and delivery. Sonya must have sensed Duncan needed to have a word with Joelle about the sleeping arrangements because she walked ahead of them, giving them some privacy.

Duncan waited for Joelle to spell out that it was risky

for them to be under the same roof. Especially after the kiss and the steamy looks they'd been giving each other.

"My resistance for you is really low right now," she whispered. "You saved my life, and you're the father of a baby we both love and want to protect."

That was it. No extra line to clarify where that low resistance would lead them. Duncan's guess was to bed since he didn't have a whole lot of resistance when it came to her, either.

And that caused him to curse.

Because she'd just confessed she was vulnerable. Of course, she was. She'd nearly been kidnapped and could have been killed. So, landing in bed was totally out since it'd be taking advantage of her.

"Yes," she murmured when he cursed again, and the response confirmed she was well aware of his thought process.

His body didn't want to give up on the "landing in bed" part, but Duncan had to shove all thoughts of that aside as Sonya opened one of the hospital room doors. When Duncan looked in, he immediately saw Molly on the bed. She was smiling and cooing down at the baby she was holding.

"Isn't she beautiful?" Molly asked, her smile widening when she looked up at them.

Duncan took one of the paper surgical masks from a wall holder, put it on and went closer. "Yep, she's beautiful all right."

And she was. A perfect little face with fingers so tiny that Duncan hoped Molly didn't insist he hold her. She seemed way too fragile for that, but he got a reminder that soon, in four months or so, he'd have to get past that fear since he'd be holding his own child.

Joelle put on a mask and walked closer, peering down

at the baby. Even though Duncan couldn't see her expression, he knew she was smiling. "Molly, she's adorable." Joelle gave Molly's arm a gentle squeeze. "Congratulations, Mom."

"It's all a little daunting," Molly admitted, "and a whole lot amazing." She seemed ready to go on about the joys of motherhood. She didn't, though. She looked at Duncan. "You want to ask me questions about the kidnapping."

"Are you up to that?" he offered. "Because it can wait—"

"I can tell you what happened," Molly interrupted, "and then maybe we can do a more formal statement after I've gotten some sleep."

Duncan nodded and decided to let Molly say whatever it was she clearly wanted to say. If he saw her energy levels draining, then he would put a stop to this and come back.

Molly dragged in a long breath. "I was asleep when I heard my security system go off. I picked up my phone, thinking that maybe it was some kind of malfunction, but it wasn't. I heard someone moving around in my living room so I hit the last number I'd called. Joelle's. Then, I saw two men coming into my bedroom."

"Two?" Joelle asked.

Molly nodded. "They were both wearing ski masks, dark clothes. Both were about six feet and with somewhat muscular builds."

That described Willie Jay. Hell, it described a lot of men, and while Duncan was certain they had one of the kidnappers in custody—Willie Jay—they obviously needed to look for his partner. And Joelle's attacker. Of course, it was possible the second kidnapper was also the one who'd fired those shots into the cruiser at Joelle.

"I tried to get to my gun that I keep in the drawer next to the bed, but they grabbed me before I could do that,"

Molly went on. "I hit one of them with my phone and then dug my nails into his arm. I guess I cut him deep enough for him to leave blood at my house."

"We've identified that blood," Duncan told her. "Willie Jay Prescott. We have him in custody."

Molly's breath hitched, maybe from relief. "And the other?"

"We'll find him," he assured her, and Duncan hoped that was the truth. They needed to find the remaining person or persons responsible for this.

Molly paused a moment, kissed her daughter's cheek and then started again. "They put a hood over my head, tied up my hands and feet, and got me into a vehicle. A truck, I think, because of the way they had to lift me to put me in it. And they drove away."

It was hell for Duncan to hear all of this. To know the terror that had to have been going through Molly's mind. She'd probably thought she would lose her precious baby as well as her own life.

"The men didn't talk when we were driving," she went on. "But we weren't in the vehicle long. Maybe ten minutes or less."

Duncan calculated that was about the time it would have taken the kidnappers to get from Molly's house to the McCullough ranch. "Did they take you to the location where we found you, or did you go somewhere else first?"

"Just that one location. Your dad's ranch," Molly muttered, looking at Joelle. "I didn't know that's where I was until the EMTs were taking me to the ambulance."

That made Duncan do more mental cursing. All those hours, Molly had been so close. But they'd had so many places to search, and Molly hadn't had any connection to the McCullough ranch. She had been taken there because the kidnappers no doubt knew it was empty.

Molly cleared her throat before she continued, "After I was in the shed, I'm sure one of them left. The one who smelled like cinnamon stayed, and the other left."

"Cinnamon?" Duncan pressed.

Molly nodded. "He was chewing some kind of gum or candy. He's the one who made the calls to Joelle." She paused. "And I honestly believed what he was saying, that he regretted kidnapping me."

Maybe he did. But obviously Willie Jay hadn't felt that.

"A couple of hours before you found me," Molly continued, "the second man came back, and they had a whispered conversation. The cinnamon guy was pleading with the other to let me go, but the second man said no. They went out of the shed, and they argued, but I couldn't make out what they were saying. Then, neither one came back in. I didn't hear anyone else until you and the deputies showed up."

Duncan could only speculate as to what'd happened. Maybe the "cinnamon guy" had stormed off. Or maybe Willie Jay had eliminated him. If so, the man's body hadn't been found on the ranch, and the CSIs and some of his deputies had been combing the place.

"If you get me a sample of Willie Jay's voice, I should be able to confirm he was one of the kidnappers," Molly offered.

"I'll do that," he said just as the baby let out a kitten-like cry. That was his cue to leave and let Molly have some time with her daughter.

Joelle gave Molly another gentle hug, ran her fingers over the baby's cheek and left with Duncan. He was about to call Slater or Luca to provide backup while they went to the sheriff's office, but Slater was already in the hall, waiting for them.

"Ruston told me about Hamlin's connection to Willie Jay," Slater explained as they headed for the exit. "He's on his way in for an interview, but he's not happy."

"Welcome to the club," Duncan muttered. But in Hamlin's case, not being happy was a good thing. Riled people often said more than they intended to.

As expected, Slater had the cruiser waiting for them right outside the ER doors, and the three of them hurried to get in. Duncan glanced at Joelle and saw that she was looking at the window next to her. And she was no doubt recalling that Willie Jay had shot through a similar window to get to her.

The bullet-resistant glass was better than nothing, but this had to be a reminder that they weren't safe, not even in the cruiser. Duncan could only hope they'd be making an arrest soon that would put an end to the danger.

Duncan kept watch as Slater drove, but he didn't see anyone he didn't recognize. If Joelle hadn't been with him and if they hadn't been in the middle of town, Duncan would have wanted to spot the missing attacker. Would have liked to have a showdown with him. But the thug apparently wasn't showing his face in broad daylight.

After Slater parked, they went into the sheriff's office. Which was nearly bare. Understandable, what with all the various components of the investigation going on and with some of the deputies needing rest after a hellishly long day. Woodrow was at his desk, working on his laptop, and Ronnie was at his. Not alone. There was a young brunette woman sitting next to him. Both Ronnie and the woman got to their feet, their attention turning to Duncan.

"This is Erica Corley," Ronnie said. "She just came in to talk to you."

The name was familiar, but Duncan thumbed through his memory to figure out if he recognized her. He didn't. And when Joelle and Slater shook their heads, he figured they didn't know her, either.

"I'm Sheriff Holder." Duncan went closer to Erica and hitched a thumb at Joelle and Slater when he introduced them.

The woman nodded, swallowed hard. "I'm Al Hamlin's ex-girlfriend. Al and I had a baby together when we were teenagers."

Duncan was certain he looked surprised because he was. Not about the baby part but that Erica would just show up like this. Then again, it was possible the PI they'd talked to had located her and sent her to them.

"I heard about the kidnapping and attacks on the news," Erica went on. "One of the reports mentioned Al, that he was on the scene when a man was taken into custody."

Duncan silently groaned. He didn't know how the media picked up on such details, but he had to admit a story like this would make good press.

"And I thought… Well, I wondered," Erica added a moment later, "if Al was involved in some way?"

Since that was exactly what Duncan wanted to know, he motioned for Erica to go into his office. Joelle came, too, but Slater muttered something about needing to check for updates, and he headed to his desk in the bullpen.

"Can I get you some coffee or water?" Duncan asked her.

Erica shook her head and took one of the seats next to Duncan's desk. Joelle took the other.

"Was Al involved in the kidnapping and attacks?" Erica pressed.

Considering that Willie Jay had worked for Hamlin, the answer was yes, but Duncan kept that to himself and went with a question of his own. "Do you believe your ex is capable of something like that?" He'd asked Brad's ex, Shanda, the same thing, and she'd more or less waffled on her response.

Erica didn't.

"I believe he's capable," she said after a heavy sigh. "I don't know why he'd do it, but..." She stopped. "It could be because of what happened with our baby. I suppose you know about that?"

"We do," Duncan verified.

Erica nodded. "I wanted to give the baby up for adoption, and Al wanted to, well, sell it."

There was some anger, maybe even shame, in those last few words, and Erica lowered her head, shook it.

"I was against it," Erica went on after several moments. "But Al kept pressing me. He said he'd gotten in touch with someone, and the person would pay us ten thousand dollars. I don't come from money, and that sounded like a fortune to me. So I went through with meeting with this person, even though I wasn't sure I could actually sell my child."

That meshed with what Duncan had read in the juvenile records that Slater had managed to get. The arresting officer had mentioned that Hamlin had been the one to orchestrate the sale and had also contacted the couple two more times to up the amount he wanted them to pay for the child. That's how the extortion had come into play.

The wannabe adoptive parents had been charged, too, since they had planned on paying for the baby, but no one involved in the case had pointed the finger at Erica as being the aggressor in the sale or the extortion. Still, she'd been convicted since she had gone along with meeting the couple.

"What happened at the meeting?" Joelle prompted when the woman fell silent.

Erica gave another of those long sighs. "The San Antonio cops found out what Al and I were doing because they showed up and arrested us." She shifted her attention to Joelle. "I think your late father was the one who told the cops."

Duncan didn't know who was more surprised by that, Joelle or him. "My father?" she questioned.

"I spoke to Sheriff Cliff McCullough shortly after I was arrested. He'd gotten a tip from a longtime confidential informant that a couple was trying to buy a baby, and he gave SAPD the couple's names, and that in turn put the cops on Al and me. We didn't even make it to the meeting with the couple because they in turn told the cops about us. We were convicted of attempted extortion and trying to sell the baby."

Joelle stayed quiet a moment. "Did Hamlin know about my father's involvement in this?"

"Sure," Erica was quick to say. "Your father spoke to both Al and me after the arrest. I'm not sure what he said to Al, but your dad was kind to me. He knew my folks had kicked me out, that I had no place to go and had been staying with friends just to have a roof over my head. He told me if I needed help with a legal adoption agency or if I decided to keep the baby, he could find me a place to go."

That part didn't surprise Duncan one bit. Sheriff McCullough had been a good man, and he would have done whatever possible to right a bad situation. If Erica was telling the truth, and Duncan believed she was, then her situation had definitely qualified as bad.

"I took the sheriff up on his offer," Erica explained. "I got out of juvie three months before Al did, and the sheriff helped me get into a home that had other girls like me.

I had the baby, legally put her up for adoption and then the sheriff arranged for me to get my GED and a job."

Joelle and Duncan exchanged glances, and he could practically see the wheels turning in her head. "How did Hamlin take that?"

"Not well." That answer was also quick. "He didn't find me until after I'd had the baby, and he was furious. Not because he wanted the child. But because he still thought I should have gotten some money for the baby. Money that I should have shared with him." Her bottom lip trembled a little. "I told Al to leave me alone or I'd ask Sheriff McCullough to help me file a restraining order against him."

Duncan figured Hamlin wasn't happy about that, either. In fact, it could have riled him to the core. Did it rile him enough, though, to carry on a vendetta to murder the sheriff and go after Joelle? Maybe. And maybe Molly played into the plan simply because she would soon give birth to a baby that Hamlin could sell.

Erica lifted her head and met Duncan's gaze. "I think Al might have pressured his sister to sell her child. That might be why Isla disappeared."

Duncan considered that for a moment and then tried to link that to what was happening now. If Hamlin had continued to dabble in selling babies, then it's possible Isla would have run from him.

"Did Al ever mention Kate Moreland?" Duncan asked.

Erica opened her mouth to answer, but the sound of a man's voice stopped her. Speaking of the devil, Hamlin came in, pushing his way past one of the deputies, and his attention must have landed on Erica.

"What the hell is she doing here?" Hamlin demanded.

Erica sprang to her feet, and Duncan thought the woman might cower in fear at the sight of her ex, but she turned and faced him head-on. "I came because I thought you might be involved in what happened to Deputy McCullough and the woman who was kidnapped."

Hamlin cursed, and he opened his mouth as if about to unleash some rage and profanity, but he quickly bit that off. He turned around, pacing a few steps, and when he turned back toward Erica, he scrubbed his hand over his face.

"Don't you see?" he asked her. "They'll use anything you've told them to try and pin these crimes on me. I'm just trying to find my sister and make the people who took her pay."

"I had to come," Erica fired back. There was no real anger in her voice, just that shamed reaction again. "I don't know for sure if you've had any part in what happened, but I wanted to tell the sheriff about our arrest. I didn't think it would come up in a normal search since we were underage."

"And it's irrelevant," Hamlin insisted. He snapped toward Duncan and repeated that. "Yes, I was convicted of doing something very stupid by trying to get money for our child. I was young and desperate, and I made a mistake. All of that has nothing to do with the attacks. I told you I was there on scene because I got a text from you. Or rather a text I thought was from you."

"It wasn't," Duncan verified. And that's why Duncan had had his phone records entered into the investigation log so it would be clear he hadn't been the one who'd messaged Hamlin telling him to go to the McCullough ranch. According to the techs, the message had come from a burner, which meant Hamlin could have sent it to himself.

That was a reminder of why Duncan had wanted Hamlin to be interviewed, but he wasn't sure if Erica had more to add to the investigation or not. "Thank you for coming in today," Duncan told the woman. "Deputy Slater Mc-

Cullough will take your statement because there are some things I have to ask Hamlin."

And Duncan didn't want to do that in front of Erica. He needed to keep this all by the book since he soon might be charging Hamlin with a boatload of felonies.

Duncan tipped his head to the interview room. "This way," he told Hamlin, and Joelle followed in step behind them. On the short walk, Duncan repeated the Miranda warning.

Hamlin muttered throughout the warning, and he was still muttering when they were in the room and seated. "Erica shouldn't have come and stirred up things like that," he snapped. "I had nothing to do with what happened to Deputy McCullough and the dispatcher."

"Nothing to do with Sheriff Cliff McCullough, either?" Duncan threw out there.

Hamlin flinched. Then, he huffed again. "Erica told you that the sheriff is the one who ratted us out. Yes, he did. He poked his nose into something that wasn't his business, but I'm going to repeat myself again. I had nothing to do with what's been going on."

Duncan just stared at the man, and after a few seconds had crawled by, he said, "Willie Jay Prescott." And he watched Hamlin's reaction.

Joelle was no doubt watching, too, which meant she saw the flicker of recognition in Hamlin's eyes. "Want to tell us about your relationship with Willie Jay?" she suggested, though it was more of an order.

Hamlin's mouth tightened, and he belted out some more profanity. "What about him?"

Duncan huffed. "Stop playing games with us. Willie Jay is in a jail cell right here in this building, and he's had plenty to say."

Of course, that last part was a lie. Willie Jay hadn't said a word, but it was obvious that the revelation of Willie Jay's arrest put some serious concern on Hamlin's face.

Hamlin stayed quiet a moment, his gaze flickering right and then left. "Mr. Prescott briefly worked for me when I first became a PI," he finally said. "I employed him to help me track down leads on my cases. The employment didn't last because Mr. Prescott turned out to be not very reliable at showing up for work or doing his assigned tasks. So, I fired him."

Duncan continued to fix his hard stare on the man. "When was this?"

Hamlin certainly wasn't quick to answer. "I officially fired him about two months ago, but he hasn't actually worked for me in nearly a year. I just quit giving him assignments." He paused a heartbeat, and some more anger flared through his eyes. "Mr. Prescott was *not* happy about me terminating his employment so I'm sure anything he told you is to get back at me for firing him."

Duncan made a sound to indicate he was giving that some thought and he shook his head. "He didn't mention anything about you firing him." And Duncan left it at that, letting Hamlin squirm.

He squirmed all right and did more cursing. "Look, I don't know what Willie Jay said about me, but I've done nothing illegal. Nothing illegal since that incident when I was a teenager," he amended when Duncan lifted an eyebrow. "The person you should be looking at is Kate Moreland. She's behind these attacks."

"So you've said," Duncan commented. "But I'm not seeing a whole lot of proof that she's guilty. You, on the other hand, have a strong connection to a hired thug, Willie Jay, who we caught red-handed. He's going down, and he's going down hard. It'll be interesting to see who he takes with him."

The anger came again, like a burst of red-hot heat, but it faded just as quickly. "The person he should be taking down with him is Kate because I didn't hire Willie Jay to go after Deputy McCullough or your dispatcher."

Joelle leaned in. "Why are you so sure it's Kate? There has to be more to this vendetta of yours—"

"She was the one who contacted me when I was seventeen and Erica was pregnant," Hamlin blurted. "I'd been asking around, and she got in touch with me. She called herself a middleman in the process. A *facilitator* was the word she used."

Interesting. Because Kate hadn't mentioned anything about that. Then again, this might all be Hamlin blowing smoke.

"Kate contacted you personally?" Duncan asked.

Hamlin nodded. "With a phone call. I'd left my number around in case anyone was interested. I spelled out that Erica and I wanted some money to cover the expenses of her pregnancy and the upcoming delivery."

Duncan raised his eyebrow again.

"All right." Hamlin huffed. "I wanted more than expenses covered. I wanted to be able to give Erica and me a fresh start. And she had already said she was giving up the baby. It wasn't as if I pressured her to do that."

Maybe. Duncan figured some pressure was involved once Hamlin realized he could get money for the baby. Still, Duncan didn't want to muddy this line of questioning.

"So, did you actually meet with Kate when you were trying to arrange for the sale of your child?" Duncan asked.

The wording clearly riled Hamlin, but Duncan wasn't planning on sugarcoating anything. "No," Hamlin snarled.

"Then you can't know for certain it was Kate Moreland," Joelle was quick to point out. She obviously wasn't sugarcoating, either.

"It was her," Hamlin insisted, but then he paused and seemed to have a lightbulb over the head moment. "It was her voice. I've heard recordings of her speaking at various social events, and I'm positive it was Kate."

"Maybe," Duncan repeated.

"There's no maybe to it. It was Kate, and after that initial call, I dealt with one of her employees."

That got Duncan's attention. "Who?"

"A man named Arlo Dennison," Hamlin said without hesitation. "I've researched him, and he used to manage one of her gyms. He doesn't any longer. In fact, he's not officially on her payroll that I can find, but she's probably paying him under the table for more black market baby deals."

"That's possible," Duncan admitted. "But other things fall into the area of possibilities, too. For instance, you're the one doing the baby-brokering deals, and you want to toss some bad light on Kate so she'll take the heat for something you're doing."

Yeah, it was a hard push, but Duncan had wanted to see how Hamlin would react. And he saw all right. Hamlin got to his feet.

"I'm going to terminate this interview right now and come back with a lawyer," Hamlin insisted. He glared at Duncan. "Unless you plan on arresting me simply because I once employed a man you now have in custody."

Duncan wished he could arrest Hamlin. It'd take one of their prime suspects off the street. But there was no way he could get an arrest warrant much less a conviction with what he had.

"Come back first thing in the morning with your lawyer," Duncan told Hamlin. "By first thing, I mean eight o'clock. Be here or I'll send someone to bring you in."

Of course, that riled Hamlin even more, and the man stormed out. Duncan immediately took out his phone to look up this Arlo Dennison, but Joelle had already done it.

"Arlo Dennison," she relayed, "is forty-two and did, indeed, manage one of Kate's gyms. He's got a sheet, an old one for assault and extortion. That was eleven years ago, so he either learned his lesson or he's gotten better at covering up his crimes. I'm texting you his number now," she added.

The moment Duncan's phone dinged with the text, he clicked on the number to call Arlo Dennison. There was a single ring before the call went to voice mail. The greeting was automated and simply told the caller to leave a message. Duncan didn't, though if Arlo checked his phone, he'd be able to figure out that the sheriff of Saddle Ridge was calling him.

"Arlo lives in San Antonio," Joelle added. "You want me to have Ruston send someone out to pick him up and bring him in for questioning?"

Duncan thought about it for a couple of seconds and nodded. "See if Ruston or another SAPD cop can do the interview."

That would save them from having to wait around for Arlo to come in. Duncan figured Joelle was spent for the day. He certainly was, and added to that, they would need to re-interview Kate and try to get Willie Jay to talk.

Joelle nodded and immediately called her brother. She'd barely had time to convey what they wanted when Duncan's own phone rang, and he saw Luca's name on the screen.

"We have a problem," Luca said the moment Duncan answered the call on speaker.

"What?" Duncan asked after he groaned.

"Woodrow found a truck on one of the ranch trails that's near the McCullough ranch. Inside it, there were two dead bodies."

Chapter Eleven

Two dead bodies.

Hearing Luca say that had given Joelle an initial hit of adrenaline. But that had been six hours ago. Now she was just wiped out and had to force herself to stay alert and focused as Duncan read the latest update he'd just gotten from Woodrow and the CSIs.

"Two males," Duncan said. He was standing behind his desk, reading from his laptop. "Both were identified through prints since they had criminal records. Darrin Finney, forty-two, from San Antonio, has a sheet for B&E, assault and drug possession. Troy Oakley, thirty-six, from Austin, has a nearly identical sheet, minus the drugs. The deaths were set up to look like a murder-suicide with Troy being the killer."

Joelle, who was seated in the chair, looked up at Duncan. "Set up?" she questioned.

Duncan nodded. "There was a note left at the scene, but the CSIs said the angles of the kill shots were wrong for it to have gone down that way."

He turned his laptop so she could read the note that had been photographed. The handwriting was basically a scrawl so it took her a moment to make out what it said. "Too many cops after us," she read aloud. "This is better than going to prison. We were wrong to go after that deputy and the other woman."

Even without the wrong angles of the kill shots, Joelle would have suspected the murder-suicide was a ruse. Sometimes, criminals did do things like this, but the truth was the cops weren't on the trails of these two. Their names hadn't even surfaced so far during the investigation.

"Both men had GSR on them," Duncan continued. "And Darrin Finney had some cinnamon gum in his pocket."

Continuing to fight the fatigue, Joelle considered that a moment. Molly had said one of her kidnappers chewed that particular flavor of gum so that probably meant these two were the ones who'd taken her.

"The truck they were in was reported stolen earlier today," Duncan added a moment later, "and there doesn't seem to be a connection between the owner of the vehicle and either of these two dead men."

Molly had also mentioned she believed they had transported her in a truck. So that matched as well.

"These two took Molly," Joelle summarized. "Maybe they did, anyway. Since Willie Jay ended up at the ranch with Molly, he could have been one of her initial kidnappers." She paused. "And that would mean the two worked together with someone else to cover both her kidnapping and the attack aimed at me. The *someone else* could be just one person. Or two."

"Probably two," Duncan said. "Because I don't believe they'd see going after a cop as a one man job. So, with two dead and one in custody, there's almost certainly someone else out there we need to find."

"You're thinking the fourth man might be this Arlo Denison Hamlin told us about?" she asked.

Duncan shrugged and then sighed. She wasn't exactly

sure the reason for the sigh until he closed his laptop and walked around the desk to take her by the arm.

"I'm taking you to my place," he said, lifting her from the chair.

Part of her wanted to argue, to try to continue to push through the avalanche of information they'd gotten on this investigation. But the baby moved just as she opened her mouth to insist she had another couple of hours in her. She didn't. And the baby was a reminder that she had already had too much stress on her body today and she needed rest.

Duncan let go of her arm once they got moving out of his office and into the bullpen. Slater, Woodrow and Luca were all there. All still working. And that gave Joelle some fresh guilt over leaving when they hadn't. Still, the exhaustion wasn't giving her much of a choice about this.

Slater and Woodrow were both on the phone so Duncan turned to Luca. "Could you follow Joelle and me to my place?"

Luca's nod was quick. "You want me to stay there with you tonight?"

Duncan considered that for a moment and nodded. "Three of the attackers are out of commission, but I believe there's a fourth one and their boss are still out there. Let's go in one cruiser."

Luca nodded as well, and after mouthing the plan to Slater, he grabbed his laptop and went out the door first with Joelle and Duncan right behind them. Following their recent travel patterns, Duncan rode shotgun and Joelle took the back seat.

It wasn't far to Duncan's house, only about two miles, but travel anywhere wasn't exactly a breeze because of the attacks. All three of them knew any time out in the open could lead to another one. Added to that, it was dark now so someone could be lying in wait.

While Luca drove and they kept watch, Joelle tried to recall if Duncan had more than one guest room. Even though Duncan had owned the small ranch for five years now, she hadn't been to his place that often. Mainly because they'd spent a good chunk of those five years keeping their distance from each other.

Clearly, they'd ultimately failed since she was carrying his baby.

From the handful of visits she had made to his ranch, she recalled the house being fairly large, but even without guest rooms, she figured they'd all end up getting some sleep somewhere in the house since they had all been going at this for way too many hours.

Duncan's phone dinged with a text. A sound that instantly put Joelle on alert in case it was a message about an attack being imminent. She tried to hold onto the hope, though, that it was good news.

"It's from Slater," Duncan relayed to them. "SAPD uncovered something interesting on Kate. About three months ago, she accused Brad and Shanda of drugging her. She talked to a detective about it, and he investigated, but nothing came of it since there were no drugs in her system when Kate came in to report it."

Joelle worked that through in her mind. "I can see this playing out two ways. Either Brad and/or Shanda did, indeed, drug the woman. Or else Kate was laying the groundwork to set them up for the attacks she was planning on Molly and me."

Duncan made a sound of agreement. "And that takes us back to Kate's motive. If the attacks are to set someone up, why not do that to Hamlin? That would get him off her back."

"True," Joelle admitted. "But maybe her motive is about getting revenge for what happened to Shanda. I know she hated Shanda," she quickly added, "but the arrest and miscarriage ultimately caused a rift between Kate and her son. Kate would want to get back at Molly and me for that, and in the process she could end up with two babies to sell."

The thought of that sickened Joelle. Kate could possibly want to use her baby and Molly's to settle an old score.

It didn't take long, less than five minutes, before Luca took the turn into Duncan's driveway, and Duncan used his phone to open his garage door. He also turned on some security lights. Lots of them at both the front and sides of the house.

Unlike her place, Duncan had neighbors—a small-time rancher directly across the road from him and another about two hundred yards to his right. Not exactly right next door but close enough that the lights from those two places also provided some illumination as well.

Luca pulled into the garage, and they all stayed inside the cruiser until Duncan had shut the garage door behind them. "I have a security system," he said, checking his phone. "And I would have gotten an alert had someone gone into the house. Still, I want to do a sweep of the place just in case someone hacked into the system."

That wasn't exactly a comforting thought, but Joelle was glad Duncan had even considered it. The problem with being so tired was that it could cause a loss of focus on something critical like this.

Duncan got out, and he searched the garage first before he went into the house. Luca and she sat in the cruiser, waiting and hoping that all was well. They'd already been through way too much. Ditto for Molly, but Joelle had talked to the woman about an hour ago, and the baby and the new mother seemed to be doing well.

"Have you heard from Bree?" Luca asked, drawing Joelle's attention back to him.

"Yes. She's planning on coming home soon." Though now that she'd given that some thought, Joelle would try to talk her sister out of it. Saddle Ridge just wasn't a safe place to be right now.

Luca made a sound that could have meant anything, but Joelle thought she detected some kind of undercurrent. And she knew why. At best, Bree usually managed to come home three or four times a year and then for only a week or two.

The exception to that "coming home" pattern had been five months ago when their father had been murdered and their mother had disappeared. Bree had then stayed in Saddle Ridge for just over five weeks. Joelle knew that Bree and Luca had seen each other then, but there seemed to be some kind of rift between them and then Bree left. Luca might be wondering if he could fix that rift and go back to the way things had been.

That was a reminder for Joelle that she needed to have a conversation with Bree. Maybe soon if the fourth gunman wasn't caught and his boss arrested. Willie Jay could speed up the possibility of that if he'd just start talking. Arlo Dennison might be able to do that as well if the cops managed to find him. So far, that hadn't happened, which led Joelle to believe that he, too, might be dead.

Duncan finally appeared in the doorway that led into the house and motioned for them to come in. That helped ease some of the tension in Joelle's body. So did Duncan rearming the security system the moment they were inside.

"All the doors and windows have sensors," Duncan explained. "Normally, I keep the alarms at a soft beep since I'm a light sleeper, but I'll change that to a full sound. If someone tries to get in, we'll hear it."

Good. That was one less thing to worry about, especially since Molly's kidnappers had broken into her place despite her having a security system.

"This way," Duncan instructed. He led them through a kitchen with stainless appliances and white stone countertops. "Help yourself to anything in the fridge. Sorry that it isn't better stocked, but I hadn't counted on… Well, I hadn't counted on this."

Since Duncan had been steadily feeding her throughout the day, Joelle wasn't hungry, but she figured she would be by morning.

Duncan continued to lead them through the living and dining rooms and toward the hall. He stopped outside the first door. "It's my office, but there's a sofa sleeper," he said to Luca. "Bathroom is there." He tipped his head to the room directly across from the office.

Luca muttered a thanks, one weary with fatigue, and went in while Duncan continued with her to the next room. "Guest room," he explained, walking in with her. The walls and the comforter on the queen-size bed were both pale blue. "I'll be right next door. The walls are thin enough that I'll hear you if you call out."

Joelle sighed, hoping there'd be no need for her to call out, that nothing else would go wrong tonight.

Duncan stayed put, studying her for several moments. "This is probably going to sound wrong, but we can sleep together if that'll help with the tension that I can practically see coming off you in waves. *Sleep*," he emphasized.

Even though it was the worst reaction, Joelle smiled.

She should have instead given him a firm look to let him know she'd be fine in here alone. But she was out of firm looks for the night. She sighed again, then shook her head.

"Tempting, but I'll be okay," she muttered. She hoped. It was possible she was too tired and had too much firing through her head to actually sleep.

The corner of Duncan's mouth lifted. Apparently, he was going for his own *worst reaction*. He compounded that by pulling her into his arms.

Her body landed against his. Familiar territory for both of them. Bad territory, too, because it instantly spurred some memories that shouldn't be spurred right now. Their defenses were down. They were both vulnerable. Yet, neither one of them pulled away from each other.

Joelle actually moved in closer, sliding her arms around his waist and dropping her head onto his shoulder. Mercy, it felt good. Not just because of the heat but because of the comfort this gave her. She wasn't a weak woman. Definitely wasn't a coward. But it felt good to be this close to someone who had her back.

She felt Duncan brush a kiss on the top of her head. Not really any kind of foreplay per se, but anything they did at this point would qualify as foreplay. Again, that was a good reason for her to move away from him,

But she didn't.

Joelle lifted her head, came up on her tiptoes and kissed him. It wasn't an especially heated kiss, but it shouldn't have happened at all. Nothing about this could stay at the comforting level. It never would between Duncan and her. The heat that stirred between them would never allow a comfort level. It would only demand to be sated.

That didn't stop her from fully kissing him. Nor did it stop him from returning the kiss and tightening his arms around her, pulling her even closer to him. Until they were touching in all the wrong places.

Duncan used his foot to shut the bedroom door, and he was the one who deepened the kiss. Joelle didn't do anything to stop that, either. In fact, she welcomed it. Needed it. She needed him, and that made the situation even more dangerous. This kind of need wouldn't just rip down barriers, it would put a permanent end to them.

That still didn't stop her.

She slid her hand around his neck, pulling his mouth down to hers so she could deepen the kiss as well. So she could take. And burn. Oh, yes. She was burning all right, and the heat continued to skyrocket when he dropped his grip to her bottom and aligned them in just the right way.

Of course, the baby bump didn't allow for the usual direct body to body contact in their midsections, but it was plenty enough for Joelle to recall in perfect detail just how good this could be between Duncan and her. Good but with serious consequences. Remembering those consequences gave her just enough steel to ease her mouth from his.

Duncan stared down at her and blinked as if trying to clear his head, and then he muttered some profanity. "I didn't think," he said. "I didn't think of the baby."

He had created a wonderful steamy heat inside her head so it took a moment to cut through that and realize what he meant. She had to smile again.

"Pregnant women are allowed to kiss," she pointed out. "And have sex."

That last part flew right out of her mouth before she even knew she was going to say it. *Stupid, stupid, stupid.* Of course, it made Duncan smile again, and Joelle gave up and smiled right along with him.

The moment seemed to freeze. Their gazes certainly

did while they were locked with each other. And the heat came at them like an out-of-control train. Cutting through what was left of any common sense.

There was a ringing sound that cut through as well, and it had Duncan and her flying apart. For one horrifying moment, Joelle thought it was the security system alerting them that someone had broken in. But it was Duncan's phone.

"It's Slater," he said when he looked at the screen and put the call on speaker. She started to move away from him, but Duncan kept his arm around her waist.

"Hope I caught you before you crashed for the night," Slater greeted.

"You did," Duncan said. "Did you get something?"

"Yes." Slater stopped, cursed. "Shortly after you left, Willie Jay got a phone call. From Kate Moreland."

"Kate?" Duncan questioned. "What did she want?"

"She wouldn't say, but I told Willie Jay she'd called and tried to get him to tell me why she wanted to talk to him. He stayed clammed up. So, I went back to my desk to see if I could get the answer from Kate. She clammed up as well and said she had to go, that the doctor ordered her to rest."

Clearly, Duncan and she would be having a chat with Kate first thing in the morning.

"I dug deeper, looking for a connection between Willie Jay and Kate," Slater went on. Joelle could hear some chatter in the background at the sheriff's office. "When I got nothing, I went to check on Willie Jay, to see if he'd changed his mind about talking to us. He was unconscious when I found him." Her brother cursed again. "Duncan, Willie Jay's dead."

Chapter Twelve

Duncan poured himself another cup of coffee—his third of the morning—in the hope that it would help get rid of the headache that was throbbing at his temples and behind his eyes. That was a lot to ask of mere caffeine, but he needed a much clearer head than he had right now.

He heard the shower going in the guest room and figured Joelle would be out soon to join him in the kitchen. Maybe she'd gotten some sleep after he'd left her in the guest room an hour or so after Slater had called with the news about Willie Jay. Maybe. But like him, she'd obviously had to try to get that sleep while processing what the hell had happened.

Duncan was still processing that.

Luca no doubt was, too, because he had downed multiple cups of coffee since getting up and was now at the other end of the kitchen table while he worked on his laptop.

Like Duncan, the deputy was digging for anything and everything that would help them make sense of this. Joelle had almost certainly done the same. She just hadn't surfaced for coffee yet, probably because she could no longer have a morning jolt of caffeine. The pregnancy had apparently put a temporary halt to that.

"The tox report came in," Luca announced just as Duncan

saw it pop into his inbox. As promised, Slater had pressed the lab hard to get those results ASAP. No easy feat since it had taken the ME nearly two hours to arrange for the body to be removed from the jail and transported to the county morgue.

Duncan was scanning through those results when Joelle came hurrying into the kitchen. Her focus was on her phone screen, and her hair was damp, but she was dressed. She was wearing the clothes she'd washed and dried the night before after she'd borrowed one of his shirts and a pair of boxers to sleep in. Once they'd gotten the news about Willie Jay, Joelle had known she wouldn't want to be scrounging up some loaner clothes today, that she'd want to focus on the investigation.

"You saw the tox report," she said after glancing at them.

Duncan made a sound of agreement. "Cyanide in the form of a capsule." Part of the capsule had still been in his mouth. "Since Willie Jay was searched before he was locked up, that means he must have had the pill concealed somewhere on him. And that he must have intended to end his life rather than spend time in jail."

That, in turn, added slightly more credence to the murder-suicide of the other two gunmen. The angles of the shots were still off, but now Duncan had to consider that the men had been willing participants in their deaths.

Why?

That's what both Luca and he were digging to find out. Joelle likely would be doing that, too.

"We start with Kate. I want to find out why she called Willie Jay last night," Duncan said, checking the time. It was nearly eight o'clock. "I've already called Dr. Benton, and he said Kate had a rough night and requested sedation. But we'll be talking to her this morning."

That seemed to be Joelle's cue to get moving to the fridge, and she grabbed an apple, and after checking to see there was no milk or yogurt, she went with some cheese. "Did Dr. Benton say anything about what had caused Kate's rough night?"

"More or less. He told Kate that she'd be going home today. She asked if the deputy guarding her would be going with her, and the doctor said he didn't think so, but he didn't know for sure. He said she became agitated after hearing that and insisted she'd be in danger if she left the hospital. He left her for a while because he had to see another patient, and when he came back, she asked for the sedative."

"Does the timing work for when Kate would have tried to call Willie Jay?" Joelle asked.

"According to Benton, it does, and he said she was holding her phone when he came back in the room." Duncan paused. "And speaking of her phone, the request came through for us to get her records."

"They just arrived fifteen minutes ago," Luca supplied, looking up from his laptop to glance at both of them. "In the half hour before Kate tried to speak to Willie Jay, she got two phone calls. One from Brad and the other from Hamlin."

Joelle huffed. "Obviously, we'll be doing a lot of interviews today."

"They're already set up," Duncan assured her. "As soon as you're done eating, we can head to the hospital and knock out the one with Kate. Then, I can have an actual breakfast delivered for you from the diner while we wait for first Brad and then Hamlin to come in."

Duncan expected they'd have lawyers with them and would deny everything. But the pieces were there, and maybe, just maybe, those pieces would fit so one of them or Kate could be arrested today.

"I do have one bit of good news," Joelle said. "I had a text conversation with Bree before I got in the shower, and I convinced her not to come home right now."

Good. That was one less person who might get caught up in this messy investigation.

"I can eat my apple on the way to the hospital," Joelle insisted. "I'm eager to hear what Kate has to say."

So was he, but Duncan took a moment to make sure Joelle was up to this. One glance at her and he knew she was. He couldn't say she looked rested, but she was clearly raring to go. So, that's what he did.

With Luca grabbing his laptop, Duncan headed to the window—again—to make sure there wasn't anyone lurking around. When he didn't see anyone, they went to the cruiser and started the cautious drive to the hospital. Only a couple of minutes. But if the missing gunman and his boss had realized Duncan and Joelle had spent the night at his place, then they might have set some kind of booby trap on the road.

Luca and Joelle no doubt expected the worst, too, because they kept watch. Joelle did the entire five-minute drive with her hand over the butt of her weapon. Thankfully, though, they made it to their destination without anyone trying to kill them.

Despite the early hour, there were already several cars in the parking lot, but Luca parked close enough to the door that Joelle only had a short distance out in the open before she hurried in through the ER doors. Duncan was right there with her, and he did a sweeping check of the ER. No one suspicious.

With Luca staying close behind them, Joelle and Duncan made their way to Kate's door, and Duncan was pleased when he saw Clyde Granger standing guard. Clyde was in his sixties now and a retired deputy, but Duncan knew the man was still plenty sharp.

"She's whining," Clyde said, his tone indicating this wasn't the first time. "She won't leave without police protection."

"So Dr. Benton told me," Duncan verified. "I'll consider it." He was stretched thin with manpower and was surprised that Kate hadn't just hired private security. The woman certainly had enough money to do that.

Luca stayed in the hall with Clyde when they reached the room. Kate immediately sat up in bed, and she had her phone gripped as if ready to call 911. She audibly released her breath when she saw it was Joelle and Duncan.

"Dr. Benton said he's releasing me this morning," she said like a protest.

Duncan nodded. "He said you believed you were in danger."

"I am," Kate was quick to verify. She glanced away, then. "Maybe in danger from my own son. Did you arrest him?"

"I'm questioning him," Duncan supplied, and he considered that the end to him answering the woman's questions. He hadn't come here for that. "Tell me why you called the sheriff's office last night and asked to speak to a prisoner we had in custody."

Kate didn't look surprised. Probably because she would have known all calls would be logged. Especially calls made to a criminal like Willie Jay.

"That PI, Al Hamlin, phoned me," Kate snarled with plenty of venom in her voice now. "He told me you'd arrested a man named Willie Jay Prescott, and that the man was going to tell you and the deputies that I had been the one who arranged to kidnap the dispatcher and Deputy McCullough."

"Did you?" Duncan demanded.

"No." That came out as a howl of outrage, followed by a groan and a lot of head shaking. "Of course not. I wouldn't do something like that."

The jury was still out on that, but Duncan tried a different angle. "Tell me about Arlo Dennison."

No howl of outrage this time, but there was plenty of surprise. "Why do you want to know about him?"

Duncan gave her a hard look to let her know she would be answering questions, not him.

Kate's mouth tightened. "Arlo managed one of my gyms. And I know what you're going to say," she continued when Duncan's look hardened even more. "That PI told you he talked with Arlo when he and his girlfriend were giving up their baby for adoption."

"He did." And Duncan made a circling motion with his finger for her to continue.

She obeyed, after she huffed. "I was very busy with work when all of that was going on, but a friend of a friend wanted to adopt a baby. So, when I got word of Hamlin and his girlfriend, I made the initial contact. Arlo followed up with them. But you should know that I had no idea Hamlin and his girlfriend wanted money for the baby. They were convicted, you know."

"And you and Arlo were questioned," Duncan reminded her. Ruston had come across that tidbit and passed it along.

"We were," she admitted, "but nothing came of it because there was nothing to find. I was trying to do this friend of a friend a favor, and I got caught up in the middle of an ugly mess. Now Hamlin thinks I took his sister and am running some kind of baby-selling business. I can assure you, I'm not."

Kate looked ready to add more to that protest, but the

sound of some loud talking in the hall stopped her. "Brad," she muttered when she obviously recognized one of those voices.

Duncan knew the other voice was Clyde's, and the deputy was clearly in an argument with Kate's son.

"I want to see my mother now," Brad demanded.

His first thought was to send Brad on his way to the sheriff's office so he could wait for the interview. But then Duncan figured it would be interesting to see how mother and son reacted to each other, especially since there were four deputies ready to intercede if Brad did try to go after Kate. Or vice versa.

Throwing open the door, Duncan silenced Brad with one of the glares he'd been doling out to Kate for the past five minutes or so. Brad froze for a moment, but then moved darn fast when Duncan motioned for him to come inside.

"I don't want him here," Kate snapped.

Duncan ignored her, but he also blocked Brad when he attempted to charge closer to Kate. "Since you clearly have something to say to your mother, say it," Duncan invited.

Brad had another momentary freeze before he speared his mother's gaze with his. "You told Hamlin I hired gunmen to go after Deputy McCullough and the dispatcher."

Kate's shoulders went stiff. "I most certainly did not." She muttered some profanity. "And I'm tired of being accused of things I didn't do," she added to Duncan.

"Hamlin said he called you and that you said I should be arrested before I tried to kill you," Brad insisted.

Kate huffed. "No." She stretched out that word. "Hamlin's the one who pointed the finger at you, and he didn't say anything to me about you trying to kill me. Hamlin, however, did warn me about that prisoner, Willie Jay Prescott. Hamlin claimed you hired him."

Silence fell over the room while they all took a moment to process that. Duncan didn't need a moment, though, since he'd already come to a conclusion.

"Hamlin could be trying to stir up trouble between you two," Duncan pointed out. "More trouble," he amended, "since it's obvious that things aren't lovey-dovey."

"They aren't," Kate muttered, and her face tightened. Duncan figured it had occurred to her that he was right, that Hamlin had called both Kate and Brad to get them at each other's throats.

And it had worked.

It made Duncan wonder if Hamlin had done that with the hopes it would get Kate to say something to incriminate herself in the illegal baby sales. Or if Brad would be the one doing the self-incriminating. If so, Hamlin could have wanted that to cover up his own guilt. In fact, all the attacks and Molly's kidnapping could be to set up either Brad or Kate so Hamlin would escape scrutiny for his pregnant sister's disappearance.

"My lawyer is on his way to Saddle Ridge," Brad muttered a moment later. "I'll talk to him about suing Hamlin for slander."

Duncan didn't tell Brad that would be a long shot and turn into a "he said, she said." Added to that, Kate probably wouldn't want all of this to be rehashed in public, which it would be if there was a lawsuit.

Brad continued to stare at Kate while his jaw muscles tightened. "Look me in the eyes, Mother, and tell me you had nothing to do with Shanda being murdered."

The anger on Kate's face had cooled a bit, but that caused it to heat up again. "No, I did not, and I'm insulted you even asked."

"I have to ask," Brad fired back, "because you hated her."

Kate opened her mouth, and must have rethought what she was about to say. "Yes, I hated her because of the person you became once you got involved with her," she finally said, her voice surprisingly calm. "You changed after Shanda lost that baby. You became obsessed with payback."

"Obsessed with getting my family back," he quickly replied. "I wanted Shanda and a baby."

"You wanted revenge," Kate spelled out.

Brad glared at her. But he didn't disagree. However, Brad did turn and head out the door. It was still open since Luca and Clyde had both been keeping a close eye on the situation.

Duncan went after Brad so he could remind the man about the interview, but when he went into the hall, he saw that Brad was practically charging toward someone.

Hamlin.

The PI was coming straight up the hall, and the men rammed into each other. That caused them to collide with a nurse carrying a tray of meds, all of which went flying.

So did the fists.

Brad managed to punch Hamlin in the face before Duncan could get to him. Hamlin retaliated, throwing his own punch, and the hall was suddenly filled with profanity-laced tirades and the sounds of the struggle. The nurse was trapped beneath the men.

Duncan reached into the heap and pulled out the nurse, sliding her toward Joelle who had moved closer to help. Once Joelle had the nurse out of the way, Duncan went after Brad next and hauled him out of the fray by the collar of his shirt. Clyde and Luca took hold of Hamlin, who came off the floor ready to run at Brad again.

"You lying SOB," Brad yelled, and he added plenty more profanity to go along with that. Hamlin was doing the same.

Duncan glanced at Joelle who was moving the nurse back toward the nurses' station. "Call for two deputies," Duncan instructed Joelle. "I want both Brad and Hamlin taken to holding cells."

That would keep both men off the streets at least until Duncan had a chance to interview them. It was possible, likely even, that Brad and Hamlin would be filing assault charges against each other. But he'd deal with all of that later. For now, Duncan needed to establish some calm and control since a crowd had gathered to see what the ruckus was all about. There were at least a dozen medical folks and patients gawking at the two men being restrained and the now-crying nurse.

"I can get this one to the cruiser now," Luca offered, keeping a firm grip on Hamlin. "Once he's in holding, I can come back for Joelle and you."

"Do that," Duncan agreed. As long as Brad and Hamlin were around each other, there'd be the possibility of another altercation.

Luca immediately got a still-cursing Hamlin moving toward the ER doors, and when Brad tried to go after the PI, Duncan had had enough. He pulled out some plastic cuffs from his pocket and restrained Brad.

"Go back and stay with Kate," Duncan told Clyde. "I'll look for a place to stash Brad until the other deputies arrive." Duncan also wanted to check on the nurse. She didn't appear to be injured, but she had taken a hard fall.

Duncan got Brad moving toward Joelle and the nurse, but he'd only made it a couple of steps before Clyde called out to him. Duncan turned to see Clyde standing in front of Kate's still open door.

"The room's empty, Sheriff," Clyde said. "Kate's gone."

JOELLE READ THE text from Woodrow to let her know that Ronnie and he had Brad out of the hospital and in their cruiser. Thankfully, she'd already gotten a text from Luca to let them know he'd arrived safely with Hamlin, and that the PI was now in a holding cell where he'd wait until Duncan and she could get back to the sheriff's office.

Whenever that would be.

There was a full-scale search going on for Kate not only in the hospital but also the grounds. Since Duncan hadn't wanted Joelle out of his sight, they had taken the patients wing with the hopes that a frightened Kate had ducked into one of them to avoid another confrontation with her son.

So far, nothing.

And that's what Clyde and some of the orderlies were reporting as they searched the grounds. Kate had seemingly vanished, and Joelle knew that couldn't be a good thing.

In the chaos of the fight, it was possible someone had sneaked in and taken Kate. There was a good argument to be made for that since Kate's phone had been left on the bed. If the woman had fled of her own accord, she likely would have taken that. Then again, she might have left it behind since the phone could be used to pinpoint her whereabouts.

If so, Kate might have left out of fear of her own arrest.

Duncan huffed when they cleared another room and there was still no sign of Kate. At least this particular room hadn't had a patient. Some of the others had been occupied, and it had to be unsettling to have two cops show up and conduct a search. Joelle had doled out a lot of apologies. Not just to the patients but the nurse who'd been shaken up in the brawl. Thankfully, the woman hadn't been hurt other than some bruising and frayed nerves.

"Three more to go," Duncan muttered when they went

back into the hall. "And supposedly none is occupied." He'd likely gotten that info from one of the nurses since Duncan's phone had been dinging every few minutes with texts.

As they'd done with the other rooms, Duncan kept his gun ready while he eased open a door and peered inside. Once he'd done the initial check of the main part of the room, Joelle stepped in to cover him so he could have a look in the bathroom.

"Empty," he said, and he stopped to read another text. "The hospital security guard is searching the roof to see if Kate went up there."

Joelle figured if the woman was going to run, it wouldn't be to the roof where she would essentially end up trapped since there was only one set of stairs leading to it. Still, Kate might not be thinking straight.

Duncan and she went back into the hall, which had thankfully been cleared of any gawkers, and they made their way to the next room. This one was easier than some of the others since the bathroom door was wide open, so all they had to do was a cursory sweep before moving on to the final room. Once they checked it, they'd be able to head to the sheriff's office where they could question Brad and Hamlin while the search for Kate continued.

They came to a quick stop outside the final room when there was a thumping sound just on the other side of the door. Duncan glanced back at her, a silent warning for her to use extra caution. She would. Because even if it was Kate in there, it didn't mean the woman wouldn't attack them. Maybe out of fear.

Maybe, though, because Kate was the killer.

Duncan motioned for Joelle to stand back, and he eased open the door. Unlike the other rooms, this one was pitch-dark, probably because someone had lowered the blinds.

Joelle barely managed a glance inside when she heard another sound. One that she instantly recognized.

A stun gun.

"Duncan," she managed to call out.

But it was too late.

The gloved hand that snaked out of the darkness jammed the stun gun against Duncan's throat. He staggered back, and Joelle reached for him, trying to break his fall, but she didn't get to him in time. Duncan dropped like a stone.

Oh, God.

"Duncan," she shouted.

Joelle automatically drew her gun. But it was too late for that, too. A bulky man wearing orderly scrubs and a ski mask charged right at her, pushing her back against the wall. In the same motion, he tried to knock the gun from her hand. She held on, twisting her body to try and get away from him so she'd have a clean shot. No chance of that since this thug might deflect the gun, and the bullet could hit Duncan.

"Officer down," she yelled, hoping that someone would hear her and come running.

The thug must have thought that was a possibility, too, because he clamped his hand on hers and her gun and started muscling her toward the exit. He was not only tall but strong. A lot stronger than she was, but Joelle knew she had to fight him.

For her baby's sake.

For Duncan's.

This goon might turn and shoot Duncan before he made that final push to get her out of the building. Kidnapping her. Just as Willie Jay had tried. And the other two dead gunmen.

Joelle didn't want to mentally play out what would happen to her if he did manage to get her outside and into a vehicle. Instead, she focused on the baby and Duncan and tried not to let the terror take over.

She stomped as hard as she could on the goon's foot, and while it slowed him down and made him curse her, it didn't stop him. So Joelle twisted around and rammed her elbow into his gut. That worked better than the foot stomp because he staggered back a step, his back smacking against the wall. He still managed to keep his beefy grip on her gun.

From the corner of her eye, Joelle saw Duncan struggling to move, and he was lifting his gun. She had no idea if he had the motor control yet to pull the trigger, and like her, he didn't have anything close to a clean shot.

The goon pushed himself away from the wall, throwing himself at her and off-balancing her. Joelle had no choice but to protect her stomach, and she did that by bending forward. Not an easy task because of the baby bump, but she used her upper torso to protect her child.

Her attacker cursed her, and as Willie Jay had done, he latched onto her hair. The pain shot through her. With his other hand on her gun, he probably hoped to use that leverage and the pain to force her to move.

That failed, thank heavens.

Joelle got another slam of adrenaline. Another punch of the fight mode, and she used that strength and her training to twist his hand. And her gun. Until she had it aimed at his right leg.

She fired.

He yelled, the sound echoing along with the blast of the shot. Staggering, he let go of her hair, and the maneuver allowed her to take aim again. At his left leg. The bullet slammed into him and caused him to drop to his knees.

Joelle heard the sound of running footsteps and Slater

calling out to her. Help would be here soon. But she didn't take her attention off the goon. She couldn't see his face, but she figured it had to be twisted in pain.

"Move and I'll put another bullet in you," she warned him, wrenching her hand from his grip.

The goon didn't listen. He moved, reaching out so fast that it was just a blur of motion. But before Joelle could pull the trigger, someone else did.

Duncan.

He was still on the floor, but he'd lifted his head and shooting hand enough to deliver the fatal shot. Her attacker slumped forward. *Dead.*

Chapter Thirteen

Duncan paced while he waited on hold with Slater. Paced and kept his eye on Joelle who was now seated at his kitchen table.

Since she'd been covered with their attacker's blood, he'd brought her here to his place instead of the sheriff's office so she could shower. That was after she'd had yet another exam to make sure both she and the baby were all right.

They were. By some miracle, they were.

So was he since he'd also needed to be checked to make sure the stun gun hadn't done any permanent damage. It hadn't.

Duncan figured he'd be saying a lot of thanks and prayers for that. After he'd put an end to the danger so Joelle could make it through a blasted day without someone trying to kidnap her again. Because that's what had happened. Another attempted kidnapping. If the masked thug had wanted her dead, he would have shot her the moment Duncan opened the door of that hospital room.

Even though she hadn't been shot or hurt beyond a few minor scrapes and bruises, it still twisted away at him that she'd come so close to being taken. He should have put more precautions in place to prevent that. And he would. He couldn't continue to put her in harm's way when so much was at stake.

That's why he'd brought Luca with him, and like before, the deputy was in Duncan's home office doing reports of this latest incident. *Incident*, he silently repeated, the anger rising in him again. A sterile word for something that damn sure hadn't been sterile. Joelle and he had been attacked, and Duncan had been forced to kill the SOB. He'd add more thanks and prayers for having regained enough feeling in his shooting hand to manage that. If not, Joelle would have had to do it, and Duncan didn't want her having to deal with that on top of everything else.

And *everything else* was huge.

She'd been attacked three times now, and while Molly thankfully hadn't been this time around, the dispatcher was shaken to the core. So much so that she'd asked Duncan to have not one but two reserve deputies stay with her. Duncan had complied, pulling the two off the search for Kate.

Kate was another investigative thorn in his side right now. There was no sign of her, and worse, she could have been the one who'd hired that thug to come after Joelle and him in the hospital. If Duncan hadn't allowed himself to get distracted by Brad and Hamlin's fight, then he might have seen the woman sneaking out.

Or being taken.

"Stop beating yourself up," Joelle muttered.

She was watching him and sipping some milk that Slater had had delivered, and she looked so small in the loaner clothes she'd gotten from the sheriff's office. Loose gray jogging pants and a black tee that was a couple sizes too big for her.

"I deserve to be beaten up," he was quick to remind her. "I should have brought you to the sheriff's office before I ever started searching for Kate."

Joelle lifted her shoulder, sighed and stood, going to

the fridge to refill her glass of milk. That meant walking right by him, and she brushed her arm against his. Probably not by accident. He took out the *probably* when he looked at her.

"Stop beating yourself up," she repeated. "I'm a cop, and I could have made the decision to go to the sheriff's office when Luca was transporting Hamlin. If I'd done that, then who's to say this kidnapper wouldn't have come after me in the cruiser. Willie Jay did."

He had to fight back the horrific images of that attempt and this one. There had been enough bad for a lifetime, and it wasn't over. It wouldn't be over until he had the culprit behind bars.

She reached up and touched her fingers to his forehead. Duncan didn't exactly recoil, but the touch hurt a little. When he'd fallen after being stunned, his head had smacked on the floor, and the gash had needed a couple of stitches. He'd gotten those in the ER while the doctor had been examining Joelle and the baby.

There was finally a crackle of sound on the other end of the phone, and a moment later, Duncan heard Slater's voice. He went ahead and put the call on speaker since this was an update Joelle would want to hear.

"The dead guy is Arlo Dennison," Slater provided.

Hell. That circled right back to Kate since the man had been one of her employees. It was possible Arlo had still been an employee, just in a different capacity as a hired gun.

"Four dead men," Slater emphasized. "That could mean whoever hired them has run out of muscle."

Maybe. But Duncan knew it was just as likely that Kate, Brad or Hamlin had found yet someone else to do their dirty work.

"Still no sign of Kate," Slater went on. "The Texas Rangers you requested arrived, and they're coordinating the search."

Good. Duncan figured if the woman could be found, the Rangers were his best shot at making that happen. Especially since Kate could be anywhere right now. She hadn't taken her phone with her, but she could have arranged for someone to meet her in the parking lot and take her to heavens knew where.

"Luca just filed yours and Joelle's statements on the attack at the hospital," Slater added a moment later.

No surprise there. Luca had been the one to take those statements shortly after they'd come to his place. Both Joelle's and Duncan's primary weapons and clothes had also been taken into evidence. All standard procedure. So was counseling, but that was going to have to wait.

"Any updates on Brad and Hamlin?" Duncan said to Slater.

Duncan already knew both men had made bail and the interviews had been rescheduled for late afternoon. Not with Joelle and him doing them, either. Going with standard procedure again, neither of them would be doing interviews and such until there'd been a review of how they'd handled Arlo's attack.

"Nothing new," Slater said. "Well, nothing other than both men's lawyers are clamoring about their clients being innocent and harassed by the cops. Same ol', same ol'," he muttered. Then, paused. "How's Joelle? And, yes, I'm asking you, Duncan, because my sister might not tell me the truth."

"I'm okay," she insisted. "Okay-ish," Joelle amended when Slater huffed and Duncan gave her a flat stare. "You should be asking about Duncan. He's the one beating himself up over what happened. I'm not. We did what we had to do to stay alive and keep our baby safe."

Duncan continued to study her, to see if she'd said that to ease her brother's mind. And his. But Joelle seemed to have processed this and just might actually be okay-ish.

"I'll keep an eye on Joelle," Duncan told Slater, not only because it was true but because he also wanted to relieve Slater's worries. It would relieve Duncan's worries about her, too.

He ended the call, and when he went to put his phone away, he saw the blood smears on the back of his hand. His own blood from the cut on his head. It was a reminder that unlike Joelle, he hadn't showered.

"Shower," he muttered when he saw that her attention, too, had landed on the blood, and Duncan decided it was time to remedy that.

Time to remedy something else, too.

Duncan pulled Joelle to him and kissed her. Really kissed her. Yeah, it was a stupid thing to do, but it was necessary. He needed to have her close, this close, if only for a moment or two.

He didn't deepen the kiss. Didn't move them body to body, even though a certain part of him immediately started urging him to do just that. Duncan just kept the kiss gentle and hopefully comforting. Because he was damn sure they both needed that right now.

When he finally eased back, he stared down into her eyes and braced himself for her to warn him they were playing with fire. Which they were. But she simply smiled.

"Shower," she muttered. "Then, we can…talk."

That idiot part of him got all excited that sex might happen. It didn't matter that it would be a bad idea.

At least, it probably would be.

Joelle likely wasn't thinking straight and didn't need to land in bed with him. But her mention of *talk* had nixed the bed thing, and unlike sex, that was probably a good thing. She no doubt had things she needed to say about the attack. Maybe things about all this kissing they'd been doing.

Duncan headed to his bedroom for that shower, but he stopped by the office to check on Luca. He was still typing up reports. "Statements from the people interviewed at the hospital," Luca muttered without taking his attention off the screen.

A necessary pain in the butt. And something might be in those statements they could use. It was a serious long shot, though.

Duncan was thankful that Joelle followed him to his bedroom. Not because of the possibility of that sex happening, but because he didn't want her too far away from him. The security system was on, and two of Slater's ranch hands were outside in a truck, watching the place—something they'd been doing since he and Joelle had arrived from the hospital. A lot of avenues had been covered, but Duncan still wanted Joelle close so he'd be able to get to her fast if there was another attack.

Joelle sat on the foot of his bed while he headed to the shower. He didn't close the bathroom door between them. Another precaution, in case she called out to him for help. He hoped like hell there wouldn't be any such need for that.

Duncan turned on the shower, and stripped while he waiting for the water to reach the right temperature. The moment it was warm enough, he stepped in so he could do this fast and minimize the time Joelle was out of his sight. He had barely gotten started on it, though, when the shower door opened, and Joelle was standing there.

Joelle, who slid her gaze down the entire length of his body.

Duncan's gaze did some sliding as well. Looking at every

inch of her. Man, she was beautiful. Always had been. But the baby bump actually added to that beauty.

He went hard as stone.

"I haven't been with anyone else but you since, well, in a very long time," she said.

It took him a moment to realize why she'd volunteered that. Then, he spotted the condom that she had likely taken from the drawer of his nightstand. It was a reminder they'd used one five months ago, and she'd still gotten pregnant.

"I haven't been with anyone else, either, in a long time," he told her and could have added that she was the only woman he wanted.

"So, not necessary," she muttered, tossing the condom onto the vanity.

Without taking her attention off him, she pulled off the loose clothes, tossing them on the floor next to his.

"I'll be careful," she said when he glanced down at the wet tiled floor. "Maybe you can hold on tight to me to make sure we don't slip."

And she stepped inside under the spray of warm water. In the same motion, she looped her arm around his neck and pulled him to her.

She kissed him.

Hard, hungry and long. This was no kiss of comfort, and yet it accomplished just that. Comfort. Then, a whole mountain of heat. She kissed and kissed until the nightmarish images just slid away.

"The bathroom door is locked," she muttered. "Our phones are right on the vanity where we'll be able to hear them. And we aren't going to think about this," she tacked onto that.

Good. Because Duncan didn't want to think. He just wanted Joelle, and he wanted her now. Apparently, she was on the same page because she added some clever touching to the deep kiss. She slid her hand between their naked bodies. Down his chest. To his stomach. Then, over his erection.

If Duncan had actually wanted to do any thinking, that would have put an end to it. The only thing on his mind right now was taking Joelle.

Joelle got that taking started by hooking her arms around his neck and pulling herself up. He gladly helped with that by putting his arm underneath her bottom and lifting her until they were facing each other.

The kiss continued, raging on, cranking up the heat even more. But that heat was a drop in the bucket compared to Joelle's wet breasts sliding against his chest and with their centers pressed right against each other.

Duncan had to fight the urge just to push into her, to give both their bodies what they were demanding. But he purposely slowed so he could savor this. He eased back on the urgency of the kiss, and he kept his touch light as he cupped her breasts and flicked his thumb over her nipple.

She gave an aroused moan, and her head lolled to the side, exposing her throat. Duncan took advantage of that and slid both his mouth and tongue down her neck. Pleasuring her. Pleasuring himself.

The angle was all wrong for him to kiss her breasts so he levered her up even more, using the shower wall to stop them from falling. Once he had her high enough, he took one of her nipples into his mouth.

This time her moan was a whole lot louder, and the kiss kicked up the urgency again. She worked her way back down, aligning their centers again, notching up Duncan's own urgency when she slid herself against him.

No way could he hold off after that so he anchored her

again by holding her bottom while he pushed into her. He got an instant slam of sensations. Pleasure. So much pleasure. But more. This was right. This was exactly what he'd been waiting for these past five months. Hell, longer. Since he'd wanted Joelle for as long as he could remember.

It was a balancing act to stay on his feet, but Duncan adjusted his position, and he started the slow deep strokes inside her. All thoughts of, well, pretty much everything vanished. Everything except this. The right here, right now. Everything except Joelle.

The need clawed its way through him, driving him to move faster. Pushing him to give Joelle both the pleasure and the release from this intense heat. It happened, and it didn't take long. Not with their bodies starved for each other. Duncan only needed a few of those strokes when he felt her muscles clamp around him. When he felt the climax ripple through her.

"Duncan," she muttered, dropping her head onto his shoulder.

And that was all he needed to push him right over the edge. Duncan held Joelle close and found his own release.

Chapter Fourteen

Joelle's entire body felt slack. Sated. Incredible. But she also knew without a doubt that she wouldn't be able to stand on what she was sure would be wobbly legs.

Duncan took care of that.

Just as he'd taken care of her with that sexual release.

He turned off the shower, scooped her up in his arms and stepped with her onto the rug. He didn't stop there, either, but rather sat her on the vanity while he pulled a huge towel around her. Since he proceeded to dry her off, that meant she got an amazing view of his completely naked wet body.

Mercy, she wanted him all over again.

This had been the problem with them for years. The heat. The need. And she'd thought that once they finally ended up in bed five months ago, the need would lessen some. It hadn't. And later, she was going to consider why that was. Consider, too, if it would ever go away.

Judging from the way her body was humming, the answer to that was no.

After he dried her off, he kissed her again. One of those scorching, heart-melting post-sex kisses that held promises of more to come. Too bad her body was absolutely onboard for that. Her mind, though, was reminding her to hold back, to guard her heart. And to put up those barriers again.

Joelle didn't do any of that.

She kissed him right back in the full-throttle mode. It lasted some very long moments, and when she eased back, she saw the fresh heat in those amazing eyes of his. The corner of his mouth lifted, flashing her a smile that also fell into the amazing category.

Of course, the smile didn't last. It faded by degrees, but at least she'd gotten to enjoy it for a bit.

"I'm guessing we'll have that talk now," he muttered, not sounding the least bit enthusiastic about that.

Neither was she, but Joelle thought they should spell out that this could be temporary. That this was "no strings attached" sex. Because she didn't want Duncan to feel this had to be the start of some grand commitment. He'd already committed to the baby, both offering child support and shared custody, and that was enough.

Had to be enough.

Joelle wasn't exactly sure what her feelings were for him... She stopped, mentally regrouped. All right, she was sure. She cared deeply for Duncan. Was perhaps leaning toward being in love with him. But this was so not the right time to delve into all of that.

"Let's put the talk on hold," she suggested. "Instead, let's go over the reports Luca's done, and I'll see if he needs help with any others."

Of course, Joelle had offered to help Luca when they'd arrived at Duncan's, and he'd declined, telling her to get some rest. Sex had been an incredible substitute for rest, and now she wanted to dive back into the investigation.

Duncan didn't seem convinced. He frowned. She wasn't sure if that was because he did, indeed, want to talk. Or maybe he wanted to keep kissing her and go for round two of sex. That was tempting. Mercy, was it.

"The sooner we make an arrest, the sooner the baby will be safe," she said, knowing Duncan was already well aware of that.

However, it seemed to be the exact nudge he needed to move away from her and start drying off. He did mutter some profanity, though, under his breath that had her smiling again.

Joelle started to get dressed, and despite the reminder she'd just given him, she didn't ignore the peep show going on right in front of her. Duncan was hot, but he was even hotter when he was naked.

He pulled on his boxers, his gaze meeting hers, and she saw the heat that was still there. She felt the tug deep within her body. Not sexual. Well, not totally. This was something different. Something just as strong. And it had her going back to falling in love with him. She probably would have had a mental debate with herself about that had her phone not rang.

She got a jolt when she looked at the screen and saw *Unknown Caller*, and part of her realized she'd been waiting for another would-be kidnapper to get in touch with her. Yes, four hired guns were dead, but Joelle was pretty sure their boss was still out there somewhere.

Out there and had possibly already hired new thugs to come after her.

Duncan became all cop, and he hit the recorder on his phone a split second before he nodded for her to take the call. She did, expecting to hear some muffled threatening voice of a stranger.

She didn't.

"Joelle?" the woman asked.

She nearly dropped the phone. "It's my mother," she said, the words rushing out with her breath. She looked at

Duncan to see if he'd recognized it as well. He did, and he looked just as stunned as she was.

"Mom," Joelle finally managed. "Where are you? How are you?" And she had so many other questions she wanted to add to that.

For five months, she'd been terrified for her mother. Not only for her mom's safety since Joelle considered that she, too, might be dead. But there had also been the worry that Sandra McCullough had somehow participated in her husband's murder. Or was on the run because of something she'd learned or witnessed.

"Joelle," her mom repeated, but she didn't launch right into answering those questions. "I need help."

The static crackled across the phone connection, but Joelle still heard that loud and clear. "Where are you?" she repeated. "What's wrong?"

Again, there wasn't a quick answer, and the static increased. There was also the sound of a revving car engine.

"I'm at the ranch," her mother finally said. "Please, Joelle, please, come and get me before it's too late."

JOELLE FELT AS if she'd had way too much caffeine and her mind was whirling from it. However, the jumble of thoughts wasn't from any coffee but rather from hearing her mother's voice.

Slater was hearing it now, too.

Her brother and Carmen had arrived within minutes after Joelle had phoned him to let him know about the call, and now Slater was standing in Duncan's living room, listening to the recording. It wasn't the first time Slater had played it, either. This was his third, and he seemed just as shell-shocked as she had been.

Still was.

"That's Mom's voice," she muttered to Slater. That was a repeat as well.

Her brother made a soft sound of agreement, and he looked up as if yanking himself out of a trance. "Yeah. But you know this is some kind of a trap."

"She knows," Duncan was quick to say.

Joelle did, indeed, and that's what had prevented her from bolting out of Duncan's house, jumping into the cruiser and driving straight to her family's ranch. Because this could all be a ploy to draw her out into the open like that. But there was a flipside to this.

Her mother could be in grave danger.

Could be.

And that was the sticking point here. Slater obviously knew something about that *could be* because he played the recording once more. Duncan and she had done the same thing when they'd waited for Slater to arrive.

"The call was almost certainly made from a burner," Slater pointed out, and Joelle made a sound of agreement. That was being checked as they spoke. Techs were also repeatedly trying to call the number with the hopes that someone would answer. So far, nothing.

"Mom never answered any of your questions," her brother added a moment later.

Joelle nodded. "And there's the static. A lot of it," she emphasized. "It seems to be coming from maybe a TV station or radio that's offline. It's too steady for the intermittent kind of static you'd get from a bad phone connection."

Slater nodded as well, and he shifted his attention to Duncan. "So, the fact that we're not charging over to the ranch right now tells me you don't believe my mother is actually in danger."

"I wish I knew for sure," Duncan said, drawing in a long

breath. "It is Sandra's voice," he verified. "But it could have been spliced together from old recordings. Maybe interviews taken from the internet."

Her mother had certainly done some of those since she'd often campaigned for bond issues to better fund the schools and libraries. Joelle couldn't recall a specific speech or such that could have been used to piece together what she'd heard, but it was possible. There was a huge *but*, though, in all of this.

"If the killer actually has her..." Joelle started, but then she couldn't force out the rest of it. Not aloud, anyway. But inside her head, the possibility was flashing bright and nonstop.

Her mother could be murdered.

She could be being held right now. Could be hurt. And she could need their help. In fact, it was possible her father's killer had taken her mother five months ago and had been holding her all this time, planning to use her to punish Joelle for whatever the killer believed she needed to be punished for. Maybe Brad for what'd happened to Shanda. Maybe Kate because her father had been on her trail for the illegal baby sales. Or Hamlin who wanted revenge for his arrest as a juvenile.

Duncan was well aware of that, too, and that's why he'd spent the past fifteen minutes assembling a team. Or rather two of them. And even though Duncan hadn't spelled it out yet, Joelle was pretty sure she knew what he was planning.

"You'll stay here," Duncan said, his gaze spearing hers. "I would take you to the sheriff's office, but this SOB could be hoping for that. To attack us along the road and try to take you."

Joelle had already considered that as well. It was the very definition of a rock and a hard place. If she went anywhere, she was a target. Ditto for if she stayed put. Duncan couldn't stop that, but he could maybe stop her mother from being killed if she was being held at the ranch.

"Luca and Carmen will stay here with you," Duncan went on. "And the two armed ranch hands will continue to guard the grounds. They'll block the driveway to prevent anyone from using a vehicle to get to the house. Stay inside and keep the security system on."

She recalled him saying all the windows and doors were rigged so if someone did attempt to break in, they'd at least get a warning. Then, whoever tried to get inside would be facing three cops.

"Slater and I will go to the ranch," Duncan continued a moment later.

But Joelle immediately interrupted him. "And you'll have extra backup with you," she insisted. "As we learned with Molly, there are plenty of places for someone to lie in wait."

Duncan didn't argue. "Ronnie and Woodrow are already on the way to the ranch. They'll hang back and use binoculars and infrared to try and spot any threats. Try and spot your mother, too, if she's actually there." He checked the time. "The plan is to make this as quick as possible."

His gaze lingered on Joelle's for a couple of moments, and she nodded. Not because she liked the idea but because there wasn't another option. The ranch had to be checked, and Duncan was the sheriff.

He went to her, and while he didn't kiss her, not with other cops watching, Duncan took her hand and gave it a gentle squeeze. "It's only a trap if we aren't ready for it, and we are," he whispered to her. "We'll take every possible precaution, and I want you to do the same."

She nodded again. "Come back to me in one piece," she muttered.

Duncan looked as if he wanted to groan at that. Because it seemed to be the start of some grand confession about her feelings for him. About how important he was to her.

Which he was.

But no way did she want to send him off with that kind of distraction running through his mind.

"Stay safe," she added, using her cop's voice, and Joelle purposely turned away from him and faced Luca. "I can help you type up the witness statements from the hospital."

That would give her something to focus on. Or rather something to try to focus on. Joelle didn't know how long this would take Duncan and the others, but she would be on pins and needles the entire time.

"I'll reset the security system with my phone once we're out," Duncan relayed to her as Slater and he went to the door. Both Duncan and her brother gave her one last look before they headed out. One last stomach-twisting look.

Joelle stayed put, listening, and she heard the sound of the cruiser ignition. Heard, too, when Slater and Duncan drove away.

And the waiting began.

"Luca, I can do some reports as well," Carmen said, drawing Joelle's attention back to the other deputies. "So email me the notes of the ones you want me to do," she added as she took out her laptop.

Carmen didn't sit in the kitchen though but rather moved to the front window. No doubt so she could keep watch.

Since the keeping watch was a good idea, Joelle tipped her head to the hall. "Duncan's bedroom has a good view of the backyard. I can work from there. And yes, I'll stay back from the windows."

Luca didn't make a sound of agreement until she added that last part. "The office has a view of the east side of the property, and since that side doesn't face any of Duncan's neighbors, I can keep an eye on things from there. I'll email you both some of the statement notes," he added, heading to the office.

Joelle took her laptop and went into Duncan's bedroom. Of course, it was a reminder that less than an hour ago they'd had shower sex. *Amazing shower sex*. But since that brought on images of Duncan, the worry came with it, and she said a flurry of quick prayers that Duncan, her brother, Woodrow and Ronnie would come out of this unscathed.

Her mother, too.

Part of her wanted to hope her mother was there at the ranch. Because if she was, then it meant she probably hadn't voluntarily left her family. But if that was the case, then it was unbearable to think of the hell her mother had gone through all these months.

Since that kind of thinking wasn't helping her already frayed nerves, Joelle got to work—away from the window, though, she did open the curtains enough for her to be able to see out. There was a small seating area in the corner of the bedroom, and Joelle turned the chair so it was facing the window. That would keep her in the shadows and hopefully out of the line of sight of any shooters.

While she booted up her computer, she glanced out in the backyard. Unlike her place, this area wasn't thick with trees. Just the opposite. There was a small barn and some white wood pasture fence. A shooter wouldn't be able to use the fence to hide or sneak up closer to the house.

But the barn was a different matter.

The door was closed, and if a determined shooter belly-crawled through the pasture, they could slip behind the barn and try to fire into the house. With that unsettling thought,

Joelle wasn't sure how much work she would get done, but she opened the file that Luca sent her, anyway.

There had apparently been thirty-one statements taken from patients, medical staff and anyone who happened to be in the parking lot at the time Arlo launched his attack and Kate went missing. Luca had sent Joelle six, nowhere near the one-third he should have given her. When she got through these, she would ask for more.

The statements were basically notes taken by the questioning officers, and they needed to be cleaned up and put in an official file that would then have to be verified and signed by those interviewers. Normally, cops did their own reports, but with so many aspects to the investigation, they all needed to chip in. Especially since she wasn't the one out there looking for Kate.

Joelle made it through the first one when she heard a soft thumping sound coming from the large walk-in closet/dressing area that was on the other side of the bathroom. The closet door was closed, and there wasn't a window in there that someone could use to break in.

She waited, her fingers poised on the keyboard while she continued to listen. Nothing.

And she was ready to dismiss it when she heard it again.

Joelle quietly set her laptop aside and got to her feet. She drew her weapon and inched to the closet door while also keeping watch of the window in the bedroom. It occurred to her that someone could be tossing something against the exterior wall to distract her so they could make sure no one was watching them if they sneaked up to the barn.

She stopped to send a text to Frankie Mendoza, one of Slater's ranch hands who was out front watching the road.

Do you see anyone on the right side of the house toward the back?

Joelle's heartbeat kicked up a few notches while she waited the couple of seconds it took him to answer. No one's there, Frankie replied.

That settled her down some, but Joelle remembered Duncan whispering to her about taking every possible precaution so she decided to get some help, especially since she was only a couple of feet away from the closet door. Even though it should have set off the security alarms, maybe someone had managed to get into the house.

"Luca?" she called out, keeping her voice calm and level. "Could you come here a second?" If it turned out to be nothing, then she would owe him an apology for interrupting him.

But it was something.

Before Joelle even heard Luca's footsteps, there were two loud thumps as if something heavy had fallen onto the floor of the closet. Her gaze whipped to the closet door as it flew open.

The two men were wearing ski masks, and they charged right at her.

DUNCAN'S STOMACH KNOTTED when he saw the McCullough ranch come into view on the horizon. Considering the god-awful things that'd happened here, the place had an eerie feel to it. The approaching storm didn't help, either. The thick clouds were an angry-looking slate gray and shut out so much of the light that it looked more like twilight than daytime.

He stopped the cruiser at the end of the road and fired glances all around while Slater sent off a text to Woodrow. According to the two messages they'd already received from

Woodrow while Slater and he had been en route, Woodrow and Ronnie had arrived at the ranch about seven minutes earlier, and they had done an immediate check with the binoculars.

They'd seen no one.

So they'd driven slightly closer to accommodate the short range of the infrared, and they were about to scan for heat sources. Since the deputies should have had time to at least start that, Duncan needed an update.

"Nothing so far," Slater relayed when he got a response from Woodrow. "They're moving closer now that we're here."

Ahead of them, he saw the deputies' cruiser start inching toward the house. Duncan did the same, driving slightly faster than Woodrow since he wanted to be right there with them in case someone opened fire.

It'd been less than ten minutes since he'd left Joelle at his place. Ten minutes of constant worry and doubts. And now Duncan hoped he could do this search as fast as possible so he could get back to her. He had a bad feeling about this whole situation, but he didn't know if the feeling was because he and his deputies were in immediate danger.

Or if Joelle was.

Possibly all of them were.

So far, their attacker had used guns and the fire at Joelle's to attempt to kidnap her, but it was possible they had something much bigger in their arsenal now. Then again, they wouldn't need bigger if they had Joelle's mom. If Sandra was truly here, she would be a damn good bargaining tool. One no doubt designed to draw out Joelle.

Slater's phone dinged again. "Woodrow spotted a heat source in the center of the barn," he told Duncan as he read the text. "If it's a person, he or she is lying down."

Hell. Lying down because she could be tied up. Like proverbial bait.

"No other heat sources," Slater finished.

Of course, that didn't mean no one was around. If the hired guns or their boss figured infrared would be used, they could be staying just out of range.

"Tell Woodrow that I'm going to pull ahead of them," Duncan instructed Slater. "I'll have to knock down a fence, but I'll drive to the barn." Maybe even into the barn itself since the person wasn't near the entrance. That would keep Slater and him protected for a while longer.

While Slater dealt with sending the text, Duncan maneuvered around the other cruiser and drove through the yard. He accelerated when he got to the fence, and the reinforced cruiser bashed right through it. Wood went flying, some of it thumping against the cruiser, but Duncan didn't think there'd be any real damage to the vehicle. He'd owe the McCulloughs a fence, though.

"Heat source hasn't moved," Slater said, giving Duncan the latest update from Woodrow.

That added some weight to the possibility of the person being tied up. Or maybe unconscious. Hell, perhaps even dead, because a body could continue to register as a heat source for minutes after dying.

Duncan was about to rev up to bash the front end of the cruiser into the barn door, but his phone rang. His heart went to his knees when he saw Luca's name on the screen.

"What's wrong?" Duncan immediately asked.

But he didn't get an immediate answer. And no answer at all from Luca. "It's me," Carmen said, and her trembling voice confirmed something was wrong.

"What happened?" Duncan snarled.

"Luca was hit with a stun gun," Carmen muttered. There

was both urgency and pain in her voice. "And someone clubbed me on the head. I didn't see the man in time, Duncan. He just charged right at me."

Duncan had to fight the fear that was clawing its way through his throat. "Who charged at you? And where's Joelle?" he couldn't ask fast enough.

"A man wearing a ski mask." Carmen moaned. "There's a hole in the ceiling of your closet, and I think that's how they got in. Through the roof."

Hell. The roof wasn't rigged with the security sensors so an intruder wouldn't have set off the alarms. No one in the house would have known they were about to be attacked.

Duncan hit the accelerator, not heading into the barn but turning around. The tires kicked up clumps of dirt and grass as he sped away.

"God, Duncan," Carmen said. "They took her. They took Joelle."

Chapter Fifteen

Joelle's heart was pounding in her chest. Her breath was gusting. And the fear was right there, clawing away at her.

So much fear for her precious baby.

But she wasn't fighting as the two thugs manhandled her out of the house, down the porch and into the backyard. Not fighting. She had to get away from them, but she couldn't do that now.

Not with one of them holding a stun gun directly against her stomach.

She had no idea what a stun gun would do to the baby, but it couldn't be good. No. She had to wait for a safer way to try to escape, and she had to pray that opportunity would happen soon. Especially since they had gotten her out of Duncan's house and were taking her heavens knew where.

At least they hadn't killed her on sight, and she didn't think they'd killed Carmen or Luca, either. While one of the goons had used her as a human shield—after he'd knocked away her gun—he had held her at bay with the stunner. The other one had used a stun gun on Luca, and Joelle had seen him drop to the floor. Hard. Maybe hard enough to crack his skull.

Carmen had come at the hulking attacker, and she'd had her gun drawn, but she hadn't got off a shot before the thug hit her with a billy club. Carmen went down, too, and then the men had dragged Joelle toward the back of the house.

Now she had to pray they didn't shoot the ranch hands.

Since the hands were at the front of the house, they didn't have the best angle to see what was going on, but if they did, hopefully they'd take cover and call—

She mentally stopped right there.

Someone would call Duncan. If not the hands, eventually Carmen or Luca would do that when they were able. And Duncan would come for her.

Which was possibly what these thugs wanted.

The chance to have her while also forcing Duncan to put his own life in danger to save her and the baby. Was that the thugs' intention? Or would they try to get as far away from Duncan and the other cops as possible? She just didn't know, but she had to be ready for either of those things to happen.

"Was that really my mother who called me?" she asked. Not that she especially wanted to know the answer, not at the moment anyway, but if one of them spoke, she might recognize the voice and then she could know who was doing this.

Not Kate.

She was the only one of their suspects who couldn't be dragging her past Duncan's barn. Of course, Kate could have hired the pair, but it was possible one of the men was either Hamlin or Brad. The smaller goon was the right size to be one of them. But neither of them spoke. They just kept moving.

Joelle tried to tamp down the panic that was threatening to consume her. Hard to do, though, when everything was at risk. Her breathing didn't help. Way too fast. Way too shallow, and it didn't help that the air felt so heavy, like wet wool.

Soon, those heavy clouds would unleash a bad storm, and she figured that wouldn't help matters. It'd mean Duncan would be driving through that to get to her.

The manhandling continued toward the back of the barn, and Joelle heard someone shout. Carmen. The deputy was calling out to the ranch hands for help. That caused both alarm and relief for Joelle. Carmen was alive, but Joelle also didn't want the ranch hands gunned down if they charged at them. Hopefully, the hands would use caution if they figured out where she was.

Once her attackers were behind the barn, they kept moving. Kept dragging her, and just ahead she spotted an old ranch trail. They were commonplace in the area, and this one had a spattering of trees flanking it. A car was there, tucked in between the shadows of those trees. Definitely not visible from the house.

"Where are you taking me?" Joelle asked, trying to make that sound like a demand.

Of course, they didn't answer, which meant they either had orders not to speak to her or there was the real possibility that she would be able to ID one of them from his voice. The men just kept moving until they reached the car, and they shoved her into the back seat.

Since the maneuver caused the stun gun to shift away from her stomach, Joelle tried to pivot so she could do something to escape. But the bulkier man pointed at her with the billy club. The threat was clear. He'd hit her if she tried anything.

She stayed put.

The big guy got in the back seat with her, and the other man jumped behind the wheel. He drove out of there fast. Not heading toward the house, of course, but rather using the trail. She had no idea where it led. They obviously did, though, since they had driven it to get to Duncan's.

She glanced around for anything she could use as a weapon. And she froze. Not because there was something that could help her defend herself but because of the photos.

Dozens of them scattered on the floor of the car.

The pictures of her father. Bleeding. Dying. The same ones that'd been left on the side of the ranch house.

Her gaze fired to the big thug, and while she could see his eyes, there was nothing. No concern that he had just kidnapped a pregnant cop. No worry that she'd just seen photos that could link him to her previous attack.

And to her father's murder.

She hadn't needed any further proof that this was a hired gun. A person capable of cold-blooded murder.

"Did you kill him?" she had to ask.

Still no reaction, though, she heard the driver. He growled out a "shut up." Maybe meant for her. Maybe meant for the big guy as a reminder not to say anything. Either way, the two words had been so low that she hadn't been able to tell if this was Hamlin or Brad who were both out on bail. It was possibly neither of them since the driver could be a hired gun as well. This way, their boss took no risks and kept their hands clean.

Her body shifted and leaned as the driver threaded the car around the ranch trail, and Joelle pushed all thoughts of their suspects aside. Instead, she tried to focus on the shifting and leaning. If she timed it right, she might be able to shove herself against the big guy. Might be able to ram her elbow into his gut and strip him of that billy club and stun gun. But any hopes of that vanished when the driver came off the trail and onto the road.

Joelle glanced around again to get her bearings, and she

recognized where she was. It was, indeed, the road that led to Saddle Ridge, and to the interstate, but they weren't heading in that direction. Just the opposite.

The driver didn't stay on the road for long, though. He took another turn onto another ranch trail. The car bobbled over the uneven surface, and Joelle knew even if she managed to somehow jump from the vehicle, she could be killed since there were thick trees on both sides of this trail.

The minutes crawled by before the car exited out onto another road. She recognized this one as well. And her heart dropped when she realized where they were going.

"You're taking me to my family's ranch," she muttered.

Neither man responded, but Joelle didn't need their confirmation. This wasn't the main route to get to the ranch. This was a much less traveled farm road, one she'd used as a teenager to learn to drive.

They were taking her to Duncan at her family's ranch.

But she immediately rethought that. Duncan would almost certainly be on his way back to his place. And he would be driving the usual faster route. He wouldn't see her. In fact, maybe these goons were taking her there to hand her off to someone. To their boss. Though Joelle couldn't figure out why they'd choose her family ranch for the exchange, she knew she had to be ready to try to escape.

The goon behind the wheel took the turn onto the ranch grounds. Again, not the usual front driveway but rather the back trail that led from the road to the pasture. It was dirt and gravel, not paved like the other, but it was in decent enough shape since it's how her father had often had hay and feed delivered to the barn.

Even though it was hard for her to see the front driveway, Joelle did her best to look around and tried to spot Duncan. Or Woodrow and Ronnie since they were backup.

She couldn't see any of them so it was entirely possible that the two deputies had followed Slater and him back to Duncan's place.

And that could be what the goons had counted on.

Maybe that's why they'd left Luca and Carmen alive. It would have ensured one of them would be able to call for help, and Duncan would come running. Once he arrived at his place, though, Duncan would see she wasn't there.

Would he think to come back here?

It was possible, but it was just as likely he'd be frantically trying to shut down the interstate exits and roads to try and stop the goons from getting her out of the area.

The driver pulled to a stop at the end of the road. Directly in front of the back door of the barn. The loading door was wide enough to accommodate a vehicle, but he didn't open it and park inside where the vehicle would be out of sight. However, he did park, and he immediately got out, throwing open the door on her side and pulling her out. He put the stun gun to her stomach again.

Goon number two made a fast exit, too, and he hurried to his partner so he could hook his arm around Joelle's waist and get her moving. Again, not into the barn but across the backyard.

And that's when Joelle realized where they were taking her.

They were dragging her straight toward the well.

DUNCAN WANTED TO smash his fist into the steering wheel. But that wouldn't help him get to Joelle. Still, the smashing would give him a hard jolt of pain that might rid him of some of the anger, fear and frustration bubbling up inside him. Then again, nothing would help that.

Nothing but finding Joelle and making sure she was safe.

Slater was on the phone to Carmen, and since the call was on speaker, Duncan was hearing what a hellish situation was waiting for him at his place. The ambulance was on the way to get Luca who apparently had a head injury. Carmen had one as well and was bleeding from being hit. And while all of that was important, it wasn't at the top of his worry list.

Joelle was.

And she hadn't been seen since two masked SOBs took her. The ranch hands hadn't spotted anyone. Hadn't seen a vehicle. That could mean the kidnappers had taken Joelle into the barn and were waiting for some kind of showdown. But it was just as likely they'd had a vehicle on one of the ranch trails and used that to escape with her. If so, she could be anywhere by now.

Duncan couldn't let that thought linger in his head. Like bashing his fist on the steering wheel, it wouldn't help, and right now, he just had to focus.

Where would they take her?

And why?

For the baby? So they could wait until she delivered and then try to sell the child? Maybe. But like the other times he'd considered that, it just didn't feel right. Four months was a long time to hold a woman, and if it was the baby they wanted, then why not wait to take her until closer to her due date?

Because this was about revenge.

Of course, that didn't rule out any of their suspects. Hamlin had been riled at Joelle's father for alerting the authorities about the sale of his baby. Hamlin could have decided to aim that anger at Joelle. But Brad hated Sheriff McCullough, too, and he had a beef with everyone in the sheriff's department over Shanda's arrest.

That left Kate.

Joelle's father had been investigating the sale of babies. Had his investigation led him to Kate, and had she silenced the sheriff before he could arrest her? If so, maybe Kate believed that Joelle would follow the same trail as her father and that trail would eventually lead her to Kate.

Of course, none of those theories addressed the baby. And maybe their child didn't directly play into this. It was possible the person doing this didn't want to kill a pregnant woman.

In the background of Slater's phone call, Duncan could hear the wail of sirens approaching his place. He also heard something else, the dinging sound that Slater had an incoming call.

"It's Woodrow," Slater said. "Carmen, I'll call you right back," he added, and he switched to the incoming.

Duncan immediately thought of the heat source they'd seen on infrared in the barn. Possibly Joelle's mother. Or another hostage. And that's why Duncan had had Slater call Woodrow and Ronnie and tell them to stay at the McCullough ranch. Not by the barn, either, in case the person inside turned out to be a gunman. But rather Duncan had wanted them to pull the cruiser out of sight and keep watch of the barn. Hopefully, things hadn't gone to hell in a handbasket there.

"Slater," Woodrow said the moment he was on the line, and Duncan could hear the urgency in the deputy's voice. "A dark blue car just approached the barn from the pasture side of the property."

It took Duncan a second to realize that Woodrow was talking about the McCullough ranch and not Duncan's place. "Is Joelle in the car?" Duncan couldn't ask fast enough.

"I'm pretty sure she is," Woodrow was equally quick to

answer. "There's a woman in the back seat that I believe is Joelle. There are two people with her, both wearing ski masks."

Hell. They had taken her there and that made Duncan even more suspicious of that heat source. The killer could be inside the barn.

Duncan slammed on the brakes, and even though the road was narrow, he executed a U-turn to get them headed back to his place. He only hoped he was in time to stop whatever was about to happen.

"We're on our way back there," Slater explained to Woodrow. He glanced at Duncan. "You want Woodrow and Ronnie to move in or wait for us to get there?"

This might turn out to be a "damned if he did, damned if he didn't" situation, and it could put Woodrow and Ronnie at extreme risk. Still, Duncan didn't have a lot of options here.

"Woodrow, move in if they get Joelle out of the car," Duncan instructed the deputy. "Do as quiet of an approach as you can manage. I want you to try to sneak up on them and see if you can get her away from them. We'll be there as fast as we can."

Slater ended the call so that Woodrow could get started on that, and then Slater phoned Carmen back to fill her in on what was happening. Or rather what they thought was happening. Duncan wasn't sure what the hell was going on, but if these SOBs hurt Joelle, he was going to rip them to pieces.

Duncan drove too fast and had to fight to keep the cruiser on the road when he took one of the many curves. He had to push. Had to get to Joelle. Because he could be wrong about the boss not wanting to kill a pregnant woman. This could be a sick attempt to use her to replay her father's murder.

Duncan had to stop thinking like that.

"We'll get to her in time," Slater muttered under his breath when he finished his call with Carmen.

Duncan prayed he was right, and he kept up the speed, eating up the distance to the ranch. He was still a good two minutes out when Slater's phone rang again.

"It's Woodrow," Slater said, taking the call on speaker.

"Ronnie and I are out of the cruiser and are approaching the barn on foot," Woodrow said in a whisper. "They just took Joelle out of the car, and one of them has a stun gun pointed at her belly."

That gave Duncan a nasty punch of fear and adrenaline. "Is she injured?" he managed to ask.

"I don't think so." Woodrow paused a heartbeat. "I don't have a clean shot," he added. "They're holding her close."

Duncan got another of those nasty punches. They were using Joelle to protect their sorry butts. "Are they taking her to the house?" Specifically, to the front door so they could recreate the murder.

Woodrow wasn't so quick to answer this time. "No. They're taking her to the well."

Duncan went stiff with surprise. Then, dread. Pure, sick dread.

They were planning to toss her in.

"If we don't get there in time," Duncan said, his voice strangled now from the tight muscles in his throat, "move in to save her. Save her, Woodrow. Don't let her die."

"I won't," Woodrow assured him.

And Woodrow would try. Even if it meant giving up his own life, both Woodrow and Ronnie would attempt to save her. That could get them all killed. But Duncan had to hold on to the hope that all of them would make it out of this alive.

Had to.

Because he couldn't imagine a life without Joelle.

Woodrow ended the call, no doubt so he could focus on getting to Joelle. Duncan focused, too, and he decided not to go with a quiet approach. That would eat up precious time since he would have to park at the end of the driveway and run to the well. Instead, he turned on the sirens, hoping it would distract the two men and cover up any sounds from Woodrow and Ronnie's approach.

Duncan took the turn into the ranch, the cruiser practically flying when he slammed on the accelerator again. Everything inside him was yelling for him to get to Joelle.

He spotted the car in the pasture by the barn. Then, he spotted Joelle. She was, indeed, being used as a shield for two masked men. But she was alive. For now, anyway. She was also right next to the well, and one of the snakes holding her stooped down to shove the cover of the well aside.

Duncan couldn't be sure, but he figured both men were looking at his cruiser now. Joelle certainly was, and he saw the mix of emotions on her face. The fear. The hope. The extreme sense of dread that their baby wasn't safe.

That none of them were.

He fired some glances around, to see if there were any other gunmen lying in wait. No sign of them, but Duncan did spot Woodrow and Ronnie. They were skulking toward the barn, staying on the side where the two thugs hopefully wouldn't be able to see them.

Duncan drove through the yard until one of the thugs motioned for him to stop. That wouldn't have caused him to hit the brakes, but then the thug's partner yanked back Joelle's head, using the choke hold he now had on her. Duncan stopped about thirty feet away, drew his gun and threw open his door. He used the door as a shield and took aim, even though he had nowhere near a clean shot. On the other side of the cruiser, Slater did the same.

Neither man spoke, but the bigger one of the two continued to hold Joelle while the other looped a rope around her. Not in the usual way someone would tie up a person. This was more like a harness that they looped around her bottom.

When the two goons started to move Joelle, Duncan's heart slammed against his chest. They were going to put her in the well. Duncan tried not to look at Joelle's face since he knew that would be too much of a distraction. Instead, he focused on the men, waiting for one of them to move so he could take the shot.

But that didn't happen.

He could only watch as Joelle clutched the rope, and the goons began to lower her into the well.

"Shoot me or my hired help, and we drop her," the smaller man said.

And that's when Duncan knew who was behind this. Because he instantly recognized the voice.

Brad.

JOELLE CURSED WHEN she heard Brad's voice. Everyone in the sheriff's office had searched nonstop to find out the identity of their attacker, and now they had confirmation of who it was with just that handful of words.

Shoot one of us, and we drop her.

And they would. They already had her over the opening of the well, but she had no idea why. If they wanted her dead, why not just kill her…

That thought immediately stopped because she knew why. A moment later Brad confirmed that, too.

"We're going to play a game, Sheriff Holder," he said, his voice dripping with venom. Brad yanked off his ski mask. "You and Slater McCullough are going to die. No way around that," he added in a snarl. "Joelle, too, but you can make her death painless or a nightmare."

It was already a nightmare. She was literally hovering over a well that was at least a hundred feet deep. The sides were narrow so it was possible she could try to hold on, but she wouldn't be able to do that for long. Brad had a grip on the end of the rope, but there were no guarantees whatsoever that he wouldn't just let her drop.

"What the hell do you want?" Duncan snarled.

"Revenge," Brad spat out just as the first drops of rain started to fall. "For ruining my life. For bringing me to this."

"You brought yourself to this," Joelle muttered.

Brad apparently heard her because he made a feral sound of outrage. "You and your fellow cops arrested Shanda. You caused her to miscarry," he shouted.

"And you killed her," Joelle said. Yes, it was a risk to agitate him like this, but the agitation might distract him so that Duncan and Slater could shoot him.

No feral sound this time. Brad made more of a hoarse sob. "That was an accident. She was going to the cops because she thought I'd killed Sheriff McCullough, and I had to stop her." He sounded genuinely sorry about that. And maybe he was.

"You had to stop her," Joelle repeated, and she managed to keep her voice calm. "But you couldn't reason with her."

From the corner of her eye, she saw Woodrow peer around the side of the barn, and she felt another surge of hope. If Duncan and her brother didn't get a shot, then maybe Woodrow could.

"Yes," Brad muttered, and it seemed for a few moments, he was lost in some memories with Shanda. "The hired guns, too, since they chickened out after taking the dispatcher who helped arrest Shanda. Not Arlo, though. He tried and tried hard. So did Willie Jay, and he knew to do the right thing after he was caught."

"I'm guessing Willie Jay knew he was a dead man once he was in custody so he ended things," Duncan said.

"He did the right thing," Brad emphasized. "Not my mother, though. She was going to rat me out, just like Shanda," he added in a mutter that was coated with pain.

"Is your mother alive?" Duncan asked.

"Of course." The pain in his eyes evaporated, and Brad's gaze flicked to the barn. "She's, uh, waiting her turn. I've already planted some records for the withdrawals from the bank to point to that idiot Hamlin hiring some muscle to carry out the kidnappings and such, and now I'll walk away," he said.

Oh, mercy. If Kate was in the barn, Brad probably didn't have plans for her to come out. He would likely kill her and pin that on Hamlin, too.

Then, Joelle had a sickening thought. What if Brad had managed to get his hands on Molly? She could be in the barn right now, gagged, unable to call out for help.

"You waited a long time to come after us," Duncan said, his gaze fixed on Brad. "It's been five months since you murdered Sheriff McCullough."

"I didn't kill him," Brad snapped, and the grip tightened on the rope, yanking Joelle back and nearly causing her to fall in the well. "Shanda thought I did, and I was afraid she'd be able to convince you that I had. Convince you enough to arrest me. But I didn't kill him. Someone beat me to it."

Joelle hadn't thought anything else could add to her grief, but that did it. From the moment Brad had revealed himself, she'd thought they had found her father's killer. Of course, Brad could be lying.

But why would he?

He'd just confessed to killing Shanda and orchestrating a plot to get revenge for her arrest. Why not just own up to her father's murder if he'd done it?

Because he hadn't, that's why.

Now it was Joelle who had to choke back a sob, and later—sweet heaven, there would be a later—she'd deal with that. For now, though, she had to stay alive and make sure Duncan, Slater, Woodrow and Ronnie did, too.

"Do you have Sandra McCullough?" Duncan asked. "Or was it a recording you spliced together?"

Brad's brief smile gave away his answer, but Brad confirmed it anyway. "Easy to fake a recording when she's blabbed on and on during interviews. I had a lot to work with to create a lure."

Part of her was relieved that Brad didn't have her mother. Joelle had to hope that meant she was alive and would be found.

"So, what now?" Duncan demanded.

"Now, you step away from your cruiser," Brad said, his voice eerily calm. He was blinking hard because the rain was getting in his eyes. "Slater, too."

"Step away so you can gun them down," Joelle spelled out. She saw Woodrow again, and he was on his belly inching closer.

"Of course." Again, Brad's voice stayed calm. "This was the best way I knew to draw them out into the open, and I'll deal with Molly later. She's the only one left, and then all the loose ends will be tied up."

"My baby is not a loose end." In contrast, there was plenty of anger in Joelle's voice. "She's an innocent victim in all of this."

"I know. And I'm sorry about that. I am," Brad repeated when she glared at him. "But I'll make this fast. Once Duncan and Slater are dead, then I can finish you fast. You won't feel a thing."

Joelle doubted that, and when Brad started to glance around, she knew she had to do something to pull his attention back to her. "Slater had nothing to do with Shanda's arrest."

Fresh rage flared in Brad's eyes. "He's his father's son, and if he'd been on duty, he would have taken part in it." He shifted those anger-filled eyes to Duncan. "You've got five seconds to step away from the cruiser." And he started the countdown. "One, two, three—"

Before he could get to four, Joelle caught onto the rope and gave it a quick hard jerk. It did what she wanted. It off-balanced Brad. But it did the same to her, and Joelle had to struggle to catch hold of the sides of the well so she wouldn't fall and plunge to the bottom. She scrambled onto the ground, clutching at the grass to make sure she didn't slip back into the gaping hole.

Brad cursed, calling her a vile name, but the sound of the gunshot stopped his profanity tirade. A split second later, there was another blast. Then, a third.

Behind her, the big thug fell. The headshot had made sure of that. Brad, however, stayed on his feet. Frozen with his face pale with shock. He dropped the rope, clutching his left hand to his chest.

Where the blood was spreading fast.

"I'm not sorry," Brad muttered, his gaze fixed on Joelle. "I wish I could have killed you." He pressed something in his pocket before he slumped lifelessly to the ground.

Behind them, fire erupted around the barn.

Chapter Sixteen

Duncan had already started running toward Joelle before he even saw Brad press whatever he'd had in his pocket. Some kind of detonation device no doubt.

The last ditch act of a dying man to kill the person in the barn.

Joelle moved fast, too, hurrying toward the barn. "Molly or Kate could be in there."

Yeah, the heat source they'd seen on infrared could definitely be one of them, but it was equally possible this was another hired gun, lying in wait to finish what his boss had started. That's why Duncan raced ahead of Joelle.

Slater hurried in to help, too. "Joelle, make sure Brad and his hired help aren't anywhere near weapons," Slater told her.

That accomplished two things. Joelle would no longer be close to the barn, and Duncan definitely didn't want Brad or the thug to try any retaliation if they'd managed to survive the gunshots. He was pretty sure they hadn't, but it was too big of a risk to take.

Woodrow hurried to help Joelle, and Ronnie stood guard, making sure no one else was about to launch an attack. Duncan reached the barn first and was thankful that most of the flames were on the sides of the building. Not for long, though. Brad had obviously used some kind of accelerant because the fire was quickly eating its way to the door.

Duncan threw open the barn door and immediately stepped to the side in case he was about to be gunned down. But no shots came his way. Smoke did, though, thick billowing clouds of it. Something that had no doubt been part of Brad's sick plan. The rain would help, some, with the flames, but if the fire didn't kill the person inside, smoke inhalation might.

Even though the storm had blocked out so much of the light, Duncan still spotted the figure on the ground in the center of the barn. "Kate," he muttered. She was trussed up and gagged, but she was conscious and trying to move.

Duncan didn't take the time to untie her. He scooped her up and started toward the door. Not a second too soon. The fire must have triggered some kind of secondary device because the back wall of the barn burst into flames. That got Duncan moving even faster, and in that short distance, the smoke was already clogging his throat and lungs.

The rain was definitely welcome when he darted out into it, and he continued to run, continued to get Kate and himself as far away from the barn as possible. Because there could be another device, one meant to bring the whole barn down, and he didn't want Kate or anyone else hit with fiery debris.

"I just called for an ambulance," Joelle said, hurrying to help him with Kate when Duncan placed the woman on the ground. He got to work on removing the ropes while Joelle tackled the gag.

"Brad's going to kill all of you and set me up for it," Kate blurted the moment she could speak. "He bragged to me about, egging on that PI so he'd look guilty of these attacks."

"Yes," Duncan confirmed. "Brad admitted to planting some evidence that would point to Hamlin."

"Did he also tell you he drugged me?" Kate asked, and Duncan shook his head, though he'd suspected that's what had happened. "He said he drugged my tea, and then he cursed because I apparently didn't drink enough of it. He wanted me unconscious so he could kill me. But I managed to get out of the house and go to Saddle Ridge."

Duncan nodded since that worked with his theory, too. Brad would have eliminated his mother so she wouldn't tell the cops about him, and then he could have chalked up her death to Hamlin.

"Brad spooked me into leaving the hospital," Kate murmured. "I thought he was going to sneak in and kill me. That's why I ran." She squeezed her eyes shut a moment and shook her head. "At least I tried to run, but one of Brad's hired thugs caught me."

Duncan hated to question the woman, but while they were waiting on that ambulance, she might be able to provide him with more answers. A big one in case any other lives were at stake. "Did Brad say anything about the PI's sister?"

"Isla," Kate was quick to say. "Yes. Brad did more bragging about her, too. He took her a month ago when he started setting all this up. He said she was insurance. That if the cops didn't arrest Hamlin for murder, he would use Isla to force Hamlin to do it. And that if the cops did arrest him, then he could still sell the baby when she had it and then get rid of Isla."

Duncan cursed. "Where was Brad holding Isla?"

Kate shook her head again. "He didn't say. Maybe at his house in San Antonio? It's a big place, and he told me he'd closed off the second floor because he never used it."

Before Duncan could even ask, Slater was taking out his phone. "I'll get SAPD out there right now to do a search."

Good. He prayed she was there and safe. He didn't want Brad to add any more victims to his list.

"My son was a very sick, very disturbed man." Kate's gaze slid to the bodies, and a hoarse sob tore from her throat.

"One of them is Brad," Duncan told her. Not the best way to do a death notification, but she had to know. "I stopped him."

Kate looked up at him, and a mix of both tears and rain slid down her cheeks. "You did what you had to do," she muttered.

He had, and while Duncan didn't need Kate's validation about that, he was glad she didn't appear to be on the verge of being hysterical with grief. But there would be grief. He was sure of that, and somehow Kate would have to try to come to terms with what her son had done.

And what Brad had done was create a nightmare.

Five dead hired guns. Duncan wouldn't mourn that. But he was desperately sorry for the hellish memories Brad had given Joelle, Molly and Kate. Hell, had given him, too, because he doubted he'd ever be able to forget the terror of Brad coming so close to putting Joelle in that well.

One thing that Duncan was certain of was that Kate had had no part in her son's plan. That was good for tying up the loose ends of the investigation, but again, Kate would have to deal with her son pulling her into all of this.

Duncan looked at Joelle, their gazes connecting, and he didn't care who was watching. He pulled her into his arms and kissed her. There was both relief and hope in that kiss. Relief that she and their baby were alive. Hope that nothing like this would ever happen to them again.

"SAPD already had officers in the area of Brad's house, and they're going in right now," Duncan heard Slater say, and he looked up to see Joelle's brother watching them. Well, watching as much as the rain would allow. It was coming down hard now.

Woodrow was heading to the back of the ranch house, and Ronnie was near the bodies. The chaos of a crime scene had already gotten started.

"Woodrow's getting some umbrellas from the house," Slater explained. "We won't move Kate any more than necessary until the EMTs give us the okay, but why don't Joelle and you go wait on the porch? No need for all of us to get soaked."

Duncan didn't care about the "getting soaked" part, but he wanted Joelle off her feet. Of course, she'd need another exam at the hospital, but he wanted to check for himself to make sure she hadn't physically been harmed.

Even though he figured it wasn't necessary, Duncan scooped her up in his arms and carried her to the porch. She didn't balk. In fact, she sighed and buried her face against his neck. He held her that way for several moments until they were beneath the porch roof. Then, he eased her back to her feet so he could kiss her.

It was another of those comfort kisses, and she didn't balk about that, either. Just the opposite. She returned the kiss, making it long, hard and deep.

"I thought Brad was going to shoot you," she said when she finally pulled back. She looked at him, examining him as he was doing to her.

Duncan didn't voice his fears about what he thought Brad would do to her. No need. They both knew how close they'd all come to dying.

"I think Brad was telling the truth when he said he didn't kill my father," Joelle muttered.

He nodded. And wished it weren't true. Because if Brad had killed Sheriff McCullough, then that would have given them all some closure. It would have closed the case, and they could have started the process of moving on. From that, anyway. In other ways, Duncan felt as if Joelle and he had, indeed, moved on.

In the best possible direction.

He hoped he wasn't wrong.

"I'm in love with you, Joelle," he said, "and I'm sorry I didn't tell you that sooner. I'm sorry that it took us almost dying for me to realize that I love you and I want a life with you and our baby."

Duncan braced for her reaction, which he knew could be a shake of her head and a reminder that the timing was all wrong for this. That the timing might never be right.

But that didn't happen.

Joelle smiled. Actually, smiled. And like the kiss, Duncan felt as if it lifted a whole mountain of weight off his shoulders. He would have kissed her again to taste that smile, but Slater called out to them.

"The cops found Isla," Slater said, adding a fist pump of celebration. "She's alive and as well as she can be. They're transporting her to the hospital as soon as the ambulance arrives."

"Did she have the baby?" Joelle asked.

Slater shook his head. "She's due in a couple of weeks." He motioned toward his phone. "Should I call Hamlin and let him know?"

"Call him," Duncan verified. From everything that Kate and Brad had said, Hamlin hadn't been responsible for any of this mess.

Slater moved away to do that, and Duncan turned back to Joelle to give her that kiss. But she beat him to it and kissed him first. She seemed to pour everything into it. Especially her heart. It turned way too hot, considering they were on a porch with a yard full of cops and the approaching sirens from an ambulance and more cruisers.

Joelle didn't break the kiss until there was a risk of passing out from lack of oxygen, and when she finally did pull back, she laughed.

"I'm in love with you, too, Duncan," she said, pinning her gaze to his. They were eye to eye. Mouth to mouth. Breath to breath. "And, no, that's not the adrenaline crash talking. Or the effects of that kiss. Though it was pretty potent," she added in a mutter.

Now he laughed, and he let the heat and the joy of the moment wash over him. Duncan knew it would be the start of more moments just like this one. With the woman he loved and their baby.

* * * * *

Don't miss the stories in this mini series!

SADDLE RIDGE JUSTICE

The Sheriff's Baby
DELORES FOSSEN
October 2024

Protecting The Newborn
DELORES FOSSEN
November 2024

Tracking Down The Lawman's Son
DELORES FOSSEN
December 2024

Under Lock And Key

K.D. Richards

MILLS & BOON

K.D. Richards is a native of the Washington, DC, area, who now lives outside Toronto with her husband and two sons. You can find her at kdrichardsbooks.com.

Books by K.D. Richards

Harlequin Intrigue

West Investigations

Pursuit of the Truth
Missing at Christmas
Christmas Data Breach
Shielding Her Son
Dark Water Disappearance
Catching the Carling Lake Killer
Under the Cover of Darkness
A Stalker's Prey
Silenced Witness
Lakeside Secrets
Under Lock and Key

Visit the Author Profile page at millsandboon.com.au.

CAST OF CHARACTERS

Kevin Lombard—West Security and Investigations private investigator.

Maggie Scott—Curator at the Larimer Museum and suspect in the theft of the Viperé ruby.

Tess Stenning—Head of West Security and Investigations' West Coast office.

Detective Gill Francois—LAPD detective investigating the theft.

Robert Gustev—Maggie's boss.

Carter Tutwilder—Chairman of the board of the Larimer Museum.

Chapter One

Maggie Scott looked around the dimly lit museum gallery, exhausted but content. She'd done it. The donors' open house for the Viperé ruby exhibit had been a rousing success. The classical music that had played softly in the background during the night was silent now, but the air of sophistication and sense of reverence still filled the room. Soft spotlights lit the priceless paintings on the wall while a brighter beam shone down on what was literally the crown jewel of the exhibit. The Viperé ruby glowed under the light like a blood red sun.

Maggie stood in front of the glass case with the almost empty bottle of champagne she'd procured from the caterers before they'd left and a flute. She poured what little was left in the bottle into the flute and toasted herself.

"Congratulations to me." She downed half the liquid in the glass. Her eyes passed over the gallery space with a mixture of awe, satisfaction and pride. The night had been the culmination of a year's worth of labor. A decade of work if she counted undergraduate and graduate school and the handful of jobs she'd held at other museums before joining the Larimer Museum as an assistant curator three years earlier. It had taken a massive amount of work to ensure the success of the display and the open house for the donors and board members, who got a first look at the highly anticipated exhibit. As one of two assistant curators up for a possible promotion to curator and with the director of the British museum who'd loaned the Viperé ruby to the relatively small Larimer Museum watching her, she was under a great deal of pressure from a great many people. But the night had been an unmitigated success, so said her boss, and she was hopeful that she was now a shoo-in for the promotion.

Maggie stepped closer to the jewel, reaching out with her free hand and almost grazing the glass. The spotlight hit the ruby, creating a rainbow of glittering light around her. She raised the champagne flute to her lips and spoke, "To the Viperé ruby and all the other pieces of art that have inspired, challenged and united humanity in ways words cannot express."

She finished the champagne and stood for a moment, taking in the energy and vitality that emanated from the works around her.

Maggie was abruptly yanked from her reverie by the sound of a soft thud. She and Carl Downy were the only two people who were still in the building. Carl was the retired cop who provided security at night for the museum. Mostly, that meant he walked the three floors of the renovated and repurposed Victorian building that was itself a work of art between naps during his nine-hour shift.

A surge of unease traveled through her. She gripped the empty champagne bottle tightly and called out, "Carl, is that you?"

A moment passed without a response.

Unease was replaced with concern. Carl was getting on in years. He could have fallen or had a medical emergency of some type.

Maggie stepped into the even more dimly lit hallway connecting the rooms, the galleries as her boss liked to call them, on the main floor. The thud had sounded as if it had come from the front of the museum, but all she saw was pitch black in that direction. She knew the nooks and crannies of the museum as well as she knew her own house. Normally, she loved wandering through the space, leisurely taking in the pieces. Even though she'd seen each of them dozens of times, she always found herself noticing something new, some aspect or feature of the pieces she'd overlooked. That was one of the reasons she loved art. It was always teaching, always changing, even when it stayed the same.

But she didn't love it at the moment. The museum was eerily still and quiet.

Suddenly, a dark-clad figure stepped out of the shadows. He wore a mask, but she could tell he was a male. That was all she had time to process before the figure charged at her.

Her heartbeat thundered, and a voice in her head told her to run, but her feet felt melted to the floor. The bottle and champagne flute slid from her hands, shattering against the polished wood planks.

The intruder slammed her back into the wall, knocking the breath out of her. Before she had time to recover, he backhanded her across the face with a beefy gloved hand.

Pain exploded on the side of her face.

She slid along the wall, instinct forcing her to try to get away even as her conscious brain still struggled to process what was happening. But her assailant grabbed her arm, stopping her escape.

Her vision was blurred by the blow to her face, and the mask the intruder wore covered all but his dark brown eyes. Still, she was aware of her assailant raising his hand a second time, his fist clenched.

Her limbs felt like they were stuck in molasses, but she tried to raise her arm to deflect the blow.

Too slowly, as it turned out.

The intruder hit her on the side of her head, the impact causing excruciating pain before darkness descended and her world faded to black.

KEVIN LOMBARD'S PHONE RANG, dragging him out of a dreamless sleep at just after one in the morning.

"Lombard."

"Kevin, hey, sorry to wake you." The voice of his new boss, Tess Stenning, flowed over the phone line. "We have a problem. An assault and theft at the Larimer Museum, one of our newer clients. Since you are West Investigation's new director of corporate and institutional accounts, that makes it your problem."

Kevin groaned. He'd only been on the job for three weeks, but Tess was right, his division, his problem. It didn't matter that he hadn't overseen the installation of the security system at the Larimer. He'd looked over the file, as he'd done with all of the security plans that West Security and Investigations' new West Coast office had installed in the six months since they'd been open, so he had an idea of what the gallery security looked like.

West Security and Investigations was one of the premier security and private investigation firms on the East Coast. Run primarily by brothers Ryan and Shawn West, with a little help from their two older brothers, James and Brandon, West Security and Investigations had recently opened a West Coast office in Los Angeles, headed up by Tess Stenning, a long-time West operative and damn good private investigator. If he'd been asked a year ago whether he would ever consider joining a private investigations firm, even one with as sterling a reputation as West Security and Investigations, he'd have laughed.

But staying in Idyllwild had become untenable. A friend of a friend had recommended he reach out to Tess, and after a series of interviews with her and Ryan West, he'd been offered the job. Moving to Los Angeles had been an adjustment, but he was settling in.

He searched his memory for the details of the museum's security. Despite West Security and Investigations' recommendation that the museum update its entire security system, the gallery's board of directors had only approved the security specifications for the Viperé ruby. Shortsighted, he'd noted when he'd read the file, and now he had the feeling that he was about to be proven right.

Tess gave him the sparse details that she'd gotten from her contact on the police force. Someone had broken into the museum, attacked a curator and a guard and made off with the ruby. He ended the call and dragged himself into the bathroom for a quick shower. Ten years on the police force had conditioned him to getting late night—or early morning, as it were—phone calls. The shower helped wake him, and he set his coffee machine to brew while he quickly dressed then pulled up the museum's file on his West-issued tablet. A little more than thirty minutes after he'd gotten the call from Tess, he was headed out.

He arrived at the Larimer Museum twenty minutes later, thankful that most of Los Angeles was still asleep or out partying and not on the roads. He showed his ID to the police officer manning the door and was waved in. Officers milled about in the lobby, but he caught sight of Tess down a short hall toward the back of the Victorian building, talking to a small man in a rumpled suit and haphazardly knotted blue tie. The man waved his hands in obvious distress while it looked like Tess tried to console him.

Kevin made his way toward the pair. In the room twenty feet from where they stood, a police technician worked gathering evidence from the break-in.

"This is going to ruin us. The Larimer Museum will be ruined, and I'll never get another job as curator again." The man wiped the back of his hand over his brow.

Tess gave Kevin a nod. "Mr. Gustev, this is my colleague Kevin Lombard. Kevin, Robert Gustev, managing director and head curator of the Larimer Museum."

Gustev ignored Kevin's outstretched hand. He pointed his index figure at Tess. "This is your fault."

"West Investigations is going to do its best to identify the perpetrators and retrieve the ruby."

Gustev swiped his hand over his brow again. "I can't believe this is happening."

The man looked on the verge of being sick.

"Mr. Gustev—" Tess started.

"You were supposed to protect the ruby."

"If you recall, we did make several recommendations for upgrading the museum's security, which you and the Larimer's board of directors rejected," Tess said pointedly.

Gustev's face reddened, his jowls shaking in anger.

"Mr. Gustev," Kevin said before the curator had a chance to respond to Tess. "We are going to do everything we can to recover the ruby. It would help if you took Tess and I through everything that happened up until the time the intruder assaulted you."

"Me? No, it wasn't me that the thief attacked."

Kevin frowned. On the phone, Tess had said the guard and the curator had been attacked.

"It was my assistant curator who confronted the thief." Gustev frowned. "She's speaking with the police detective in her office right now."

"Oh, well, why don't you tell us what you know, and we'll speak to her once the police have finished."

Gustev ran them through a detailed description of the party that had taken place earlier that night. Kevin pressed the man on whether anything out of the ordinary happened at the party or in the days before, but Gustev swore that nothing of note had occurred.

The curator waved a hand at Tess. "I have to call the board members." He turned and hurried off down the hall, ascending a rear staircase.

Tess's eyes stayed trained on the retreating man's back until he disappeared on the second-floor landing. She let out a labored sigh. "This is going to turn into a you-know-what show if we don't get a handle on it fast."

Kevin's stomach turned over because she was right. "I'm not sure we can avoid that, but I'll do my best to get to the bottom of things as quickly as possible." He turned to look at the activity taking place in the room to the right of where they stood.

Glass sparkled on top of a podium covered with a black velvet blanket. A numbered yellow cone marked the shards as evidence. A crime scene tech made her way around the room, systematically photographing and bagging anything of note.

Tess groaned. "Someone managed to break into the building and steal the Viperé ruby, a ruby the size of your fist and worth more than the gross domestic product of my hometown of Missoula."

His eyebrow quirked up. "Sounds like a lot."

"Try two hundred fifty million a lot."

Kevin gave a low whistle. "That's a lot."

Tess cut him a look. "A lot of problems for us. I'm afraid Gustev—" she nodded toward the staircase that the curator had ascended moments earlier "—is going to throw himself out of a window."

The curator was more than a little bit on edge, but who could blame him. "The thief attacked the assistant curator but left her alive?"

Tess nodded. "The night guard and one of the assistant curators were knocked unconscious by the thief, apparently."

Kevin frowned. "What was an assistant curator still doing here so late?"

"That I don't know." Tess shrugged. "But the museum had a party tonight to kick off the opening of the Viperé ruby exhibit. The board, donors and other muckety mucks, drinking, dancing and, undoubtedly, opening their wallets."

"Undoubtedly," he said, turning his attention back to the crime scene technician at work.

Tess shook her head. "The guard was out cold when the EMTs arrived. They took him to the hospital. He's on the older side, former cop, though, so he's tough. The curator is in her office. Declined transportation to the hospital."

"Sounds like she's pretty tough, too."

Tess shrugged. "Or stupid. Detective Gill Francois is questioning her now."

He frowned. He hadn't had the pleasure of working with Francois yet, but he'd heard of him. The detective was a bulldog.

Tess chuckled. "Don't do that. Gill's good people. I've

already talked to him. He's agreed to let us tag along on the case, as long as we play nice and keep him in the loop regarding anything we find out."

He felt one of his eyebrows arch up. "And he'll do the same?"

Tess rolled her eyes. "You know how it goes. He says he will but…"

"Yeah, *but*." He did know how it went. He'd been one of the boys in blue not so long ago.

"Listen, I made sure West Investigations covered its rear regarding our advice to the board of directors of the museum to upgrade the entire system." Tess waved a hand in the air. "I told them that the security they'd authorized for the Viperé ruby left them open to possible theft, but they didn't want to spend the money and figured the locked and alarmed case along with the on-site twenty-four-hour security guard was enough."

"Didn't want to pony up the money?"

Tess tapped her nose then sighed. "Still, this is going to be a black mark on West Investigations if we don't figure out what happened here quickly. I know you've barely gotten settled in, but do you think you're up for the job?"

"Absolutely," he answered without reservation. "The first thing I want to do is get the security recordings and the alarm logs and get the exact time when the case was broken. We'll also need to figure out what the thief used to break the glass." He pulled the same type of small notebook he'd used when he was a police detective out of his jacket along with the small pen he kept hooked in the spiral. His tablet was in the computer case that hung from his shoulder, but he preferred the old-fashioned methods. Writing out his notes and thoughts helped him remember things better and think things through. "Of course, shatterproof glass isn't invincible, but it would have taken a great deal of force and a strong weapon to do it." He scratched out notes on his thoughts before they got away from him.

Tess cleared her throat. "The alarm went off just after eleven, triggered by the curator after she'd regained consciousness. Getting more specific than that is going to be a problem, at least with regards to the alarm logs."

Kevin looked up from his notebook. "Why?"

Tess looked more than a little green around the gills.

His stomach turned over, anticipating that whatever she was about to say wasn't going to be good.

"Because the alarm didn't go off," she said.

"The alarm didn't go off." Kevin repeated the words back to Tess as if they didn't make any sense to him. Then again, they didn't. "How is that possible?"

"That is a very good question."

He and Tess turned toward the sound of the voice.

A man Kevin would have made as a cop no matter where they'd met descended the back staircase.

Kevin's gaze moved to the woman coming down the stairs next to him, and his world stopped.

The man and woman halted in front of him and Tess.

"Hello, Kevin." The words floated from Maggie's lips on a wisp of a breath.

"Hello, Maggie."

Maggie Scott. His college girlfriend and, at one point, the woman he'd imagined spending his life with.

Chapter Two

Kevin's eyes swept over Maggie, drinking her in. Her dark hair was mussed and fell in tangled ringlets around the soft curve of her cocoa-colored cheeks. When he'd thought of her over the years, it had always been as he'd remembered her. A co-ed in jeans that hugged her voluptuous curves and CalSci T-shirts that he'd loved peeling off her. But now she was dressed in a black sheath cocktail dress and heels that accentuated long, smooth legs that had him remembering the ecstasy he'd felt having them wrapped around his waist.

"You know each other?" Detective Francois's voice pulled him back to the present. The detective's gaze darted between Kevin and Maggie.

"Yeah," Kevin answered.

At the same time, Maggie said, "We were acquaintances in college."

Acquaintances. They'd been much more than acquaintances. For a while, he thought they would spend the rest of their lives together. But then the NFL had come knocking, and he'd let hubris and arrogance turn him into a fool. He'd wanted to start his new life unencumbered, so he'd broken things off with Maggie.

It was, to date, the biggest mistake he'd ever made in his life.

Pale skin shone under the thinning wisps of hair on the top of Francois's head. Kevin put him somewhere in his early fifties, but the intelligence that sparked in the man's eyes said it wouldn't be easy to get anything over on him. It was clear he suspected there was more than a mere college friendship between Kevin and Maggie, but the detective didn't push. At least, not yet.

"What is this about the alarm not going off?" Francois looked at Maggie with suspicion in his gaze. "I thought you said you triggered the alarm when you regained consciousness?"

"I did," Maggie said, defensiveness in her tone. She wrapped her arms around her torso.

"She did," Tess interjected, "but the alarm should have gone off automatically when the intruder entered the building and when the case with the Viperé ruby was opened, but it didn't."

"And why didn't it?" Francois demanded.

Tess rubbed her temples. "We are looking into it, but it appears that someone turned the system off just before the theft occurred."

"Turned it off?" Detective Francois said. "Can someone just hit a switch and shut the thing down?"

"It's not that easy," Kevin said, his eyes straying to Maggie again. The shock he'd seen in her eyes when they'd first landed on him was gone, replaced by a guarded coolness. She had the beginnings of a shiner growing around her left eye. A bandage was affixed to her right temple.

He fought the urge to hurt the person who'd put their hands on her.

"We can discuss this further in a moment. I was just going to have an officer take Ms. Scott home." Francois nodded at a uniformed officer, who hurried over.

"If it's okay with you, Detective, I'd like to ask Ms. Scott a few questions," Kevin said.

Francois made a face. "I'm sure Ms. Scott is exhausted. Maybe it can wait until tomorrow?"

"It's okay," Maggie said. "I'll do whatever I can to help. I can't believe someone stole the Viperé ruby."

"Let's start there. I'm sure you've told Detective Francois already, and Tess of course knows about the ruby from having set up the security, but would you mind telling me about the gem?"

"The Viperé ruby from the Isle Dení," Maggie started, appearing to perk up just a bit. "It's a rare, priceless jewel with a rich, contested history."

"Contested." Kevin looked up from the notes he'd been taking.

"Isle Dení is a small island off the coast of Greece. How exactly the jewel got into the hands of the British government is hotly debated to this day, but somewhere around the turn of the nineteenth century, the ruby went missing only to be 'found'—" Maggie made air quotes "—in the private collection of a British millionaire. I'm going to jump over a ton of history here. Let's just say the ruby changed hands multiple times, ultimately ending up property of the British government but the subject of multiple lawsuits arguing that it was stolen from the Dení people and is rightfully theirs. A number of lawsuits have been pending for years."

"Got it," Kevin said, making notes. The story didn't sound all that unusual. He knew that a lot of cultural artifacts had contested ownership.

"Beyond the pricelessness of the piece, the ruby is also the subject of a legend," Maggie continued.

A legend. Well, that was interesting.

"Many of the citizens of the island believe that the jewel was the reason their land was prosperous and safe for many centuries before the British discovered it. Since the ruby was discovered in British hands, the island has contended with many of the issues other small islands have had to contend with. A struggling economy. Youth fleeing for greener pastures. Globalization."

"It doesn't seem fair to blame that on a ruby," Detective Francois said. "As you said, many places are dealing with the same issues."

Maggie shrugged. "Fair or not, that's what the legend holds."

"This is great background. Let's jump ahead a few hundred years or so to what happened here tonight," Kevin said with an encouraging smile.

Maggie let out a long, deep breath.

Kevin watched as the tension that had left her shoulders when she'd been talking about the ruby returned.

She crossed her arms over her torso. "I don't know where to start."

"Just start at the beginning," he said soothingly. "I understand you had some kind of party here at the museum tonight."

Maggie nodded. "Yes, a donors' open house. We have them before every big opening. We invite the big donors and those we hope will become big donors, the board, politicians, reporters and anyone else we can think of that could help us with funding and getting the word out about the museum and the work we do."

"How many people would you say were in attendance tonight?"

"Um…a hundred fifty. Maybe a little more. We are constrained by space limitations."

"Okay." Kevin nodded encouragingly. "When did the donors' open house end?"

"The last board member and Mr. Gustev left around nine thirty. The caterers were here for another forty-five minutes."

"But you stayed later? Why?"

A faint smile ticked her lips upward. "I wanted a moment to celebrate my success. The exhibit was my baby. Robert and the board had the ultimate sign-off on the loan of the Viperé ruby from the London Natural History Museum, but I was the one who broached the exchange and shepherded it through the thorny maze of contracts, permits and diplomacy that these kinds of trades require."

Kevin nodded. "That makes sense. So you were here in this room?" He jerked his chin in the direction of the shattered glass around the display case.

"Gallery, we call each of the rooms *galleries*. And yes, I was in the gallery that hosted the exhibit when I heard a thud. I stepped out into the hall to investigate, and a man in black just appeared out of the shadows." A small tremble went through her.

He had a sudden urge to wrap her in his arms.

"It all happened so fast. I know that's a cliché, but it really did happen so fast. The guy hit me, twice I think, maybe three times. I know I lost consciousness but not for too long." Her face scrunched. "At least, I don't think it was too long. The next thing I remember was waking up on the floor here in the hall. It took me a minute to stand without my head spinning, then I made my way to the security office where Carl usually sits. He was on the floor, blood around his head. I grabbed the office phone and called 911."

Kevin scribbled out everything she'd said in his notepad. "Can you describe the man?"

She shook her head, then stopped, wincing. "He was dressed in all black and had a mask over his face. I'm sorry that's all I can tell you."

"But you're sure it was a man?"

"Yes."

That was something, but not much.

"Did you, or maybe Carl, turn off the alarm after everyone left?" Tess said. "Maybe so you could take the jewel out of the case?"

Maggie's forehead furrowed. "Absolutely not. I mean I can't speak for Carl, but I don't know why he would. And I can say for a fact that I didn't turn it off. Why?"

"It looks like someone did," Detective Francois said.

Maggie's big hazel eyes widened even further. "Someone shut off the alarm?"

"Using an administrative code on site," Tess said. "I'd have to talk to Mr. Gustev to find out exactly who the code belonged to."

Maggie's arms tightened around her midsection, and her face blanched. "There's only one code. Mr. Gustev, Kim and I, we all used the same code." Tess's expression darkened. "But I showed Mr. Gustev how to create unique codes for each employee he wanted to have access to the system. That way, we could track who turns it on and off. I showed him how to do it."

"And Kim and I told him that we should all have our own codes, but he didn't think that was necessary. Said it would mean changing codes every time someone left for a new job and that having more than one code meant there was more chances for a code to get into the wrong hands."

"But it's the exact opposite." Tess's voice rose. "One

code makes it all the more likely that someone could get their hands on it!"

Maggie's expression was apologetic, even though it didn't appear she had anything to be sorry about. "I know, but Mr. Gustev has never been very accepting of new technology. We only got the upgraded security system because it was a condition in the loan of the Viperé ruby."

"I'm sorry. Who is Kim?" Kevin interjected.

"Kim Sumika," Detective Francois answered his question.

"The other assistant curator here," Maggie added. "She helped me set up, but she had a terrible migraine come on and had to miss the opening gala."

Detective Francois asked, "Were you, Ms. Sumika and Mr. Gustev the only three with the code to turn off the alarm?"

"And Carl and the day guards." Maggie's chin jerked up. "Wait. You can't possibly think that someone who works here had anything to do with stealing the Viperé ruby?"

No one spoke.

Maggie shook her head vehemently. "That's not possible. None of us would do this. We're like a family here. We've all had thorough background checks, and we've all worked for the Larimer for years."

Kevin had seen too much to discount anything. It was often the people closest that had the greatest power to betray the most.

The expression on Tess's and Detective Francois's faces said they were thinking along the same lines.

"Okay, let's set the alarm aside for now," he said, taking charge of the questioning again. "Was the man carrying anything? A hammer or some sort of baton?"

Maggie shook her head slowly this time, whether it was because she was thinking or to keep from wincing a second time, he wasn't sure. "No, nothing that I could see, but I was startled and terrified. He could have had something with him. I know he hit me with his hand. His fist actually, it is one thing I can remember very clearly."

Kevin's anger flared again. He hoped he found out who this guy was before the cops did. He'd make sure to get a few shots. Any man who hit a woman didn't deserve to be called a man in his book.

Maggie raised a shaky hand to the bandage on her forehead.

"I think that's enough for tonight," Detective Francois said.

Kevin nodded his agreement and closed his notebook. "Maggie, why don't you let me give you a lift home?"

"Thanks, but I have my car."

"You've been through a lot tonight. Let Kevin drive you home," Tess interjected. "If you give me your car keys and address, I'll make sure your car is in your driveway before you wake up tomorrow morning."

Maggie hesitated.

"Really, Maggie. It would be my pleasure to see you home safely." He gave her what he hoped was a reassuring smile. Tess was right. She'd been hit over the head hard enough to black out, and he wanted to make sure she got home safely.

She hesitated for a second longer. "Well, if you're sure. Yes, thank you, I'd love to go home now."

He waited for her to fall into step next to him, staying on guard in case she needed a hand. Head wounds could be tricky, and the last thing he wanted was for her to get woozy and fall.

Chapter Three

Kevin drove them through the early morning traffic with ease. It was far too early for most commuters to be on the streets, thankfully.

Maggie sat in the passenger seat, her head resting against the side window. She'd answered with a soft "thank you" when Kevin held the passenger door open for her to get into the car but hadn't spoken otherwise. She could tell Kevin had more questions he wanted to ask her, but she was grateful when he didn't push.

It was a struggle to take in oxygen. She knew the Viperé ruby was gone, but she still struggled to process exactly what that meant. For her and for the Larimer.

Her throat constricted even further. Once word got out that the museum had let the priceless jewel be stolen, they'd never get another museum to agree to let them showcase their pieces. Not to mention the donors who would drop them, unwilling to be associated with a museum surrounded by scandal.

She would probably lose her job. Heck, the museum might close altogether.

Her head began to spin. She could feel a panic attack coming on. Great. That was just what she needed. To embarrass herself in front of the security specialist.

Breathe, breathe, she ordered herself. After several minutes, the spinning stopped, and she felt her pulse slowing to a normal speed.

She looked across the car to see if Kevin had noticed her near meltdown. His chiseled chin was still in profile, his dark brown eyes trained straight ahead at the windshield.

"Thank you for driving me home," she said, breaking the silence as they neared her street. "It's kind of you."

"I'm just doing my job."

Just doing his job. He was still painfully clear about where his priorities lay, and it wasn't with her.

"Of course. Your job."

His career was the reason he'd broken up with her in college. Or the career he'd planned on having as a wide receiver in the NFL. Unfortunately, a torn ACL during the preseason had ended his career before it really began. She was embarrassed to remember how she'd harbored a hope that he'd return and somehow they'd find their way back to each other. But he hadn't returned or reached out to her. He'd enlisted in the military. And she'd met and married Ellison, moved on with her life, but she'd never stopped thinking about him.

"I didn't mean it like that. I just meant West Security and Investigations was hired to provide security to the Larimer, and as far as I'm concerned that includes its employees. That's you. I'm sorry we failed you tonight."

They made the rest of the drive in a long awkward silence. Finally, he turned into the long driveway that led to her rental, a former carriage house situated behind Kim's much larger Tudor-style home. He stopped in front of the carriage home and put the car in Park.

He hit his seat belt release. "Let me help you into the house."

She unlatched her own seat belt and waited for Kevin to open the passenger door.

He offered his hand to help her out of the car. The skin-to-skin contact set off fireworks in her. Did he feel it too?

She gave herself a mental shake. It didn't matter. He couldn't have been clearer. Just doing his job. Heck, she'd seen his face when Detective Francois had implied she or someone from the Larimer might be involved in the theft. He wasn't attracted to her. He suspected she was involved in the Viperé's theft.

She pulled her hand back. "I think I've got it."

Kevin shut the car door, and they started for the cottage. "This is a nice place. How'd you find it?"

"Through my friend. Kimberly Sumika." She was moving slowly. Her entire body aching.

He frowned. "The other assistant curator?"

She nodded. "Yes. She owns the big house." She cocked her head toward the Tudor. "I rent the carriage house from her. She and I were friends in grad school, but lost touch after graduation. When Ellison died, she reached out."

Kevin shot a glance across the dark interior of the car. "Ellison. Your husband?"

"Ex-husband. We'd been divorced for a few months when he died. He'd…had some troubles at his job before his death. He had been charged with embezzling five hundred thousand dollars from his accounting firm." She shifted in the passenger seat. It was awkward telling Kevin about Ellison, but she'd rather he heard the story from her.

She cleared her throat and continued. "Even though Ellison was gone, the scandal that swirled around him wasn't. A lot of people in New York thought I was in on the theft or at least knew about it. It was horrible. I lost my job. No museum in New York would hire me. Kim got in touch and told me about an opening at the Larimer, where she worked. She put in a good word for me, and I got the job, so I moved back to California. She really went to bat for me to get the job."

"And she gave you a place to live. Sounds like a good friend." Kevin helped her up the two front steps.

She reached into the front pocket of her purse for her keys. "At a steep discount off market rates. She is a great friend." Worry niggled at her.

After dialing 911, she'd called both Robert and Kim, but Kim hadn't answered her phone. Maggie had left a message for her explaining the break-in. Kim loved the museum as much as she did. Why hadn't she at least returned the call?

She turned to look at the Tudor. The back door stood open.

She grasped his forearm. "Kevin. Something is wrong."

She felt his body tense beside her. He slipped in front of her, pinning her between the front door of the cottage and his large body.

"What is it?"

"Kim's back door is open." She pointed. "She'd never forget to lock her doors."

His body stiffened even more. "You go inside. I'll check it out."

He bounded off the porch stairs and moved like liquid across the lawn and up the Tudor's back porch staircase.

She was exhausted and injured, but there was no way she was going to cower in her house when Kim could need help. She followed Kevin across the backyard and into the Tudor.

The back door opened directly onto the kitchen. The Larimer didn't pay them anywhere near enough to afford a four-bedroom, three-bathroom detached home in the Los Angeles suburbs. Kim had inherited the house from her parents, and the mortgage-free home had allowed her the ability to use her salary to make extensive upgrades. The kitchen was modern, designed so that the appliances blended in with the cabinets.

The interior of the house was dark, and Kevin had disappeared somewhere inside.

Dread twisted in Maggie's stomach. She took a deep breath, attempting to calm her nerves, and made her way down the short hallway from the kitchen to the front of the house.

Kevin met her at the entrance to the living room. "You shouldn't go in there."

"Why? What's wrong? Where is Kim?"

Kevin tried to move her backward, but she skirted around him.

A sob caught in her throat.

Kevin wrapped his arm around her shoulders and turned her away from the living room. But not fast enough.

Kim was slumped on the sofa. She appeared to be asleep, but her skin was ashen and gray. Her eyes stared forward, empty, at nothing.

Kim wasn't asleep.

She was dead.

Chapter Four

Kevin took Maggie back to her cottage and got her settled before returning to the front porch of the Tudor to wait for the authorities. EMTs and officers responded quickly, as did Detective Francois. He pulled up right behind the ambulance although there was no need for anyone to hurry. Kim Sumika was beyond help.

The property around the house had been taped off with yellow crime scene tape, drawing neighbors out of their homes to gawk at the goings-on despite the early hour.

Francois paused on his way into the house only long enough to have Kevin recount how he and Maggie had found Kim's body and to ask him not to go anywhere. That had been thirty minutes ago, and Kevin was itching to go check on Maggie. He was just about to let the heavyset, young, uniformed officer with puffy eyes who manned the door know that he could be found in the cottage at the rear of the property when he heard Francois call out for him to come inside.

Kevin stepped into the house and found the detective standing in the entryway to the living room. The detective was alone in the room, the crime scene technicians having not yet arrived.

Francois turned his gray eyes on Kevin. "You're a former cop."

It wasn't a question, not really. He was sure the detective had checked him, Tess and West Investigations out. "San Jacinto PD. Seven years."

Francois nodded. "Tell me what you see."

Kevin looked at the scene. Kim's body sat on the sofa. She was in her late thirties or early forties and fit. It looked almost as if she'd been settling in for a relaxing night in front of the television. She wore loose-fitting pajama pants, a Clippers T-shirt and slippers that showed off electric blue toenails. An open bottle of wine and a mostly eaten bowl of popcorn sat on the coffee table. The television facing the sofa was off. An ordinary night except for the needle on the carpet at Kim's feet and the belt that was looped around the dead woman's right arm like a tourniquet. On the coffee table in front of the couch were various other indicators of drug use.

"Possible overdose."

Francois's bushy brows made a V over his nose. "Possible?"

Kevin shrugged. "I don't like making assumptions. It looks like an overdose based on the limited information in front of me. The television was off when I found her. You should check to see if it's one of those energy savers that turns itself off after a certain amount of time sitting idle."

Francois smiled slightly and made a note on his phone. "Would you like to take a closer look?" He waved for Kevin to come farther into the room.

He would. He stepped into the living room, careful to stay on the pathway that Francois had already marked off with police tape. The fact that Francois had made sure to delineate a confined pathway for the techs and any other required personnel marked him as a true professional. It was important to make sure that no one muddied the scene more than necessary.

Kevin scanned the room, turning slowly, marking the space on a mental grid and noting anything that seemed out of place or relevant. The first thing he noticed was that the carpet appeared to have been vacuumed recently. As in so recently that there were still lines in the material from the vacuum wheels.

He stepped closer to Kim's body. There were indications of track marks on both her arms, but they appeared to be old and scarred over. She had clearly been a drug user at some point in her life. Had she relapsed? It was possible. Relapse among former drug users was common even after years of sobriety. Many former users didn't realize that starting up with drugs again after years of being clean could have immediate and devastating effects on a body that had already been through so much.

Kevin turned back to Francois. "Can I take a look around the house?"

Francois nodded. "Certainly. We can look together."

They moved as carefully through the rest of the house as they had in the living room. There wasn't much to see. Four bedrooms and two bathrooms upstairs. A den, dining room, bathroom and kitchen on the main floor. The basement was unfinished, and it looked as if Kim used it as a gym and storage space.

No sign of anything amiss or disturbed anywhere except in the living room.

He and Francois stepped back into the foyer just as the crime scene technicians walked through the front door with their equipment.

"You should make sure they get photographs of everything in the living room, including shots of the carpet leading from the doorway to where Kim is sitting," Kevin said to Francois, hoping the detective didn't get piqued and decide he was overstepping.

Francois cocked his head to one side. "Why?"

"Look at it." Kevin, Francois and the crime scene tech turned toward the living room. "Doesn't it strike you as odd?"

"Odd?" Francois said.

"I see what you mean." The tech, a tall, easily six-foot-six, woman with vibrant green hair, nodded excitedly.

"Well, I don't." Francois frowned. "Can someone clue me in?"

"There are vacuum lines in the carpet but no footprint impressions," Kevin answered. "How could she have gotten to the sofa without mussing the vacuum lines or leaving footprints? Why would she even try? It's her house."

"She couldn't have." The tech shifted from foot to foot excitedly. "Someone vacuumed after this woman died. Probably trying to get rid of any evidence he or she might have left." The tech snorted. "As if." She looked to Detective Francois. "Can I get started?"

"Yes, and you heard the man." Francois sighed. "Lots of photos and be careful. This is shaping up to be a homicide."

MAGGIE OPENED THE front door and let Kevin and Detective Francois into her small home. She'd fallen in love with the cottage the moment she'd stepped into the house. The gleaming hardwood floors, soaring ceiling and wall of windows looking out of the back onto a sea of green grass had sold her on the place. Kim had helped her make a fresh start when she'd been convinced her life was over.

And now her friend was gone. Maggie beat back another crying jag. She'd already indulged in a good one while waiting for Kevin and Detective Francois to come for her.

She waved the men to the sofa. "I've made coffee. Can I get either of you a cup?"

"Please." Detective Francois smiled.

"None for me," Kevin answered.

"Still not a coffee drinker, I see." A faint smile crossed her lips. He'd always said it tasted like liquified mud when they were in college.

"Never acquired a taste for it." Kevin smiled back.

It only took a moment to pour two cups of coffee, one for the detective and another for herself. She arranged the cups, a small carafe of cream and a sugar bowl on a tray and carried it into the living room. She settled the coffee on the table beside the sofa and took her cup to the only other seat in the room, a blue easy chair she'd found at the Salvation Army that had still been in good shape. Or at least good enough shape.

Detective Francois took a long sip of coffee.

Maggie held the cup in her hand, staring at the dark liquid inside but not drinking. "Kim is dead." She didn't need confirmation of that. "How?"

"We are very much still in the preliminary stages of the investigation." The detective set the mug aside and pulled out his cell phone. "Can you take me through what happened from the time you and Mr. Lombard left the museum?"

Maggie let out a shuddering breath and began. Kevin remained quiet while she recounted their steps from the museum to finding Kim, but she could tell he'd already gone through the story with Detective Francois.

"Did Ms. Sumika do drugs?" Detective Francois asked.

Maggie jolted at the detective's question. How could he know? She shook her head. "No. Not anymore. She'd been clean for years. A decade."

Francois pinned Maggie in his gaze. "But she used to do drugs."

Maggie hesitated.

"I know you might not want to say something that could paint Kim in a bad light," Kevin said, "but anything you can tell the detective could help to figure out exactly what happened here."

"Kim didn't do drugs." Maggie believed that despite what she'd seen when they'd found her friend's body. "Not anymore. She had a problem when she was an undergraduate. Before we met. She dropped out of college for a while, but she went into rehab, and she was clean by the time we met in grad school, although she was up-front about her addiction."

"I believe you," Kevin said.

She searched his face and found nothing, but he seemed sincere. Unfortunately, she couldn't say the same about Detective Francois's expression. To say he appeared skeptical was an understatement.

"Do you know where or from whom she got her drugs?" Detective Francois asked.

She gritted her teeth. "I don't. I told you that was before we met. I wouldn't have moved in here if I didn't believe that she'd conquered that demon."

Detective Francois stopped typing the note he'd been putting in his phone. "What do you think happened then?"

Maggie stayed silent. That was the question, wasn't it? She thought Kim had beat her addiction, but relapses among addicts weren't uncommon. She'd been busy planning for the opening and the Viperé exhibit. Maybe she'd missed the signs. Maybe she'd failed her friend. Or maybe there hadn't been any signs because Kim hadn't relapsed. Maybe her overdose wasn't an accident. Maybe it was murder. But that was just too hard to comprehend.

"I don't know." It wasn't satisfactory for anyone, but it was the only answer she could give the detective.

"We'll have to wait for the medical examiner's report to be sure, but the scene has all the signs of an overdose, and at the moment, we are proceeding as if it is such. We will of course explore every avenue and go wherever the evidence takes us," Detective Francois said.

He moved on. "Did Ms. Sumika do her own housework?"

The sudden change in subject threw Maggie. "Housework?"

"Yes, you know." The detective waved the phone as he spoke. "Laundry. Cooking. Doing the dishes. Cleaning. Vacuuming."

She had no idea why that information would be relevant to Kim's death but wanted to do anything she could to help the detective. "No. She had a service come in twice a week."

"Huh. Sounds expensive," Francois remarked. "I don't expect that she would have made the kind of money to afford the house, a twice-a-week cleaning service, and I saw a very nice Audi Sport in the garage."

Maggie let out a frustrated breath. Kim shouldn't be the one on trial. She was a victim. "Kim came from money. The house was her childhood home. She inherited it when her parents died a couple years ago within months of each other. A real love story."

Maggie had been almost as devastated as Kim when,

first, Kim's mother had passed then, two months later, her father, both from heart attacks, although Kim believed her father's had been brought on from the devastating loss of his soulmate.

"Ah, well that makes sense then."

Kevin cleared his throat, drawing the attention in the room to him. "Was Kim right- or left-handed?"

"Oh..." Another question out of left field. "She was right-handed. Why?"

The men shared a look, but neither answered her.

That wasn't going to do for her. She stood. "Look, I want to help. I want to know what happened to Kim, and if someone..." She swallowed the sob that bubbled in her throat. "And if someone hurt her, I want them brought to justice more than anyone. I can help you."

Both men stood.

"You are helping," Detective Francois said. "By answering my questions."

She shot a glance at Kevin and then back at Francois. "You're letting him into the investigation. Why not me?"

"Mr. Lombard is a former police officer and trained security specialist."

And Kevin wasn't a suspect in a major jewel theft. The detective didn't say that, but Maggie had no problem hearing it in the silence that fell. She had a feeling she was going to get good at hearing the things Francois didn't say.

Detective Francois tucked his phone into his suit pocket. "It's been a long night. We'll go and let you get some sleep, but I'll likely have more questions for you in the coming days. About the theft and Ms. Sumika."

She crossed her arms over her torso and followed the men to the front door.

Detective Francois stepped into the night, headed to the Tudor without a glance back.

Kevin stopped on her small front stoop. “Hey, he’s right about one thing. You’ve been through more than any one person should have to deal with in one night. Try to get some rest. Maybe call a friend to come stay with you.”

Maggie shook her head and finally let the tears she’d been holding back fall. She met his gaze, surprised to find sympathy there. “Rest isn’t what’s going to help me get through this. Helping to find Kim’s killer will.”

Chapter Five

Kevin arrived at police headquarters just after ten the next morning. Tess had set up a status meeting for them with Detective Francois. His boss had been busy in the hours since he'd seen her last. The Larimer Museum's insurance company had agreed to employ West Investigations to find the Viperé jewel, although Tess had stressed that the working relationship was tenuous. West's reputation had taken a hit with the theft, but they had a longstanding relationship with this particular insurance company, and that had gone a long way in convincing them to allow West to take the first crack at the case.

The Los Angeles Police Department had also agreed to let West work with them. They had more than enough to deal with without adding a jewel heist to their ever-growing list of investigations. They'd still take the lead with respect to Kim Sumika's possible homicide, but Kevin would work with Detective Francois on the jewel theft and have full access to the detective. Kevin was surprised Tess had been able to pull off such access, and she'd admitted that his prior experience as a police officer had helped her convince the powers that be in the LAPD to let him help. Despite the show of faith from the insurance company and the police departments, both he and

Tess knew that the reputation of West's new West Coast office was on the line.

He gave his name to the young officer who sidled up to the bulletproof glass separating the clerk's desk from the public. After showing his identification and going through the metal detectors, he took a precarious ride on a rickety elevator to the fourth floor.

The elevator doors opened onto a depressingly gray hallway where Detective Francois and Tess waited.

"Sorry. Am I late?" Kevin said, stepping out of the elevator.

"Not at all," Detective Francois answered. He held a black leather folio in one hand. "Tess was on her way up when I got the call that you were right behind her, so we figured we'd just wait and take the walk to the conference room together."

Detective Francois started off down the hallway. Kevin and Tess followed closely behind. The detective waved them into a small conference room at the end of the hall. He offered water and coffee, which Kevin and Tess declined. They settled in around the conference table, Francois pulling out his phone while Tess pulled out a tablet. Kevin went old school with his trusty lined notebook.

"The lab is still running tests on the evidence collected from the Sumika scene, but the medical examiner was able to give me a preliminary time of death, 10:04 p.m."

Tess wore a questioning expression. "That's unusually specific for a time of death."

Francois read from his phone. "We lucked out there. Ms. Sumika's watch was also one of those heartbeat, pulse thingies. We were able to get the exact time her pulse and heartbeat went to zero."

"Lucky for us. Not so lucky for Kim Sumika," Tess said.

Kevin noted the timing. "That is about forty minutes before Maggie Scott and the guard at the Larimer were attacked."

Francois nodded. "Give or take."

Tess's gaze bounced between the two men. "Just so we are all on the same page, everyone here is suspicious of the timing of the theft and Ms. Sumika's death. I mean, I know we don't have a definitive ruling of homicide—"

"Yet—" Kevin said because he wasn't just suspicious. He'd thought about it all last night, and it was too convenient to believe that the assistant curator just happened to overdose on the very night a priceless jewel was stolen from the museum where she worked.

"It's hard to believe they are unrelated," Tess continued.

Francois shifted in his chair. "It seemed unlikely, but we have to keep an open mind and explore all possibilities."

"Of course," Tess said without conviction.

"I pulled background and credit checks on Kimberly Sumika, Maggie Scott, Carl Downy and Robert Gustev." Francois pulled several sheets of paper from his folio and slid them across the table to Tess and Kevin.

"Did you go home at all last night?" Tess joked.

"No," Francois answered seriously.

The detective was dedicated. Kevin respected that.

"Scott, Downy and Gustev all look clean, but Sumika has run up quite a bit of debt."

Kevin flipped to Kim's financials. Francois wasn't joking about the amount of debt. Nearly three hundred fifty thousand dollars' worth.

"Maggie said that Kim had an inheritance from her parents. How did she get into so much debt?" Kevin asked.

"It looks like the inheritance was limited to the house, which to be fair, in this market isn't paltry," Tess said, reading through the packet Francois had given them.

She cocked her head to the side, thinking. "But a house isn't liquid. Getting cash out would require taking a mortgage or selling."

"Exactly." Francois nodded. "It looks like Sumika maxed out her credit cards and a home equity line of credit."

Kevin frowned. That didn't make sense. "The house is worth a lot, but Kim didn't make the kind of money to pay that loan back. But why did she need that much money in the first place?"

Francois pointed a finger. "That's the three-hundred-fifty-thousand-dollar question."

"Maggie might know the answer," Kevin offered.

His thoughts had strayed to Maggie more than once during the night. She really should have gone to the hospital to have her head wound checked out. If she had a concussion, they could be tricky, and it didn't seem as if she had anyone to check up on her. His thoughts hadn't been exclusive to her health. He'd also wondered if she could have had anything to do with the theft of the Viperé ruby. At least, she couldn't have been involved with Sumika's death, not directly anyway. The time of death made that impossible.

"I plan on questioning her again today. Maybe she'll remember something helpful," Francois said.

"Do we think that Ms. Scott or the guard had a hand in the theft?" Tess asked.

Even though he'd been entertaining the idea himself, the knowledge that Tess and Detective Francois might also be considering it didn't sit well in Kevin's gut.

"I mean, we have to consider it," Tess added, though she couldn't have known how he was feeling.

"I'm definitely considering it." Francois frowned. "Ms. Scott's financials don't throw up any flags, but I find it strange that she works with and lives on the same property as our victim. Not to mention she also knew the code for the security system and knows how valuable the Viperé ruby is."

Tess propped her tablet up. "I downloaded the security footage from our server. We can see what happened up until the time the cameras were shut off."

Tess cued up the video, and the screen sprang to life. They watched Maggie enter the empty gallery and have a drink in front of the Viperé ruby. After a couple of minutes, she suddenly jerked as if something startled her then walked toward the hallway. The screen went black after that.

"Any footage of the guard's attack?" Francois asked.

Tess shook her head. "No cameras in the area where the security office is. None of the other cameras picked up anything or appeared to have been tampered with."

"So someone gets into the museum without being seen—"

"That might not have been difficult. The intruder could have come in during the donors' open house and hidden himself or herself until the party was over."

"It's as good a theory as any," Francois concurred. "But the intruder had to know that there weren't cameras in the hall leading to the security office and to hide there."

Kevin frowned. "If you're thinking about Maggie Scott, the timing doesn't work. The video we do have clearly shows her in the gallery with the ruby when the camera shuts off."

Francois's shoulders rose then fell. "Maybe she figured out a way to shut the camera off remotely. Or maybe she had help."

"Kim Sumika." Tess said what Francois had left unspoken.

Francois's shoulder went up and down again.

A protective instinct flared in Kevin's chest. That would not do. Francois was right to explore the possibility that Maggie Scott had something to do with the theft. The detective wouldn't be doing his job if he didn't. And neither would he if he ignored the possibility because he had a misplaced attraction to the pretty assistant curator.

"Maggie and Kim working together doesn't get around the timing issue," Kevin said, hoping his voice sounded nothing but professional. "Maggie couldn't have killed Kim, and if Kim was somehow involved with the theft, where is the ruby?"

"There could be a third player," Tess offered. "In fact, there is likely at least one other person involved whether or not Maggie Scott or Kim Sumika was. Whoever stole the ruby would need a fence to sell it."

"Maggie Scott probably knows a lot of people in the antiquities world, including dealers." Francois rubbed his chin.

"Everyone involved in this case probably knows art dealers. They are all involved in the art world," Kevin growled.

"Point taken." If Francois noticed the tone in his voice, he kept it to himself. "Still, I think that reaching out to the local dealers is a good idea."

"Me too," Tess said.

"Agreed," Kevin rumbled. "We also have to consider that the jewel wasn't stolen in order to be sold."

Francois tapped his phone screen. "That someone stole it because of the legend and dispute surrounding it."

"Exactly," Kevin said. "I did a little research of my own last night after leaving Maggie Scott's place, and there are very passionate groups on both sides of the issue. The government of Isle Bení has been in litigation with the British government for decades arguing that the jewel should be returned to the people of the island. So far, they've been unsuccessful."

"Someone could have gotten tired of waiting and decided to take matters into their own hands." Tess spun the tablet around and closed its cover. "But it's not as if they could just give the ruby back to the Bení government."

"No," Kevin agreed, "but it wouldn't stop them from returning the jewel to the island. The general public might not know it was there, but if the thief is a true believer, they may not care. The ruby being back on the island may be the goal, not public acknowledgment that it is there."

"So, we have two possible theories right now," Francois summed up. "One, the ruby could have been stolen to sell it."

"Or two," Tess picked up the detective's line of thought, "it could have been stolen by someone who believes in the legend and wants to return it to what they believe is its proper place on the island."

"We still have more questions than answers," Kevin said, looking from Francois to Tess, "but one thing that seems to be clear is that Maggie Scott is in the middle of whatever this thing is."

Chapter Six

The next day dawned bright and clear, and if she didn't look out of the cottage's front windows, Maggie could pretend that it was just another ordinary day. But when she inevitably did look, she could see the yellow crime scene tape still strung around the perimeter of Kim's Tudor, and the events of the night before washed out any fantasy she might have had.

The Viperé ruby was still missing, and Kim was dead. And she was a suspect in both crimes if she'd read Detective Francois and Kevin correctly.

That was more than enough to make anyone want to hide in bed indefinitely, but she couldn't. She wasn't sure whether the police would allow them back into the Larimer so soon, but Colin Rycroft, director of the London Natural History Museum, the museum that had loaned the Viperé ruby to the Larimer, would be in town that afternoon for a private tour of the exhibit. She hadn't spoken to Mr. Gustev since the night before, but surely he would have notified Rycroft and the London Natural History Museum of the theft by now.

She had switched on the television as soon as she'd awoken that morning, and there'd been a short segment on the break-in, although thankfully no mention of exactly what had been stolen. Rycroft was sure to be apoplectic about the missing Viperé, and the Larimer's reputation in the community would be ruined. They might never convince another museum to agree to an exchange again.

She'd just finished showering and dressing when her phone rang. Boyd Scott's gruff, smiling face filled the screen.

It had been several weeks since she'd spoken to her father. She knew her father loved her. He'd been a single parent since his beloved wife, her mother, died when she was ten. It had been a crushing blow to father and daughter. Boyd had dealt with losing his wife by entering into a series of short-term, ill-fated marriages that had led to them moving around the country a lot. In her sophomore year of high school, they'd moved to Los Angeles, Boyd's sixth wife's hometown. The marriage was over by the start of her senior year, but she convinced her father to stick it out in the city until she graduated. He'd made it a whole week after her graduation before taking off. These days, her father generally only called when he needed something from her, usually money. Her father's itinerant lifestyle hadn't exactly laid the foundation for a stable, well-funded retirement.

But she couldn't help hoping that this time was different. That her father had heard about the robbery at the Larimer and that he was calling now for no other reason than to make sure his only daughter was safe.

She answered the call.

"Hi, sweetheart," her father said cheerfully. "How's my favorite girl?"

"Tired. I didn't get much sleep last night, and today isn't likely to be any better."

"Oh?" A note of surprise sounded in her father's voice.

"That's too bad. It's important to get the proper amount of sleep."

So this call wasn't to check on her. Her father had no idea about her assault at the Larimer or the stolen ruby.

She sighed. "I do my best, Dad. So what can I do for you?"

"Nothing. Why do you always assume I'm calling you for something? Can't a father call his daughter just to check in on her?"

A father could, but her father didn't. But she kept that thought to herself. She was in no mood for an argument.

"Sorry, Dad. Like I said, I didn't get a lot of sleep."

"It's okay, sweetie. I won't keep you. I did have a little favor I wanted to ask you."

And there it was.

She loved her father. She really did. She wouldn't say her childhood was stable or financially secure, but she'd never worried about having a roof over her head or food on the table. Her father had always been there for her, helping her with homework, showing up at every performance the semester she was in the school play, and coming home every night even when she might have wished he'd pull an extra shift or two just to have a bit of savings in the bank.

But that was just it. Boyd Scott didn't believe in saving. "You can't take it with you" was his favorite saying. And to her father that saying was a license to spend, spend, spend. He spent money as fast as he made it, which often led to the need to borrow money from his daughter in order to deal with those pesky obligations like rent, electricity and car insurance, to name a few bills she'd forked over money to cover in the last year. She knew she should refuse. As long as her father knew she'd be there as a safety net, he'd never get his own financial house in order, but it was hard to say no to Boyd Scott. As evidenced by his six wives.

"How much do you need?" she asked, resigned to their respective roles in this scene.

"Nothing," he said with a touch of indignation in his voice that almost made her laugh. "I don't need any money." He took a pregnant pause. "I got engaged."

Maggie sat down hard in the chair at her kitchen table. She'd figured her father's days of getting hitched were over. It had been sixteen years since his divorce from wife number six, and while he'd had a few serious-for-him relationships since then, they hadn't ended in marriage. She knew it was immature; her father was only fifty-nine, hardly an old man, but...*ewww.*

She stifled her first reaction and instead said, "Engaged?"

"I know it's a shock. It was a surprise to me too. Well, not a surprise, I've been seeing Julie for nine months now."

She vaguely remembered her father mentioning a girlfriend in one of their prior calls, but honestly, she'd stopped attempting to remember his girlfriends' names long ago. *Julie*. It didn't ring a bell.

"We took a weekend getaway to Vegas, and one thing led to another, bing bang boom, I'm going to be a married man. Again."

Again.

"I..." Maggie wasn't sure what to say. Her father married again on top of everything else was too much to process, so her mind just didn't. "Congratulations, Dad."

"Thanks, baby. Now about that favor I mentioned. I want you and Julie to meet."

"Dad, now is not a good time. I..."

"Maggie, it doesn't have to be today, but soon. I want my two best girls to get to know each other. I know you and Julie are going to love each other. As much as I love you both."

The doorbell rang, saving her from having to come up with an answer right away.

"Dad, there's someone at my door. I'll call you back."

"Okay." She noted the hint of disappointment in her father's voice, guilt flooding through her. "Hey, sweetie. I love you."

"I love you too, Dad. I'll call soon, and we'll set something up."

She ended the call and went to the door.

Lisa stood on the stoop with a to-go cup in each hand. "Open up!"

Maggie swung the door open. "What are you doing here?"

Lisa pushed her way into the house and threw her arms around Maggie, careful not to spill as she did. "What am I doing here?" she said, pulling back. "I wake up to a text that says, 'Theft at the museum. I'm banged up but fine. Call you later,' and you think I'm not going to come and check on you? What kind of bestie do you think I am?"

Maggie grinned. "You are the best bestie there is."

She and Lisa had met not long after Lisa moved to Los Angeles at an event at the Getty. Maggie had never found it particularly easy to make friends, especially as she'd gotten older, but Lisa Eberhard was a force to be reckoned with. She'd been admiring the painting *Portrait of a Woman* when Lisa had walked up and begun rattling off the history of the painting and the Dutch artist who'd painted it, Jan Mytens. She'd learned that Lisa was a writer, a ghostwriter to be exact, and that she had the same love and appreciation of art that Maggie recognized in herself. She'd walked the rest of the exhibit with Lisa then they'd gone for coffee. It had been an instant connection, and they'd been friends ever since.

"Damned straight." Lisa thrust one of the to-go cups at Maggie. "Dark roast. Figured you'd need strong stuff today."

Maggie took the cup and sipped. "You figured right."

"What's with the caution tape around Kim's house? Is she doing renovations again?" Lisa asked, settled in on the sofa in her usual spot.

Maggie sat. Kim and Lisa were cordial, but they'd never really taken a liking to each other. Still, it hadn't seemed right to mention Kim's death in the text she'd sent to Lisa last night. She'd planned to call her friend and catch her up on everything that had happened later that day.

"Lisa, Kim overdosed last night. She's…gone."

Lisa sat stunned for a moment. "Overdosed? But I thought she'd kicked her habit a long time ago."

"I don't know what happened." She felt tears welling in her eyes.

"Oh, honey." Lisa set her cup on the coffee table and scooted forward on the sofa so she could wrap Maggie in a hug. "I'm so sorry."

Maggie let herself cry on her friend's shoulder for a minute before straightening. "It doesn't make any sense. Kim was clean. I know she was. This whole thing, the theft, Kim's death, it's like the world has gone crazy. None of it makes sense."

Lisa studied Maggie while she sipped her coffee. "Maggie, are you really okay? You know you can come and stay with me for a while. Or I can stay with you."

"I love you for offering, but we're going to be all hands on deck at the museum dealing with the fallout of the theft and Kim's death."

"You can't possibly be thinking about going into work today?"

"I have to. At least, if the museum is open. The director of the museum who loaned us the Viperé is scheduled for a private walk-through of the exhibit."

Lisa made a face. "Yikes."

"Exactly. I'd planned to call Mr. Gustev at nine thirty to find out what he wanted to do."

"If you are going to work, what are you planning to do with that black eye?"

Maggie touched two fingers to her eye. It was still tender. "I tried to cover it."

Lisa made another face. "You did not succeed."

"It looks worse than it is."

"It looks pretty bad."

It did. She'd tried to cover the worst of it with makeup, but that had only seemed to make the purplish bruise stand out more.

Lisa stood abruptly. Everything Lisa did had an abrupt quality about it. She was one of those people who vibrated with energy even when she was standing still. "Where's your makeup kit? I'll see what I can do with it."

Maggie did all right with her day-to-day makeup, but Lisa was a wiz at makeup. She had the patience for layering, blending and whatever else professional makeup artists did that made a face full of products look barely there.

She followed her friend into the bathroom and sat down on the closed toilet seat while Lisa rifled around in her makeup bag, lamenting the slim pickings.

"Ah-ha." Lisa turned with concealer in one hand and foundation in the other. "Now tell me all about last night."

Maggie did as Lisa asked while she did her best to cover her black eye. As a ghostwriter, Lisa had penned books for a handful of celebrities as well as a few politicians. She was good at what she did, and one of the many skills she'd developed from working with recalcitrant rich people was a knack for interrogation without seeming to be prying. By the time she'd finished covering the worst of the shiner, she'd pulled the whole story, detail by excruciating detail, from Maggie. By the end of the tale, though, Maggie felt marginally better.

"Ta-da." Lisa pulled Maggie to her feet and over to the bathroom mirror.

She could see a dark ring around her eye, but it looked more like she'd had a rough night and less like she'd been in a cage match.

"Thank you."

The doorbell rang.

Lisa's brow arched. "Expecting someone?"

She wasn't. She and Lisa walked to the front door together. Maggie looked out the peephole while Lisa went to the front widow and pulled back the curtain.

Kevin Lombard stood on the front stoop, a to-go cup and white paper bag in one hand.

Lisa let the curtain drop and shot her friend a crooked grin. "Girlfriend, have you been holding out on me?"

MAGGIE OPENED THE door to Kevin. "What are you doing here?"

He held up the coffee and bag. "I came to check on you. And I brought breakfast. Can I come in?"

Maggie hesitated for a moment before moving aside to let him cross the threshold.

Lisa cleared her throat, still standing by the window. Kevin spun in her direction.

"Hello, I'm Lisa, Maggie's best friend. And you are?"

Kevin quirked a brow. "Kevin Lombard."

"He's the security expert I told you about. With the firm that provides security for the Viperé ruby."

Lisa tsked. "You guys are in a spot of trouble then." She ambled to the sofa and slung her purse over her shoulder. "I have to go. I have a meeting with a prospective client that I can't reschedule, but if you need me to, I can come back this evening. Stay the night. We can have an old-fashioned sleepover."

Maggie wrapped her arms around her friend and pulled her into a tight hug. "I'll be fine. I'll call you tonight."

"You better," Lisa said, stepping back and heading for the door. "Bye, Kevin Lombard."

"I'm glad to see you asked a friend to stay with you," Kevin said after the door closed behind Lisa.

"I didn't actually call." Maggie turned and walked to her small kitchen, sitting at the table. "Lisa just showed up."

"The sign of a true friend," Kevin said, sitting across the table from her. He slid the coffee and bag to her. "It's a blueberry muffin. I don't know what you like, but who doesn't like blueberry muffins?"

"Thank you." She pushed the coffee to the side, it was too soon for a second cup, but she did like blueberry muffins. She pulled the muffin from the bag. "You didn't get yourself anything."

"I had a muffin on my way here."

"So—" she swiped her hands together, dusting off crumbs "—why are you here?"

"I have a few more questions I'm hoping you can answer."

"Why isn't Detective Francois asking the questions?"

Kevin frowned. "The LAPD has agreed to allow West Investigations to work with them on this case. Specifically, looking into the jewel theft. Detective Francois has enough on his plate looking into your friend's death."

Despite feeling more exhausted than she'd ever been in her life, she'd barely slept all night, thinking about the ruby and Kim. The two situations had to be connected. Had the thieves killed Kim? But if so, why?

"I can call Detective Francois if you'd be more comfortable speaking to him?" Kevin said, pulling her attention back to the present.

"No, it's fine. What did you want to ask me?"

"I'm sure Detective Francois asked you this last night, but can you think of anyone who had a grudge against the Larimer or anyone who took an unusual interest in the ruby?"

"Actually, Detective Francois did ask me that question already, but I was in such a daze last night—"

"Shock," he offered. "You'd just been through a scary and traumatizing experience."

She hugged her arms around her middle. "That's for sure. I told Detective Francois that I couldn't think of anyone who'd steal the ruby, but that's not true. At least, I don't think they would go so far as to steal the ruby, but..."

Kevin pulled a small notebook from his pocket. "Who are they?"

"The Art and Antiquities Repatriation Project."

Kevin laughed. "AARP? Really?"

Maggie held her hands up, palms out, a smile tipping her lips. “Hey, I didn’t name the group. They’re a nonprofit that works to return art and other cultural artifacts back to their countries of origin.”

“And they had a problem with the Larimer Museum?”

She nodded. “They have a problem with a lot of museums. They were upset that we were hosting the Viperé exhibit. They staged a protest outside the museum a few weeks ago. But, like I said, they’re a passionate group but reputable. I don’t think they’d break the law. At least, not this way.”

Kevin jotted something in his notebook. “You never know how far people will go if they feel they don’t have any other choice. I’ll check them out. Let’s change focus for a moment. Assume that the thief doesn’t want to repatriate the ruby but wants to sell it instead. How would they go about doing that?”

Maggie shook her head. “That wouldn’t be easy. You can’t just take a well-known, stolen gem to a pawnshop and trade it in for cash.”

“Of course not, but these things can be sold on the black market. We both know that.”

“Are you asking me if I know any shady antiquities dealers who’d be willing to offload the Viperé ruby on the black market?”

“I’m sure you and the Larimer only do business with reputable dealers, but you are in this industry. At this point, any lead would be helpful. Rumor. Speculation. Can you think of anyone who’d be willing to resort to theft to get the ruby?”

She shook her head again. “That might be a better question for Colin Rycroft.”

She watched Kevin write the name in his notebook. "Colin Rycroft. Who is he?"

"He's the director of the London Natural History Museum. They loaned the ruby to the Larimer for the exhibit. Mr. Rycroft will be in town this afternoon. I can ask him if he'd be willing to speak with you."

Although, she was sure Colin Rycroft would be in no mood to do her or anyone affiliated with the Larimer any favors. But maybe in the interest of getting the Viperé back quickly, he'd agree to speak to Kevin. He'd almost certainly have to speak to Detective Francois.

"That would be helpful. Back to the dealers."

Maggie held up a hand. "I don't know any dealers who would risk their reputations, not to mention a lengthy jail sentence, to fence the ruby, but I will ask around. Maybe someone has heard something."

"Thank you again. You mentioned that the ruby is the subject of several lawsuits over ownership. Have any of the parties involved in the lawsuits contacted you? Maybe someone was upset enough about the exhibit to go to extremes."

"We had a few emails and phone calls from people expressing disagreement with the museum's decision to feature the ruby in an exhibit given the disputes over provenance and expatriation."

"Did you keep a list of those names?"

She shook her head. "I didn't, but I could probably generate one."

"That would be very helpful."

Maggie chewed her bottom lip. "Can I ask you something?"

"Sure."

"Why were you and Detective Francois asking all those

questions about Kim's cleaning habits and whether she was right- or left-handed?"

Kevin hesitated.

"Kim was my friend," Maggie pressed. "I deserve answers."

"There are some indications that Ms. Sumika may not have voluntarily overdosed."

Her mouth went dry. "Are you saying Kim was—"

"I'm not saying anything other than that Detective Francois's investigation is ongoing and he's investigating all possibilities."

She wasn't sure what to do with the information he'd just dropped on her. It was clear that he and Detective Francois at least suspected Kim's death might not be an accidental overdose, but if it wasn't… She wasn't sure she could deal with that blow on top of everything else.

Maggie balled up the now empty muffin wrapper. "Is there anything else?"

She still needed to call her boss and find out if going into the museum was possible, but Kevin didn't need to know that.

"Just one more thing," he said, looking up from his notebook. "Detective Francois pulled Ms. Sumika's finances, and it appears that she was in serious debt."

"No." He had to be wrong. "Kim never mentioned anything about being in debt. Her parents passed, so I don't know the particulars about her inheritance, but I got the feeling her parents left her a substantial amount."

"It appears she inherited the house free and clear, but there was very little money. She took out a mortgage on the house, and combined with her credit card debt, she owed more than three hundred thousand dollars."

"Three hundred—" she sputtered "—thousand?"

"It looks that way. You don't have any idea what the money was for or where it went?"

She had an idea of where the money could have gone, but it was just speculation, and she wasn't sure she wanted to share it with him, not yet at least. "She did some renovations to the house."

Kevin's eyes narrowed on her. He was shrewd. A former cop? She could see him in a uniform. Warmth flowed through her. Even with everything that had happened the night before, it hadn't escaped her notice how attractive he was. His penetrating dark gaze, athletic body and full beard was hard not to notice.

"Maggie," Kevin said, pulling her from her thoughts of him. "Holding back is only going to make it that much more difficult to find the ruby."

And possibly Kim's killer, although Kevin stopped short of saying that. But she was sure he didn't believe the ruby's theft and Kim's death were unconnected.

She sighed, reluctant to share her friend's confidences with Kevin if it would help them find Kim's killer. "Kim had a problem with gambling."

"Gambling."

"Kim was a good woman, but everyone has their troubles. Kim had an addictive personality. She kicked the drugs, but she replaced that habit with online gambling." Maggie rose, gathering the trash from the breakfast Kevin had bought her and tossing it into the trash can. Even though Kim was gone, it felt too much like she was betraying her friend.

"It started off small, just some online stuff." She leaned against the kitchen counter, wrapping her arms around herself. "I know Kim's parents helped her pay off an earlier debt about a year before they passed away. I had no idea she'd fallen back into that vice again."

It seemed there was a lot she didn't know about Kim even though they'd been living only footsteps apart for the last two years. How had she been so blind? Guilt swam in her chest. She hadn't been a good friend.

Kevin's pen scratched over the paper. "Three hundred thousand is a lot to spend online. Did she gamble anywhere else?"

She felt her face twist into a scowl. "She had a bookie. I haven't seen him around in years, so I don't know if they still communicated but…"

"It's a place to start. Do you remember the bookie's name?"

Maggie pushed away from the counter and stepped back to the table. "I do."

Kevin's eyebrow quirked up. "Will you share it with me?"

She shook her head. "No." She owed Kim more than that. She'd been her friend, and when she'd needed her, Maggie had failed her. She wanted to have a hand in bringing the person who'd hurt Kim to justice.

"No?"

"No, I won't tell you Kim's bookie's name, but I will take you to him."

Chapter Seven

Kevin did his best to get Maggie to let him talk to Kim's bookie on his own, but she wouldn't budge. He'd finally given in, and now he was following the directions barked out by his GPS system to the address Maggie had given him. At least the address was in the NoHo Arts District, a North Hollywood neighborhood, and not in a seedier area of town where Kevin would have assumed a bookie would reside.

Maggie called her boss as he drove them across town. The call wasn't on speaker phone, but he could hear both sides of the conversation easily. The police were planning to release the crime scene at noon, and although the museum wouldn't open to the public for at least several more days, Robert Gustev wanted to meet with the staff that afternoon. Colin Rycroft's tour of the exhibit was still on. Apparently, the director of the museum that lent the Viperé ruby to the Larimer was insisting on seeing the scene of the crime with his own eyes.

Miraculously, he found a parking spot on the street a half a block from the address Maggie had given him just as she ended her call.

This area of Los Angeles had undergone a renaissance in the last couple of decades. New shops and businesses had sprung up almost as fast as the rehabbed condos and apartments that had been bought and rented by hip millennials and Gen Zers.

Maggie strode ahead of him on the sidewalk, reaching for the door of a redbrick building in the middle of the block of buildings that housed various shops and businesses.

Kevin pulled up short. "Are you sure this is the right place?"

The sign above the door Maggie reached for read The Cupcake Bar.

She shot a grin at him over her shoulder. "Trust me. This is it."

He followed her through the doors. It was obvious that at some point this place had actually been a bar. The space was a mixture of light and dark: wide pine plank floors, dark red exposed brick walls and a long oak bar that ran the length of one side. The front of the bar had been retrofitted into a glass-fronted display case for the cupcakes inside. Behind the bar was a mirrored wall, but instead of the expected shelves of various and sundry liquors, the shelves were also lined with cupcakes.

The shop was empty, but the bell tinkling as they walked in brought a man in a pink apron with Cupcake Bar emblazoned on it through the swinging doors behind the bar.

"Good morning. Welcome to the Cupcake Bar. How may I help—" The clerk's gaze moved from Kevin to Maggie. "Oh, Maggie, it's you."

"Anthony, we need to talk to you," Maggie said.

Anthony's eyes moved back to Kevin, sliding over him appraisingly. "Who is *we*?"

Kevin stuck his hand out. "Kevin Lombard. My firm

has been hired to provide security at the Larimer Museum. Maggie and I have a few questions for you about Kim Sumika."

Anthony gave his hand a brief shake and sighed. "Maggie, you know I can't talk to you about my business with Kim."

"Anthony, Kim is dead."

Anthony's eyes went wide, and his mouth fell open. "What? How?"

"She was found last night, or this morning I guess. It looks like she accidentally overdosed, but—" Maggie shot a questioning glance at Kevin, her eyes asking how much she could tell Anthony.

He should have briefed her on what to say and not to say before they'd entered. Interviewing a witness could be a tricky business. Asking the right questions but doing so without leading the person in any particular direction was a learned skill. It was too late now.

He jumped into the conversation before Maggie said too much. "The police are still investigating. Maggie says you and Kim were…friends. We were wondering if you'd seen any signs that she was using again?"

Anthony looked confused. "If you work security for the Larimer, why are you asking me questions about Kim's death?"

"Because the Larimer was also robbed yesterday," Maggie answered.

"Damn." Anthony walked around the bar to one of the tables and sat.

Kevin and Maggie took seats across from him.

"A very precious ruby was stolen, and a guard and I were attacked," Maggie continued.

"Damn. I'm sorry to hear that. So you think Kim's

death is connected to the theft? It would be quite a coincidence if it wasn't, I guess." Anthony answered his own question.

"As I said, the police are exploring every possibility. My firm, West Investigations, is helping with the investigation into the theft," Kevin said. "So, about Kim's possible drug use."

Anthony gave a wan smile. "If Maggie brought you here, I'm sure she would have told you about my relationship with Kim. We weren't friends, not in the traditional sense."

"She told me you are Kim's bookie."

Anthony's shoulders went back, and he stayed silent.

"Okay." Kevin held up his hand. "During your nontraditional friendship, did you notice any signs that Kim might be using again?"

Anthony cocked his head to the side and thought for a moment. "I can't say I did, but I only saw Kim for short stretches of time. She'd come in, grab a cupcake, maybe a little something else—" he looked away guiltily "—and leave."

Kevin sighed. The whole baker-bookie thing was cute, an innovative way to stay under the radar, but he was investigating a theft and possible murder. He didn't have time for cuteness. "Look, man. I'm not a cop. I don't care about your bookmaking business unless it led to Kim Sumika's death. I just want some answers."

Anthony's expression hardened.

Maggie reached across the table for the clerk's hand. "Anthony, I know we haven't always seen eye to eye. I don't like your side hustle. I don't like what it did to Kim, but this is bigger than all that. There's a chance..." She shot a glance at Kevin, and he gave a slight nod. Sometimes giving a little led to getting a lot. He suspected this was one of those times. "A good chance Kim didn't accidentally overdose. That someone set it up to look like she did."

Anthony pulled his hand from Maggie's grasp, his expression incredulous. "You can't possibly be suggesting it was me?"

"Was it?" Kevin pressed.

"No. Of course not!"

Maggie straightened in her seat. "Kim was in a lot of debt."

"She'd been placing a lot of bets lately that didn't pan out, sure, but I wouldn't kill anyone over that. Most of my clients aren't good gamblers. It's how I stay in business."

"People have been killed for a lot less than three hundred thousand dollars."

"What?" Anthony stood so quickly his chair fell over backward. "Three hundred thousand. Uh, uh. No way. Kim didn't owe me anywhere near that amount of money."

"Sit," Kevin directed. He waited for Anthony to right his chair and reclaim his seat. "How much did she owe you?"

"A couple thousand. Look around, man. You think I'd be slinging cupcakes if I had three hundred thousand dollars to front one person? I'd be in Tahiti or something."

Kevin believed him. Three hundred thousand was a lot of cupcakes. "Do you have any idea why Kim would be in that kind of debt?"

Anthony's eyes darted to the ceiling.

"Anthony, please," Maggie said.

Anthony sighed. "I'm small-time, okay? I did the bookmaking thing to earn enough money to open the shop, and I continued taking bets from a select number of clients after I opened, but it's not my main source of income, you know."

"Okay." Kevin wished the man would just come out and say whatever it was.

"She was obsessed, addicted to gambling. I've seen it before, and I tried to steer her away from getting in too deep but..." He shrugged.

"She started placing bets with another bookie," Kevin said, seeing where this was going.

Anthony nodded. "Yeah."

"Do you know who?"

Anthony's gaze strayed again. "I don't know for sure..."

"You have an idea," Maggie said. "Tell us."

"Look, like I said, I don't know for sure, but she did ask me about Ivan Kovalev."

"Russian mob?" Kevin didn't know the name. He hadn't been in Los Angeles long enough to get to know who the major players in the local underworld were, but the Russian mob had long tentacles in the US. And they weren't the kind of men you wanted to owe money.

Anthony shrugged then nodded. "When Kim asked me about Ivan, I warned her to steer clear."

Maggie was chewing her bottom lip again. "What exactly did Kim want with this Ivan person?"

"She wanted to know if I knew him. Could I make an introduction." Anthony twisted his hands in his apron. "To be clear, I don't. I stick to my small-time hustle and don't mess with those guys."

"Smart," Kevin said.

The bell on the door tinkled, and four women walked in, chatting.

Anthony stood. "Listen, I have to go. I don't know anything else that can help you. I hope you figure out what happened to Kim. She had her issues, but she was a nice woman."

Anthony headed for the bar display case to help the new customers.

Neither Kevin nor Maggie spoke until they were back in his car.

"Do you think Kim got involved with this Ivan person? Could he have killed her? Or had her killed?"

It was definitely a possibility, but he could see the idea was already weighing on Maggie.

He reached across the car and squeezed her hand. The electric currents that he'd felt the first time he'd touched her were back, even stronger.

"I think our talk with Anthony the baker slash bookmaker raised more questions than answers."

Chapter Eight

Kevin called Tess from the car as he drove toward the museum and updated her on what they'd learned from Anthony.

"Ivan has his hands in a number of pies in Los Angeles and beyond. He owns several seemingly legit businesses, including a bar in downtown Los Angeles. Nightingale's. Conducts his shadier business at night out of the party room."

"Think you can get a meeting with him?" Kevin asked.

"I'll see what I can do," Tess answered before ending the call.

"If we know this Ivan guy hangs out at Nightingale's, why don't we just go there tonight and ask to speak to him?"

"Because, *a*, you don't just drop in on a mobster. And, *b*, we are not going to talk to him." Kevin glanced across the car. "He's someone you should stay away from."

She rolled her eyes. "Are you planning to go to talk to him? Find out if he knew Kim and lent her money?"

"Maggie, listen to me. Ivan Kovalev, the people he probably works for, these are not men you want knowing you even exist. I'm not going to let you anywhere near them, do you understand?"

"Let me?"

He sucked in a deep breath then let it out slowly, which only infuriated her more.

"I didn't mean it that way. I'm just trying to protect you. We don't know what Kim got herself into, but it is starting to look very dangerous."

As if it hadn't been dangerous before now. She'd been clocked in the head, her friend was dead, likely murdered, and a precious historical jewel was missing. She hadn't exactly been living in Shangri-la.

They made the rest of the ride in silence. He pulled to a stop in front of the museum a few minutes after twelve thirty.

"I can come back and pick you up at the end of your workday if you'd like," he offered, stiffly.

"That's nice of you," she responded, already reaching for the door, "but I'll get a ride from a colleague or call an Uber."

She hopped out of the car and headed for the museum. It actually wasn't that far of a walk from the museum to her cottage. She'd made the walk before.

The police tape was gone from the front of the museum, and her employee identification, which doubled as a key card, opened the door to the employee entrance without any trouble.

Her head was still swirling with news that Kim might have gotten herself involved with mobsters. She was so caught up in her thoughts that she gave a startled scream when the door to the ladies' room swung open as she passed and Diyana Shelton stepped out.

"Oh my gosh, Maggie. I'm so sorry. I didn't mean to frighten you," Diyana said, a flush pinking her pale cheeks. Diyana was in the UCLA graduate art history program and interning at the Larimer for the semester.

"No, it was my fault," Maggie said, her hand still pressed to her racing heart. "I wasn't paying attention."

"How are you?" Diyana cocked her head to the side, her expression one of concern. The graduate student was pretty in a somewhat unconventional way. Dark brown eyes were set a little wide and her lips were thin lines, but her olive-colored skin was smooth as silk, and somehow the individual features worked together. "I heard you and Carl were here when the ruby was stolen and that the thief attacked you both." Her eyes strayed to Maggie's injuries. This close, Maggie had no doubt Diyana could see the results of her encounter with the thief clearly enough.

"I'm okay and, thank goodness, so is Carl. It's the museum I'm worried about." Maggie started walking again toward her office.

Diyana fell in step next to her. "You're right to be. The theft is huge. I mean, I'm not sure what Robert is going to do. I heard him talking to Colin Rycroft on the phone earlier, and it did not sound like a friendly conversation. How could this have happened?"

Maggie stopped in front of her office. She didn't usually mind Diyana's curiosity, but she was simply in no mood for it today.

"I don't know, but I'm sure the police will find out. I can't chat right now, Diyana. I have to get ready for the staff meeting. I'll see you there." She slid into her office, closing the door behind her firmly before a wave of guilt hit.

She'd been a little abrupt, possibly bordering on rude. Diyana didn't deserve that. She'd apologize after the meeting.

Remembering her promise to Kevin to reach out to the dealers she knew about the stolen Viperé ruby, she put a call in to several dealers, including her friend Apollo Bouras. She left him a message asking him to call her back as soon as he could. No doubt he and every other dealer in the Los Angeles area had already heard about the theft of the Viperé ruby, and they'd either want to stay as far away from her and the Larimer as possible given the situation or they'd call back quickly, eager to snatch up any crumb of gossip to spread.

Messages left, she got busy wading through the hundreds of emails she'd received overnight. Several were from colleagues at other museums asking if she was okay and wanting the skinny on the break-in. She'd respond to those later. More than a dozen were from news organizations, several from the same reporters. Interview requests. She deleted those without opening most of them. All too soon, it was time for the staff meeting.

She was surprised to find Carter Tutwilder, chairman of the Larimer's board of directors, standing in front of the room next to Robert.

"Come in, come in. Find a seat. Quickly please," Robert said, waving her inside.

Maggie grabbed the empty seat next to Diyana and shot the young woman what she hoped was an apologetic smile. Diyana smiled back wanly.

"Okay, before we get started with the meeting, Mr. Tutwilder wanted to say a few words."

"Thank you, Robert." Mr. Tutwilder buttoned his suit jacket. "I won't impose for long. I just wanted to acknowledge the heinous crime that has been perpetrated against the Larimer and those of us who love the museum. Of course, no one more than Maggie and Carl." Mr. Tutwilder extended a hand in her direction. "Maggie, the Larimer and the board stand behind you one hundred percent. Whatever you need, we're here for you."

"Thank you," she said, touched by the show of concern.

"As soon as things settle down, we'll also be planning a memorial for our colleague Kim Sumika. The board has made grief counselors available to anyone who feels they need to talk." Mr. Tutwilder turned back to Robert. "I'll hand things back over to you, Robert."

"Thank you, Carter."

A polite smattering of applause broke out as Mr. Tutwilder left the room.

"Okay," Robert said. "Let's get started."

Robert began the meeting with an update on Carl's condition. He was admitted to the hospital with a serious concussion, but the doctors expected him to make a full recovery. The doctors planned to release him from the hospital in a few days, but it might be a couple weeks before he was up to returning to the job. Then Robert turned to the theft of the Viperé ruby and did his best to set everyone's concerns at ease, although Maggie wasn't sure how much he accomplished. They all knew that the longer it took for the police to find the ruby, the worse things would get for the Larimer. And there was a fair chance that the ruby would never be found. It would be a coveted possession amongst the sordid world of private collectors, a notoriously secretive bunch of people who collected treasures that should rightly be seen by the masses. A lot of these extremely wealthy collectors didn't much care how they came into possession of items, just that they obtained them.

It was a short meeting. Maggie pulled Diyana aside before she left and apologized for her abrupt dismissal earlier.

"It's okay." Diyana smiled sweetly. "We're all under a huge amount of pressure right now."

Maggie returned the intern's smile. "Thank you for understanding."

"Maggie." Robert stepped up next to Maggie and Diyana. "I'd like to speak to you for a moment, please."

Diyana nodded and scurried from the conference room. All the other staff members had already left the room.

Robert gestured for her to sit and she did. He sat across from her, folding his hands on the table in front of him. She felt like a child being admonished by the principal. She smoothed the front of her slacks nervously. Was he going to fire her? He wouldn't. She wasn't responsible for the theft. She was a victim as much as the Larimer.

She sat silently, waiting for him to start.

"I'm glad to see you weren't hurt badly."

She tried for a smile and failed. "No. I'm fine."

"Good, I'm happy to hear that, although I have been thinking that it might be a good idea if you took a leave of absence."

"A leave of absence?"

So he wasn't firing her. At least, not yet. But a leave of absence was no consolation.

"Well, some time off, really. Vacation time."

"Vacation time? Now?" She was confused. It was quite possibly the worst time for her to take a vacation. With Kim…and the media storm around the theft. "Robert, what is this about?"

He sighed heavily. He looked as if he'd aged two decades in the last twelve hours. "The Larimer is under a tremendous amount of pressure at the moment. All eyes are on us with the theft and Ms. Sumika's untimely death. And well, there are already rumblings that Kim might have had something to do with the theft, and that's what led her to do—" Robert rolled his wrist "—what she did."

"You can't believe that! You worked with Kim for years. You know as well as I do how much she loved the Larimer."

Robert avoided meeting her gaze. "I have a hard time believing anyone associated with the Larimer would have committed such a heinous act, but the fact is someone did. And your relationship with Ms. Sumika—"

Maggie felt her back stiffen. "My relationship with Kim was that we were friends and coworkers."

His lips thinned. "Be that as it may, I have an obligation to look out for the best interests of the museum, and we simply cannot afford to have even a hint of impropriety at the moment."

"Impropriety—"

"I believe that it would be best for you to separate yourself from the Larimer, at least for a time." He stood as if that put an end to the conversation.

Maggie got to her feet as well. "Well, I have a contract, and I expect it to be honored. And if you try to fire me or force me to take vacation time, I have no problem taking my grievances up with the board of directors."

"Now, just a moment—" Robert held his hands out as if they might stop the onslaught of words coming his way.

Her heart pounded wildly. She'd been through this before when Ellison was charged with embezzling from his accounting firm. Guilty by association. She couldn't go through it again. "No, no moments. I will not let you suggest that I am somehow involved in the theft of the Viperé ruby."

"I never said—" he spoke quickly.

"You came close enough. And if I'm suddenly placed

on leave or taking a vacation, those same people who are rumbling about Kim maybe being involved with the theft will be rumbling about me next. I will not have my reputation impugned when I did nothing wrong."

"No one is saying you did anything wrong."

"Great." She flashed a smile at him that she was pretty sure looked more feral than friendly by the way he took three quick steps backward. "Good. Then I'll head back to my office. Mr. Rycroft should be here any minute, and I'm sure we both want to be prepared for that meeting. I'll see you soon."

She stepped out of the room and marched back to her office. Inside, she rested her back against the closed door, shaking from a combination of anger and adrenaline. It had felt good standing up for herself, but she knew if Robert really wanted her out, there wasn't much she could do to stop him. He had far more sway with the board members than she had, and they'd likely do whatever he suggested if it meant a chance at saving the Larimer's reputation. Even if it ruined hers.

She pulled herself together moments before the security guard on duty buzzed to say that Colin Rycroft had arrived. She let Robert know then picked Rycroft up from the reception desk.

The Brit was not happy.

She and Robert spent the next two hours walking Rycroft through the exhibit and explaining how the Viperé ruby's theft couldn't have been foreseen. Rycroft made them walk through the security measures they'd had in place three times, and he read them the riot act for the failure of the cameras. It would have been nice to have Tess or Kevin there to explain the security system in more detail, but neither she nor Robert had thought of it in time. And given Tess's disgust at the museum's decision not to go with her original plan for securing the ruby, they might have been better off without a representative from West Investigations. Rycroft insisted that they set up a meeting with the insurance company and West Security and Investigations to go over the steps that were being taken to recover the ruby. Of course, the Larimer had obtained an insurance policy on the Viperé, but Rycroft wasn't incorrect that money was poor consolation for a piece as rare as the Viperé.

Maggie promised to set up a meeting between the parties in the coming days and hoped that Kevin's and Tess's obvious experience and expertise might work to mollify the Brit at least a little.

By the time Rycroft finally left the museum and headed back to his hotel—he planned to be in town for the next several days—she was wiped. It wasn't quite five thirty, officially quitting time, so she headed back to her office with every intention of going home. All she wanted was a big glass of wine.

She knew the moment she entered her office that someone had been there. The air felt different. There was a slight chill to it. Maybe that was why she'd shivered as she'd stepped over the threshold.

Or maybe it was the blood-red envelope that lay, center stage, on her desk.

A get-well card probably. She was overreacting to a colleague's caring gesture.

She grabbed the envelope and slipped the piece of paper from it.

Her heart stuttered to a stop as she read then reread the words on the card.

Beware the Viperé curse. You are next to die.

Chapter Nine

Kevin stepped into his apartment, dropping his keys on the table next to the door. He still had a lot of work to do, but luckily West Investigations equipped each of their employees with a fully secure laptop so they were able to work from practically anywhere in the world.

But it didn't seem likely that he was going to get a lot of work done at the moment. The television in his living room blared.

"Tanya," he called from the doorway. He couldn't see his sister from the entrance, but this wasn't the first time he'd come home to find her camped out on his sofa, the television loud enough to wake the dead.

He slipped out of his shoes and padded into the living room. "Tanya," he yelled at the back of his sister's head.

Tanya turned and grinned at him over the back of the sofa. "Hey, bro."

People were always surprised when they found out he and Tanya were brother and sister and outright shocked when they found out they were twins. He was tall, six two and dark—dark brown hair, eyes and skin. Tanya, in contrast, was petite at five foot one, with skin the color of café latte, piercing hazel eyes and light brown hair streaked with blond. Two sides of the same coin their mother liked to call them, pointing out that where it really mattered they were very much alike. They were both driven, bossy, stubborn and thought they knew best. Kevin couldn't really dispute their mother's assessment. He and Tanya were very much alike, which tended to both draw them close and lead to a fair amount of arguing. But there was no one more loyal than Tanya, and he would do anything to protect his younger-by-seven-minutes sister.

Kevin dropped down on the sofa next to his sister. He didn't bother asking her what she was doing there. The red beans and rice she was shoveling into her mouth was all the answer he needed.

Tanya was an emergency room doctor at the nearby hospital, and given that she was still in her scrubs, her crocs lined up neatly by his front door, he inferred she'd come over directly at the end of her shift. When he'd announced he was leaving the Idyllwild Police Department and accepting a job with West Security and Investigations that would put him in Los Angeles and closer to her, Tanya had conveniently found him the perfect rental just minutes away from the hospital. Since the place had two bedrooms, he'd offered to let her move in with him, but she'd declined, saying that they needed their space. That hadn't stopped her from accepting the spare key he'd offered her and stopping in whenever she wanted, most often to bum leftovers off of him. He chided her about her visits, but the truth was he loved spending time with her. She was more than just his sister, she was his best friend.

"You look tired," she said, peeling her gaze away from the rerun of *The Office* playing on the television screen.

He put a hand to his ear and leaned toward her. "I'm sorry, I can't hear you. What did you say?" he yelled over the sound of the television.

She rolled her eyes but reached for the remote tucked under her legs and turned the volume down to something reasonable. "Better?"

"Yes, thank you. You know turning the sound up that loud isn't good for you."

"I wanted to hear the show while I was in the kitchen heating up dinner. You really outdid yourself, by the way. This is good." She shoveled more beans and rice into her mouth.

"You know, I seem to recall giving you the recipe for this dish. And showing you how to make it. And a few others. I know you are far more skilled in the emergency room than the kitchen, but for a smarty-pants doctor like you, red beans and rice can't be that hard to master," he teased.

"It's not hard to master," she said around a bite of food. "But you know what is easier? Coming over here and eating your food." She grinned at him again. "Anyway, you cook enough for a small army."

"I wonder why." He pulled the throw pillow from behind his back and tossed it at her before slouching down until his head rested against the back of the sofa.

Tanya shifted, crossing her legs on the sofa and facing him. "New job putting you through your paces?"

"I caught a particularly thorny case."

Tanya had gone to CalSci University with him and Maggie. Although they'd tried to give each other space to explore who they were outside of being Kevin's twin sister and Tanya's twin brother, Tanya had been there throughout his relationship with Maggie and had been there for him when he'd decided to end things with her. She'd even tried to talk him out of ending things, arguing that she could take out loans and work her way through medical school. But he hadn't wanted her to be burdened with the kind of debt that most medical students graduated with. He'd spent three years playing college football, making who knew how much money for the university, and he figured it was time that some of those big bucks benefited his mother and sister. Professional athletes were always on borrowed time, and he didn't want to waste any of his. So he'd left school after his junior year and directed his entire focus toward his NFL career. A career that, unbeknownst to him at the time, would only last for two years.

"Can you tell me about it?" Tanya asked.

"Some things. Have you heard about the theft at the Larimer Museum?"

Tanya squinted, the sign that she was thinking. "Yeah, I think I saw a post about it while I was scrolling through social media during my break."

"Well, that's my case. West Investigations provided the security for the exhibit."

Tanya sucked her teeth. "Not good."

"Definitely not good." He hesitated for a moment, but knew it was better that she heard it from him than stumble on the information somewhere else. "Maggie Scott is one of the curators at the Larimer. She's actually the curator responsible for the exhibit. She was hurt during the commission of the theft, not badly, but the police are also very suspicious of her at the moment."

"Kevin." Tanya closed her eyes and let her head fall to her chest.

"I know what you are going to say."

She opened one eye. "Do you?"

"Okay, what are you going to say?"

She lifted her head, both eyes open and pinned on him now. "I'm going to say that you should recuse yourself from this case. You and Maggie have a fraught history, and that is putting it mildly. I saw how torn up you were after you broke up with her. It took you years to get over her. This can come to no good for either of you."

"I wasn't torn up. I broke up with her."

Tanya snorted. "That may be, but you were broken-hearted." She held her hand up in a stop motion. "Save it. You threw yourself into football, but I know you. Heart. Broken."

"Whatever. That was a long time ago. We're both different people now."

"Yeah, that's why you haven't had a serious relationship since that relationship ended," his sister said pointedly.

"I've had relationships."

She rolled her eyes at him. "I said a serious relationship. One where you bring the woman home to meet Ma."

"This is a pointless conversation. This is my job. The other assistant curator, Maggie's friend, was found having apparently accidentally overdosed the same night as the theft, and Maggie insists on being involved in the investigation. There's nothing I can do."

Tanya set her now empty bowl aside. "Kevin, there's something you don't know."

He watched something flicker behind his sister's eyes. "What?"

She studied him for a long moment. He knew her well enough to see she was struggling with whatever it was she wanted to tell him.

He took her hands in his. "Hey, you know you can tell me anything, right? I'm your big bro. There are no secrets between us."

Tanya gave him a faint smile, slipping her hands from

his. "I know. I was just going to say that Maggie was really hurt when you left her."

His twin instinct told him that she was holding something back, but she spoke again before he could press her on what it was.

"I don't say that to make you feel bad or guilty. It is just a fact. I saw her a few times after you left, and she was devastated. Just be careful. Be sure. I know you don't want to hurt her again."

She unfolded from the sofa and carried her bowl into the kitchen.

Be careful. Be sure.

He wasn't sure about anything at the moment except that Maggie wouldn't hurt anyone, especially not someone she considered a friend. And she wouldn't be involved in theft.

The Office's distinctive theme song began playing, the credits rolling on the television screen, just as his cell phone rang. He groaned when he saw Tess's name.

"What's up, Tess?"

"You need to get to the Larimer right away. We have a problem."

IT FELT LIKE the situation had just taken a darker, more sinister turn. Stealing a priceless ruby was one thing, and they couldn't be sure yet if Kim's death was in any way connected. But coming after Maggie now? When the thief should be concerned about getting away with the gem without getting caught, that meant they weren't dealing with a run-of-the-mill criminal.

"Do you know anything about the curse that's mentioned in the note?" Francois had directed the question to Maggie.

She looked shell-shocked, which made Kevin ache to wrap his arms around her. Tess eyed him. He kept his hands down by his sides.

The four of them stood in Maggie's office. After finding the letter, Maggie called Tess and the detective. She'd explained that Robert Gustev had held a staff meeting and kept her after for a brief discussion. He got the feeling that it hadn't been a positive discussion, but Francois didn't ask what it was about and Kevin hadn't wanted to step on the detective's toes. She'd found the envelope when she'd returned to her office.

Kevin assessed the space. It was neat and orderly. A handful of files were stacked on the corner of the desk, pens, a stapler and tape dispenser lined up in a row across the top edge. The books on the bookshelf behind the desk had been organized alphabetically by the author's last name. A printer sat on a credenza to the right of the door. There were no personal items at all. No photos of Maggie or a pet. No artwork on the wall, which he found surprising. But according to Maggie there was also nothing out of place or missing. Whoever had left the note had come in, dropped it on her desk and walked out. Their mystery person had likely touched nothing and spent less than twenty seconds inside the office.

Which meant there wouldn't be much to go on.

Maggie's voice pulled him out of his thoughts. "I have no idea what it means. I told you about the legend associated with the ruby, but I don't know anything about a curse."

Francois rubbed his chin. "Maybe the note writer meant the legend."

"The legend doesn't mention anything about people dying," Kevin pointed out.

"Yes, well..." Francois shrugged and slid the note into a plastic evidence bag.

Kevin could tell that Francois didn't think much of the threat, but it put him on edge. Even more on edge. Someone had come into Maggie's private space and lobbed a direct threat of violence. He couldn't just dismiss it as idle. The fact that there were no cameras in the areas only accessible by staff meant that any one of a number of people could have left the note, including someone who worked with Maggie.

Kevin had spent the last hour shadowing Francois while he'd questioned the staff members, but no one had admitted to seeing a stranger or anyone enter Maggie's office. He wasn't surprised by that. One thing he and Francois would probably agree on was that it seemed more and more likely that the person behind the theft, and now the threat against Maggie, was someone well known by Maggie and the employees of the Larimer. Someone who was pretty confident their presence in the areas of the museum restricted to employees wouldn't be notable if they were seen.

"I'll take the note in to be fingerprinted," Francois said.

"That's it?" Maggie shot back.

"There's not much more we can do, Ms. Scott. I'd urge the museum to increase its security measures. It wouldn't be a bad idea to install cameras in the employee work areas, at least the hallways here."

"Francois, this is a direct threat aimed at Maggie," Kevin said.

Francois darted a look between Kevin and Maggie, assessing.

Okay, so maybe he'd come on a bit too strong, but he didn't think the detective was taking this situation seriously enough. "And the LAPD is doing what it can to address the threat, but you know how these things go. Without more, my hands are tied." Francois looked at Maggie again. "Ms. Scott, you should remain vigilant about your surroundings. If you see or are approached by anyone suspicious, call me immediately." He handed Maggie his business card and shot a glance at Kevin. "Or I'm sure you can also call Mr. Lombard if you're feeling unsafe."

Kevin fought back the urge to punch the man.

"Kevin, a word please." Francois stepped out of Maggie's office and moved away down the hall where they wouldn't be overheard.

"Don't you think you might be getting too emotionally involved with this case?" Francois said, shooting a pointed glance at the door to Maggie's office.

"No, I don't." The lie hung between them. "Have you considered that your suspicion of Mag—Ms. Scott," Kevin corrected himself but not before Francois's brow cocked, "might be leading you to dismiss the danger she could be in?"

Francois scowled. "I'm not dismissing anything, including the possibility that Ms. Scott left this threatening letter for herself."

"Oh, come on." Francois was exasperating. "Why would she do that?"

"To take suspicion off herself." Francois held up a hand. "Look, I'll keep an open mind if you will. I think we can agree that whatever we're dealing, with Ms. Scott is at the center of it whether she wants to be or not."

"At the center, how?"

"Well, just look at the situation." Francois began ticking off his points using his fingers. "Ms. Scott advocated for bringing the ruby to the Larimer. She designed the exhibit and knew all about the security measures."

"She was one of several people who knew about the security measures for the Viperé."

"I'll give you that. She was at the museum the night the ruby was stolen."

"She was also attacked that night."

"True. She lives on the property where another museum employee was found dead, possibly murdered." Francois continued his list. "She was married to a man charged with embezzlement, who subsequently died, and no one can find the money. And now she has received a mysterious threat citing a curse no one seems to have heard of."

"None of that proves she had anything to do with the things that have happened."

Francois's scowl deepened. "I'm not a man who believes in coincidence. I'd think as a former law enforcement professional, you'd appreciate that."

"I think you're wrong about Maggie," Kevin said. "I think she's in real danger, and the reference in this threat to a curse might explain why."

"You think we might be dealing with some sort of conspiracy nut? A fanatic who's heard of or even made up some curse and associated it with the Viperé ruby?"

"I think it's possible. The internet can put all sorts of questionable ideas in people's heads, especially when there is already the hook of the so-called Viperé legends. I think it's definitely worth looking into."

Francois shook his head, but he was also rubbing his chin, a sign Kevin now knew that the detective was considering the point he'd made. "I have enough on my plate. I can't start chasing down curses. And—" he shot Kevin a pointed look "—I think you might be stretching here."

"Then I'll do it, but if I bring you something concrete, you have to promise you'll give it real consideration."

Francois considered for a moment longer before nodding. "Okay, but no cowboy stuff. If you find something, you bring it to me right away."

They shook on the deal.

Francois started to walk away then stopped and turned back. "Lombard, a word of advice. I know you think you can handle it, but it's very easy to lose your objectivity around a woman like Ms. Scott. I'd be careful if I were you."

Maggie was still standing exactly where she'd been when he'd left her office with Detective Francois. She looked scared and unsure. The urge to take her in his arms hit him again, even stronger this time.

"Come on. I'll take you home."

"Detective Francois thinks I left the note for myself, doesn't he? He thinks I was involved in the theft and that this is all just some big game I'm playing with everyone." Her voice was edging toward hysteria. "He probably thinks I killed Kim."

"Hey." Kevin reached out to her, and despite knowing what Detective Francois would say if he walked by and saw them, he pulled Maggie to his chest. "Francois is just doing his job. He'll come to see you had nothing to do with any of this."

Maggie pulled back just enough to look up at him with teary eyes. "You believe me though, don't you? You believe that I had nothing to do with any of this?"

He held her gaze. "I believe you."

Chapter Ten

I believe you.

Kevin's words bounced around in Maggie's mind during the drive from the Larimer to her house. She knew he'd been suspicious of her at first, but a good part of the weight, the fear, that she'd been carrying inside since she'd been attacked was alleviated by those three words.

I believe you.

She'd never developed such strong feelings so quickly for a man, but her attraction to Kevin was palpable and intense. She needed to keep it in check though. He seemed like a good investigator, as good a man as he was all those years ago, but it would be folly to trust him with her heart again.

He pulled to a stop in front of her cottage, and she exited the car, careful to avoid looking over at Kim's house. She didn't know how long she could keep living in the cottage, because of her feelings about Kim's death occurring only steps away and because she wasn't sure whether whatever relative of Kim's who inherited it would allow her to stay on the property. Just the idea of having to find a new place to live and move was too much to deal with, so she put the thought out of her mind. She just wanted to go inside and block out everything and everyone for a while.

She opened the door and turned back to Kevin. “Thank you for the ride.”

“You’re welcome. I’ll be back in the morning to take you to work.”

She jolted with surprise. “You don’t have to do that.”

“I know I don’t have to, but in light of the assault against you and the threat today, I think it’s best to err on the side of caution.”

“I—”

She was cut off by the sound of her ringing phone. It was Apollo Bouras, the dealer she’d called earlier.

“It’s one of the dealers I reached out to earlier today. I have to take this.” She accepted the call.

Apollo was about twenty years older than Maggie, a Greek immigrant who knew everything there was to know about Southern European antiquities. He also did a fair amount of business as a go-between for sellers and buyers of rare gems.

“I’m sure you’ve heard about the theft of the Viperé ruby,” Maggie said, jumping right into the heart of the call.

“Yes. Shocking,” Apollo answered.

“Well, the museum is working with an investigator, and we’d like to pick your brain.”

“Of course, of course. I will do anything I can to help you. You know that. Why don’t you stop by the shop tomorrow? I’ll be in all day as usual.”

“Wonderful. Say tomorrow morning around nine thirty?” She looked at Kevin and got a nod from him confirming the time worked.

“Nine thirty is perfect,” Apollo answered. “See you then.”

She ended the call and turned back to Kevin.

"So I guess you will need that escort after all." The full-wattage smile he gave her sent her heart fluttering.

She returned the smile. "We could meet there." She was flirting, and it felt, well, it felt a little strange under the circumstances, but also exciting.

His gaze lowered to her mouth, and she noticed a subtle change in his expression. When his eyes met hers again there was a spark of desire there. The cool evening air warmed. She took a small step toward him, and he did the same, slipping his hand behind her head and lowering his mouth to hers.

The kiss was better than anything she had imagined, and she had to admit that she'd imagined kissing Kevin again several times over the years. She'd never forgotten what it felt like to be in his arms. The warm sensation quickly intensified into something fiery. She slid her hands up his chest and around his neck, pulling him closer and melding her body to his.

She'd forgotten how good a kisser he was. Extraordinary really. Need boiled inside of her. This couldn't be normal. The smoldering desire between them had to be some sort of response to the intensity of the situation they found themselves in.

She pulled back from the kiss. "I should go in."

He stepped back, his eyes shrouded. "I'll pick you up in the morning."

"Good night, Kevin."

His dark brown eyes were piercing. "Sleep tight, Maggie."

MAGGIE SPENT A fitful night tossing and turning. The few snatches of sleep she was able to get alternated between grief-riddled dreams of Kim and memories of her past relationship with Kevin. Her past and present were colliding in an emotional tumult that felt like it had the potential to spin out of control. She awoke more exhausted than she'd been when she fell asleep.

She was working on her second mug of coffee when Kevin rang her doorbell, and she let him in.

He held out the to-go cup in his hand. "Looks like you don't need this," he said, handing her the cup.

She smiled and took the cup. "Not right now, but probably later."

He cocked his head to the side. "Didn't get much sleep last night?"

Heat crept up her neck as she recalled the dreams she'd had about him. "Not much, no." She turned away from him, carrying her empty coffee mug to the sink. "We should get going."

Even with her back to him, she could feel Kevin's frown. After a moment, he rose and tossed his trash in the garbage bin.

She grabbed her purse from the sofa as they passed through the living room and headed for the front door.

A police cruiser and an unmarked black sedan pulled into the driveway as she locked up.

Detective Francois stepped out of the sedan and walked toward her and Kevin. He stopped at the bottom of her stoop.

"Ms. Scott." He held a piece of paper out to her. "I have a warrant to search these premises."

AS A FORMER police officer, Kevin was used to search warrants, but he wasn't usually on this side of the execution.

"Can I see that?" He gestured to the warrant in Maggie's shaking hand. She was looking at it, but he could tell she wasn't seeing the words. She handed him the papers.

He skimmed them, looking for the most important piece of information. The suspected crime that Francois listed to justify the search. Felony theft. Second-degree murder.

Murder.

That must mean the police had determined that Kim Sumika hadn't accidentally overdosed.

He skimmed the rest of the warrant, noting the items the officers were allowed to seize. It was pretty typical. Electronics. Diaries. Writings. Receipts. Medications. Disposable gloves. Cleaning products. Vacuums. The warrant also gave Francois the right to search Maggie's car and phone.

So Francois thought Maggie could have killed her best friend, cleaned up after herself then pulled off the theft of a priceless ruby.

He caught Francois's eyes, but the man was good. He saw nothing there.

"I don't understand. I didn't do anything," Maggie pleaded.

Francois turned to her. "Ms. Scott, I understand this has to be upsetting for you. You are welcome to stay as long as you do nothing to interfere with the search in any way. We should only be an hour or two since your residence isn't terribly large."

"Should I have a lawyer present?" Maggie's gaze darted to him.

The knot in his stomach grew. He wished he could do or say something to help her in that instant, but he knew there was nothing. Francois had a warrant, and that gave him the power to be there. They could only make the situation worse. "You could," he started to say.

"But we do not have to wait for your attorney to arrive before beginning our search," Francois declared, correctly.

Kevin worked to check the anger he felt toward the detective at the moment. "Detective Francois, could I speak with you for a moment. Please," he added when the detective looked ready to refuse.

Francois hesitated for a moment then nodded.

They walked to the end of the driveway, away from the two officers who had shown up with Francois.

"It's not personal," Francois said. "I'm just doing my job. Maggie Scott had the means and opportunity to carry out the theft of the ruby and the murder of Kim Sumika."

"Let's slow down for a minute. You know for sure Kim Sumika's death was a homicide?"

Francois looked as if he was kicking himself for having said too much. He pressed his lips together tightly.

"Francois. Detective, please. I would really appreciate it if you could tell me what you can."

Francois sighed heavily. "The coroner found heroin and Rohypnol in Kim Sumika's system. The killer may have thought we wouldn't check, but Dr. Brown is thorough."

"So the killer sedates Kim with the Rohypnol then injects her with the heroin, making it look like she overdosed."

"That's the working theory at the moment."

"You still have a timing issue. Maggie was at the museum when Kim Sumika was killed."

"Sumika's house is only ten minutes from the museum. That gives Maggie plenty of time to get to Kim's place, slip her the overdose and get back to the museum in time to be 'assaulted'—" Francois made air quotes "—giving her a pretty good alibi for the theft and murder."

"Come on!" Kevin shook his head, accentuating the absurdity of the idea.

"You know how this goes, Lombard. If she's innocent, we'll find nothing and move on, but you know I have to do this."

He understood where Francois was coming from. He'd stood in his exact spot hundreds of times and not that long ago. That didn't mean he liked it now.

"I'm going to take Maggie out of here."

"That's fine. You'll have to take your car though. We'll need hers for searching and processing. It's included in the warrant. And, Ms. Scott, we'll need your phone before you leave. If you give me a minute, I can have a tech copy the hard drive now, and I can give it right back."

Kevin appreciated the gesture.

He started back toward Maggie, but Francois's hand on his arm stopped him.

"Lombard, I am keeping an open mind here, I assure you," Francois said with a seriousness that hardened his jaw. His gaze darted to Maggie then back to Kevin's face. "You would do well to do the same."

Chapter Eleven

The sky was cloudless, the day already warm even though it was only midmorning. Maggie stared out of the car window as Kevin drove. They stopped at a red light, and she watched a group of kids, about middle school age, amble down the sidewalk, chatting and laughing, backpacks strapped to their backs. It was a picture-perfect day, and yet Maggie felt like she was in purgatory. She hadn't understood most of what was written in the search warrant, but several words had stood out.

Theft.

Second-degree murder.

Detective Francois thought she'd killed Kim.

She was a murder suspect.

Despite her question about having a lawyer present at the search, the reality was she didn't have the money for a lawyer. She was barely getting by. If not for Kim offering her a cut-rate rent far below the going market, she wouldn't have been able to afford to live in such a nice neighborhood so close to the Larimer.

A lump grew in her throat, but she was determined not to cry. He'd suggested they head out to meet with her dealer friend as they'd planned, and she'd agreed. The last thing she wanted to do was stand around while strangers pawed through her belongings.

Her phone dinged, indicating she'd received a text message. Her father had made a 1:15 p.m. lunch reservation at a restaurant she wasn't familiar with in Chinatown.

She couldn't hold back the groan that escaped as she read it.

"What is it? Is everything okay?" Kevin darted a look at her from the driver's side of the car.

"No, but yes. Nothing for you to worry about. It's just my father."

Kevin grinned. "How is Boyd?"

"Getting married."

Kevin's grin widened. "I guess he's pretty good then."

She groaned. "He wants me to meet his fiancée today over lunch. What kind of woman willingly becomes a man's seventh wife? The man is clearly incapable of making a real commitment to anyone."

"I know Boyd was a nontraditional father, but he's a good guy. A bit impulsive, but he embraces life."

"Of course you'd take his side. He always liked you, probably because he saw so much of himself in you."

A heavy silence fell over the car.

"I'm sorry. I shouldn't have said that."

"You don't have to be sorry for how you feel. I hurt you. From your perspective, I can see how you view me and your father as alike. But, Maggie, I was a twenty-year-old idiot when I walked away from you. I didn't realize what I had until it was too late. And I was even stupider for not crawling back to you on my hands and knees once I realized what a fool I'd been. But I want a second chance."

"Kevin, I can't do this right now."

"No, I know. It's terrible timing, but let me do one thing. Let me go to lunch with you."

She was surprised. “You want to be my date to lunch to meet my father’s fiancée?”

“Yes, you said it yourself, your dad and I get along well. I can help keep the conversation going, smooth over any awkward bumps and be a sounding board for your inevitable meltdown afterward.”

She slid a sidelong glance at him. “I’m not going to melt down.”

“Of course you won’t. So what do you say?”

It wasn’t a bad idea. He could be a buffer if she needed one.

“Okay.” She hesitated. “But about this second chance.”

He reached for her hand. “I meant it. I’m not going to run away this time. I know that I want a second chance with you. You may not want the same, and I’ll have to live with that if you don’t, but I’m putting it out there. Just think about it, okay?”

She nodded. It was going to be hard not to think about it, but there was a more pressing situation facing them at the moment. She forced herself to focus on it.

Kevin parked in the lot behind the store, and they made their way to Xanthe’s Treasures. The chime from the security system rang out as they stepped through the doors.

Antiques filled every shelf and cabinet, and Maggie knew each item had been carefully curated by Apollo Bouras. The items that were worth substantial amounts were locked in glass cases strategically placed in the space.

Apollo flashed a quick smile as she and Kevin entered, before turning back to the customer he’d been working with, an older woman who reeked of money in a black-and-white-checked Chanel suit, string pearls and low-heeled pumps.

They milled around the store while Apollo finished with his client.

It took close to fifteen minutes for Apollo's customer to finally settle on her purchases and pay. Apollo kept a cheery smile on his face until the woman had left the store and disappeared from sight.

"Finally. Mrs. Lowell is richer than a sultan, but the woman is just so indecisive."

"It's fine. We didn't have a problem waiting." She exchanged air kisses with Apollo.

"Maggie, my God! How could something like this have happened?" Apollo said, holding her at arm's length. "I can't believe it."

"Me either, but I'm hoping you can help. Oh, excuse my rudeness. This is Kevin Lombard. His firm has been hired by the board of directors of the museum to try and locate the Viperé ruby."

The two men shook hands.

Apollo focused on Maggie again, confusion wrinkling his brow. "And you're here because of the Viperé?"

"Well, we think it's possible the thief has plans to sell the Viperé on the black market."

Apollo looked thoughtful. "That would make some sense. It's quite valuable. Even more so if the thief is able to find someone who will cut it for him."

Maggie brought a hand to her throat, a small gasp escaping.

Apollo chuckled. "Don't stroke out on me. It's just speculation."

"I honestly hadn't thought about the thief cutting the ruby," she answered.

"Why would it be more valuable cut?" Kevin asked.

"It would be easier to conceal and move for one thing.

The authorities are on the lookout for a large ruby, not several small rubies," Maggie answered.

"And the thief could likely get more money overall as long as he finds someone who knows what they are doing when they cut the stone. It's like those investors who buy a company, chop it up and sell it for parts. Sometimes the parts are worth more than the whole. In this case, smaller stones can be set in several different settings, obscuring the origin of the whole."

Kevin nodded his head in understanding, but Maggie was still dealing with the shock of realizing the Viperé stone might not even exist any longer. At least, not in its original form.

"We're actually here looking for your help," Kevin said, giving her a look.

"Yes." She shook the shock away. Until she knew otherwise, she was going to assume the ruby was intact. And pray it stayed that way. "I know you have handled transactions involving jewelry and gems of a certain significance. Have you or any other dealer you know of had an inquiry from someone asking about the Viperé ruby?"

Apollo looked uncomfortable. "You know I keep my clients' information in the strictest of confidences."

Kevin's mouth tightened. "We could have the police visit."

Apollo frowned.

Maggie placed a hand on his forearm. Apollo required honey, not vinegar. "Apollo, I know you have the utmost integrity. We're not asking for confidential information. Just whether there's been anyone asking about the Viperé."

Apollo still did not look happy. "No. Not asking about the Viperé."

"But someone was asking about rubies?" she pressed.

"Not rubies per se, but whether I knew about any large, precious gemstones that might be on the market, or coming onto the market soon. I didn't have, or know of, a current seller, so I couldn't help the potential buyer."

"And who was this potential buyer?" Kevin said.

Apollo hesitated again.

"Please, Apollo," Maggie said.

Apollo gave a resigned sigh. "I can't imagine he'd have anything to do with the theft anyway. The Larimer is his museum, after all."

Maggie felt herself leaning in. "His museum?"

Apollo nodded. "Carter Tutwilder. He's the potential buyer who made the inquiry."

CARTER TUTWILDER'S OFFICE was in Los Angeles's financial district. Maggie called ahead to Tutwilder Industries, explaining who she was and that she'd like to speak to Mr. Tutwilder at his earliest convenience, that day if it was at all possible. Tutwilder had agreed to give them ten minutes.

The Tutwilder family had a long and storied history on the West Coast and in the Midwest. The family had built their fortune in agribusiness. They had their hands in farming, fuel, fisheries, grain and other commodities, as well as biotechnology, to name just a few industries that had contributed to their multibillion dollar fortune. Still, the family somehow managed to remain under the radar and out of the public eye.

Kevin pulled into a garage two blocks from the Wilshire Grand Center, and he and Maggie walked to the building.

Office space in the Wilshire went for thousands of dollars per square foot, and Kevin had no doubt that Tutwilder's offices would be among the grandest. He wasn't disappointed. Tutwilder Industries' offices comprised floors twenty-five through twenty-nine.

He and Maggie signed in with security in the lobby then took the elevator to the twenty-ninth floor.

The office suite was decorated in rich, dark colors of walnut and burgundy that gave the space an elegant and expensive feel.

An attractive young brunette looked up from her computer monitor as they made their way to her desk.

"Good afternoon and welcome to Tutwilder Industries. How may I help you today?" She smiled.

"We have an appointment with Mr. Tutwilder," Maggie said.

"And your names?"

Maggie gave their names, and the receptionist clicked a few keys on the computer. "Yes, of course. One moment, please."

The receptionist reached for the phone. She spoke softly into the receiver before hanging up and standing.

"Mr. Tutwilder is ready for you now. If you'll follow me, please."

Kevin looked at Maggie with raised eyebrows. He hadn't expected it to be so easy to get in to see a man like Tutwilder, but he'd been impressed when Maggie had convincingly argued to whichever gatekeeper she'd spoken to about arranging this meeting that Mr. Tutwilder would want to do whatever he could to help them find the Viperé ruby. And from all appearances, it had worked.

The receptionist led them down a long corridor full of large offices and busy-looking people in them. They stopped at the only office with a frosted-glass door and no nameplate.

The receptionist rapped on the door and waited until a brisk "come in" came from the other side.

She pushed open the door, and he and Maggie stepped around her and inside a spacious office outfitted with buttery black leather furniture and a massive glass-topped desk. But the showstopper was the view. A glass wall of windows overlooked downtown Los Angeles.

Carter Tutwilder rose from behind his desk.

"Ms. Scott," he said, circling the desk and offering his hand. "And you must be Kevin Lombard. Tess Stenning had said wonderful things about you. I trust you are getting close to finding the criminals who have absconded with the Viperé ruby."

"I am doing everything in my power along with the police," he said, shaking the man's hand.

The receptionist slipped from the room, shutting the door behind her.

Tutwilder made his way back behind the desk, and Kevin took the opportunity to really study the man.

He had the presence and confidence of someone who'd been born into wealth and privilege. He stood tall in a black suit that looked like it had been made specifically for him, which it probably had. The tailoring was impeccable, but it didn't quite mask the soft upper body. His face showed the beginnings of a double chin, and his hair had been combed over to hide a bald spot at his crown, again expertly, but there was only so much that could be done to fight a receding hairline.

Tutwilder sat, waving them into the chairs across from his desk. "So, how can I help you?"

"You are the chairman of the board of the Larimer Museum," Kevin started them off.

"Correct. And one of the museum's largest donors."

Maggie smiled. "You and the members of your family are very generous, and the museum appreciates it more than I can say."

Tutwilder relaxed, leaning back in his chair. "I'm happy to do it. The arts are so important and artists so underappreciated by society. There never seems to be enough funding."

"As one of the biggest donors, you received an invitation to the open house two nights ago, correct?"

Tutwilder smiled, but it wasn't as bright as the smile he'd given them when they'd entered. "I see where you're going with this. I did receive an invitation to the opening, of course, but unfortunately I had a prior commitment and could not make it."

"But you have an extensive art collection—" Kevin paused with intention "—that includes a collection of rare gems, I understand."

Tutwilder's eyes narrowed. "I do, although it's not common knowledge. I'd sure like to know how you came across that information."

He returned Tutwilder's narrow gaze. "I am an investigator."

"A very good one it would seem," Tutwilder said in a clipped tone.

"Mr. Tutwilder—"

"Ah, now, Ms. Scott. Please call me Carter."

"And I'm Maggie. Carter, please know that we mean no offense. Kevin and I thought that with your knowledge of gems you might be able to help point us in a few directions that we might not otherwise think of."

Kevin studied Tutwilder and saw that he wasn't buying Maggie's buttering him up. You didn't run a multibillion dollar corporation and not develop well-honed instincts for when someone was attempting to pull one over on you. He'd conducted enough suspect interviews to know that the best way to get information out of Tutwilder would be to go directly at him. He'd definitely anger the man, but it would be that anger that tripped him up.

"Where do you keep your collections?"

"That is need-to-know information, Mr. Lombard."

"I'm sure the LAPD will feel they need to know. I can call Detective Francois."

"Carter—" Maggie started then stopped abruptly when Tutwilder held up a hand.

"What are you suggesting? That I had something to do with the theft of the Viperé ruby?"

"I'm not suggesting anything," Kevin shot back. "I'm asking questions and seeking answers."

"Well, I don't like your questions."

"And I don't like your answers. We have it on good authority that you were asking about the purchase of rare jewels just a few weeks ago."

"We?" Tutwilder's angry gaze slid to Maggie's face.

Maggie wrapped her hand around his forearm and squeezed. "Carter—" she tried again.

And again Tutwilder cut her off. "I don't know where you are getting your information, but it appears you aren't as good an investigator as I first thought."

"So you haven't been looking to acquire more jewels for your private collection?"

"Mr. Lombard, what I am or am not looking to acquire is none of your concern." Tutwilder looked at Maggie. "Or yours, Ms. Scott. Now, I squeezed you into my schedule because I thought I might be of some help. I can see that I was mistaken. I really don't have any more time for you today."

Tutwilder slid on the glasses lying on his desk, an obvious dismissal.

Maggie gripped his arm tighter, goading him to stand.

Tutwilder could kick them out of his office, but he couldn't stop them from looking for more information on his collection.

"What the hell were you thinking?" Maggie whirled on him the moment they stepped into the elevator. "That man is my boss's boss, kind of. He's basically the head of the museum, and I'm already on thin ice. I can't afford to lose my job."

He didn't break eye contact. "Your job is the last thing you should be worried about right now. You could be on the verge of losing your freedom if we don't give Detective Francois someone else to focus on quickly."

Maggie stalled hard then focused on the closed elevator doors.

He sighed internally. This had not gone the way he'd hoped. "Look, I'm sorry if I came on strong in there, but Carter Tutwilder is lying."

Maggie didn't answer. They made the walk back to the car silently. She didn't speak until he'd paid the parking fee and they were headed out of the garage. "Even if he is lying, how are we going to prove it?"

His stomach churned because that was the million-dollar question and one he didn't have an answer to. "I don't know, but I will."

Chapter Twelve

Maggie would have liked to continue pushing ahead on the case, but it was 12:40 p.m. They were meeting her father and his fiancée at 1:15 p.m. Of course, when it came to her father, 1:15 p.m. more likely meant 1:30 p.m. or even 2:00 p.m., but she didn't want to be the one who was late to the party, so to speak.

"Do you need to stop by the museum before we head to the restaurant?" Kevin asked.

"No. There's no time and no point."

She really should call Robert and let him know she wouldn't be in until later in the afternoon. They didn't punch timecards at the museum. There were times when they were expected to stay late or come in early, so everyone just kept their own schedule. It wasn't unusual for any of them to take a half day for personal reasons, so it shouldn't be a problem that she hadn't gotten to work yet. *Shouldn't*, though, was the operative word. It still hurt that Robert had tried to sideline her. She skipped the call and shot Robert a text telling him she'd be in after lunch.

The restaurant was in Chinatown.

She and Kevin were the first to arrive, but they were seated immediately. The hostess had just walked away from the table when the door to the restaurant opened and Boyd Scott entered.

Her father and a woman who could only be Julie walked into the restaurant holding hands, and Maggie was instantly thankful that Kevin had invited himself to come along.

The panic must have shown on her face because Kevin leaned over from where he sat by her side and said, "You doing okay?"

She couldn't form words at the moment, but she smiled and nodded.

Just be polite and keep it together for one lunch. That was all she had to do. That wasn't hard. She was an adult, after all.

"Maggie," her father said, coming to a stop beside the table. He wore a sports jacket and khaki pants. The dark brown skin on the top of his head hadn't seen hair for more than two decades, but he still wore a neatly trimmed mustache above his top lip.

Maggie stood and let him pull her into a bear hug. He smelled as he usually did, like cigars. The familiarity of it put her more at ease. This was her father, Boyd, a new woman on his arm, but he was the same as always.

"This," her father said, reaching behind him for the hand of the woman he'd come into the restaurant with, "is Julie." He pulled Julie to his side.

Julie wore a ruffled white shirt, a peasant skirt with colorful flowers all over it and gold goddess sandals that laced up her legs. Her makeup was as colorful as her outfit—bursts of pink on her lips, her eyelids and her cheeks. Her blond hair was streaked with gray and piled atop her head in a messy updo. The thing that surprised Maggie most though was her age. Her father's girlfriends had trended down in age for the last decade and a half. Based on that, Maggie had been expecting a woman in her mid to early thirties. She had to be at least a decade older than thirty, which still made her more than a decade younger than her father, but at least she wasn't younger than Maggie like the last woman her father had insisted she meet. She knew it wasn't forward-thinking or liberated to care about the age difference between two consenting adults, and usually she didn't, but this was her father. Maybe it was childish and immature, but it was weird to think about her father dating someone younger than she was.

A wave of sickly sweet perfume came at Maggie as Julie threw her arms around her. "It's so nice to finally meet you."

"Oh! It's, ah, it's nice to meet you too."

"I'm sorry," Julie said, taking two steps back. "I'm a hugger. Especially when I'm nervous. I just want us to get along."

"Honey, now don't you worry about that. I know you and Maggie are going to get along swimmingly. Just you wait and see. Kevin!"

Several heads at the tables around them turned. Boyd Scott was a man with a personality that grabbed attention even when he didn't mean to.

Kevin stood. "Mr. Scott." Kevin extended a hand.

Body shook it heartily. "It's been a long time. I'm glad to see you and Maggie are spending time together again. Maybe you two will finally get your acts together then."

"Dad."

"Boyd, darling. Let's sit," Julie said, seeming to catch on quicker than her fiancé to Maggie's distress at his comments. "We have all lunch to catch up with the kids."

Maggie frowned. Now she was one of the kids. This woman barely knew her.

Kevin squeezed her hand. "You can do this," he mouthed.

She sucked in a deep breath and let it out slowly as they settled in at the table.

Maggie reached for the wine list. There was no way she was getting through this lunch without liquid help.

"Let's have champagne," her father said. "After all, we are celebrating. And it's on me."

Maggie's eyebrows arched. The restaurant her father had chosen wasn't going to be getting any spreads in a magazine, but it wasn't cheap either.

Her father laughed. "I know. I know. But I got a job."

Maggie's brow climbed higher.

"I didn't want to tell you until I got through the probationary period, but I've been working for a nonprofit for older adults. The organization provides classes—computer, horticultural, painting—and social activities like dances and cocktail hours. It's like summer camp for us mature individuals, but since most of the people who sign up are retired, we can do it all year round."

Maggie set the wine list down. "Wow, Dad, that's great. Congratulations."

Her father beamed. "Thank you, baby. That's actually how Julie and I met. She teaches the gardening and horticulture classes at the center."

"My husband and I used to own our own landscaping business," Julie added.

"Oh, that's great." What she knew about gardening could fit on a Post-it. She didn't even have plants in her house, couldn't keep them alive. But if Julie had owned a business, she wasn't under the illusion that marrying her father would be some sort of financial windfall.

"I started going to the center to have something to fill my days with," Boyd continued telling the story of how he and Julie met, "and when the office assistant moved to Phoenix to be with her children, the manager offered me the job."

Their waiter arrived. Her father ordered champagne for the table, and they each placed their orders. The restaurant had pretty standard American fare. Her father and Kevin ordered burgers and fries, Julie got the salmon and Maggie ordered the chicken salad.

"So, how long have you two been dating?" Kevin asked once the waiter had hurried off the put in their orders.

Boyd's brow arched. "I could ask the same question of you two."

"We're not dating, Dad."

"No? Then what is he doing here? No offense there, Kevin, but it's been a minute since I've seen you and my daughter together. Always liked you, though. I figured when you disappeared and Maggie stopped talking about you that she'd thrown you back into the ocean, so to speak."

"We're friends, Dad. I thought we were here to get to know Julie," she said, attempting to divert her father's attention from her love life to his own.

Kevin's shoulders shook with suppressed laughter.

"We are, we are. I want my two favorite ladies in the whole wide world to get to love each other as much as I love you both. But—" her father held his hand out palm up "—you can't just show up with your long-lost first love and expect me not to ask questions. I am your father."

Maggie massaged her temples.

"Boyd, darling, I think you're embarrassing Maggie.

She is your daughter, but she's a grown woman who may not want to talk about her love life with her father."

Maggie shot Julie a look of gratitude. Maybe she wasn't so terrible.

"So, Julie, why horticulture?" Kevin said, finally doing what she'd brought him along to do—keep the situation from going off the rails.

Julie explained that her husband had started the business before they'd met, and after they married she'd joined him. He'd passed away from a heart attack four years earlier. Their three children were scattered across the country, and none of them had the green thumb their parents had, so she'd sold the company after her husband's death.

The waiter came back with the champagne as she'd talked, and they toasted to the engagement.

Maggie had to admit, Julie wasn't what she'd expected and her father seemed genuinely happy. Not that he hadn't seemed happy at the beginning of the relationships with his other wives, but he did seem different with Julie. More grounded. The woman was an expert at rooting things. Maybe she'd found a way to give her father roots.

They ate and chatted, and Maggie found herself genuinely liking Julie. In addition to her job at the center, Julie liked to sew and paint and to visit with her grandchildren. Maggie was reeling a bit from the realization that once her father and Julie married, she'd have stepsiblings. At the age of thirty-six, she was finally going to have a sister and two brothers. And five step nieces and nephews. As much as she'd always wished she'd had more family, it was all suddenly a bit much to take in.

More than anything, she was thankful that the theft at the museum didn't come up. She was not surprised her father didn't know about the theft or Kim's death. He wasn't much of a paper reader and didn't particularly care for art. She didn't want to worry him nor did she want to hash through the mess that was her life at the moment.

Her head spun, and she felt sick to her stomach. She pushed her chair back from the table abruptly. "Excuse me for a moment."

She rose and made her way toward the restrooms.

"Maggie." Julie rushed to catch up to her at the door to the ladies' room. "Your father wanted me to check on you and make sure you were okay."

"I'm fine." She tried for a smile. "I think I might have had a little too much champagne."

Julie laid a light hand on Maggie's forearm. "I just wanted to let you know that I love your father and I plan to do my very best to make him happy. And I hope that we can forge our own relationship."

Maggie didn't have to force a smile this time. "I hope so too."

Maggie's phone rang.

"I should be getting back to the table. I'm sure the guys are eager to know you're okay."

The call was from Robert. "I'll be there in a moment. This is my boss. Probably wanting to know when I'm coming in today."

Maggie accepted the call as Julie made her way back to the table.

"Hi, Robert. I know I should have called you and let you know that I was going to be in late today, but this morning has been hectic."

"That's one way to put it. I just got off the phone with Carter Tutwilder."

Crap.

"I know I should have called you first—"

"It wouldn't have made a difference. Carter was not pleased to hear that the police searched your home this morning."

"How did Carter even know about that?"

"Are you saying it's not true?" Robert shot back.

"No. The police did search my home this morning, but I had nothing to do with that. They are investigating—"

"Yes, they are. And in order for them to have gotten a search warrant for your home, they'd have to have some sort of evidence that you could be involved in a crime. I'm sorry, Maggie, we just can't have that kind of rumor and supposition associated with the Larimer."

Her jaw clenched. "Robert, we've discussed this."

"That was before. Carter and the board agree. Until this matter is resolved, you are being placed on administrative leave."

She was sure Carter had agreed. She didn't know how he found out about the search of her house, but she had no doubt that his decision to have the board put her on administrative leave was motivated by the meeting they'd just had.

"Until the matter is over. Robert, police investigations can take months. Even years."

Administrative leave meant no paycheck. They may as well have fired her. They probably would. They just wanted to get their ducks in a row before they did.

"I'm sorry, Maggie. I'll have the personal effects from your office shipped to your house."

The line went dead.

"Maggie?"

She turned to find Kevin behind her.

"You okay?" he asked, concern crinkling the skin around his eyes.

She shook her head. "No, no, I'm not." It was happening again. Losing her job. Being suspected of having committed a crime. Being ostracized. Just like it had in New York with Ellison.

She swallowed and said the words that sent panic streaking through her. "I just got fired."

Chapter Thirteen

Maggie went back to the table and pleaded sickness to her father and Julie, promising that they'd get together again soon. Now she and Kevin stood outside in front of the restaurant.

She turned angry eyes on him. "I just lost my job. The board has voted to put me on administrative leave until the police case is over." The words burned their way out of her throat.

"I'm sorry. I—" Kevin reached out to her, but she stepped back, away from his touch.

"You went into Tutwilder's office like a bull in a china shop and basically accused the chairman of the board of the museum of what? Stealing a priceless artifact." She shook with anger.

Kevin held his hands out. "Look, I could have been more diplomatic. I wasn't thinking."

"That's just it. You never think about me. When we were together in college, it was all about you."

Kevin's face hardened. "It was never about me. It was about making money so my mom didn't have to struggle anymore and so Tanya wouldn't have to worry about paying for medical school."

"Was it?" she shot back at him. "That's why you played

football. Why you went into the NFL. But it doesn't explain why you dumped me." Her voice dropped low. "We were planning a life together after graduation. A family. And then, just like that—" she snapped her fingers "—you were out. Gone." She looked at him and all the hurt she'd felt the moment he told her it was over welled up again. "And what? Now you want a second chance?"

"Walking away from you was the biggest mistake of my life. I have and will always regret it and I am more sorry than I can ever express. I know I hurt you—"

"You have no idea," she hissed. Hot tears rolled down her cheeks. She wished she could stop them, but she was well past controlling her emotions. Or the words that were tumbling from her mouth. "I was pregnant."

Kevin stilled, the color fleeing from his face.

"I found out a week after you broke up with me," she continued. "And the next week, I miscarried."

"You were pregnant?" His voice was barely audible. "Why didn't you tell me?"

"Because you weren't there." The accusation whipped from her lips.

He flinched.

"And then it didn't matter."

Anger flashed in his eyes. "It mattered. You should have told me."

"No." She pointed at him. "I was nineteen, pregnant, and the man I thought was going to love me forever had just walked out on me. You of all people do not get to judge my choices."

His jaw clenched. "I had a right to know."

She stepped forward, holding his gaze. "Then you should have been there."

A long moment passed.

"Is that why you married Ellison after we broke up? Because I wasn't there?"

She shook her head, some of the anger she felt toward him dissipating. It was useless being angry. It wouldn't get her job back, and it wouldn't change anything. "I'm not doing this with you. The past is in the past, and that's where I'm leaving it."

She turned and started away from him.

"Where are you going?" He jogged to catch up with her.

"Home." She pulled out her phone and called up the rideshare app. "I'll get there myself."

"Maggie—"

"No." She turned to him, looking him in the eye. "I don't want to be around you right now, Kevin."

KEVIN CAUGHT TANYA at her apartment the next morning before she left for her shift at the hospital. Tanya already had her coat on, thermos of hot coffee in hand, when she opened the door to him.

"Kevin? Hi, what's up? Are you okay?" she asked, stepping back so he could enter the apartment.

He didn't waste time or mince words. "You knew about Maggie's miscarriage? About the baby, didn't you?"

"How did you—"

"Maggie told me. That's what you were going to tell me the other day before you stopped yourself."

Tanya sighed and set her thermos down on the side table next to her purse. "I knew."

"Why didn't you tell me?" Fury rose in his tone.

"Because I couldn't. Maggie came into the student health center once she realized she might be pregnant. You know I held a work-study job there while we were in school. I was on duty. Patient confidentiality laws prohibited me from saying anything to you or anyone about a patient's medical history."

He glowered at her. "You're my sister. It's been years."

She shook her head. "It doesn't matter who I am or how many years it's been. Confidentiality still applies. And, to be honest with you, I'm not sure I would have told you if I could have."

He threw up his hands. "Is everybody losing their minds?" he yelled.

"Kevin, there was nothing you could have done. Miscarriages are common, much more common than most people even realize. Telling you would have only left you feeling guilty for something that you had no control over." She reached out, placing a hand on his arm. "Something that was not in any way your fault, do you understand me?"

He understood her just like she understood where his anger emanated from. Fear. Fear that his decision to break up with Maggie had upset her enough to cause a miscarriage.

"If I hadn't left—" he said softly.

"She would have still lost the baby," Tanya said firmly.

"I should have been there for her."

"What is it Mom always says, 'the shoulda, woulda, couldas will drive you up a wall if you let them'?" She gave him a small smile. "You can't change the choices you made, and you shouldn't want to. Right or wrong, they made you, and to some extent Maggie, who you are now. And you're not that bad." She gave a little sister shrug he knew was intended to draw a smile from him.

He wasn't ready to smile, but talking to his sister did make him feel a little better. It didn't alleviate all his guilt. He wasn't sure anything could do that, but he felt a little lighter than he had when he'd walked into her apartment. He pulled his sister into a tight hug.

"So Maggie finally told you," Tanya said after they pulled apart. "Interesting."

"What's interesting about it? She was mad at me for getting her fired, and she shot it at me like a bullet."

Tanya's mouth fell open. "You got her fired?"

He ran a hand over his head. His life felt as if it was spinning out of control, and he didn't like it. "Not on purpose. I came on a little strong when questioning her boss's boss, and he's taking it out on her."

"You remember what I said about you. Maggie. This case." She threw her hands up in a gesture simulating an explosion. "Kaboom."

"I know, I—"

"Should have listened to your younger, but wiser, sister." She pressed her palms to her chest. "Yes, you should have."

"Didn't you just say something about 'shoulda, woulda, couldas'? I'm trying to remember what that was."

"Point taken. So what are you going to do now?"

"I have to get my head on straight and focus. West Investigations has been hired to find the ruby, and I'm convinced its theft is somehow tied to Maggie's friend's murder."

"And Maggie is intent on helping solve said friend's murder." Tanya looped her purse over her shoulder and picked up her thermos. "Well, maybe you'll have the rarest of opportunities, big brother. You might be able to rectify some of your 'shoulda, woulda, couldas.'"

Chapter Fourteen

"Thanks for coming in," Detective Francois said, settling into the chair on the opposite side of the table from Maggie.

Maggie had spent the first morning of her forced leave giving her house a deep clean and chastising herself for letting her anger get the better of her the day before with Kevin. Detective Francois had shown up on her doorstep around noon, requesting her presence down at the station for a formal interview. He'd posed it as a question, but she'd gotten the distinct impression she didn't have a choice.

She'd hesitated a moment, wondering if she should have a lawyer present, but had dismissed the idea quickly. She had nothing to hide. The faster Detective Francois saw that she'd had nothing to do with the theft or Kim's murder, the quicker he could turn his attention to viable suspects.

So she'd ridden to the police station beside him in his unmarked police sedan.

He'd shown her into an interrogation room and offered her coffee and water, which she'd declined. She considered a lawyer a second time when Detective Francois read her Miranda rights, but she again rejected the idea. She didn't have the money, and she didn't have anything to hide.

"There are just a few things I want to clarify." He looked up from the notepad in front of him and gave her a smile she guessed was meant to be disarming. To her, it looked a little more predatory. No matter how polite Detective Francois was, she wasn't going to make the mistake of thinking that he was her friend. He was looking for a thief and a murderer, and right now she knew she was his best suspect.

She flashed him a quick smile. "Anything I can do to help, Detective. Have you made any headway with Kim's case?"

His smile tightened. "I assure you we are doing everything we can."

"I'm sure you are," she lied.

"Just so I'm sure I have things correct, can you go over the night of the theft and finding Ms. Sumika's body again?"

Maggie bit back her frustration and walked the detective through the worst night of her life once again.

"And when was the last time, before you found Ms. Sumika, that you were in her house?"

Maggie thought for a moment. "Two evenings before. Kim invited me over for dinner. She did that on occasion. She did seem a little distracted."

Detective Francois perked up. "Distracted? How?"

"Like she had something on her mind. I asked her about it, and she said it was nothing." Guilt hung heavy on her heart. "I wish I'd pressed her on it."

"You have no idea what might have been worrying her?"

"No. I was assigned to take the lead on designing the Viperé exhibit, but we were all under a bit of stress with the donors' open house coming up and making sure everything went as scheduled. I remember thinking that it could just be that."

"Huh." He wrote something she couldn't read on the notepad.

Detective Francois's eyes narrowed to slits. "So, two days before. That was the last time you were in Ms. Sumika's house."

"Yes, that's what I said."

"And the last time you saw her was the day of the donors' open house?"

"That's right. Right before the event, Kim complained of a migraine. I had everything under control, so I told her to go home and rest."

Detective Francois cocked his head to the side and gave her a contemplative look. "That didn't seem odd to you? I mean, this donors' open house is a big deal, right?" Maggie nodded. "So suddenly Ms. Sumika is too sick to attend, and neither you nor Mr. Gustev thought that was odd?"

Maggie fought to keep her annoyance in check. Detective Francois hadn't known Kim or how devoted she was to the museum. Then again, it seemed like there was a lot she hadn't known about Kim either. She hadn't thought it was suspicious for Kim to miss the event at the time, but now… Maybe she should have paid a little more attention to Kim in the last days of her life.

"Kim suffered from migraines," she answered. "I didn't think it was suspicious that the stress of the new exhibit and the party got to her."

Detective Francois frowned. "What do you know about Ms. Sumika's finances?"

Maggie shrugged. "Nothing, really. I mean, I knew she'd inherited the house from her parents. I know how much a place like that would go for, so I assumed Kim wasn't financially strapped, even with the gambling. At least, not on paper."

The detective leaned forward. "What do you mean 'at least, not on paper'?"

Maggie found herself instinctively leaning away from the detective. She could see why he'd insisted on having this conversation in an interrogation room. It was effectively intimidating.

"I didn't mean anything. Just that houses like Kim's sell for quite a bit these days. Neither of us made a fortune working for the Larimer, but I figured Kim at least had the house as an asset."

"And your rental income."

"Yes, although she wasn't charging me anywhere near market rate."

"Right." He pulled stapled sheets of paper from between the pages of his notebook. "Have you seen this before?" He passed the pages across the table to her.

Last Will and Testament. The first paragraph looked to be standard boilerplate language with Kim's name typed onto a thick black line.

"I've never seen this before this moment, no."

Detective Francois reached for the papers and flipped the pages until he got to a section highlighted in yellow. "Please read this paragraph for me."

Maggie read, her heart picking up its pace until it was thundering as she read the last words.

Kim had left her house and all personal possessions to Maggie.

She met Detective Francois's gaze. "I didn't know."

"You had no idea you were the sole benefactor, save for a few charitable bequests, of Kim Sumika's will?"

"I had no idea, Detective. You have to believe me."

Detective Francois studied her.

She couldn't tell if he did, in fact, believe her, but she was stunned. Kim hadn't even hinted about the arrangements she'd made. Maggie knew she'd been an only child, but she recalled Kim speaking about a cousin in Indiana. Heck, she was surprised her friend even had a will. She'd only had one drawn up after Ellison had died without any instructions regarding his final wishes. Since they were divorced by then, she hadn't had any say in how his property was distributed. She'd heard his sister got everything, but it hadn't been her place to inquire.

Detective Francois took the will from her and slid it back between the pages of his notebook. "One of your other colleagues mentioned that there was a group that wasn't happy with the Larimer exhibiting the Viperé ruby. They staged a protest in front of the museum several weeks ago."

The sudden change in topic was jarring. She just looked at the detective for a moment.

"Yes," she answered finally. "Ah, the Art and Antiquities Repatriation Project people. They've staged protests at various museums in California and elsewhere against exhibits that show items that are the subject of cultural or repatriation claims."

"Are you a member of this organization or any similar organization?"

Maggie frowned. "No."

"Several of the board members I spoke with mentioned that you'd made an impassioned argument against the Larimer mounting this exhibit. Why is that?"

She didn't try to hide her irritation this time. "I wasn't arguing against the exhibit. I just thought that the board should be aware of and prepared for the fact that not everyone was going to agree with a decision to exhibit the Viperé."

"Huh." He tapped his pen against the notepad. "And did you agree with the board's decision to move forward?"

"I didn't disagree. It's a complex issue, as evidenced by the various lawsuits."

The detective leaned forward in his seat. "So you sympathize with the plaintiffs in these lawsuits and organizations like the one that was protesting your museum."

"I do," she gritted out, regretting her decision to speak with the detective without a lawyer.

It was clear that Detective Francois wasn't broadening the scope of the investigation. He was narrowing it. On her.

She reached for her purse at her feet. "Detective, I don't think I wish to answer any more questions without an attorney."

Detective Francois spread his hands out. "Ms. Scott, I'm just trying to get to the bottom of the crimes that seem to be swirling around you."

She stood, her chair scraping against the linoleum flooring. "And I hope you do get to the bottom of these crimes. For Kim's sake. But I promise you, when you do, I won't be the person you find there."

His expression clearly said he didn't believe that, but he stood and opened the door for her.

She marched down the short hallway leading away from the interrogation rooms and toward the front exit. She came to a stop just past the front reception area.

Kevin was leaning against the side wall, his arms crossed over his chest.

He straightened when he saw her.

"What are you doing here?" she asked, approaching

warily. Guilt gnawed at her. She didn't regret the choice she'd made in not telling him about her miscarriage when it happened, but it had been unkind to drop it on him like she had.

"I heard Detective Francois brought you in for questioning." He took a step closer to her.

"Do I want to know how you knew that?"

"I have my spies." He gave her a tepid smile. "Are you ready to get out of here?"

She definitely was, but they had so much they needed to talk about, and she wasn't in the right headspace to tackle it at the moment.

"It might be best if I get an Uber. I know we have things we need to talk about, and we will, but I just can't right now."

Kevin held his hands up. "I'm just offering you a ride home. We don't have to speak at all if you don't want."

She hesitated for a moment more before her shoulders relaxed and she returned his tepid smile with one of her own. "Okay then, thank you. A ride would be great."

He led her out the front doors of the police station and to the parking lot. The farther they got from the station, the more she relaxed.

"Do you mind if I ask you what Detective Francois asked you in there?"

She looked up at him, her throat constricting with fear. "He thinks I killed Kim. He pretty much said as much." She stopped walking, and Kevin paused alongside her. The man walking behind them shot them a dirty look and veered around them. "Kevin, Detective Francois had Kim's will, and she left me everything."

Kevin stroked his chin. "And I take it you had no idea she was going to do this."

"None at all." She pulled him to the side, out of the path of another pedestrian heading their way. "I mean, I knew Kim didn't have much family to speak of, but I never expected her to name me in her will."

Kevin's eyes darkened. "And because she did, it now looks like you had a motive for wanting her dead."

She nodded. "That seems to be what the detective is thinking. Kevin, I'm scared. Detective Francois isn't looking at anyone else. He thinks I did this. The theft and killing Kim."

He pulled her into his arms and dropped a kiss on the top of her head. "We're going to get to the bottom of this. I promise you."

Maggie wrapped her arms around him. Let his warmth seep through her. And tried to believe that he was right and that they'd find the real culprit.

Chapter Fifteen

Kevin led Maggie toward his Mustang. Tess had called him less than an hour earlier with the contact information for Josh Huber, head of the organization that had staged the protest against the Larimer Museum. She'd also informed him that Detective Francois had brought Maggie in for another round of questioning. He'd asked Tess to give Huber a call and set up a meeting for that afternoon and hopped in the car, headed for the police station.

Of course, the cops wouldn't let him into the interrogation room with Maggie, but he'd refused to leave. Detective Francois seemed to have homed in on Maggie as his prime suspect, and he wanted to be there if she needed support or, worse, needed someone to get her a lawyer. He'd breathed a sigh of relief when she'd walked out of the back of the police station.

But now he wasn't sure what he wanted to say to her. He was still upset with her for having kept her pregnancy from him, even if he was beginning to understand why she'd done so. More than anything, what he felt was remorse. Remorse for having not been there for her when she'd needed him. Guilt at having broken up with her at all. As much as he'd tried to convince himself that he'd had to leave everything behind and focus all his efforts and attention on football, he knew now that he'd just been scared. Scared of the intensity of his feelings for her. So he'd pushed her away. Ran away from her, actually.

But it hadn't worked. He'd never stopped thinking about her.

And now? Now that she was back in his life, he wasn't willing to let her go.

They both got in his car, but he made no move to start the engine.

"Maggie, about yesterday—"

She reached across the console for his hand. "Kevin, I'm sorry. I shouldn't have sprung the miscarriage on you like that," she interrupted.

"No, you have nothing to apologize for." He turned her hand palm up and ran his index finger along her wrist.

"I do. I was angry about losing my job and frustrated with everything that's going on right now, and I lashed out at you. I wanted to hurt you, and that was wrong."

He entwined his fingers with hers. "There are a lot of things I want to say, but I'm not sure how to say them at the moment."

"We do need to talk, but maybe right now isn't the best time. We both need time to process, and then there's this." She gestured toward the police station.

"So let's make a deal. After this—" he made the same gesture that she had toward the police station "—is all over, we'll talk. Really talk. Deal?"

She smiled at him, and his heart turned over.

"Deal," she said.

He wanted to kiss her. He always had loved kissing Maggie.

His phone beeped and he groaned inside. He pulled it from his pocket and looked at the screen. "It's a text from

Tess. She's set up a meeting for me with Josh Huber. He's the director of the Art and Antiquities Repatriation Project. The group that protested the Viperé exhibit at the Larimer. He has time to speak with me now." He looked at her with a question in his eye. "To see us now?"

"What are you waiting for?"

The Art and Antiquities Repatriation Project was housed in a rundown slip of a building that had seen better days. In fact, the entire block looked as if it had seen better days. There was a hotel on one corner, its front window so filthy the Vacancies Available sign was nearly obscured, and a corner store on the other. Several of the storefronts had signs proclaiming them For Rent, but a handful of businesses seemed to be holding on. A tarot card reader, a yoga studio and a fabric store were among them. Seeing this area, Kevin regretted bringing Maggie with him and even considered blowing the meeting off and rescheduling. But Maggie wasn't wrong about one thing: the pressure was building to give Francois anyone other than her to focus on as a suspect. And he hoped he could find that someone among the workers and volunteers at the Art and Antiquities Repatriation Project.

He parked at the curb in front of the address he had for the AARP. It took a minute for a voice to come over the intercom after he pressed the buzzer, but the door unlocked as soon as he identified himself and Maggie.

The space was uncomfortably warm bordering on sweltering, but it was clear that someone had done their best to do what they could with the AARP offices. The walls were a bright white made brighter by the recessed lighting illuminating the space. Fresh flowers sat in a vase on the desk just inside the doorway. The space was empty, save for several mismatched desks, some wood, some metal, in what was clearly a shared workspace. A number of file cabinets lined one wall, and a table in the back held a coffee maker, paper cups and other assorted items.

A man stepped out of the office at the back of the workspace. He was short, no more than five foot five or six, middle-aged and bald.

"Kevin Lombard?" The man approached them warily.

Kevin held out his hand. "Yes. And this is Maggie Scott. Thank you for meeting with us, Mr. Huber."

Josh Huber was the director of the Art and Antiquities Repatriation Project. Since he'd done his homework, Kevin knew that Huber had a degree in art history and that he'd spent more than a decade lecturing at a local college before taking on the position at the AARP. The protest at the Larimer was one of many the group had staged over the past several years. They'd seemingly had a few successes, getting a couple of museums and private collectors to donate smaller pieces to museums in the countries from which the pieces originated. But through his research into the group, he'd learned that repatriation was a tricky, costly and sometimes politically fraught endeavor.

Huber led them into his office. The space was cramped and stuffy.

"Sorry about the heat in here. Seems like no matter what I do, this office is always too hot." Huber dropped down into his office chair.

There was only one visitor's chair. He let Maggie take it and stood next to her.

"It's fine," Kevin said. "We don't want to take up too much of your time. We're hoping you can answer some questions for us."

"About our protest at the Larimer." Huber leaned back in his chair, pen in hand.

"Well, yes. I'm sure you're aware the Viperé ruby was stolen the night before last."

Huber frowned. "And you think that the Art and Antiquities Repatriation Project had something to do with that? Sorry to deprive you of an easy answer, but no way."

Maggie leaned forward in the chair. "We're not looking for an easy answer, Mr. Huber. We just want to get the ruby back."

Huber spun the pen in his hands. "I'm afraid I still can't help you. I'm not even sure I would if I could, but I can't."

"We know your organization believes that these types of items belong to the people of the countries from which they came," Kevin said.

"They do." Huber straightened. "They were stolen during periods of colonization." He pounded a fist on his desk.

Kevin caught the glance Maggie sent him. "Mr. Huber, we really aren't here to debate you on your views."

"I work at the Larimer," Maggie cut in. "I think you make some very good points, and I did articulate them to the board when they were considering whether or not to go forward with the exhibit."

Huber looked surprised. "Didn't seem to do much good though."

"From your point of view, no, I guess it didn't," Maggie conceded.

"Mr. Huber, was there anyone in your group who was particularly upset that the protest didn't have the desired effect of getting the museum to cancel the exhibit?"

Huber sighed. "Now why would I tell you that? You'll just use it to paint a target on the back of our volunteers."

"I promise you that's not what we intend to do," Maggie spoke up. "If you're aware of the ruby's theft, I'm sure you also know that one of my coworkers was found later that night having died of an overdose. I don't think it was an accident."

"You think your coworker was killed by whoever stole the ruby." Huber shook his head. "There's no way anyone associated with our group would be involved in what you're suggesting. No way."

"If that's true, then there's no harm in helping us," Kevin responded.

"Please," Maggie added when Huber continued to hesitate.

Huber sighed again. "Look, like I said, no one in this group would be involved in a theft. That would make them no better than the people who took these artifacts from their countries in the first place."

They weren't going to get names of members from this guy. Kevin wasn't surprised about that. Maybe Francois would have better luck. Still, he needed to get what he could from Huber. "What about people not associated with the Repatriation Project? There are always people who think that lawful protest simply isn't enough. Has anyone like that expressed an interest in the ruby lately?"

"You are right. There are always people who think that more…aggressive measures should be taken to address wrongs." Huber paused, thinking. "I can't think of anyone though who expressed an interest in the ruby per se."

Kevin's ears perked up at the hedge. "But you can think of someone who fits the description of the kind of person we're talking about generally."

"There was a girl, a woman, early twenties. Just out of college. Idealistic, you know the type." Huber was back spinning the pen between his fingers. "I don't know her name. She came to one of the protests we held, oh, maybe a month or two ago. Really aggressive. Said talk wasn't enough. We needed to get our hands dirty in the fight if we wanted to affect real change." Huber scoffed. "I've been doing this kind of work for more than twenty years. Maybe longer than this woman had been alive. I think my hands are plenty dirty."

"Do you know her name?" Kevin asked.

Huber shook his head. "No. She only came to the one protest. She made such a scene I had to ask her to leave. Never saw her again."

"Can you describe her?"

Huber shrugged. "Brunette, shortish hair. Not too tall."

That probably described thousands of women in the Los Angeles area, and they weren't even sure the woman was from here.

He and Maggie thanked Huber for his time and left.

"What do you think?" Maggie asked when they were back in the car.

"I think Francois will get the names of the members of the organization, but I don't think this group has the know-how to pull something like this off."

"So where does that leave us?"

Continuing to spin their wheels looking for a suspect that wasn't her. Since that was an answer he wasn't willing to give her, he started the engine and pulled away from the curb without a word.

Chapter Sixteen

Kevin glanced at the clock on his bedside table: 11:10 p.m. He sighed and climbed out of bed. Maybe some calming mint tea would help him finally get some sleep.

He couldn't stop thinking about Maggie.

He hoped she was getting more rest than he was, although he doubted it. Even though she insisted she wasn't going to be run out of her home, he'd seen the fear in her eyes. Everything inside of him wanted to make her feel safe.

He'd crossed the line from professional to personal the moment he'd kissed her on her front porch. Scratch that. He'd crossed that line the moment he'd realized she was the curator who had been attacked during the theft of the Viperé ruby. From that moment on, he'd wanted nothing more than to catch the man who'd put his hands on his Maggie and make him pay.

His Maggie.

That was how he used to think about her all the time. He wasn't sure when he started thinking about her like that again, but sometime in the last several days, he had. And he realized something else. He wanted another chance with her. Now he just had to figure out a way to convince her to give him one.

He glanced at the phone, wondering if it was too late to call. Of course it was. But he wasn't sure he could wait until the more socially acceptable time the next morning.

It wasn't just the nearly uncontrollable desire to at least hear her voice. This case, everything about it, bothered him.

The theft, Maggie being attacked and the threat against her, Kim Sumika's murder and now Carter Tutwilder's possible inquiries into buying a gem like the Viperé only weeks before it was stolen. None of it made sense. Especially not the attacks on Maggie. If the thief was the same person who'd made the threat against her, why had he hung around to do so? And if the thief and the person threatening Maggie weren't the same person? He wasn't sure what that would mean, and he didn't like not having answers. Not when it came to Maggie's safety.

There were simultaneously too many clues and not enough. Carter Tutwilder had been keeping something from them, he was sure of that, but was his secret relevant or just something the billionaire didn't want to see in the papers? Kim Sumika had a gambling problem, but so did thousands of other Los Angelenos. It might not have anything to do with the theft or her murder. And if Kim had reached out to Kovalev to be her new bookie, Kim would have brought real trouble down on her head by not paying up. But the timing was just too coincidental for him to shake off.

The tea kettle whistled. He poured the tea into a travel mug and carried it to his bedroom to change.

Midnight might be too late for a phone call, but nothing was stopping him from taking a drive by Maggie's house to make sure all was quiet there.

MOONLIGHT WAS STILL peeking around the edges of the blinds when she opened her eyes. She'd gone to bed at ten, exhausted. The dream she'd been having involved her and Kevin walking hand in hand on a beach, which had led to a romantic dinner, which had led to the two of them in bed. It had felt so real she almost expected to see Kevin lying in bed beside her, but of course he wasn't there. She touched the cold spot next to her with longing before chiding herself. She couldn't fall back into things with Kevin.

A shadow shifted outside her window. She stilled, her heart in her throat. A long minute passed and she relaxed. Just shadows.

The last several days had put her on edge, and she hated it. Hated looking over her shoulder all the time. Hated feeling unsafe in her own home. And it didn't feel like she and Kevin were getting any closer to discovering who was behind the theft of the ruby, Kim's death or the terror campaign against her.

Something caught her eye outside the window. It wasn't just a shadow. There was someone out there. A glance at the clock showed that it was 11:25 p.m. No one with good intentions would be lurking around her house at this time of the night.

She slid from her bed as quietly as she could, her heart in her throat.

Grabbing her cell phone, she moved into the living room, not turning on any lights. As long as the person outside thought she was still asleep, she had the element of surprise.

She waited impatiently, her eyes moving from the windows at the front of the house to the ones in the back, looking for any movement, as Kevin's phone rang. After what seemed like hours, he picked up.

"There's someone here," she whispered frantically as soon as the call connected.

"I'm two minutes away." She wondered how he could already be so close, but any thought of asking the question was cut off by the sound of the glass pane in her back door shattering.

She dropped the phone and lunged for the end table in the living room where she kept a Maglite flashlight.

"Maggie? Maggie, are you there? Answer me, Maggie."

She grabbed the flashlight, which was heavy enough to double as a weapon if it came to that, and clicked it on. She turned the light toward the back door just as the hand jutting into the house through the broken pane found the lock and turned it. She jerked the beam toward the intruder's face.

He wore a mask, but this one was different from the one the thief at the Larimer wore. It covered the top of the intruder's head and his neck and came up to his nose, but left his forehead and eye area uncovered. Something tugged at the back of her mind for a fleeting moment, but the intruder's startled jerk chased it away.

"The cops are on their way, and I have a gun. If you come any closer, I will shoot." She could only hope the intruder couldn't hear the lie in her voice.

Luck was on her side. A pounding sounded on the front door as the last words left her mouth.

"Maggie!" Kevin yelled.

"I'm okay," she shouted back. "He's at the back door."

The intruder's eyes went wide. He pulled his hand out of the door and lurched away.

She waited several seconds before going to the door and peering out of what was left of the window.

The intruder hoisted himself over the back fence and disappeared into the darkness of the neighbor's lawn.

Kevin rounded the side of the cottage.

She jerked the damaged door open and pointed at the house behind the cottage. "He went over the fence."

Kevin looked her up and down quickly.

"I'm fine. He didn't make it inside."

"Call 911, tell them you had an intruder and ask them to call Detective Francois," he said before taking off after the intruder.

Into the darkness.

KEVIN WAITED UNTIL he saw Maggie slip back into the house and the door close. Then he headed for the back fence, vaulting over it with one hand, his gun in the other. The neighbor's yard was shrouded in darkness. The little bit of illumination came from the bulb over the neighbor's back door and created eerie shadows and shapes. He froze, listening for the sound of an animal bigger than the usual night creatures moving about. For several long moments, all he heard were the chirps of crickets. Then, almost as if they were warning him of impending danger, the chirping to his right fell silent.

He turned in that direction and saw the shadow moving quickly along the side of the porch toward the front of the house. He started for it, but the man must have seen or heard him coming.

The intruder took off running.

Kevin gave chase.

The intruder didn't seem to be worried about being quiet or stealthy anymore. He just wanted to get away now. And he was fast. In a matter of seconds, he'd managed to put a good distance between them.

It struck him that the intruder seemed familiar with the neighborhood. Was that because he'd been staking out Maggie's home or could there be another reason? He'd be sure to ask, as soon as he had the man in custody.

He picked up his pace, trying to close the distance. Even though the sun had long since set, the night was warm, leaving him sweaty even though he'd only run two blocks. He kept in shape, running several miles every week. But his heart was pounding, and the adrenaline rushing through his body wasn't helping him pace himself. And he was worried about Maggie. What if the intruder was leading him on a wild-goose chase just to get him away from her house? He could have a partner or double back. Maggie was all alone. Where the hell was the patrol that was supposed to be keeping an eye on her house?

Coming to the corner, Kevin turned in the direction he'd seen the intruder flee. The street and sidewalk were empty.

"Damnit." The intruder couldn't have disappeared.

He hadn't heard the sound of an engine turning, so he doubted the person had escaped in a car. He scanned the street.

A thick hedge ran along the property line of a nearby house.

Kevin crossed to it; it was dark, but it only took him seconds to find the narrow path leading between two neighboring houses. The shadow at the end of the path turned in time for Kevin to catch the whites of the man's eyes before he darted away again.

Propelled by a new surge of adrenaline, he raced down the path after the man. He had to catch the intruder and put an end to him terrorizing Maggie.

He got to the end of the path and found himself surrounded by trees. The path had ended at what appeared to be the beginning of a wooded area behind the homes. Maggie's intruder could be anywhere. Hiding among the trees. It wouldn't be safe for him to plunge into the thicket.

A moment too late, he sensed someone behind him.

Before he could turn, something hit him hard over the back of his head.

He went down to his knees, dizzy, stars flashing behind his eyes. Thankfully, he didn't lose consciousness. He could hear footfalls heading back down the path. He struggled to his feet, disoriented and woozy.

The footsteps faded into silence.

Chapter Seventeen

When he arrived back at Maggie's house, she was already speaking to one of the police officers that had responded to her call while the other officer searched around the perimeter of the house. Detective Francois arrived minutes later, and Maggie described the attempted break-in, with Kevin taking over the tale once the foot chase began. Francois sent the officers out to scour the neighborhood, but Kevin wasn't surprised when they returned without having spotted the intruder.

"Do you need to get checked out at the hospital, Lombard?" Francois asked.

Kevin rubbed the back of his head where he'd been hit. There was a little bump there, but he'd had worse. "I'll be fine."

Francois gave him a look that said he disagreed with his decision, but he didn't push. "Ms. Scott, the police department is doing everything it can to get to the bottom of the current situation, but it appears we are dealing with someone who wants to hurt you and who may have already killed Kim Sumika. I'd strongly advise you to stay with a friend for a while. Just until we have a better handle on the situation."

Maggie made a face. "I could ask my friend Lisa, but

her place is an hour away and small. And she has a cat that hates me." She shook her head, seemingly rejecting the idea even as she mentioned it.

"You can stay with me." Warning bells went off in his head immediately. Having her only feet away from his bed was probably not the best idea he'd ever had. Not when he couldn't have her in his bed. But he could see she was afraid, and he could keep his libido in check if that was what it took to make her feel safe.

"I don't know," she said hesitantly.

"I do. I have a guest room. It's yours for as long as you want it."

She gave him a grateful smile. "Thank you."

He waited while Maggie packed a bag and locked up the cottage. She didn't want to be stranded without a car, so she followed him to his place in her own car. When they got there, he ran inside the apartment building to get her a visitor's parking permit, then called Tess and updated her on the night's events as Maggie pulled into one of the reserved spaces while he kept an eye out.

"None of this is making a whole lot of sense," Tess said when he'd finished his update.

"On that, we agree."

"Well, I do have some news that's good. My source was able to get a location on Ivan Kovalev. He's partying at the bar he owns, Nightingale's. My source says the way the booze and recreational drugs are flowing, Ivan is likely to be there until closing at four. The source can get you into the club, but he can't guarantee Ivan will meet with you."

"But Ivan knows I want to speak with him?"

"Oh, he knows. There isn't much Ivan doesn't know. Once you're in the club, if Ivan is open to talking to you, he'll find you."

Kevin watched as Maggie got out of her car and went to the trunk for her overnight bag. "The timing sucks. Maggie is going to stay with me for a while. I want to get her settled, and I'm not sure about leaving her alone."

"We know where Ivan is going to be tonight. I can send someone else if you really can't make it, but you know the details of this case back and forth."

And he didn't want to leave Ivan's questioning to anyone else. Finding out what he knew might be the key to figuring out what was going on and stopping it. Maggie was heading for him now. He glanced at his watch: 12:18 a.m. That gave him time to get Maggie settled, wait till she fell asleep and head to the club.

"And you're sure he's going to be at Nightingale's?" Kevin asked.

Maggie stopped in front of him and waited.

"That's what the source said."

"Okay, got it. Maggie is here. I've got to go." He ended the call.

"Who was that?" Maggie asked.

"Tess." He slid her bag from her shoulder and tossed it over his own. "I was filling her in on the attempted break-in at your house and you staying with me for a while."

"I don't know if it will be awhile. Let's just take it one day at a time."

"Whatever you want. You ready to go up?" He led her to the elevators into the building.

"I heard you and Tess talking about Nightingale's. That's that trendy club in Hollywood where all the celebrities hang out right? Who is going to be there tonight? Clooney? Pitt? One of the many, many Chrises?" Maggie asked jokingly after the elevator doors closed and they'd started their ascent.

"Tess's informant got a location on Ivan Kovalev. He owns Nightingale's, a club in Hollywood."

"Are we going to talk to him?"

Kevin raised his hands. "Ivan Kovalev is a dangerous man. I don't want you anywhere near him."

Maggie frowned. "He may have answers to who killed Kim and is trying to destroy my life."

"I get it, but we have to be careful. Your safety is my number one priority."

"Kevin—"

The elevator stopped on the twelfth floor, and the doors slid open.

"We don't have to speak to Ivan tonight. Tess said he's at the club nearly every night." He felt a moment of guilt about the white lie then shook it off, remembering that, while she may not have lied to him, she'd kept a pretty major piece of information from him. At least he was doing it to protect her.

He could tell from her deepening frown that she didn't like that answer, but she nodded.

They got off the elevator, and he led her to a door at the end of the hallway.

He opened the door, flicked on the light and led her into the space.

"You have a nice place," Maggie said, her eyes roaming over the space.

"Tanya found it for me. It's five minutes from the hospital, which is its best feature. At least, in her opinion."

Maggie shot him a wan smile.

"You have to be exhausted. The guest room is just down this way." He led her down the short hallway to the left of the front door.

His guest bedroom wasn't much, just a bed, dresser

and nightstand, but it was warm and comfortable, and she'd be safe in his place.

He set her bag down at the foot of the bed and stepped back into the hall.

Maggie touched his arm as he passed by her, sending sparks of electric desire through him.

"Thank you," she said softly.

He pressed a kiss to her forehead then stepped back. He'd wanted to do much more, but she needed to rest. "You don't ever have to thank me. I'll always be there when you need me."

He retreated to his own room but didn't change into pajamas. He knew she'd be angry with him, but there was no way he was going to take her to Ivan's club. Especially when he wasn't sure Ivan wasn't behind everything that had been happening. He just had to wait for her to go to sleep, and then he could slip out of the apartment.

He heard Maggie's bedroom door open and her footsteps as she headed for the single bathroom in the apartment. She took a long shower then he heard the bathroom door open and the floor creak as she headed back to her room.

The bedroom door snapped shut, and the apartment fell quiet.

He lay back on his bed, planning to wait a few minutes for her to fall asleep before he left. While he waited, he ran through the events of the night in his head. The attempt to break into Maggie's home was bold, and it had terrified him. Whoever was behind everything that was happening seemed to be obsessed with Maggie. And obsessions only ended one of two ways. The person was caught or the object of the obsession was eliminated.

Fear and fury burned in his chest.

He would not let anything happen to Maggie.

The sound of the guest room door creaking open sent him on instant alert. Light spilled out of the guest bedroom. He sat up in bed, watching as Maggie's shadow moved closer and closer to his room.

She crept forward, headed for the bathroom, he guessed.

Maggie continued to creep forward, but not to the bathroom. She stopped at his bedroom door. "Kevin?"

"You okay?"

"I can't sleep."

He swung his bare feet to the floor. "I can make you some tea. Something soothing that might help you fall asleep."

She came into the room, and he got a good look at her. She was wearing a satin nightie that hugged her plump breasts and showed miles of long silky leg.

His lower body sprung to attention.

She stepped up to the side of the bed, her thigh brushing against him. "I was thinking about something else that might help me sleep."

"Maggie." His voice came out low and rough. He was surprised he was able to form words with her standing so close. So nearly naked. "This might not be a good idea."

But even as he spoke, he couldn't help reaching out and drawing his hand lightly over Maggie's hip.

"I don't want to think about rubies or death or tomorrow. I just want right now. With you."

She lowered her mouth to his, and his control snapped.

The years, the fears, the secrets, they all melted away with that kiss. All that was left was desire.

With those words, he closed the remaining distance between them, capturing her lips in a fervent kiss.

It was as if time hadn't passed at all. Her mouth claimed

his, her tongue exploring with hunger. She kissed him like a woman desperate.

He knew the feeling because he felt it too.

Her hands rose and pressed against his chest, coaxing him back on the bed. He let her take the lead. She straddled him, and it was a fight not to lose control.

How many nights had he dreamed of this? Too many to count.

He wrapped his hands around her hips, pulling her against the hardness and heat between his thighs. He wanted her to feel how much he wanted her. To feel the weight of his arousal.

Her mouth left his, but her hold on him remained firm. She began a sensual exploration down his neck, her tongue caressing and igniting a thunderous beat in his chest and ears.

There were countless reasons why he should pull away. But he curled around her hips, fitting her tightly against him.

As if she sensed his hesitation, she whispered in his ear, "I want this. I need you."

What little control he had left shattered. Kevin flipped them so she was under him. He kissed her with raw desire, unchecked by any more reservations.

Already shirtless, he removed his pants, letting them fall to the floor.

A soft gasp escaped her lips.

He tugged on the hem of her nightie, pulling it over her head.

It joined his pants on the floor.

He took her breast into his mouth, tasting her. As his tongue caressed her, she arched toward him, eager.

The events of the past and the last several days vanished, leaving only desire.

He kissed a scorching trail down her stomach, causing her breath to catch.

He reached for the nightstand next to his bed, where he kept protection. The next time, and there would be a next time, they'd go slow, but right now…right now he had to sink into her or he felt like he might explode from pent-up need.

After sheathing himself, he settled between her thighs, entering her slowly so she had time to adjust to every inch of him.

Seated fully, he gazed down at the woman beneath him.

Her eyes burned with passion.

"You are so beautiful," he said huskily.

"Kevin," she moaned.

Their eyes locked.

He withdrew and thrust into her, hard and fast. He withdrew again and plunged again, the rhythm desperate, greedy. The need had swelled too rapidly for him to hold back.

Her legs wrapped around him, her nails digging into his shoulders as their pleasure surged and intensified.

Their bodies met again and again.

He kissed her, caressed her, driving her to the precipice of desire—

And then her release crashed over her, and she gasped his name, her release unleashing his own.

He had expected pleasure. But this…this was something beyond his wildest imagination.

The world spun away as her body quivered under him, waves of ecstasy rippling through her. He was there with her, growling out her name, holding her just as tightly as she held him as pleasure consumed him.

He lifted his body, supporting his weight, and gazed down at her. “Are you okay?”

She leaned up, and he was amazed that his arousal surged again. She swept her lips over his and said, “No thinking. Tonight, there is only this.”

Chapter Eighteen

Maggie woke up alone in Kevin's bed.

"Kevin?"

Only silence answered her.

She rose and padded from the bedroom. The kitchen and living room were empty. She glanced out of the front window of the house, her suspicions rising. Kevin's car wasn't in the driveway where he'd parked it.

Then she remembered the earlier call from Tess. Her ire peaked. She had a pretty good idea where Kevin had gone. She was happy she'd followed him to his place in her own car.

She pulled up the address for Nightingale's on her phone and got dressed. The club looked nice, upscale, not the kind of place where she could wear the jeans and sweater she'd arrived at Kevin's house in. Luckily, she'd had the foresight to pack a dress that was nice enough for a night out.

Foresight or wishful thinking? She'd seen the dress, one of her favorites because it hugged and gave in all the right places, while packing, and a thought had flashed through her mind. Her in the dress sitting across from Kevin at a candlelit table. Ridiculous under the circumstances, but she'd thrown the dress in her bag just in case.

She put it on then hopped into her car. She didn't know exactly how much of a head start Kevin had on her, but the restaurant wasn't far from his house.

She made a right turn and noticed that the dark SUV behind her did the same.

She told herself to relax, that it didn't mean anything. The driver could be going in the same direction.

She made a left at the light, and the SUV did the same. She made another left and the next immediate left. The SUV followed.

Okay, that wasn't a coincidence. There was no reason for the SUV to circle the block unless it was following her.

Her phone rang and she started, tapping the break. The SUV fell back but continued to follow her as she drove. She reached for the phone with one hand, the other still on the wheel.

"What do you think you're doing?" Kevin's voice boomed from the phone.

"What are you—"

"You didn't think I'd leave you without protection, did you? One of the other operatives from West Investigations was watching the house. He said you took off in your car before he could stop you."

She glanced at the rearview mirror. "Is that who's following me?"

"Yes. Pull over," he demanded. "I'm a block away."

She pulled to a stop at the curb, as did the SUV. It was less than a minute before Kevin's black Mustang rolled to a stop behind the SUV.

He stopped at the driver's side of the SUV and said a few words to the driver before heading for her car.

Maggie stepped out, slamming the door behind her. "Who do you think you are? Sending me off to bed like a child and then sneaking out of the house like some sneaky sneak."

Okay, so it wasn't the strongest admonition, but she was a novice at telling someone off.

Kevin looked angry, but she thought she saw the ends of his mouth tip up slightly, which only stoked her ire.

She poked him in the chest. "I am not a child. Kim was my friend, and the Viperé ruby was my responsibility. I am a part of this whether you want me to be or not. I'm not going to hide from this maniac, no matter how much—"

The rest of her rant was cut off by Kevin's lips crushing against her mouth.

For several long moments, she was lost in his kiss. Finally, Kevin stepped back.

She shook the fog of his kiss from her head. "If you think that's going to stop me from going—"

Kevin held up his hand. "I know nothing is going to stop you." He caressed her cheek with the pad of his thumb. "Nothing ever stops you from doing what you think is right. It's one of the things I lo—"

This time it was she who pressed her mouth to his. She wasn't ready to hear what he was about to say.

She pulled back after a moment. "So, Nightingale's."

He took her hand. "I'll drive. I've already got someone coming to take your car back to my house. Miller will stay with your car until he gets here."

Heat crept up her neck at the realization that Miller had seen them kissing. She left the keys to her car with Miller and got into the Mustang beside Kevin.

Nightingale's looked like a typical bar. A long bar ran along one side of the space and white tableclothed tables filled in the rest in a seemingly random pattern.

Kevin led her toward the bar. They slid onto stools and ordered drinks, tonic water for him and white wine for her.

"Shouldn't we tell someone that we're here?"

"Ivan Kovalev knows when each and every person walks through his doors. Trust me, he knows we are here, and if he doesn't know already, if we give him a few minutes, he'll know who we are."

They continued to sip their drinks at the bar, exchanging a few words but mostly waiting. It seemed like forever, but it had probably only been ten or fifteen minutes when a large man with biceps the size of tree stumps and a raised scar running along the right side of his jaw appeared beside Kevin.

"Sir. Mr. Kovalev is ready to see you now."

The man turned and started away, clearly intending for Maggie and Kevin to follow him.

She slid from the barstool. Kevin palmed her elbow, angling his body between her and the man they followed.

The man led them through the bar's main area and down a narrow hallway toward the back of the building. They passed the kitchen and heard the clank of dishes and the sound of raised voices on the other side of the swinging door. Finally, the man stopped in front of a door. A private dining room.

There were no windows and the walls were dark wood paneling. With the dim lighting, the overall feel was menacing, which Maggie was sure was the point.

A circular table dominated the space, and in the seat facing the door sat a man who Maggie had no doubt was Ivan Kovalev.

He waved them into the room and toward the table without rising. "Mr. Lombard. Ms. Scott. So good of you to join me," Kovalev said as if he'd invited them to dine with him.

Kevin squeezed her elbow, in caution or as a soothing gesture, she wasn't sure.

He pulled out a chair on the opposite side of the table for her and waited until she was seated before taking the seat next to her.

Ivan Kovalev looked to be in his early sixties, maybe a little older, lean with hair that had gone more white than gray and eyes that were shrewd. If she'd passed him on the street, not knowing that he was part of the Russian mob, she would have still given him a wide berth. Everything about the man screamed he was dangerous.

A waiter hurried in with glasses of wine and a breadbasket. He set the glasses of wine in front of Maggie and Kevin—Kovalev already had a full glass—and left the breadbasket in the middle of the table before slipping back out of the room.

"Thank you for seeing us," Kevin said.

Kovalev waved a hand in dismissal. "It is nothing. I'm sure we were destined to meet at some point with you being the new head of West Security and Investigations' corporate accounts."

It was a show of power. Kovalev knew exactly who they were.

"I've been thinking about upgrading the security at my various buildings. Maybe I should give you a call."

"West would be glad to help," Kevin responded.

Kovalev smiled. "I'm sure you would. But am I incorrect in thinking you are not here to solicit my business?"

Kovalev's gaze swung to Maggie. She was used to men assessing her, but the look Kovalev swept over her was more than just a man appreciating a woman; it was predatory, and it left her feeling as if she needed a shower. Immediately. She shook off the feeling.

Out of the side of her eye, she saw Kevin's jaw tighten. He hadn't missed the way Kovalev had looked at her.

"We're here to ask about Kim Sumika," Kevin gritted out.

Kovalev shot Kevin a smile, taking pleasure over having gotten under his skin, no doubt. "Such a shame. I'm sorry for your loss." Kovalev tipped his head at Maggie.

"Thank you," she said. "It's come to our attention that Kim may have borrowed a sum of money from you. I'm hoping you can tell us more about that."

Kovalev frowned. "I'm not sure that's any of your business."

"We've made it our business," Kevin shot back.

Kovalev's frown turned into a hard scowl.

"Mr. Kovalev, please," Maggie jumped in, hoping to dispel some of the tension. "Kim was my friend. She wasn't close to the little family she had left. I'm all she had, and I feel an obligation to find out what happened to her."

Kovalev's gaze lingered on Kevin for several seconds longer then shifted to her. His face softened, but only a fraction. "Your loyalty is admirable, but maybe misguided. You should allow the police to look into these sorts of things."

Maggie shifted her gaze to the table and said softly, "Would you? If you were in my situation?"

Her words hung there for a moment, silently. She looked at Kovalev through her lashes and waited.

Finally, he spoke. "Point well taken, my dear. What would you like to know?"

Since Kovalev seemed more willing to share with her

than with Kevin, she took over the questioning. "We know Kim had a gambling problem. She'd maxed out her credit cards and a home equity line of credit, and we were told she might have borrowed money from you."

"It appears that Anthony Cauley knows more than just wine and cupcakes. Seems to know more than I've given him credit for."

Maggie sucked in a breath. The last thing she wanted to do was to get Anthony in trouble with Ivan Kovalev. She started to speak.

Kovalev waved her off. "It's nothing. People talk. Mr. Cauley is of no concern to me." He took a sip of wine before he spoke again. "Yes, Ms. Sumika owed me money. Or she did. She paid off her debt, in full, with interest, about a week before her untimely death."

Maggie shot a surprised look at Kevin. For his part, his expression remained unchanged.

"Would you mind telling us how much that was?"

Kovalev's frown returned. He was silent for a beat. "Fifty thousand dollars, give or take."

Maggie swallowed hard. That was, she knew, nearly Kim's entire salary for a year. Where did she get that kind of money?

The Viperé ruby. If she was involved, maybe the fifty thousand was her cut. Or part of it. The ruby was worth multiples of fifty thousand dollars.

"Is there anything else you'd like to know? I'm sorry but I have a busy evening ahead of me." Kovalev downed the remainder of his wine. He'd clearly lost interest in them. It was time to go.

But there was one question she wanted to ask. Something she needed to know.

She started to speak, but Kevin reached for her hand. This time, it was clear what he intended to convey.

He stood, pulling her with him. “Mr. Kovalev, thank you for your time.”

Kovalev waved at them again, a clear dismissal.

Big biceps waited for them outside of the room. He led them in a reverse trek down the hall and through the bar’s dining area to the door.

She guessed Kovalev didn’t want them to stay for a nightcap.

The door to the bar banged closed after them.

“Why didn’t you let me ask him if he’d killed Kim?”

“Because he wouldn’t have told you the truth,” Kevin said, his arm around her, leading her to the car. “And I already know he didn’t kill Kim.”

She stopped walking. “You do? How?”

“Kovalev knew who we were before we stepped foot in the bar. He knew who you were. That tells me he’s done his homework, and I have no doubt that he knows you inherit Kim’s estate.”

She wasn’t following. “So?”

“So, if Kim hadn’t paid him the money she owed him, he’d have made it clear that he expected you to pay out of the money she left you. Men like Kovalev don’t just let a debt die when the person who owes the debt dies, not if they can help it.”

“So you think he was telling us the truth about Kim paying off her debt.” Maggie let out a breath of frustration. Her prior thought about where Kim had gotten the money to pay off that debt came swimming back to her. “Which means he didn’t have a motive to kill Kim or steal the ruby.”

“Exactly,” Kevin said, walking them to the car.

"So what now?"

Kevin pulled open the passenger-side door for her, but she made no move to get into the car.

He looked her in the eye. "Now we keep pulling threads until we find the one that unravels this whole mess."

Chapter Nineteen

Two hours after leaving Ivan Kovalev, Maggie lay in Kevin's bed, one leg slung over his, her head resting on his chest. He snored lightly, but she hadn't been able to fall asleep after they'd made love. She knew that the more time she spent in his arms, in his bed, the harder it would be to walk away from him when the time came. And it would come. No matter how electric their lovemaking or how safe she felt with him, she wasn't willing to risk her heart again. She'd tried love twice and failed both times. That was enough for her.

Repressing a sigh, she eased herself out of Kevin's arms, slipping from the bed. She wrapped herself in the quilt from the bottom of the bed and padded from the room, closing the door behind her. After a quick stop in the guest bedroom where she was supposed to be sleeping to grab her laptop, she settled onto the living room sofa.

She opened the laptop and logged on to Facebook. She'd tried to avoid the news about the Larimer, but curiosity was finally getting to her. She went to the museum's Facebook page and scanned the comments. Most of them were sympathetic, dismay and disgust about the theft the chief responses. But a few almost seemed to celebrate the ruby going missing. She scanned the thumbnail photos of the commenters, wondering if one of the posters was the aggressive brunette that Josh Huber had told them about. None of the photos jumped out at her.

She navigated to the AARP page. There were several posts about exhibits that the group was against and pictures from the many protests that they'd held. She scrolled through the posts, not sure what she was looking for. Probably nothing, but maybe mindlessly scrolling would slow her racing thoughts enough that she'd be able to go to sleep.

The last several days of her life had been nothing but chaos. One of her coworkers and closest friends was dead, quite possibly because she'd been involved in stealing the Viperé. Why hadn't Kim come to her if she was in trouble? After everything Kim had done for her since the scandal in New York, Maggie would have lent her money to get out of debt if she'd needed it. It might not have been enough, but it had to be better than borrowing from a mobster or, worse, getting involved in a major jewel theft.

If that was what Kim had done. Maggie still didn't want to believe it. She wasn't sure she would believe it until there was incontrovertible proof.

She scrolled past a photo of a protest then paused, swiping down so the photo came back onto the screen. The picture was of two young women and a young male holding protest signs. The man and one of the women were blond, but the brunette with them, she looked familiar.

Maggie clicked on the photo, and it popped up in its own browser window, filling her computer screen. The bigger picture was sharper, the faces in it clearer.

Clear enough that there was no doubt.

The brunette woman in the photo was Diyana Shelton.

MAGGIE HAD AWAKENED him at four in the morning with the photo of Diyana Shelton, the intern at the Larimer, at an AARP protest. He had to admit that she did fit the description of the young brunette that Josh Huber had given them, but he'd cautioned Maggie against jumping to any conclusions. Maggie had been ready to drive to Diyana's apartment and confront the woman before dawn. He'd convinced her to wait until a more reasonable time that morning, but just barely. At seven thirty, they headed to Diyana's apartment, hoping to catch her before she left for the day.

Maggie had given the intern a ride home several times when they'd both had to stay late working on the exhibit, so he hadn't had to tap into West Investigations' vast resources to find an address for the young woman. Diyana lived in a nondescript garden-style apartment. Each of the apartments had a balcony, and the grounds seemed to be fairly well kept. He wasn't sure how much interns made, but it must be a decent amount if Diyana was able to foot the rent here. Residents had to buzz the front door open for their guests, so their appearance at her apartment couldn't come as a complete surprise to Diyana.

Kevin pressed the button for apartment 303, the top floor of the three-floor building, and they waited. It was just after eight, and Maggie had been pretty sure that Diyana would still be at home since the intern didn't usually arrive at the museum until nine thirty.

He was about to press the buzzer again when a voice came over the intercom mounted on the outside wall.

"Yes?"

"Diyana, it's Maggie Scott and Kevin Lombard. I'm sorry to drop in on you so early in the morning, but there's something important we need to discuss with you. Can we come up?"

Diyana didn't respond, but static crackled on her end, so he knew the line was still open.

Maggie shot him a look then said, "Diyana, please."

"Okay."

The line went dead, and a moment later there was a buzz then the door unlocked.

He and Maggie took the stairs to the third floor.

Diyana waited for them outside of apartment 303, barelegged in fuzzy pink slippers, an oversized sweater wrapped around her. "What is it?"

He couldn't blame her for the irritation he heard in her voice. He wouldn't have been happy at having people drop in on him at eight in the morning on a workday. And, if Diyana had a hand in the theft of the Viperé ruby, it was likely him and Maggie showing up at her apartment at this time of the morning had spiked a bit of fear in her.

Good.

He didn't take Diyana for a criminal mastermind, which meant that fear was likely to drive her to make mistakes. And mistakes were good for him and Maggie.

"Again, I'm sorry for dropping in on you, but you know I'm not allowed at the museum, and we really do need to speak with you," Maggie said again without smiling.

Diyana shrugged, but the movement made her appear scared more than nonchalant. "Okay, so what is so urgent?"

"We might want to have this conversation inside," Kevin said.

Diyana hesitated for a moment then stepped back and let them pass into the apartment.

Maggie had printed out a copy of the photo she'd found

on Facebook. She pulled it from her purse now. "This." She handed the piece of paper over to Diyana. "That's you at a protest organized by the Arts and Antiquities Repatriation Project."

Diyana's eyes widened. She licked her lips, panic in her eyes. "So?"

"So what were you doing there?" he snapped.

She shifted her weight from one leg to the other, chewing her bottom lip. "It was a protest. Like some museum was profiting off of the stolen artifacts from Mexico."

"AARP is the group that staged the protest against us a few weeks ago."

"So?" Diyana repeated, her gaze skittering away from Maggie's.

The girl was a terrible liar.

"Look, you can tell us what you know, or I can call Detective Larimer and tell him what we know about you. I'm sure he will have no problem hauling you down to the police station."

"But I didn't do anything!"

"Then you have nothing to worry about," Maggie said.

Diyana pressed her lips together.

"Fine." The intern was working his patience. He pulled his phone from his pocket. "I'm calling Detective Francois."

"No. Don't do that." Diyana reached for his hand, stopping him from bringing the phone to his ear. "My parents will kill me if I get arrested."

"Well, you should start talking then," Kevin shot back.

Unless she'd been involved in the theft, she wasn't going to be arrested, but Detective Francois would want to talk to her anyway once Kevin told him about their visit with the intern. He didn't share that piece of information with her.

"Fine," she huffed as if she were a five-year-old. "Look, all I was going to do was add a couple of names to the guest list for the donors' open house."

Maggie's forehead furrowed. "What names?"

Diyana rolled her eyes. "I didn't do it, okay? Like, you guarded that list like it was gold or something. I knew I wouldn't be able to sneak the names onto it without you noticing, so no harm, no foul, right?" She crossed her arms over her chest defensively.

"I don't understand," Maggie said. "Whose names were you going to add to the list and why?"

"Just a couple friends of mine. They wanted to get inside the party, and when the board members and whatnot started up with the speeches about how great it was to have the Viperé ruby at the Larimer, they were going to chant and stuff. Like just civil disobedience."

"What are these friends' names?" Kevin asked.

Diyana pressed her lips together again.

He waved his phone at her. "Detective Francois is not going to ask as nicely."

"Fine." She gave him two names. "You're making a big deal out of nothing. I couldn't get their names on the list, so the protest didn't happen."

"But the theft of the Viperé did," Maggie pointed out.

Diyana held her hands out in a surrender pose. "Hey, my friends had nothing to do with that. All they were going to do was, like, yell a little until security dragged them out. That's it."

If her friends were anything like Diyana, Kevin doubted very much they'd know the first thing about stealing a precious jewel. "Were you and your friends members of the AARP?"

Diyana shrugged. “We were but they do their own thing mostly now.”

“Why did they leave the group?” Maggie followed up.

Diyana snorted. “I mean, Josh has been doing this work for, like, twenty years, and he isn’t exactly getting it done. They felt like they could do better on their own.”

“And you?” Maggie said. “Why did you leave the group? Or did you?”

Diyana shrugged again. “I don’t know. I mean, I think that these artifacts should go back where they belong, but I also want to be a curator someday.”

Welcome to adulthood, he wanted to say. One hard choice after another.

“Are you going to tell Robert what I almost did?” Diyana looked at Maggie with a plea in her eyes.

“I’m on leave from the museum right now, but I really think you should tell Robert. I can’t promise you that things will work out for you the way you want them to, but I know that it would show a lot of maturity and integrity if you did. I think Robert would appreciate that.”

Diyana chewed her bottom lip. “Maybe.”

They left the young woman contemplating her next move.

“Are you going to tell your boss about Diyana’s actions?” Kevin asked Maggie once they’d stepped back outside.

“Well, since I’m on administrative leave, I don’t think there is any conflict in giving her a little time to work up the courage to do it herself. But if she doesn’t—” Maggie nodded “—yeah, I’ll have to.”

“I think she was telling us the truth,” he said, holding the passenger-side door open for Maggie.

She let out a deep, frustrated breath. “Yeah, unfortunately for me, I do too.”

Chapter Twenty

Maggie followed Kevin into his house. She could feel a panic attack coming on. Her throat constricted, her lungs burning from a lack of oxygen. Kevin wanted to speak with the people Diyana had planned to get into the donors' open and confirm their alibis, but Maggie's gut told her that no graduate students were behind the Viperé's theft and Kim's death. And the two were connected. She was absolutely sure of that.

No. The things that were happening now had been orchestrated by someone who'd meticulously planned it out. Planned it to seem as if she'd played a part in the theft and in killing her friend.

She tossed her purse on Kevin's kitchen table and collapsed into a chair.

Breathe. Breathe. She gulped in air.

Kevin slid into the chair next to her. "Maggie, I know this is tough for you, but don't give up hope."

She stared into Kevin's eyes. "I don't know how much more of this I can take."

"Hey." He reached across the table for her hand. "You are one of the toughest people I know. You can do this. We are going to prove your innocence."

"How? Every lead turns into a dead end. Nothing

makes any sense. If the person who stole the Viperé ruby is behind this, why kill Kim? Why stick around and leave that note for me at the office?"

"I don't know, but we will figure it out." He squeezed her hand. "You're going to make yourself sick if you don't de-stress some. Why don't you take a swim?" He slanted his head toward the sliding glass doors and the pool in the backyard beyond.

Maggie shook her head. "I don't have a swimsuit."

"There should be a couple swimsuits in the dresser in the guest room. Tanya bought a few suits to keep here, and she's never used any of them. You two are about the same size."

She looked longingly at the crystal blue water in the pool. She loved swimming, although she rarely found the time to make it to the pool at her gym. Actually, she couldn't remember the last time she made it to the gym at all.

"Are you sure Tanya wouldn't mind me stealing one of her swimsuits?"

Kevin smiled and her heart did a flip-flop. "I'm sure Tanya won't even notice. And while you swim, I'll whip us up a late breakfast. I have to go into the office at some point this morning, but you're welcome to stay here as long as you want."

"Thanks. I'm not sure what I'll do with my time now that I don't have a job to go to. I guess I need to go to my place and check on the cottage."

"If what Francois said about Kim's will is true, the cottage and Kim's house are yours now. You'll have some decisions to make whether or not you go back to the Larimer."

A knot formed in her throat. No matter what happened,

her life was never going to be the same again. She found Kevin's gaze and held it. No, too much had changed and too many feelings she'd thought were dead had been resurrected. Kevin was back in her life, and as much as she wanted to protect herself from the kind of hurt she'd felt when he'd walked away years ago, she could feel herself falling for him again. Falling just as hard as she'd fallen as a twenty-year-old coed, and she wasn't sure she had the strength to stop falling in love with him again.

She wasn't sure she wanted to stop falling in love with him again.

Maggie rose and went to the guest room, where her suitcase lay open on the bed just as she'd left it. A reminder that she hadn't slept in the guest bed at all the night before.

Memories of the prior night in Kevin's arms floated back at her as she changed into a swimsuit and headed out to the pool. The six-foot privacy fence on Kevin's side of the property line was buffeted by evergreen trees that towered at least three feet higher, giving the backyard the feel of a remote oasis.

She'd found a swim cap and goggles in the drawer, along with several swimsuits with tags still attached. She adjusted the swim cap and pulled the goggles down over her eyes before pushing off the side and gliding into the water. The water was surprisingly warm, and by the third lap, she could feel some of the stress she'd been carrying in her body easing. By the tenth lap, she was in a zone where there was nothing but the sound of the water and her breathing.

She knew the moment Kevin stepped out onto the patio. She finished her current lap then waded to the side of the pool. She pulled herself up and out. An innocuous move, but she watched desire flare in Kevin's eyes. He stood next to the chaise longue, backlit by the light coming from inside the house. His chest and feet were bare, a pair of nylon shorts hung low on his hips.

He grabbed the towel she'd left on the lounger and padded barefoot toward her. He dropped the towel over her shoulder then lowered his head and captured her mouth in a smoldering kiss that heated every inch of her skin.

His hands wandered to her hips, pulling her against him so she could feel how much he wanted her. She wanted him too. Even if she knew she shouldn't. Even if she knew it wouldn't last. She wanted him, and that was all that mattered at that moment.

He walked them toward the chaise and sat, pulling her onto his lap. The intensity of his kiss stole her breath. She thought she might like to kiss him forever. But then he pressed his hips to her, grinding against her core, and she wanted to do much more than kiss.

He shifted and flipped her so she lay on her back underneath him on the lounger.

She spread her legs wider, giving him space to seat himself comfortably against her.

She rubbed against him, rotating her hips, creating a delicious friction between their bodies. She rubbed her hands along his spine and broad shoulders, then down lower over the curve of his back to his firm behind.

His hands slipped under her bikini top. He kneaded her breast and pinched her nipple hard, sparking a pain that only heightened her pleasure. He moved on to her other breast, replaying the same movements.

It felt so good to have his weight on her body. His hands on her body. His mouth on her body.

They'd never had any problems in the bedroom. Their

physical attraction had always been explosive. This was the part they always got right, she reminded herself. It was all the other stuff that they'd struggled with.

Kevin slid his hand under the fabric of her bikini bottom, stroking her core, and she stopped thinking at all and just felt. And it felt good.

She let out a little mewling sound, and Kevin smiled sexily in return.

His gaze slid down her body. He untied her bikini top and lavished each of her breasts with kisses now that they were free. His mouth on her sent sparks shooting through her.

He slid down her body, pulling the strings that held her bottoms together. Lifting her slightly, he pulled the bottom of her bathing suit free and tossed it on top of her bikini top. She flexed her hips, enjoying the sensation of the bulging erection under his shorts.

He groaned, his jaw tightening. "Maggie, you feel so good."

"I'd feel a lot better if you weren't wearing so many clothes."

He reared up, pulling protection from his pocket before shedding his shorts.

She marveled for a moment at his hardened body and his thick erection before reaching out to pull him back down to her.

Kevin fit his hips between her legs, his length against her thigh. He held her gaze as he inched inside of her, setting a slow rhythm that sent her heart racing. His tongue darted in and out of her mouth, mimicking the pace set by the thrusting of their hips in time with each other.

He increased his rhythm, surging in and out of her until her orgasm hit with a force she'd never experienced before. She panted, clinging to him as pleasure sparked through every inch of her body. She clung to him, her legs wrapped tightly around his waist.

Kevin didn't stop making love to her. He increased his pace, pushing her toward a second orgasm that threatened to be even more powerful than the first.

His body tensed in time with hers. They quivered in each other's arms, tipping over the precipice of ecstasy together.

KEVIN STRODE THROUGH the doors of West Security and Investigations' West Coast offices the next morning, shooting a smile at the receptionist and heading for his office. He'd been reluctant to leave Maggie alone, but he needed to give Tess an update on the Larimer case and to check on several other cases that he'd been neglecting while he'd been focused on Maggie. Making love had been a much needed stress release for both of them, but he knew that neither of them would be able to completely relax until they'd cleared her name. And Maggie was right about one thing: they were really no closer to doing that than they'd been when he'd started the investigation.

He wasn't surprised to see Tess's head pop around his doorframe before he'd even booted up his computer.

She gave a perfunctory knock on the frame, the keys in her hand jingling, before speaking. "Morning, Kevin. Do you have a moment to give me an update on Maggie's case?"

He waved his boss into the office. "Of course. I was planning on stopping by your office in a minute or two anyway."

He'd been keeping Tess updated via quick calls and text messages throughout the investigation, but now he filled in all the details he'd skirted over in those prior communications. He also told his boss about Maggie having found a photograph of Diyana at one of the Art and Antiquities Repatriation Project's protests and the graduate students' thwarted plans to protest at the donors' open.

Tess massaged her temples. "This is a real mess."

"There's a logic to it," Kevin said, feeling his own frustration bubbling in his chest. "At least to our thief and killer. We just have to figure out what it is."

"I think it's safe to say that the theft of the Viperé ruby is certainly connected to Kim Sumika's death. Given the woman's gambling debt, it must have crossed your mind that she could have had a hand in the theft."

Kevin sighed. "It has, although I've been reluctant to share those thoughts with Maggie. But Kim had the same access to the ruby as Maggie did, and I do find it strange that Kim would miss the donors' open house."

"Migraines can be debilitating," Tess said, playing devil's advocate.

"Yeah," Kevin responded, his tone indicating that he still didn't buy it.

"Maggie seems to believe her friend and fellow curator was telling the truth about the migraine, and we don't have any direct evidence to the contrary. Although..." Tess shot him a pointed look. "Maggie is definitely too close to this case. I've given you wide latitude here, but do you think we should be letting her have a role in this investigation?"

"I don't think we have much of a choice. She's not going to sit back and stay out of it, and I don't think it's in her or our interest to have her out there trying to conduct her own investigation."

"Definitely not."

"She's been a help. Her dealer contact led us to Carter Tutwilder."

Tess twirled the keys. "Yeah, but so far I haven't been able to dig up anything on him that would suggest he had anything to do with the theft or Kim Sumika's death."

"He has the money to hire someone to pull this kind of thing off."

"Yeah, and if he hired someone, you can bet the money trail is buried under dozens of layers. We'll never find it."

Kevin let out a frustrated sigh. "The same could be said about Ivan Kovalev, although shockingly I believed Ivan when he said that Kim paid off her debt."

"He doesn't have a reason to lie." Tess's keys jingled, twirled and jingled again.

"No, he doesn't. But that raises another question. Where did Kim get the money to pay off the loan from Ivan?"

"And we're back to the ruby's theft," Tess said, catching the keys in the air and leaning forward in the chair. "If Kim had a hand in stealing the ruby, maybe she used her cut of the money to pay off her debt."

"And then what? Whoever she was working with killed her?"

Tess shrugged. "It wouldn't be the first time. No honor among thieves and all that."

He couldn't deny he had thought about this scenario. Heck, it was the one that made the most sense so far. Maggie was going to hate it, but it seemed clear that Kim Sumika had some role in stealing the Viperé ruby. How exactly that had led to her death was still an open question.

Tess leaned back in her chair, twirling her keys again. "You know I said that Maggie was too close to this case, but I've also wondered whether you're too close to it as well. You and Maggie? I haven't wanted to delve too much into your personal business, but it's clear that your 'past relationship'—" Tess drew air quotes around the last two words "—isn't so much in the past. Are you sure you can handle this case?"

His and Maggie's past relationship wasn't at all in the past anymore. And he planned to make sure a relationship with Maggie was his future, but he didn't tell Tess that. Not yet at least. He and Maggie still hadn't had a heart-to-heart, and despite the mind-blowing sex they'd shared, he didn't know what she was thinking. Heck, if he was being truthful with himself, he was afraid to find out exactly what she wanted. He could only hope she was feeling at least some of what he was feeling.

He realized he'd been silent for a beat too long. "I can handle it."

Tess cocked her head to the side and gave him a slight nod before rising. "Okay, then. Let me know if you need anything."

She turned back to him at the door. "Finding the ruby is why we were retained by the insurance company, and I don't think Maggie had anything to do with the theft. But we don't have unlimited time. If we don't find the ruby soon, the insurance agency will pull us and hire another firm."

He understood what she was saying. They'd lose access to the files and likely the people who could help clear Maggie's name. And another firm might think Maggie wasn't innocent.

"You need to find answers," Tess added. "Fast."

Chapter Twenty-One

"I can't imagine dealing with everything you've gone through in the last several days," Lisa said on the other end of the phone. "What can I do to help? Do you want me to come back down there?"

Maggie had just spent the last hour catching her best friend up on the events of the past several days and venting on the phone.

"No. I don't want to put you out." Lisa just having made the offer to drop everything and come stand by her side was enough to remind Maggie why she loved her friend. "I just needed someone to talk to."

"And I'm always here for that or whatever you need. You know that, right?"

"I do."

A beat of silence passed over the line.

"I feel like there's something else you want to say but aren't." Lisa always was perceptive.

"I slept with Kevin."

Lisa snorted. "That's not a surprise. I saw the way you two looked at each other."

"Yeah, it's not that simple." Maggie took a deep breath and told Lisa about her past relationship with Kevin while they were undergraduates and her miscarriage after they'd broken up.

"Maggie, I'm so sorry."

"I never expected to see Kevin again, but now that I have, I can't deny that there is still something there between us. But even if there is, does that mean it's healthy? Shouldn't I be looking forward, not backward?"

Lisa's sigh sounded through the line. "You know I don't believe in regrets or looking backward, but is that what this really is? I mean, you just said that there is something there between you two. Something in the here and now. I wouldn't necessarily say that it's unhealthy to explore what that might be."

"When has reuniting with an ex-boyfriend ever worked out in the end?"

"Frida Kahlo and Diego Rivera married, divorced and remarried, staying together until she passed away."

Maggie chuckled. "Of course you know that."

"What can I say? I know my art history."

Maggie couldn't help but be buoyed by Lisa's teasing.

"But really," Lisa said, becoming more serious. "I think you should think about what you really want. Forget the past. Think about the now and your future. And give yourself permission to forgive Kevin for walking away all those years ago. I'd hate for you to miss out on a good thing today because of choices you and Kevin made when you were just kids."

Maggie's phone beeped that she had a call coming in. She checked the screen and saw her father's photo.

"Lisa, I have to go. My dad is calling. But I heard you. I'll think about what you said."

"Good. Love ya."

"Love you too."

She ended the call with Lisa and clicked over to her father. She knew instantly that something was wrong.

"Dad?"

"Maggie?" Her father's words came out groggy.

"It's me, Dad."

"Maggie?"

"Dad? Are you okay?"

The silence on the other end of the phone spiked her anxiety.

"My head…my head hurts."

"Is Julie there, Dad?"

"Julie?"

Concern prickled at the back of her neck. Something was clearly wrong with her father.

She shoved her feet into her sneakers and grabbed her purse. "Did you fall? Dad, where are you?"

"Maggie, can you come over? My head hurts."

"I'm on my way, Dad. I'll be there in ten minutes. Stay on the phone with me, okay?" She was already moving to the front door.

"I think I need to lie down."

"Dad? Dad!"

The line went dead.

She dialed Kevin's number. The call went straight to voicemail.

"Kevin, something is wrong with my dad. I'm headed to his house now."

The drive from Kevin's house to her father's was fifteen minutes, but she made it in ten.

Her father's car wasn't in the driveway. She let herself into the house with her key.

"Dad? Julie? Anybody home?"

The house was quiet. Her heart galloped.

"Dad?"

A soft groan came from the back of the house.

"Dad?" She dropped her purse by the sofa in the living room as she hurried toward the back bedrooms.

Her father was on the floor of the main bedroom, next to the bed. She knelt next to him. "Oh my God, Dad. Here, let me help you up."

Her father gripped her arm tightly. "Hit me." His words slurred.

"Hit you? Did someone hit you, Dad?" Anger swelled in her chest. "Did Julie hit you?"

Her father shook his head. "Not…Julie. He hit me. From behind."

It was a struggle to get her father to his feet, but with his help she was finally able to get him onto the bed.

He rubbed the back of his head.

She put her hand to his head and felt a bump.

"He who, Dad?" she asked, panting slightly from a mix of exertion and rage. "Who hit you?"

"Ellison."

Her body went cold. "That's not possible. Ellison is dead."

Her father shook his head, but whether he was just trying to clear it, or he was disputing her claim about Ellison, she couldn't tell.

A thump came from the front of the house.

Her pulse quickened. Her father might have been confused about who hit him, but someone had. Someone who was still in the house.

She glanced around the room for a weapon but found nothing. Her purse was in the living room where she'd left it after she'd entered the house.

"Dad." She lowered her voice to a whisper. "Where is your phone?"

Her eyes darted around the room. Her father had called

her using his cell phone, but it was nowhere to be seen now. It didn't look like there was a landline in the house. At least, not in the bedroom.

The bedroom window was big enough for her to shimmy through. She could get out, run to a neighbor's house and call the police. But she couldn't leave her father.

She had to get to her purse and her cell phone.

"Stay here, Dad. I'm going to get my phone."

Her father gave a slight nod and squeezed her hand. She could tell he was in a lot of pain. Probably had a concussion. She needed to get him help quickly.

She forced herself to walk to the bedroom door and stuck her head out carefully, peering into the hallway.

It was empty.

She slid into the hall, closing the bedroom door after her. The hallway carpeting was the stiff, scratchy kind. It seemed to snap and crackle with each footstep.

There was a second bedroom across the hall from her father's room that was full of moving boxes.

Forcing herself to step as quietly as possible, she made her way down the hall toward the living room. Her father's house wasn't large. The living room could be seen from the kitchen and dining area. If the intruder was in any of those rooms, he'd see her as soon as she stepped out of the hall.

She stopped at the point where the hall opened onto the living room. Her heart hammered. She couldn't hear anything other than the sound of her own breathing, and that sounded like thunder rumbling through the entire house.

The living room looked to be empty.

She darted across the open space and grabbed her purse. She always kept her phone in the front pocket, but when she plunged her hand inside she felt nothing.

"Looking for this?"

Terror was a strange thing. Rationally, she knew she was more scared than she'd ever been in her life. Yet, at the sound of the voice that was almost as familiar to her as her own, a certain calmness washed over her.

She turned and, for the first time in three years, faced her ex-husband.

"ELLISON."

Ellison stood in the passageway between the living room and the kitchen, a misshapen smile on his face. In one hand, he held her phone, and in the other, a knife.

"Ellison." Although her eyes were telling her that he was there, alive, her brain was struggling to catch up with the sight.

She was looking at a dead man. A very alive, dead man.

He looked different. His blond hair was now dark, almost black. The piercing blue eyes were now covered by brown contacts. He'd aged far more than the three it had been since she'd seen him. His skin darkened by a tan, but leathery looking. It looked like he'd been living hard, but being on the run would do that, she supposed.

"Ellison." She said his name again in an effort to make it all make sense in her head. "What...what are you doing here? How are you here?"

"I'm here for you," Ellison said, the words sending a sliver of fear through her. "You and the ruby."

"You...you stole the ruby?"

Ellison let out a laugh that sent a shiver down her spine. "You can get away with so much when you are dead."

She swallowed hard, already knowing the answer to the question she was about to ask. "And Kim?"

"I needed her help to steal the ruby. Wasn't hard to

convince her. But I couldn't take the chance that she'd turn on me later."

"You killed her?"

He shrugged, but it was more than enough of an answer. He'd killed her friend. And he planned to do the same to her.

She could make a run for the front door, but that would mean leaving her father, and she wouldn't do that. Even if she tried, she had no doubt that Ellison would catch her before she could get the door open. And he had a knife.

She looked into Ellison's eyes and saw a stranger. And hate. The man standing in front of her hated her. But why? She had to try to reach the man she'd married. He was still in there somewhere. At least, she hoped he was.

"Ellison, my father needs help. Let me call an ambulance for him."

"You want to help him? Where were you when I needed help?"

"I tried to be there for you."

"You tried? I lost my job. My reputation. My so-called friends. My home. You," he spat.

"We were divorced before the scandal."

"I never wanted that. I did everything for you. The money? That was all for you."

Maggie jerked with the realization of what he was saying. "I never asked you to steal for me. I wouldn't have."

"You didn't have to ask," he roared. "That's how much I loved you. And when I needed you, you deserted me."

"I tried to be there for you. I called. I reached out. But the pressure. The police suspected I'd helped you steal that money. The police and the press hounded me. I had to move to the West Coast to get away from it. Even after you died."

Ellison smirked. "Looks like that wasn't far enough." He tapped the knife against his thigh twice then flipped it, blade out.

"You don't have to do this. You have the money and now the ruby. Just take them and go."

"The money is gone. It takes a lot of money to live on the run. Why do you think I came for the ruby? And as for this?" He waved the knife at her. "I've had a lot of time to think about your betrayal. You have to pay."

She wasn't going to be able to reach him. If she wanted to get herself and her father out of this alive, she was going to have to fight.

She leaped toward the door, then as Ellison lurched after her, she spun, lashing out with a kick to his side. He hopped and stumbled backward, cursing. She pushed past him into the kitchen. There was another door there and, more importantly, a host of possible weapons she could use to defend herself.

She got lucky. Her father hadn't gotten around to cleaning up after lunch. The sink was full of dishes, including a large butcher knife. She grabbed it and turned just as Ellison stumbled into the kitchen.

"You're going to pay for that," he snarled, starting toward her.

Keys jangled in the front door.

Ellison froze.

"Boyd? Baby, are you okay?"

Maggie screamed, "Julie, run!"

She lunged at Ellison again, swiping out with the knife.

He jumped back, untouched. But the introduction of another person changed his odds. He swore then ran for the back door, shooting a venomous look over his shoulder at her before disappearing out of it.

"Maggie? What's going on? Are you okay? Where is Boyd?" Julie's eyes darted back and forth between the open back door and Maggie.

Maggie slid down onto the kitchen floor, her back against the lower cabinets.

Fire burned up her right arm. She looked down, catching sight of the bloody gash slashed there. He'd stabbed her.

She felt like she was going to throw up. Blood trickled from the wound on her arm and her head spun. "Dad, he needs help. Call 911," she stammered.

Then she passed out.

Chapter Twenty-Two

Maggie had regained consciousness by the time the EMTs arrived, her pride only a little worse for wear for having passed out at the sight of her own blood. She rode to the hospital in the ambulance with her father, Julie driving her car close behind. She'd called Kevin while the EMTs loaded her father into the ambulance and given him a quick summary of Ellison's attack on her father. Kevin was already there when the ambulance pulled up in the emergency room drive, standing next to his sister, Tanya.

She was relieved her father had a doctor that she knew cared. Tanya took charge immediately, barking out orders to the nurse and EMTs helping to move her father into the hospital. Kevin was by her side the moment she stepped out of the ambulance.

"I think my heart stopped when I got your message," Kevin said as they followed the gurney into the hospital. "Are you okay?"

"It's just a scratch." She held up her arm so he could see. The white bandage the EMT had applied in the ambulance was much bigger than was necessary. "I gave everyone a scare by passing out though."

A smile cracked through his worried expression. "Still can't stand to see your own blood."

"I'm not sure how anyone can."

She filled him in on her father's call and Ellison attacking her when she arrived at her father's house.

The shock she felt at seeing Ellison was mirrored on Kevin's face. "Ellison? How?"

"Apparently, he faked his death to get out of the embezzlement charge. I don't know how he did it, but, Kevin, I'm telling you he's alive." A tiny shiver shook through her.

"I'm not doubting you."

The doors to the waiting room opened, and Julie rushed through before he could say anything else. Julie scanned the visitors in the waiting room until her eyes landed on Maggie and Kevin in the far corner.

She rushed forward. "Has the doctor seen Boyd yet? Have they told you anything about his condition?"

Almost as if Julie had conjured her, Tanya stepped through the glass doors separating the emergency room from the waiting room.

"Maggie." Tanya stopped in front of the trio. "It's good to see you, although I wish it was under different circumstances."

"It's good to see you again too. I'm sorry to be so abrupt, but how is my father?"

"Nothing to be sorry for. Your father suffered a pretty serious concussion, but otherwise looks to be in good health. Because of his age, I want to keep him overnight just to keep an eye on him."

Maggie let go of the breath she felt like she'd been holding since she'd walked into her father's house and found him on the floor.

Julie squeezed her hand, tears of relief streaming down her face. "Can we see him?"

"You can see him now but only two at a time, and I'd

suggest you keep the visit brief. He needs to rest, but I anticipate releasing him tomorrow."

Julie and Maggie thanked the doctor.

"You two go," Kevin said. "I'll wait here."

Maggie froze when she saw her father in bed. His eyes were closed, and he looked so small and frail. His face was gray and ashen. His mortality slapped her in the face. Ellison's attack could have ended so much more tragically, and no matter what, one day her father wouldn't be here.

Julie squeezed her arm and gently pulled her forward toward her father's bed. "It's okay. He's okay," she whispered, seemingly reading the angst on Maggie's face.

"Dad," Maggie whispered.

Her father's eyes opened. It took several seconds for him to focus, but when he did, a small smile crossed his lips.

Julie slipped to the other side of the bed. Each woman took one of his hands.

"Did somebody die?" he quipped, looking from Maggie to Julie and back.

"I'm so sorry, Dad." Tears pooled in Maggie's eyes.

Her father pulled his hand from hers and cupped her face. "Hey, hey. You have nothing to be sorry for. This is not your fault."

"But Ellison…he was using you to get to me. He…"

Her father's face darkened. "He's out of his mind, but that's not your fault. I don't want you to blame yourself."

Her father's eyelids dropped.

Maggie shot a glance at Julie, who gave a slight shake of her head.

"Dad, I'm going to go and let you get some rest."

Her father's eyes opened again. His hand slid down to the bed and grasped hers. "Be careful. Stay safe."

She returned her father's squeeze. "I will. I promise. You get some rest." Maggie's gaze shifted to Julie. "You're going to stay with him?"

Julie smiled, looking down at Boyd with so much tenderness and devotion that it made Maggie's heart clench. "You just let them try to put me out of here."

Maggie was pretty sure that nothing less than a small army would be capable of dislodging Julie from her father's side. Still, the hospital wasn't a bunker. If Ellison wanted to get in, there were dozens of opportunities.

"I'll be back to check on you later."

"No need. I'm just going to be sleeping anyway. You just stay safe."

She leaned forward and pressed a kiss to her father's cheek. "I love you, Dad."

"I love you too, honey."

Kevin was on the phone when she returned to the waiting room. He hung up as she sailed through the doors.

"How is your father?"

She opened her mouth to answer, but all that came out was a choked sob.

Kevin pulled her into his arms and let her cry for several minutes. Once the deluge of tears slowed, she pulled back.

"Feel any better?" He grabbed a tissue from the box someone had left on the waiting room's coffee table.

Maggie dabbed her eyes and blew her nose. "A little. It was just…seeing my father so helpless."

"It can be hard to see our parents in a vulnerable state, but he's going to be okay according to the doctors, right?"

She nodded. "Right. Julie is staying in his room with him, but I'm scared that—"

"Ellison might try to hurt your father again as a way

to get to you. I thought of that too. Tess called Detective Francois, and she is sending one of our guys from West Investigations to guard your father until Ellison is in custody."

A boulder of stress rose from her shoulders. "Thank you." Ellison's screed at her father's house came back to her. "Ellison killed Kim," she said, a sob catching in her throat. "He admitted it to me."

From the look on his face, it appeared Kevin had already figured that out. He set his notebook aside and pulled her into another hug. "I know, sweetheart. I'm sorry."

"It's my fault. Ellison, he blames me. For the divorce. For pulling away during his embezzlement scandal."

Kevin lightly gripped her shoulders. "Hey, don't do that to yourself. You aren't to blame for any of this. He is. No one made him steal that money. Or the Viperé ruby. He took Kim's life. That's on him and only on him, understand?"

Her head understood, but her heart felt as if she should have known. The heavy weight of guilt wouldn't be lifting soon.

The doors to the waiting room opened again, and Detective Francois and Tess strode in.

"Ms. Scott, I'm happy to see you are relatively unharmed," the detective said. "Wishing your father a speedy recovery."

"Thank you, Detective," Maggie replied.

"Heard you kicked butt." Tess offered a tight smile. "Good girl."

Maggie sighed. "I don't know about that, but thanks."

"I know this is a trying time, but are you up for some

questions?" Detective Francois asked, taking out his phone.

Maggie sighed. More questions were the exact opposite of what she wanted to do at the moment, but she knew the detective was just doing his job. "Whatever I can do to help."

She went through the details, reiterating everything she'd told Kevin only minutes earlier. Francois's questions were nearly identical to Kevin's, but worded differently enough that a few smaller details she hadn't recalled before came back to her.

Detective Francois finally put his phone away. "Well, we have one major problem here."

Kevin's and Tess's slight nods showed they'd picked up on whatever the major problem was, but Maggie found herself left in the dark alone.

"Anyone care to fill me in on the problem?" Maggie asked.

"Ellison has been living off the grid and hiding his tracks for a long time," Tess started.

"He's practiced at being invisible. That's going to make it harder for us to find him," Kevin finished.

"I had patrols out driving a ten-mile radius within minutes of the 911 call, but he got past us somehow," Francois said, the frustration in his voice evident.

"Like I said, he's had a lot of time to practice being invisible. And since we can be sure he isn't using his real name, but we have no idea what name he is using, we don't really have a place to start looking," Kevin said.

"He's planned this for a long time." Tess frowned. "Harbored anger toward Maggie. He's not going to stop until he gets her."

"Tess," Kevin hissed.

Maggie pushed back the fear bubbling in her gut. "No, Tess is right. There's no point in sugarcoating it. Ellison is obsessed. He took the ruby because he needed the money, but he's stayed because he wants me. Dead."

Their quartet was silent for a long moment.

"We need to draw him out on our terms," Tess finally said.

"No," Kevin barked.

"The brass would never sign off on something like that," Detective Francois said, shaking his head.

"So it doesn't have to be an LAPD operation," Tess shot back.

"I said no." Kevin's bark had turned into a growl.

"Excuse me." Maggie raised her hand as if she were a pupil in school. "Again, could someone tell me what it is we are talking about here?"

Tess looked at her. "Bait. Specifically, using you as bait to draw out Ellison."

"How many times do I have to say it—"

Tess held up a hand. "You didn't have to say it the first time. I know you're against it, but if we weren't talking about Maggie, would you be as opposed to the idea?"

"It's too dangerous," Kevin said.

"Not an answer," Tess shot back. "Maggie is already in danger, and we don't know when Ellison is going to pop up again. He's waited years to come out of the shadows. He could very well go back into hiding, wait until our guard is down and pop up again. We have an opportunity now, and we should press it."

"She's right," Maggie interjected.

"She is not right."

"Look, I don't like it either, but she's right about Ellison going back underground. I don't want to live my life looking over my shoulder. If we have the chance to grab him now, I say we take it. All the better if we can get the Viperé ruby back at the same time and save West Investigations' reputation."

"I don't give a damn about West Investigations' reputation," Kevin growled.

"Not the best way to get on your new boss's good side," Tess chided.

"He doesn't mean that," Maggie said, shooting Kevin a look.

"If I thought he did, I'd fire him," Tess responded.

Detective Francois took a step away from the group. "I need to get back out there and try to catch Ellison Coelho using less…radical means. LAPD can't be involved in dangling Ms. Scott as bait, but if I can be of any help, you have my number."

Maggie guessed that meant he didn't suspect her in the crimes any longer. That was some relief. "Thank you, Detective."

Detective Francois gave her a brisk nod then strode from the waiting room.

"This is a terrible idea," Kevin said.

"If you have a better one, I'm all ears," Tess shot back.

His frown said it all.

"I'm in," Maggie said. She reached for Kevin's hand and looked him in the eye. "I'm in. I trust you and Tess, and I want to end this now."

Kevin gripped both her hands and leaned down until his forehead rested against hers. He closed his eyes. Out of the side of her eye, Maggie saw Tess slide away.

"I don't want to lose you," he whispered.

"I don't want to lose you either. This is the best shot that we have right now."

They stood for a moment more before Kevin pulled back. His gaze tracked to Tess standing a polite distance away now. “What do you have in mind?”

Chapter Twenty-Three

Kevin sat in his office, frustrated. Detective Francois hadn't been willing to dangle Maggie as bait, but the police department was willing to bend the truth a bit to get the public off their backs. Francois put out a press statement saying the department believed they knew who the suspect was in the theft of the Viperé ruby and Kim Sumika's murder. The statement made it clear that the crimes had been targeted and that the police believed the culprit had likely fled the country.

And in the week since Ellison had attacked Boyd Scott, Kevin could almost convince himself that the police's statement was correct and that Ellison had done the rational thing and run. Neither West Investigations nor the LAPD had been able to find a single trace of Ellison.

But Kevin's gut told him that after everything he'd done, Ellison wasn't going to give up on getting to Maggie.

Despite his attempts to convince her not to, Maggie had moved back into her cottage. West Investigations had set up discreet surveillance on her at home and at work. Since Detective Francois had made it clear Maggie was no longer a suspect, Maggie was pushing to get her job back. Gustev and Tutwilder were both dragging their feet and resisting though. Neither were happy to have her back at the museum, but Maggie was determined to fight for her job. She wasn't going to allow Ellison's actions to ruin the life she'd built for a second time. Kevin admired her for that gumption.

There was a knock on the door to his office. Tess stood there, practically vibrating. "Hey, we have a lead on the ruby."

His pulse quickened. A lead on the ruby meant a lead on Ellison's whereabouts. "What's the lead?"

"A source tipped me to an underground auction for black-market art. My source says the guy running it was bragging about some, and I quote, 'big, honking gem that's going to bring in a boatload of money.'"

Kevin grinned. "LAPD?"

"I've already called Detective Francois, and he spoke to my source and found him credible. The cops are working on search warrants right now." Tess's smile grew wider. "And since I've been such a Good Samaritan, Detective Francois has allowed us to tag along."

Kevin rose, moving around his desk before she'd finished the sentence. "Let's go."

POLICE VEHICLES CROWDED the parking lot of the elementary school a half block away from the target house. They were lucky that the estate homes sat several yards back from the street. Kevin and Tess joined the half a dozen uniformed officers standing at the trunk of one of the patrol cars listening to Detective Francois give instructions.

"Okay," Francois said, fastening the strap on the bulletproof vest he wore. "Our source says that there is a high-value auction of various stolen goods going on inside the property three homes down from here. The real estate records show it's owned by a foreign national from Sweden who is supposedly out of the country. We are going to breach quickly and detain everyone inside. We want to take everyone in safely and make sure we don't damage any priceless art or jewels or whatever else they are selling in there." Detective Francois gestured toward where Kevin and Tess stood at the back of the pack. "These two are headed in with us. They are on the trail of the Viperé ruby."

A ripple fluttered through the group as heads turned to check them out.

"We're going in as four teams of four. Two through the front and two around the back." Francois checked the magazine on his gun then looked up at the group. "Everybody ready?"

Kevin adjusted the bulletproof vest he wore and checked his own gun.

There was a ripple of agreement before everyone peeled off into groups of four. One of the officers carried a ram. The teams advance toward the house, quickly and quietly, the first two teams peeling off and heading around the house toward the back. The front rooms of the house were empty, the lack of lights making it appear empty, but the house was large, easily six to seven thousand square feet, with two aboveground levels.

Kevin and Tess's team brought up the rear heading to the front of the house. The two teams stopped on either side of the front door waiting for the breach signal. It was late, and the neighborhood was quiet. Cool air brushed over his skin, but adrenaline and anxiousness had beads of sweat forming on his temple despite the breeze.

"Team three and four in position," the radio on one of the uniformed officer's shoulder crackled.

Detective Francois held up three fingers. The first finger dropped soundlessly. Then the second. With the last finger, Francois barked, “Go! Go! Go!”

The officer with the ram advanced, swinging it at the door at full speed. The door cracked under the force and swung open. The rest of the team wasted no time flooding through the open door, yelling out commands for the inhabitants of the house to “freeze” and “put their hands up.” The other two teams flooded in from the back of the house.

The teams that had come through the back door moved forward, clearing the rooms on the main floor quickly. But it was clear from the angry shrieks and screams that came from the basement that was where the action was.

Kevin followed Tess, their team leader, and one of the other teams down the basement stairs. The basement was finished with marble floors, two chandeliers and a full bar running along one of the rear walls.

A small stage had been set up at the other end of the basement. People, most clad in business attire, were scattered in the rows of chairs facing the stage. Three paintings, abstracts that looked like nothing more than paint splatters, rested on easels in a semicircle on the stage. A gold statue of a dragon held a prominent place on a podium in front of the paintings. Anyone could be forgiven for thinking they’d walked into an auction house or gallery instead of the basement of a multimillion dollar home in the suburbs of Los Angeles.

“Nobody moves!” Francois called out. “Keep your hands where we can see them.”

Two of the men in the crowd stood, but the third team of uniformed officers hustling down the staircase quickly snuffed out any errant thoughts of fleeing.

Kevin scanned the faces of the men in the crowd looking for Ellison, but Maggie's ex wasn't there.

"Lombard. Stenning. Over here. I think there's something you'd like to see," Detective Francois called.

He followed Tess. Detective Francois held back a curtain separating the front of the stage. Several more items waited behind the curtain for their turn on the stage. Kevin's eyes were drawn to one. One sparkling, large, red jewel. The Viperé ruby, nestled in a black velvet cushion in a locked glass case.

Tess turned to him with a grin. "Bingo!"

It wouldn't be official until the insurance company's gemologist evaluated and signed off on it, but it looked like they'd just found the Viperé ruby.

MAGGIE WAS FRUSTRATED. Without a job, she was listless and unsure what to do with her days. She couldn't spend every minute with Kevin, and wouldn't want to if she could. He had a job, and even though he was spending the majority of his time searching for Ellison, he had other cases he had to oversee for West Investigations.

Her father had been released from the hospital, and at her urging, he and Julie had gone to Julie's son's house in Arizona. Kevin assured her that he had a man he could trust watching over the family, although Maggie had chosen to keep that piece of information from her father. She didn't want to worry him more than necessary, but she was relieved that her father and Julie were safe. Both of them assured her that they didn't blame her for Ellison's attack, but Maggie couldn't shake the guilt. She'd brought Ellison into their lives in the first place, and it was her Ellison was really after.

Since moving back into her cottage, she was under

constant surveillance by the West team, but so far Ellison hadn't taken the bait. With time on her hands, she spent it researching and racking her brain for where Ellison could be hiding out. In this day and age, it was nearly impossible for a person to go completely off the grid. They just had to figure out where Ellison would go. She knew him best, and she was their best chance of doing that.

The doorbell rang, and then someone pounded on the door. "Ms. Scott? It's Detective Decker."

"Yes."

"Ma'am, I received a call from Detective Francois. He believes Ellison Coelho is in the area. He'd like me to stick close to you until he gets here. Do you mind if I come in?"

Her pulse rate picked up its pace. Ellison was close. That meant they had a chance to catch him and end this nightmare tonight.

She looked out the peephole. The detective stood too close for her to see his face, but he held his badge up so she could see it.

She unlocked the dead bolt. As she opened the door, a hard push came from the other side, wrenching the doorknob from her hands and sending the door crashing open.

Ellison stood on the other side of the door, a gun in his hand. "Surprise."

She turned to run but didn't get far.

Excruciating pain vaulted through the back of her head. Then everything went black.

When she awoke, Maggie's head hurt worse than it ever had before. Her hands and feet were tied, and there was a piece of masking tape over her mouth. She was on her side, bouncing against a hard surface. In a car. The trunk of a car, to be specific.

Ellison had her. He intended to kill her.

And Kevin had no idea where she was.

Panic started to rise in her chest. She pushed it back down. She needed to keep her head if she had any hope of getting out of this alive. She needed a plan. It was dark in the trunk, but Ellison had tied her hands together in front of her.

She groped around the floor of the trunk hoping to find something, anything, to defend herself with. But there was nothing.

The car stopped abruptly, slamming her into the back of the trunk then rolling her forward.

She heard the car's door open then slam closed. Gravel crunched.

Ellison was coming.

The trunk popped open, and she blinked rapidly. Her eyes adjusted to the moonlight filtering in the open trunk, and she looked up into the mottled face of the man she'd once thought she'd loved.

"I'm going to get you out of the trunk. If you try anything, I will shoot you." He held up the gun to underscore his point. "Do you understand?"

She nodded.

Ellison grabbed her tied hands and yanked her up. He lifted her out of the trunk then roughly dropped her to the ground next to the back tires of the car.

She took the opportunity to scan the area. They were on a dock. Next to a warehouse that looked to be closed.

He slammed the trunk then reached for her again.

He pulled her to her feet, pushing her toward the warehouse.

Chapter Twenty-Four

He had her.

Kevin tried to control his panic, but it was a losing battle. It was all he could think about. Ellison had Maggie and was doing God only knew what to her. She might not even still be alive.

He pulled to a stop on Maggie's street, which was full of vehicles—squad cars, marked police sedans, black West Investigations SUVs and an ambulance.

Please, God, don't let that be for Maggie.

He got out of the car and ran toward Detective Francois.

"Maggie, is she—?" He couldn't bring himself to say the words.

The tech who'd been monitoring the security system at Maggie's house had called as soon as he'd realized the man at Maggie's door wasn't a police officer. He'd said that Ellison had knocked Maggie out and carried her out of the range of the camera, but what if he'd been wrong. What if Ellison had just taken her out of the range of the camera to—

"The ambulance isn't for Maggie," Tess said, stepping in front of him and stopping him from racing for the ambulance.

Francois radiated anger. "It's for the man I had on her

house tonight. Detective Decker. He took one gunshot to the torso through the car window. The EMTs are preparing to take him to the hospital now."

As if they'd heard Francois's words, the ambulance's sirens whooped, and the vehicle lurched forward and down the street, increasing in speed as it went.

Kevin worked to slow his racing heart. It wasn't Maggie in the back of the ambulance on the way to the hospital. That was good. "What do we know?"

"Our cameras caught Ellison walking up to Maggie's door at 9:25 p.m.," Tess started in a calm, focused voice. "Kept his head down, but he had Decker's badge around his neck and a holstered sidearm, so our tech thought it was Decker at first. Maggie must have thought so too. She opened the door to him after he held his badge up to the peephole. It wasn't until he pushed open the door and clocked Maggie over the head with the gun that the tech realized something was wrong."

Kevin tamped down the anger that swelled in him at hearing that Ellison had hurt Maggie. He needed to remain professional, clearheaded, if he was going to find her in time.

"The tech tried to reach Decker, but he didn't answer."

The ambulance was gone now, but they all instinctively turned to look at the unmarked sedan with the missing driver-side window that CSI was now crawling over.

Tess cleared her throat. "When he couldn't reach Decker, he called Francois."

"I had a squad car dispatched immediately. The unit found Decker when they arrived, one uniform started CPR while the other went into Ms. Scott's house."

"Ellison and Maggie were gone by then." Tess picked

up the story again. "He parked out of view of the cameras, so we don't have a tag, make or model."

"That suggests that Ellison knew where the cameras were. And if he was able to sneak up on a trained detective—"

"He's probably been casing the house and neighborhood," Tess finished his thought.

"How is that possible?" Kevin wanted to scream. The LAPD and West Investigations, one of the best security firms in the nation, were supposed to have been protecting Maggie, and they both failed?

Tess frowned. "There are always blind spots. You know that. We're doing the best we can, but Ellison has had years of practice being invisible. Hiding himself from people he didn't want to see him."

"I have officers canvassing the area for possible witnesses," Francois spoke up. "It's possible someone saw something or someone's security system caught the car."

"And if no one did?" Kevin asked although the answer was obvious. If they didn't get a break, they were screwed.

"Detective Francois, sir," a uniformed officer called. Francois ambled away.

"Kevin, I think you should head back to West headquarters," Tess said.

"The hell I will."

"You are too close to this. You've been too close to this case. I should have taken you off days ago. And now..." She shook her head. "I can't use you if your personal feelings for Maggie are going to cloud your professional judgment."

He glared at Tess. "I'm not going anywhere."

Tess glared right back. "I can make it an order—"

"Lombard. Stenning." Francois waved them over. "I think we got something here."

Kevin whirled away from his boss, stalking over to where Francois stood with the uniform. He hadn't noticed him earlier, but a teenaged boy stood with the two men. Long wisps of curly red hair fell in the boy's face, and he fidgeted from one foot to the other.

"This is Allan. Son, can you repeat what you just told me?"

The teen let out a heavy sigh. "Again?"

"One more time," Francois encouraged him.

"Okay, I mean, like, I was out, okay, I snuck out to see my girl, and I'm just walking, right?" He looked at the adults around him as if walking might not be familiar to the old folks.

"Got it, kid. You were walking," Kevin said, hoping to urge the story on faster.

"So yeah, I'm walking. My girl lives a couple blocks down that way." He pointed south of where they stood. "Then all of a sudden, I hear this lady scream, and then I see a man carrying a woman, like, fireman style over his shoulder and whatnot. And I'm like, whoa, that's probably not cool."

Kevin was finding it hard not to shake the story out of the kid to get him to talk faster. Tess must have sensed his agitation.

She gave a slight shake of her head.

"So then I was like, I can't let him see me, you know. So I ducked down behind that car there." The boy turned and pointed at a black Range Rover. "But like I said, something didn't seem right, so I snapped a picture of the car."

"You have a photo of the car the man put the woman in?" Francois said, testily.

"Oh, yeah." The teen reached into his coat pocket and pulled out his phone. "I must have forgotten to tell you that part. I got a photo of the tag and everything. Wanna see?" He held the phone up to his face to unlock it.

Kevin didn't wait for the teen to find the photo. He snatched the phone from the boy's hand.

"Hey, man! That's mine."

Kevin ignored the teen, navigating to his photo gallery while Tess assured the boy that he'd get his phone back in a moment.

He found the photos quickly. A silver, four-door Toyota Corolla. A dime a dozen, but the teen had captured a clear picture of the license plate. He sent copies of the photographs to himself, Tess and Francois before handing the phone back to the boy.

"You did a good job," he said to the teen. "Stop sneaking out at night though. You're going to get yourself in trouble." Kevin turned and started after Tess, who, like Francois, was already on the phone probably having someone pull the registration for the license.

THE CAR BELONGED to Charles and Louise Bennett, a couple in their seventies. The computer guru at West Investigations tracked down an address and phone number for the couple, worried that they might have become Ellison's victims too. Luckily, they were out of town in their winter home in Florida. As far as they knew, the car was parked in the garage at their San Pedro home.

The Bennetts had given permission to search their property. They had a larger home on several acres that afforded them the privacy that was elusive in much of Los Angeles. Ellison had to have spent a significant amount of time formulating his plan. If they dug deep enough, they'd probably find some connection between him and the Bennetts, even a tenuous one. How else would he know that they spent part of the year in Florida? He'd had years to come up with a nearly foolproof plan. Who knows how much time they had to find Maggie before it was too late for her? It might already be too late for all they knew.

Kevin, Tess, Detective Francois and several other officers fanned out in the house. Despite the size of the home, it didn't take long to determine that Ellison and Maggie weren't there. It was equally clear, though, that someone had been living in the house while the Bennetts were away. Dishes cluttered the countertops. The bed in the main bedroom was unmade. Wet bath towels lay on the bathroom floor. A dark blue Tucson was parked in the garage, but the silver Toyota Corolla that should have been next to it was gone.

"Damnit! Where are they?" Kevin's chest felt as if it were caving in on itself. He'd never been more afraid.

Tess clasped a hand on his shoulder and squeezed. "Keep your head in the game. We'll find her."

He nodded, taking several deep breaths then joining the search of the house for clues to where Ellison may have taken Maggie.

He crossed the sunken living room to the home office. One long wall was a floor-to-ceiling bookcase that matched the oversize walnut-colored desk that dominated the room. A sleek silver computer sat on the neat-as-a-pin desk.

Kevin sat in the leather executive chair and turned on the computer. The login and password were taped to the monitor. What better way for Ellison to stay off the grid than to use someone else's Wi-Fi and login information.

Kevin opened the browser and went to the history, frustrated to find that it had been deleted.

"Try the cache," Tess said, coming up behind him at the desk.

"The cache?"

"Move." She shooed him out of the chair, taking the seat for herself and clicking the mouse. "Everyone knows to clear their browser history if they don't want someone to come behind them and see what they've been searching. But most people don't think about the cache. That's where the computer stores certain data—images, fonts, that sort of thing—that make it easier for you to download the same pages again later. That can tell us a lot too."

Tess clicked the mouse a few more times, and a logo popped up on screen.

"MaxPrint," Kevin read the name off. "Never heard of it."

"Let's see." Tess opened a browser and put the name of the company along with "Los Angeles area" into the search box.

The search engine returned a webpage. Bright red letters at the top of the page screamed that, as of a few years ago, MaxPrint had closed its doors permanently. Tess copied the address for the company and pasted it into a map search box.

A map pinpointing the defunct business's location opened up in a new tab. She zoomed in on what looked like an industrial area of mostly businesses.

"That must be where he took her." Tess looked up at him from where she sat. "The building is probably still empty. Ellison would have made sure of that. And since it is late, he'd have all night before anyone from one of the surrounding businesses showed up."

"Francois!" Kevin yelled, already heading for the door.

The detective met him in the foyer of the house. He quickly explained what he and Tess had found and their theory.

"I'll get squad cars rolling that way now." Francois was already dialing a number on his phone.

"Tess and I are on our way," Kevin said.

Maggie was in that warehouse. He could feel it.

Hang on, baby. I'm coming.

THE CONCRETE FLOOR was cracked, little more than rubble in several places, and the air was sour and smelled of mold. The space was mostly empty, but there were signs of the business that used to inhabit the space. Broken wooden pallets, a metal desk and office chair. Wires hung precariously from the ceiling, and most of the windows that lined the top of the wall had been broken, jagged shards of glass protruding dangerously.

She heard a squeak as they entered, followed by the pitter-patter of paws that signaled she and Ellison were not the only two animals in the space.

But rats were the least of her problems.

Ellison led her to the chair and pushed her into it. "Don't move. I'm going to take the tape off of your mouth. If you try anything…" He held the gun up.

She yelped when he ripped the tape off.

"Why are you doing this?"

He glared at her. "I already told you why."

"Ellison, this…this has to stop. I'm sorry if I hurt you. But this, you aren't going to get away with it. The police know you're alive. They know you stole the money, the ruby, that you killed Kim and attacked my father." She said the last words with more than a little bitterness. She'd never forgive him for hurting her father.

He chortled. "Then what's one more notch on my record, huh? It was so much harder to live on the run than I expected. Five hundred thousand dollars doesn't go nearly as far as I'd have hoped. New identities. Constant moving. Staying off the radar. It's expensive." He propped himself against the side of the desk. "When I saw that the Larimer would be exhibiting the Viperé and that you were curating the exhibit, well, it had to be a sign."

"A sign?"

"Yes. The ruby is priceless. And if I could steal it and make it look like you'd done it then disappear, well, that had a certain symmetry to it, don't you see? Only you wouldn't just be pretending to be dead like I was."

"No one will believe I stole the ruby now, and if you kill me, Kevin will hunt you to the ends of the earth."

Ellison's laughter grew louder. He threw his arms out wide and tipped his head back. "Let him come." He looked her in the eyes. "I lost everything when you walked out on me. I have nothing left to lose."

They were the words of a man who was lost to madness. There was nothing behind Ellison's gaze. She knew he would kill her if she didn't do something.

She lunged up out of the chair at him, ready to fight for her life.

Luck was on her side. She caught Ellison off guard. By the time he thought to raise the gun, she was driving her shoulder into his stomach.

He yelped and staggered backward.

She'd never punched anyone in her life, didn't know the first thing about doing it properly, but she made a fist and swung for Ellison's face, catching him on the chin.

He had four inches and at least thirty pounds on her, but she knew that if she lost this fight, it would be her last. She used that knowledge, that fear, as fuel, punching and kicking like a wild animal.

Ellison put his hands up in self-defense, the hand with the gun coming around in a circular motion and catching her in the temple.

Now she staggered, falling down to her knees.

She looked up to find Ellison pointing the gun at her. His lips moved, but she couldn't hear him. It sounded like the world had exploded into screams.

All she could see was the gun pointed at her.

Then Ellison jerked backward, the gun flying out of his hand.

Thunder rolled over the warehouse, and it took a moment for her to realize that it wasn't thunder but a helicopter. The screams had come from the police officers that had stormed into the warehouse.

Then Kevin was there, on his knees beside her.

"Maggie, baby, are you okay? Talk to me."

She looked past Kevin to where Ellison lay on the floor. She couldn't see him because he was surrounded by half a dozen armed officers. "Is he dead?"

"Don't worry about him." Kevin slid one arm around her waist and another under her legs. "Let's get you out of here."

She rested her head on his shoulder and let him carry her to safety.

Chapter Twenty-Five

Maggie didn't complain when Kevin insisted she go to the hospital and get checked out this time. Ellison faking his death, stealing the Viperé ruby and attempting to kill her had made international news. She'd had to turn off her cell phone, and Detective Francois had stationed several officers at Kim's house, her house, to keep the vultures off the property.

Ellison was dead. The police were still searching the home he'd been hiding out in, but it appeared he'd documented his plan to steal the Viperé and his growing hatred for Maggie in a journal. From what the police had already been able to piece together, it appeared that Ellison had decided that the best way to avoid the consequences of his embezzlement back in New York was to fake his death. He'd done a sufficiently good job at hiding most of the money, so he had the means to live comfortably if he scaled back his lifestyle. Unfortunately, scaling back was the opposite of what he'd done. In less than three years, he'd blown through almost all of the half a million dollars he'd been able to squirrel away. With no money and nothing but time, his thoughts had turned to how to get his hands on more money.

The browser history on his computer showed that he'd

been keeping track of Maggie and her new job, his bitterness toward her perceived slight of him during the embezzlement investigation growing. When he saw the announcement for the upcoming Viperé ruby exhibit, a plan to steal it began to take shape in his head. Being dead allowed Ellison a lot of latitude for sneaking into Maggie's life. He discovered Kim's gambling habit and debts and, using a fake persona, convinced Kim to give him the security code for the museum's cameras as well as details about the donors' open house. Maggie wasn't initially a target. Ellison had no idea she would still be there on the night of the theft, but seeing her ignited all the animosity he'd built up toward her, and his rage had taken control. He'd decided that she had to pay for what he saw as abandoning him. He was the one who had broken into her house and attacked her father.

There was a knock on her hospital room door. She looked up to find Kevin standing in the doorway. He held a white paper bag in one hand and a coffee cup in the other.

Her stomach growled, and she realized that she was starving.

Kevin put the bag and coffee down on the bedside table then leaned over and kissed her lightly on the lips. "How are you feeling?"

"Like I'd like to get out of this hospital bed and into my own bed."

Kevin kissed her again. "Soon. Let the doctors run all their tests then I'll take you home."

She smiled up at the man she'd loved since she was twenty, the man she now knew she'd always love. "That sounds good." She wiggled her eyebrows.

He laughed. "I wasn't suggesting anything." He sobered a touch. "But I do think it might be a good idea if you stayed with me. Just for a few days. It's a bit of a madhouse at your place right now."

She sighed. "So I've heard. I talked to my father and Julie and let them know I was okay."

Kevin nodded. "I know. Tess agreed to keep a man from West on them for another day or two. Just to be on the safe side."

Maggie let out a breath of relief. "Thank you. I know Ellison is no longer a threat to me or my dad, but…"

"But you need time to process everything. I get it." Kevin reached for her hand. "Take your time. I'm not going anywhere."

She squeezed his hand, for the first time in days feeling light, despite being in a hospital bed. "That's a promise I'm going to hold you to."

Kevin leaned down, his lips grazing hers. "Hold me tight."

Epilogue

Maggie stood in the small party room with Julie and Julie's daughter, Sara. She felt butterflies soaring in her stomach. She could hear the sound of the harpist and the buzz of the wedding guests floating on the breeze being carried in from the garden. Everyone was waiting.

She looked in the mirror, touching her hair, which had been twisted into an elaborate updo with curls falling forward to frame her face.

"You look gorgeous," Julie said from the other side of the room.

Maggie turned and smiled at the bride. "We're supposed to be telling *you* that."

Julie really did make a beautiful bride. She wore a champagne-colored tea-length dress and red satin heels with a sparkly buckle. She'd spent the last three months all but glued to Maggie's father's side, nursing him back to health. Her father and Julie had decided that they didn't want to wait any longer than necessary to make their relationship official, although as far as Maggie was concerned, Julie was already officially part of their family. There was no need for a quick wedding, but since that was what her father and Julie wanted, Maggie made it her mission to make it happen. She'd thrown herself into wedding planning with gusto.

Kevin had gently suggested, more than once, that her enthusiasm for wedding planning might be an offshoot of the lingering guilt she felt over Ellison's attack on her father. It was true that she still struggled with guilt from having brought Ellison into their lives, but she was working through it. And she did want her father and Julie to have the wedding of their dreams. Even if they only had three months to make it happen.

Thankfully, Julie's daughter and sons had also been on board with making their mother's wedding everything she wanted. And Boyd and Julie wanted to keep the nuptials small and intimate. They'd divided up the to-do list, and together they'd been able to get the flowers, cake, food, venue, dresses, tuxedos and musicians on board in less than ninety days. And in the process, Maggie had begun building the first threads of a bond with her soon-to-be stepsister and stepbrothers.

"My hands are shaking," Julie said.

"Here, Mom," Sara said, thrusting a champagne flute in her mother's hand. "Drink this. It will calm your nerves."

Julie took a long sip and pressed her palm flat against her stomach. "Whew. I don't want to be tipsy going down the aisle."

Sara waved away her mother's concern with a laugh. "Don't worry. Rick can carry you down the aisle if he has to."

Maggie joined her soon-to-be stepsister and stepmother in laughter. At six three and built like a professional football player, Julie's oldest son, Rick, would have no problem carrying his mother down the aisle. But Julie dispelled that notion quickly.

"No way." Julie set the half-full champagne glass down

on a side table. "I want to get to the end of that aisle on my own steam and greet my groom."

Maggie's heart swelled with the love she saw in Julie's eyes. "Well, let's get this show on the road then."

The women shared a quick three-way hug before marching into the anteroom where Rick, Julie's younger son, Thomas, and one of Boyd's friends from the senior center waited to escort them down the aisle.

Maggie slipped her arm through Thomas's and grabbed her bouquet of pink and off-white roses. Together, the wedding party stepped forward as the harpist began playing the wedding march. They walked into the garden, which was full of colorful flowers, and faced the sparkling manmade lake that was the centerpiece of the resort's attractions. It was the perfect backdrop for Julie and her father to exchange their vows, but all Maggie could see was Kevin.

He looked more handsome than she'd ever seen him in a dark blue suit that looked as if each thread had been spooled just for him. His smile lit up his face, and his eyes never left hers as her father and Julie pledged their undying love to each other. Maggie was ridiculously happy. Not just for her father, but because she and Kevin had decided to give their relationship another shot. They'd both been through a lot and made mistakes when they were younger, but she knew that they were wiser and stronger as individuals now. They'd spent a lot of time talking, about what they'd done wrong and about what they wanted out of a relationship and life now. She felt in her heart that it would last this time. They'd agreed to take it slow, but she knew Kevin was the man she was supposed to spend her life with. He'd always been that man.

Later that night, with the reception in full swing, Kevin

swept Maggie outside onto the patio where her father and Julie had exchanged their vows just hours earlier. They walked hand in hand to the edge of the lake, a bottle of champagne in Maggie's hand and two champagne flutes in Kevin's.

She tapped her glass against Kevin's before taking a sip. "It was a beautiful wedding, wasn't it?"

"I don't know," Kevin answered. "All I could see was you."

She set her champagne glass on the patio and kissed him.

After a long moment, Kevin broke off the kiss. "I worried that it was too early, but I don't think I can wait any longer." He fell to one knee and slid a little black box from his trouser pocket. "I want to spend the rest of my life with you. Marry me?"

A single tear fell from Maggie's eye, but her heart swelled and the smile she wore lit up her insides. "Yes," she answered, gazing down at the man she loved.

Kevin slid a brilliant square-cut diamond onto her finger then stood, sweeping her into his arms. "Since you're now an expert in pulling together beautiful weddings quickly, how about we set the wedding day for three months from now?"

Maggie laughed, her insides flip-flopping at the thought of another wedding. "I'm not sure I can wait that long to be your wife."

Kevin's grin spread from ear to ear. "That's just what I hoped to hear."

* * * * *

Don't miss the stories in this mini series!

WEST INVESTIGATIONS

Under Lock And Key
K.D. RICHARDS
October 2024

The Perfect Murder
K.D. RICHARDS
November 2024

Keep reading for an excerpt of a new title
from the Intrigue series,
SMOKY MOUNTAINS MYSTERY by Lena Diaz

Chapter One

Keira Sloane two-handed her service weapon, elbows bent, pistol pointing up toward the ceiling as she flattened her back against the wall outside the motel room. The dim lights from the dark parking lot one story below glinted off the rusty railing across from her. Chuck Breamer, one of two fellow officers with her, mirrored her stance on the other side of the door. In front of him, Gabe Wilson held his gun pointed down. He glanced at Chuck, then Keira. After receiving their nods, he rapped loudly on the door again before jerking back to avoid potential gunfire.

"Maple Falls Police. Last chance. Open the door." As with the first knock, there was no response.

Gabe held up three fingers, silently counting down. *Three, two, one.* He delivered a vicious kick to the doorknob. The frame splintered. The ruined door flew open and crashed against the wall, making the large window beside the door rattle.

All three ran inside, sweeping their guns back and forth.

The metallic smell of blood struck Keira immediately. A wounded or dead man lay on the bed closest to the window. She quickly checked behind the chair in the corner for any hidden suspects while her fellow officers checked under both beds.

"Main room clear," she announced.

Chuck jogged to the doorway on the back left. Gabe checked the one on the back right.

"Bathroom's clear," Chuck said.

"Closet clear," Gabe echoed. "No one else is here." He motioned toward an indentation in the cheap floral comforter covering the empty bed where it appeared that someone had sat at one time. "At least, not anymore."

Keira holstered her pistol and rushed to the side of the victim's bed, grimacing in sympathy at the extent of his injuries. Dressed only in navy blue boxers, the approximately thirty-year-old Black man was mottled with bruises and cuts on all of his extremities, with most of the damage to his chest.

Beneath him, the formerly white sheet was turning red. Blood dripped down, adding to a growing wet tangle of carpet. When she pressed her fingers against the side of his neck, to her surprise it was warm. There was a weak, thready pulse.

"He's alive. Get a bus out here."

Chuck radioed for an ambulance.

Keira grabbed the edge of the comforter and used it to apply pressure to what appeared to be bullet entrance wounds on his chest. Someone had beaten and tortured this man before shooting him. He'd lost so much blood it was a miracle that he was still alive, even more of a miracle if he made it to the hospital.

A hand grabbed her wrist, making her jump. She was shocked that it was the man on the bed. He stared up at her with pain-glazed dark brown eyes, his hand clutching hers. But whatever strength he had immediately drained away. His hand fell back to the mattress.

"Hold on," she told him. "Don't go into the light, buddy. Help's on the way."

His face turned ashen as his lips moved. But she couldn't make out what he said.

She leaned close. "Say it again," she encouraged him.

"L… Lance," the faint whisper sounded.

"Lance," she echoed. "Hang on, Lance. I'm Keira. I'm a cop. We're here to help you and—"

"Move." Chuck roughly pushed her out of the way.

"He's bleeding," she said. "His chest—"

"I've got it." His prior experience as an EMT kicked in as he maintained pressure on the victim's chest with one hand and checked his airway with the other.

Keira watched with a growing feeling of helplessness as Chuck assessed the victim. She wanted to help. But of the three of them, Chuck had the best chance of keeping him alive until the ambulance arrived.

She turned to check on Gabe and saw him reaching for the top drawer of the cheap particle-board dresser opposite the two beds.

"We need a warrant," she reminded him. "Exigent circumstances are over." Even though the motel manager was the one who'd called 911, he hadn't formally given them permission to search once they'd responded to the report of "shots fired."

Gabe shrugged and dropped his hand. "The lieutenant's on his way. Knowing him, he'll already have the warrant anyway."

She smiled at his statement. They both knew no one, not even their scarily efficient supervisor, Owen Jackson, could have gotten a warrant that fast.

Chuck straightened and stepped back from the bed. "He's gone. On top of being treated like a punching bag and sliced with a knife, he was shot at least three times. There's nothing anyone could have done to save this guy."

Keira blew out a shaky breath. Her wrist tingled as if the man were still holding it. He'd wanted her help. But she hadn't been able to do anything to change his fate. "Lance. His name is Lance."

Chuck frowned. "You know this guy?"

"No. He whispered it. Lance. Might have been Vance or Vince. But I think it was Lance."

"Did he say it was *his* name? Maybe it was the killer's name."

She winced. "I hope not. I called him Lance."

"We'll know soon enough, once we get a warrant to search for his wallet. Assuming it wasn't stolen." He started typing a text, no doubt updating their boss on the current status.

She glanced around the small room. Even the blood spatter on the wall behind the victim didn't mask the years of grime. But, aside from the twisted, bloody covers on the bed, everything else was neat and orderly. The dresser and nightstand drawers were closed. No belongings had been dumped onto the floor and rifled through. The second bed was made with the pillows and comforter in place.

"The room doesn't look tossed," she said. "His business suit's lying over there on that chair, as if he'd planned on wearing it tomorrow. It's rumpled, so the killer may have checked the pockets. But if this was a robbery, you'd think they'd take the suit. It's not cheap. Could fetch a few hundred at a consignment shop."

Gabe joined them. "I doubt a robber in this part of

town would recognize the value of a suit or want to bother with it. But they'd definitely have taken the fancy Mercedes out front that the manager said belongs to this guy. Why would a man who can afford a car like that stay in a nasty, cheap motel?"

Keira glanced at the man on the bed, wishing he could answer those questions, that he'd wake up in the morning and call his family, his friends. Tell them who'd attacked him and why. "Maybe he was hiding out from someone who'd never expect him to stay in a place like this." She shrugged. "That's one of many things we'll have to figure out."

Gabe gave her a doubtful look. "What makes you think Owen is finally going to let you play detective?"

She stiffened. "I can play whodunit as well as anyone else. I'm ready."

He held his hands up in a placating gesture. "No argument here. It's the LT you have to convince."

Chuck slid his cell phone back in his pocket. "We need to identify potential witnesses before they scatter like ants in a thunderstorm. Gabe, you take the rooms to the right. I'll go left. Names and addresses, verified with ID. We can't force them to hang around. But at least we can follow up with them once we have more manpower."

"Or woman power," Keira said. "I'll help."

Chuck frowned. "You're on guard duty. If the EMTs get here before we're back, try to keep them from destroying evidence. Once they verify our victim is DOA, get them out of our crime scene."

Gabe sent her an apologetic glance as he closed the door behind him and Chuck.